THREE DOORS

J.L. VANDERS

Copyright © 2019 ~ J.L.VANDERS

This is a work of fiction.
Names, characters, places, and incidents
are either the product of the author's imagination
or are used fictitiously.
Any resemblance to actual persons, living or dead,
events, or locales is entirely coincidental.

All rights reserved.
ISBN: 9798791032218

No part of this book may be reproduced or used
in any manner without written permission
of the copyright owner.
Contact: threedoorsbooks@gmail.com

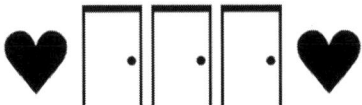

With all my heart,
I dedicate this book to my loyal readers.

fan·ta·sy
/ˈfan(t)əsē/ *noun*

1. an imagined, enjoyable scenario deemed improbable or impossible

2. this book

~ • ~

I felt his thick tip teasing me, then I gasped as he pushed deep inside. I was wet, I was ready, and it was incredible.

I wasn't sure which of the friends I'd been with so far, but his cock felt bigger as he stretched me and filled me.

He was a talented kisser. He licked my soft lips and twisted his hot tongue around mine in the dark. Kissing was a fine art, and he could paint a masterpiece with that mouth.

The kiss alone would've made me wet had he not already been fucking me. Maybe we could kiss more next time.

Of course, I couldn't tell him that.

I arched my back as he took my firm nipple between his hungry lips.
He nibbled and sucked in that artful way until I almost cried out in pleasure.

I couldn't cry out, though, so I panted in soft, labored breaths instead.

Later, after we both crashed down from our highs, I stared into the pitch-black nothingness of the bedroom and wondered to myself...

...how did we get here?

~ 1 ~

"Fuck the endocrine system," Judge groaned. "Fuck the whole fucking thing."

Evan didn't bother looking up from his fancy laptop. "Come on, man. It's not that bad."

"Like hell it's not," Mia muttered under her breath.

Shay was over it, too. She stretched her short arms above her head and yawned through a gripe. "There's just *so* fucking much."

"We're almost there." I smiled with encouragement, feeling determined to get through this latest lesson. "Let's just keep at it."

"Right, Callie." Judge shot me a tired frown. "Who needs sleep anyway?"

"I don't, but I *do* need more coffee." Shay nodded to the kitchen with a not-so-subtle hint in my direction.

"It's medical school," Decker scoffed. "We're not expected to sleep."

The six of us had piled into the cozy living room that I shared with my roommates, Mia and Shay. The space was a clusterfuck, pretty much the standard during our regular study sessions. We'd littered the black coffee table with our handwritten index cards and stacked our empty pizza boxes in the corner by the television.

I assumed my role of unofficial barista and agreed to make a fresh supply of fuel, then hopped up from my seat on the floor and ventured to the kitchen. The endocrine system was no fuckin' joke, and we were all running on fumes, especially with our first big exam of the spring semester scheduled for tomorrow. I loaded the old-school coffeemaker with black grounds and leaned against the counter with a yawn as the pot brewed. The grumpy bunch in the living room argued about adrenal glands, and I cracked a smile to myself.

"Are you sure that's right?"
"Yes. Look at the diagram."
"Well, it doesn't look like a gland."
"He's right. Wishbone on CT scan. Right there."
"You gonna argue with the textbook publisher?"
"I'm sorry. I'm just hella tired."
"We all are. Suck it up."
Oh, these fuckin' friends.

~ • ~

Mia, Shay, and I had first encountered the guys at a mixer for our student housing after we'd first landed on campus. I'd caught Judge shamelessly undressing me with his eyes as he bantered with the other boys, sneaking peeks of my assets as I sucked from my freelicious drink. Sure, I'd been hoping to impress in my tight dress. My body was desperate for attention that I hadn't enjoyed in months, and Judge made no effort to hide his interest. I'd playfully rolled my eyes in response to his creeping and heard him laugh from all the way across the room.

The guys had taken us by surprise when they boldly approached and introduced themselves as fellow medical students. Evan could've just stepped from the beach, missing only a surfboard beside his sunny skin, stylish blond hair, and crystal blue eyes. Decker had said little, seeming bored and distracted like a snobby art major with his mysterious Italian features. Judge was cocky as fuck, flexing his dark muscles a bit more than the others and smiling flirtatiously with the deepest dimples I'd ever seen.

Needless to say, my girls and I were secretly smitten from the start.

~ • ~

"How long could coffee take?" Evan bitched. "What the hell are you doing in there, Callie?"

"Oh, calm the fuck down." I refilled the beggars from the hot pot, refreshed my mug on the end table, and returned the nearly empty supply to the kitchen.

"Creamer?" Deck requested.

I plopped back down and picked up my spiral notebook. "Nope. We polished it off last round."

"You ladies prefer it black anyway, right?" Judge man-giggled at his own corny joke.

"Don't you fuckin' wish," Shay laughed.

We finally called it a night after grinding through the last sections together. We'd have about four hours to sleep before the early alarm ripped us from our peace. All things considered, that wasn't too shabby.

~ • ~

The Friday morning endocrinology exam was fucking grueling, as expected, but the weekend would provide some temporary rest and relief. We met in the evening to nurse our wounds over drinks and wallow in the shared miseries of first-year medical students. The guys rolled in right on cue, furnishing a case of cold beer to thank us for hosting.

"I feel like I've been punched in the face," Mia sighed, sinking into our big blue chair and scooping long brown locks from her neck. "This semester is gonna kick my ass."

"Nothing a little alcohol won't cure, I hope." Deck smiled with consolation as Judge passed cans of cold brew.

"I barely finished on time," I complained as I popped my tab. "I think I answered a million questions."

"Same here," Evan chimed in. "I kept thinking that I was almost there, and then boom, another fucking page."

"I'm ready for a six-pack and about eighteen hours of sleep." Shay rubbed stress from her temples. "Thank God for the weekend."

Judge stretched his thick body on the sofa next to me. "Speaking of, are we doing anything tomorrow night?"

"I'm out," Deck declined as he sprawled out on the loveseat. "I think my bar-hopping days are over with this schedule."

Mia rolled her eyes over her beer. "I don't feel like going out and getting manhandled on the dance floor. Not enough quality return for that investment."

"Speak for yourself," Judge said with a shrug. "I've been flying solo for months now and it blows."

"Hard for me to admit," Evan said, "but yeah, it's been rough out there."

"Aww, poor guys," Shay mocked. "Not enough strange willing to put up with your cocky asses?" The guys muttered under their breath like deprived children.

"Please," I piped up in defense of my neglected pussy. "It's harder being a girl. Trust me."

"Nah," Deck said with a shake of his head. "Girls can go without sex much longer than guys."

Mia choked on a drink. "Oh, you think?"

"Girls don't need dick at all," Judge reasoned with typical male arrogance. "They just need hugs."

Evan raised his red can. "*And* compliments about their shoes."

"Right? Don't forget to look at the fuckin' shoes!" The trio erupted in ridiculous laughs at our expense, and Evan hopped up for another round.

"I can't *believe* none of you have been getting laid," Mia said with dripping sarcasm. "It's shocking, really."

"I don't get it. Why do men assume women don't want casual sex, too?" Shay wondered aloud.

Good question.

Judge tossed a palm. "Face it. It's just not in your nature."

"Oh, come on," Mia bitched. "That's some sexist bullshit."

"He's right, though," Deck said. "It's not your fault."

"Maybe it's because society labels us as sluts and you as champions?" I snapped back.

"That's exactly what it is," Evan said as he distributed more chilled cans. "Ask my twin sister."

Shay blinked up at him. "What happened?"

He took a quick sip and leaned against the living room wall. "Ellen lost her virginity to the biggest tool in our high school. They practically threw a parade in his honor, but they shamed her into a corner."

"So, what did you do?" I wanted the scoop, as always.

Evan shot us a prideful grin. "I broke his fuckin' nose."

We shared another laugh, and then I circled back to the crucial topic at hand. "Honestly, I would love a quick romp sometimes, but I think guys assume there will be drama, so they don't jump in."

A naughty glimmer flashed in Deck's dark brown eyes. "Maybe they're just not that into you, Callie," he teased.

"Oh, really? You wouldn't bang me, Deck?" I pressed a palm to my chest and faked disappointment.

Evan raised his hand with no shame. "I would."

"Fuck, at this point, *I* would," Shay laughed.

Judge offered a mock toast in her direction. "Hell, I'm good with that option."

"Okay, question." Decker shifted forward and rested his elbows on his knees. "Have you girls ever considered that? Getting down together?"

"Now that you mention it, Shay *does* have nice tits," Mia giggled.

Shay glanced down at her perky rack and tipped her can with appreciation. "Why, thank you!"

"I think chick porn is hot, but I gotta have the meat eventually," I explained.

"Right? Who doesn't love some girl-on-girl porn?" Evan agreed. "It's all good."

"Hell, I know I love it." Shay stood and stretched. We raised our hands in unison when she offered to grab the next round.

"So, same question, Deck," Mia said with a sly grin. "You guys ever cuddle up on cold, lonely nights?"

Yeah, right.

"Sure." He smirked over his can. "Judge steals the blankets, though."

Judge shook his head with amusement, then placed another level on his tower of empty red cans. I listened to the cheeky crosstalk and grinned as I imagined our beefy boys tonguing.

"I think it's hot as fuck when guys kiss," Shay admitted after she delivered our next servings.

"Me, too," Mia said. I nodded with approval and recrossed my legs, carefully avoiding Judge's work of alcohol art.

"So," Deck continued with the interrogation, "which one of us is the sexiest? Spill it."

I shrugged. "That's easy. You are."

"Damn, girl." Judge gawked at me. "You just put it right out there."

"I mean, don't get me wrong, you're all hot," I assured them. "But sex appeal? Deck just has this way."

"Well, I guess that settles it." He shot me a smooth wink to confirm my claim and chugged a victory drink.

"Fuck that," Shay challenged as she waved me off. "Evan is the sexiest. *By far.*"

"You're both fuckin' crazy," Mia claimed, jumping in on the defense. "It's Judge. Hands down."

Evan offered a smug smile and shifted his weight against the wall. "No need to argue, ladies. There's enough of us to go around."

If fuckin' only.

Judge stacked his latest layer on the leaning tower. "Okay, one more for me, then I gotta bail."

I hopped up and hurried to grab the last refill for the group. After months of mild flirtations, we'd never ventured down this revealing avenue with the boys, so I was dying to hear more.

Shay dug deeper. "You guys wanted in our panties when you first met us, right?"

"You know we did," Decker answered on behalf of all three.

"Did you hash it out?" Mia giggled. "Which guy for which girl?" I perked up and loaded the cold beer against my chest, the frosty aluminum chilling my nips.

"Of fuckin' course," Evan laughed. "We thought we had it all synced."

I returned with the stack, then slid into my sofa seat next to Judge. "Oh, we gotta hear this."

"Alright." Deck raked fingers through his thick hair and fessed up first. "I was into Shay."

"Aww." Shay fanned herself. "Really?"

"It's those eyes, girl. Just gorgeous." I had to agree. Shay's striking Asian features were worthy of a runway.

Judge hit me directly with those dark dimples next. "I was a little obsessed with you after that eye roll, Callie."

Mild warmth flushed over my cheeks, but I covered it with a tease. "Only a little?" I flirted, rubbing his thigh with mock seduction.

"Nice. Now, just a bit higher…"

This guy.

"It was all Mia for me." Evan gestured to our Latina beauty with his beer. "Her hair is so pretty."

Mia beamed with surprise and playfully fondled her shiny locks. "Aww, that's so sweet!"

"Well, I guess we'll spill, too," Shay said. "Judge had me weak in the knees with that smile."

He flashed his brilliant trademark grin. "You mean *this* one?"

I figured that I should play along. "And I thought Evan was fine as hell."

He turned those bright eyes to mine. "Wow. I'm fuckin' flattered, Callie."

"So, you wanted me bad, Mia?" Deck flexed his buff biceps.

Mia swallowed a drink and nodded. "Oh, I had all kinds of dirty thoughts about you, Deck."

An easy silence filled the space as we considered those initial reactions. Our mutual attraction was obvious from the start, but once we developed genuine friendships, the lust had shifted to the side in favor of this remarkable group dynamic. Sure, we still gushed about the guys sometimes during our late-night tipsy talks, but the potential peen took a backseat to the books.

"Hell, now we know why we never hooked up," Judge chuckled as we reluctantly stood to straighten our mess.

"Well, as soon as you opened your fuckin' mouths," Shay laughed.

"It was over when we tasted your nasty cooking," Evan roasted back. Fair point, to be honest.

"We doing this again tomorrow?" Deck yawned and helped me gather empties.

"Sure. You bringing more beer?"

Judge sidled up next to me and bumped my shoulder. "We'll get beer, and you order food. And I do mean *order*."

"Smartass."

"Chinese?" Mia suggested.

Evan nodded. "It's a date."

~ • ~

The guys left for their downstairs apartment, and I shuffled to the bathroom with my best friends to begin our bedtime rituals. Shay glanced between us in the mirror before rubbing her eyes with makeup remover. "Be honest, girls," she began. "Now that we know them better, which one would you fuck?"

"Tough call." I loaded my toothbrush as Mia rubbed moisturizer over her bronzed cheeks beside me. "They each bring something hot to the table."

Mia smiled at our reflections. "Hell, I'd probably bang all three."

"Same," Shay whispered.

"Same," I added with a guilty giggle.

We shared shameless laughs through our beauty routines, then hugged goodnight in the hallway as we always did. I retired to my bedroom and buried myself deep under my ruffled white comforter, the guys crowding the corners of my brain.

Which one?

I eased my hand into my skimpy panties and strummed my plump, warm clit with experienced fingers. My vivid imagination summoned Judge sucking on my pink nipples with those sensual lips, Deck gazing between my thighs with those brooding eyes, and Evan grinding into my ass with that thick cock I noticed in his fitted pants. I bent my knees and rocked against the soft sheets as ripples of a potential peak pooled in my pelvis.

Oh, a girl could dream...

~ 2 ~

"Get your ass up!" Shay barked from my bedroom doorway the next morning.

"What the fuck?" I yanked the warm blanket over my head and cuddled deeper against my plush pillow.

"*You're* the one who wanted the early appointment, Callie."

Great. Mia had joined in, signaling that they were both up and fuckin' raring to go. I threw back my white comforter to sit up in protest and quickly realized that I wasn't wearing pants. Or panties, for that matter. Fuck. I jerked the blanket across my lap and scooted upright against the headboard.

"I just saw your cooch," Mia casually informed me.

"Why are you both here?"

Shay laughed and pointed a smartass finger. "A better question would be why you're all naked under there."

"That's not a better question."

"Fine. Nail appointments?" Shay reminded me. "You insisted we do it early before the shop got busy?"

"Ugh. That's today?"

"Yeah." Mia grinned. "Now, back to the naked thing."

"Let it go."

Shay laughed and met Mia's eyes before smiling at me. "I think Callie was tipsy touching herself last night."

Mia giggled and glanced my way. "Ya think?"

"Definitely," Shay teased. "Look, she's blushing."

"I'm not blushing," I lied as my cheeks burned. It was common knowledge that my friends and I were in a sex slump, but I'd never offered up visual evidence of my frequent self-satisfaction.

"Damn, someone got you all hot and bothered," Mia taunted with annoying amusement as she relaxed against the doorframe.

Shay wanted the dirt. "Alright. Who was it?"

"Just get the fuck out!"

"Fine. You have fifteen minutes."

Mia pulled my bedroom door closed as they stepped out, and I slid from the sheets with hesitation, half expecting them to crash back in for more cooch roasting. I vaguely remembered wiggling out of my panties last night for better finger access, so I shook my bed linens until a purple thong landed on the rug below. I grabbed black leggings and an oversized hoodie from the laundry basket of folded clothes by the closet, then I shrugged my long gray robe over my bare bottom.

"Twelve minutes, Callie!" Shay called from the hallway. I rolled my eyes, jerked open my door, and caught her perky ass sashaying toward the living room.

"*And* you're still not dressed."

I whipped around to the opposite side to find Mia palming her hips in front of her bedroom. "I need to shower first, ya fuckin' stalker," I bitched, gesturing to my tangled bedhead.

"No." She shook her head. "Rinse off. No hair washing. Let's go."

"Fine."

Shay just *had* to inject her smug comment from the front of the apartment. "And don't be playing with yourself in there! We'll be late!"

"I hate you both."

~ • ~

We strolled in the brisk morning sunlight to the nail salon a few blocks away. Shay and Mia looked like fuckin' rock stars, apparently unaffected by the lack of sleep over the last two weeks. Shay's jet-black hair fell in shiny, smooth streaks down her sleek coat. Of course, her simple, stylish flats coordinated perfectly, and her flawless makeup was practically camera-ready. Mia had straightened her silky brown locks and tucked them all to one side over her shoulder. Tight jeans hugged her ass just right, and her golden complexion always glowed in the sun. Yep, my best friends ruled the street like exotic goddesses.

I, on the other hand, looked like they'd found me in the gutter and picked me up as a project. I hadn't attempted to sort my ratty blond mop, so I left it piled in a bobbing mess on top of my head. I'd unknowingly chosen leggings with a small hole in the knee, and remnants of last night's mascara still shadowed my sleepy eyes.

Mia bumped my shoulder. "So? Whose dick were you dreaming of?"

I buried my freezing fingers in my hoodie pocket. "I don't even know."

"You can tell us," Shay reassured me. "We had to burn ya, but we play in our own playgrounds, too."

"Mostly Evan." I gave it some thought as I squinted against the bright rays. "I think the other guys were up in there, too."

"I bet Judge has the biggest shaft. That's just how he carries himself."

Mia laughed. "No fuckin' way. He's too cocky."

Shay scrunched her shoulders as the wind whipped around us. "Well, if his dick matched his arrogance, we'd all be in line."

"True story," I admitted. "I would be."

"Have you girls noticed Evan's bulge?" Mia widened her big brown eyes as we approached the salon entrance. "Especially in those rich boy khakis he wears?"

"I've noticed it," I sighed. "The outline looks hella promising, for sure."

"Fuckin' listen to us," Shay giggled. "We *really* need some action." Mia and I agreed under our breath and stepped inside for some well-deserved pampering.

~ • ~

Later, after studying until my brain rebelled and showering away my earlier slump, I arranged takeout containers on the kitchen counter for our dinner company. We tried to reserve Saturday nights for breaks from the hectic weekdays, occasionally inviting the guys if they hadn't mentioned plans. Considering the interesting revelations from last night's venting, I was pumped to see where this evening would lead.

"My nails look amazing," Mia said as she examined her nude polish.

"Mine, too. That's definitely gonna be our new place."

Shay glanced up from her manicure. "We should probably change."

"Why?"

"Haven't you checked your phones? When I texted the boys about the food, I asked them to wear pajamas."

Mia's eyes brightened. "Seriously?"

Shay tossed palms and laughed. "Sure! Why not?"

Well, this sounded fucking interesting.

Mia chewed her bottom lip with thought. "Wait. Sexy pajamas or comfy pajamas?"

"Whatever you want," Shay said. "I'm hitting the middle with the pink slip nightgown."

Oh, come on.

"That's super sexy!" I told her.

"Not compared to my other stuff."

"I have that white satin short set," Mia suggested. "It's cute, I guess. Shows some skin."

Stop right fuckin' there.

"Dude, those are both 'fuck my friend' kinda outfits," I noted with dramatic air quotes. "What am I missing here?"

"Look, I know we're all just friends, and nothing's gonna happen, but if the guys wanna jerk off to me later, I've decided that I'm okay with it." Shay smirked with a not-so-innocent shrug.

Brilliant.

My plain ass didn't own any sultry sleepwear like my girls, certainly nothing worthy of spank bank material. "Fine, but I don't have hot pajamas. Any ideas?"

"Just grab something of ours," Mia offered with a nod toward the hall.

"Yeah, help yourself." Shay stifled a laugh with pinched lips. "You can't be diddling yourself in my good gear, though."

"Is that gonna be a thing now?"

"Yep. I'm telling everyone."

Great.

"I have that black, stretchy nightgown. You want that?"

"Will it cover my ass?" I asked.

Mia grinned slyly. "Well, it barely covers mine."

I was starting to dig the potential of this plan. If we weren't gonna get fucked, we could at least dress pretty and play pretend. I wiggled into Mia's form-fitting lingerie minutes later and watched my little tits jiggle in the thin black fabric. This certainly showed more than my boring study night sweatshirts.

"Bra or no bra?" I yelled from my room.

"No bra!"

"Fuck yeah, ladies!" Mia squealed. "Let those girls out to play!"

We were still primping when the guys arrived. They let themselves in after a brief knock, as usual, and I heard them shuffling around the space like they owned the joint. I was ready first, for once in my life, so I sucked in a nervous breath and joined them in the living room. We'd never blatantly flaunted our goodies for the boys before, but I was dying to see their reactions.

"Fuck, Callie. Look at you." Decker eyed me with raised brow surprise. Christ, he was a fuckin' treat, leaning against the sofa in plaid pajama pants, muscular forearms crossed over his chiseled chest. His happy eyes found my nips in the borrowed black slip. *Nice call on the no bra.*

"Hey, guys!" I smiled through a proud blush.

Evan and Judge crouched over a big gray cooler of ice on the living room floor. Judge paused and whistled at me, then ripped open a new case. Evan muttered a greeting under his breath as he buried red cans of beer.

Shay strolled in like a perfect porcelain doll, the satin pink nightie swishing over her shapely hips as she approached. "Why did you bring a cooler?"

"So we won't have to keep running to the fridge," Evan said without looking up.

"What the fuck?" Mia pointed at the project as she joined us, her flat belly peeking out from the crop top. "That's the epitome of laziness."

Evan loaded the last few drinks, then stood when he finally noticed our slinky sleepwear. "What the hell, girls? I thought you'd be wearing flannel and old lady nightgowns."

Shay smirked. "Do I look like I own any flannel, Evan?" I was pretty sure her prissy ass did not.

I met his sexy blue eyes. "Are you complaining?"

"No," Deck insisted. "None of us are complaining. Trust me."

Mia fingered the sleeve of Judge's pajama top. "I like your threads, mister." He glanced down at his burgundy button-down sleep set, complete with coordinating slippers, then tugged on the cuffs with pride like he was showing off a new suit.

"I think he looks like a douche."

"Fuck you, man," Judge scoffed at Evan. "Mom got these for me. I loved these pajama sets when I was little."

Shay scoped Evan's basic tee and basketball shorts. "Hell, at least he made a fuckin' effort."

Evan laughed and pointed to his pelvis. "This is what I sleep in. You'd know if you ever stopped by my bedroom."

Well, damn. Here we go.

~ • ~

We stuffed ourselves with shared boxes of sticky rice and mystery meat as we finished the first case of alcohol. My orange chicken hit all the right spots, and my insides buzzed blissfully from the icy beer.

Deck relaxed back into the sofa cushions beside me and rubbed his tight abs. "I don't know what all I ate, but it was fuckin' good."

"I sure as hell don't look hot now." Shay pulled the pink satin material tight against her lower belly. "Check out this food baby."

Mia laughed. "Nah, you're still hot."

I kicked back beside Deck and tucked my ankles under my ass. "What did you guys do today?"

Evan lifted the cooler lid beside him and passed a fresh round. "Hit the gym. Studied all day. Made a beer run."

Judge took a quick drink from his cold can. "Did you girls do anything fun?"

The three of us displayed our pretty fingers and toes to the room. "Manicures and pedicures this morning," Shay explained, "then we crammed until the food came."

Mia shot me an evil grin. "We were almost late to the salon." I narrowed my eyes with a warning, but she continued anyway. "Callie was playing with herself and wouldn't get outta bed."

"Oh, get the fuck out!" I waved her off, willing away the inevitable blush that followed. I'd grown accustomed to the playful sabotage with my girls and had delivered hefty doses myself over the years, but the guys added an entirely new level of sexual tension. "I just overslept. It was innocent."

Shay smirked in my direction and gathered empty plates from the coffee table. "Are you saying that you *didn't* play with yourself, Callie? Cause I'm pretty sure you did."

Red heat rushed to my cheeks. "I mean, yeah, but that's not why we were running late. That was last night."

"Last night?" Deck asked with interest beside me. "When we left?"

"Maybe."

"Such a refreshing fuckin' conversation," Judge mumbled as the guys exchanged surprised smirks.

When Shay requested the next refill, Decker offered an alternative. "Do you have six shot glasses?"

"I think so. Check in the cabinet above the sink."

Judge perked up. "Hour of Power? With the girls? *Nice*."

I'd never heard of it. "What's Hour of Power?"

Evan grinned. "A shot every minute, on the minute, for a full hour."

"Shot of what?"

"Beer," Decker answered with a cocky grin.

Mia furrowed skeptical brows. "Who shoots beer? That's weak as hell."

"And for just an hour? That's like three beers total," Shay noted after quick mental calculations.

"It sounds mild, but trust me, it's not," Judge explained. "Just an easy way to get fucked up."

I had to laugh. "It's like eight-thirty."

"So, maybe we'll do another round later," Deck said, tossing palms with a taunt. "*If* you girls can handle it, that is."

Oh, come the fuck on.

We collectively huffed over Deck's chuckles as he shuffled to the kitchen, adding bitchy, exaggerated brags about our undergrad days. He found our shot glass stash and distributed it randomly around the room, then stood before us and covered the logistics. "We'll set a countdown on my phone and shoot every minute, on the minute."

Evan patted the gray cooler with pride. "I'll be the beer man. Here, grab a cold one to start."

I filled my frosted pink shot glass as nervous, horny energy hummed in my belly. We'd been tipsy with the boys before, but combining alcohol with both the pajamas and the admitted need for fucks? *Christ, what are we doing?*

Deck counted us down as he displayed the timer. "Three, two, one! Go!" We clinked and slammed as the Hour of Power began.

~ • ~

"I love beer," I mumbled to myself as the quick buzz settled in.

Mia extended her streaky brown strands in front of her face. "Should I cut my hair?"

Evan laughed and shook his head. "Absolutely not."

"How many is that?" Judge asked as he wiggled his empty can.

Decker checked his phone. "Twenty-two."

"I love this game," Shay sighed.

"Yeah, but this is tough for me," Evan confessed, falling back against his big cooler with slumped shoulders.

I ruffled his blond hair and smiled down at him. "What's wrong, mister?"

"We're all best friends now. I feel guilty for wanting to fuck you girls."

Aww.

"Don't feel bad," Shay consoled him. "We'd probably fuck you guys, too."

True.

"Drink!"

Mia refilled her serving. "I've never had guy friends like this. It's awesome."

I tipsy-giggled. "I know! And they're all so fuckin' hot!"

Shay called me right the fuck out. "So hot that you dream fucked all three, right?"

Judge shot me surprised brows. "Wait, what?"

I shrugged with unconvincing innocence, the beer fueling my confidence before the mouthwatering men. "I needed some inspiration, and I couldn't decide."

Decker scowled beside me. "I don't know whether to be flattered or pissed."

"Why pissed?"

"Pissed that I wasn't satisfying enough by myself."

"Drink!" Evan yelled.

Shay spilled the real stuff after another half hour of shots. "Truth? I'd screw any of you, but it would totally jack up our friendship." She sprawled back across the loveseat arm, her pink nightie sliding to the top of her thighs.

"I know," Judge sighed with a guilty peek at her panties. "We could never get back to this."

Unfortunately fuckin' true.

Mia hopped up and wiggled her sultry hips. "Dance with me, Callie!"

I scoped her moves underneath the shimmery fabric, accepted her extended hands, and then bailed after a few wobbly steps. "I can't, girl. Dance with Evan instead."

"Oh, alright."

She loosened her grip on my fingers, and I toppled back directly onto Decker's lap. "I'm so sorry!" I cringed, shifting my weight on his thighs and sliding over his impressive package.

Fuck.

"If this is the only way I can get you on top of me, Callie," Deck whispered against my neck from behind, "I'll take it."

Chills of arousal rushed down my spine, then I clumsily scooted back beside him. "You're such a tease."

He smirked and nudged me with his knee. "You're one to fuckin' talk."

Judge checked the phone and clapped. "Down to the last shot! Get your asses up!"

We gathered around the coffee table and filled our glasses once more. Half of us were a second or two late, to be expected, but in the end, we were all still standing.

"Fuck yeah!" I cheered.

Mia was ready for the next round. "Let's do it again!"

"Damn, girl. Really?" Judge looked at her with disbelief.

Shay nodded. "I don't wanna lose this buzz."

Mia licked her pouty lips with a grin. "Evan's dancing made me all hot. I think everyone should dance."

Evan raked his hand through his thick blond hair. "You're killing me, Mia. *Fuck.*"

~ • ~

Overtime unleashed our frisky sides. After the third shot, the guys ripped off their shirts to prove who was more stacked. I cuddled with the girls on the couch, licking my lips as they flexed and posed in front of us. In the end, with our drunken, narrowed eyes, we decided that they were all fuckin' winners.

After several more slams, the strictly timed shots started to slow. Evan piped some bumpin' club music through our wireless speaker and added an extra layer of temptation to the wild evening. We jumped at the opportunity to touch each other, pairing off with no prompting and grinding like horny teenagers at prom. I became enthralled with the filthy action of the unofficial couples around me. Decker and Shay stole my attention first as they practically dry-humped near the hallway. My lustful eyes stared as she rocked against his groin, his big hands groping her round ass and urging her closer. Judge stroked Mia's exposed abs from behind as they swerved together in time to the thumping bass. She chewed her bottom lip and rolled her head back against his chest as he thrust rhythmic pumps against her shorts. Fuck, watching alone was enough to dampen my needy pussy, but I had my own partner to quench my thirst.

"You look so sexy tonight, Callie," Evan rasped against my neck from behind, his wandering hands roaming over my curves. "I can't fuckin' take it."

I became quite familiar with the infamous bulge as he enveloped my small frame against his towering muscles. He teased with demanding fingertips, sliding my nightgown higher and scratching at my waist as I circled my perky cheeks against his steel cock. My core burned with a heated throb at the thought of our naked, sweaty skin clinging together a few steps away in my bed. I reached back around his neck and urged his scruff to my shoulder, displaying my writhing body for anyone's viewing pleasure.

"You feel *so* big," I whispered, the urge to french him thick on the tip of my tongue. "I love how you move."

Evan inhaled sharply, but Shay interrupted our moment. "Drink and switch!"

We paused for a few beats to fill our glasses and slam another beer shot. I must've missed the whole 'switching' plan, but Judge stepped right up to claim his round. Fuck, I didn't mind this series of events at all.

"My turn," he demanded with that velvety voice, wrapping one rippled arm around my waist. I noticed a savory cologne that I couldn't quite place.

"Are you as drunk as I am?" I blinked up at his warm brown eyes as we started moving to the music.

"I think so," Judge assured me with a dimpled smile, the thin burgundy bottoms failing to shield his shameless desire as our bodies meshed. His stiff length grazed my lower abs and coaxed my curves closer, my center begging for that sweet, slick friction. I dragged fresh nails over his bare pecs and licked my lips with an invitation as our mouths hovered just inches apart. He looked straight down my black gown at the soft spot between my breasts, and the fantasy of him sucking my hard nipples came roaring back, sending a rush of moist heat to my aching slit.

"*Fuck*," I moaned under my breath.

"Drink and switch!"

Another pause, another shot, and another partner.

Deck strolled over with blazing confidence to enjoy the fruits of his friends, and my already throbbing pussy ignited with fresh sparks of heat. By that point, after Evan and Judge had worked their magic, I was ready to fuckin' ride him. He brushed fingertips across my abs, then slid behind me and growled against my ear. "You ready for me now, Callie?"

Goddamn.

"If we were alone, I'd show you," I challenged with a lustful whisper.

Deck groaned through my blond waves with hot breath, shipping another wave of wetness to my panties, then guided me by the hand to the dining room. He pressed my round tits against the wall with his powerful chest, his hard cock riding firm against my ass. "I don't want you watching them," he rasped over my shoulder with authority. "I want you focused on me and only me."

Deck's selfish demand rocked me to my core. I yanked the black stretchy nightgown up over my hips, giving him full access to the tiny t-back underneath. He hooked his thumbs in the side strings, then pumped his pelvis against me with merciless grinds, his shaft sliding between my clenched cheeks as he tugged back on my bottoms. I flattened palms and parted lips against the paint, then moaned with desperation to feel him thrusting inside me. He upped the ante of our dirty secret and traveled north, massaging my tingling nipples in the hidden space against the wall. I eased my hand over his and forced one of his fingers deep in my mouth, licking and sucking as I imagined his smooth, thick tip tapping the back of my throat.

"Fuck, Callie," he groaned against my ear.

"Last shot! I'm fuckin' dying here!" Evan shouted over the thumping music. Decker was kind enough to cover my ass when he peeled his body from mine, then we joined the tipsy group around the coffee table.

~ • ~

"This has been one hell of a night," Mia sighed. She propped her smooth legs in my lap as we parked back in the big blue chair. Our party of six draped over the furniture like discarded clothing, still kinda drunk and reflecting on our dirty deeds.

Decker spoke up with concern from the sofa. "Does anyone feel weird?"

"I don't," I answered confidently. I couldn't pinpoint my reasoning, besides my fading buzz, but as I looked between the satisfied smiles on the faces of my friends, I felt unusually fuckin' comfortable.

"Hell, I had the best night of my life," Judge bragged.

"And I'd do it all again tomorrow if we didn't have class on Monday," Shay said.

Evan was his usual skeptical self. "Yeah, we had a blast, but let's be real. It can't stay like this." I tried to focus on the logic, but those bare, puffy muscles were quite the distraction.

Deck raked frustrated fingers through his shaggy hair. "I don't think so, either. There's solid reasoning that this hasn't happened before, and we all know it."

"Why not?" I pleaded on behalf of my confused puss. Of course, I realized the risk to our friendship, but I was willing to talk it out.

"Because we're gonna need to fuck at some point," Mia laughed and smacked my thigh.

"Hell, I'm at that point now," Judge snickered under his breath. "Literally, right now." I covered my giggles as he adjusted his junk.

"I mean, who *doesn't* wanna fuck?" Shay fluffed her black hair and crossed her legs over the arm of the loveseat. "I get it."

"I just don't wanna screw things up," Evan pressed. "I like our little thing here."

Mia shamelessly spilled her thirst. "I like it, too, but I wouldn't complain if one of you bent me over, either."

Same.

The guys exchanged apprehensive glances. "I don't know if I could fuck one of you and go right back to studying next week," Deck reasoned with an uneasy voice of logic. "The whole dynamic would change."

Tipsy me felt the need to speak freely, so I did. "It would've been nice to bang one out tonight, but I'm attracted to all three of you. I don't even know who I would want. That's just the truth of it."

"Right," Shay sighed. "That's exactly how I feel."

"I bet we *all* do," Evan said quietly. We nodded in agreement like we were fucking geniuses.

Judge stood and stretched his muscled arms. "Well, regardless, I need to go home and take care of my business."

"That's some *big* business you're involved in," I joked. We all eyed the tent in the front of Judge's special pajama bottoms, and he took a ridiculous bow.

"I have an idea before you guys leave," Shay said. "Since we were up on each other anyway, let's share goodnight kisses."

Oh.

Evan couldn't hide his excitement. "You mean I get to kiss all of you?"

She shrugged. "Sure, if my girls want...unless someone will act all jealous and shit."

Decker relaxed back on the sofa with a satisfied smirk. "Hell, no jealousy here."

"Me neither," Mia said. "So, how do we do it?"

Judge laughed and gestured to the door. "I guess we'll just line up like an assembly line of meat."

Nice.

Deck shifted to serious mode. "Let's be clear that no one has to do this. No pressure."

I took a deep breath and dove in. "Fuck it. I want to." When had I last been kissed? Hell, I think it was by a random frat boy during graduation week last spring. Christ, I was dry.

Mia slid from her seat beside me and raised an eager hand. "Can I go first?"

Decker turned to Shay. "It was my idea, Deck," she laughed. "Obviously, I'm in."

The guys flexed back into their tops and helped pick up the party mess. We were starting to sober up, and all six of us were wearing cheesy ass grins of anticipation. Our "dates" lined up near the doorway, and I admired each of them through the lens of this newfound arousal. Evan's cover-worthy, flirtatious smile begged to be kissed. Decker oozed sex as he fingered the waistline of his plaid pants with a wicked tease. Judge could coax me from my panties with only one lick of those luscious lips. They stood together in a trio of tall muscles, whispering and waiting for this unspoken line to be crossed. Fuck, I'd always thought they were appealing, but tonight had definitely opened my eyes.

I didn't have a standout favorite, so I didn't mind when Mia pressed her perky tits against Evan and stuck her wild tongue down his throat. Shay grabbed Judge by his button-down and reeled him in next.

Deck didn't wait for my move, stepping forward and scooping me in his arms. He paused over me with frustrating discipline as the others got busy, fixated on my parted lips as I panted with anticipation. He finally slipped his fingers under the short hem of my nightgown and cupped my ass with appreciation, then smothered my hungry mouth with his. He taunted me with his determined tongue, stealing the breath from my aching chest second by second as my body begged him for more. I scratched at the back of his neck and urged him deeper, but he simply pulled away and winked as he waited with a cocky grin for his next kiss.

Christ.

Evan didn't hesitate to assume control as soon as I was available, grabbing my hips aggressively and crashing his open mouth to mine. He scraped his teeth against my lips and tugged at my blond hair with unexpected dominance that weakened my shaky knees. Sparks of longing pulsed in my pelvis as I submitted to his every whim. I whimpered with little resistance as he choked me with that hot, swirling tongue, then he eventually released me to his waiting friend.

Fuck.

In contrast, Judge offered the softest kiss I'd ever tasted. His tongue tip twirled skillfully against mine, inspiring fantasies of all the juicy, tempting ways he could cure my exhilarated pussy. Our mouths fell into a delicate rhythm of unspoken desire, the tension of the erotic evening melting in the inferno between our lips and legs. By the time we parted, I was considering slipping my naughty hand down his waistband for just one desperate caress of bare cock.

I wasn't sure how the light of the sober morning would reflect on the dark deeds of this drunken night, not knowing yet if these first, memorable kisses together would also be the last. By the time the guys waved with actual goodbyes and slipped out our door, we were left somewhat breathless and quite confused.

~ • ~

Mia piled her hair into a high, loose bun as we gathered in the bathroom. "What the fuck are we doing, girls?"

I shook my head in disbelief and retrieved my toothbrush. "I have no fuckin' clue, but it was hella hot."

"Well, whatever that was, I loved it," Shay said, whipping a brush through her long locks.

Mia smiled and squirted moisturizer on her fingertips. "I did, too, but we should hash this out tomorrow."

I dribbled white, minty foam in the sink and grinned. "All I know right now is that I want more."

Mia laughed with an enthusiastic nod. "So, *so* much more…"

"…with *all* of them," Shay added.

After the traditional hug goodnight, we retired to our bedrooms to crash. It took about thirty seconds before my panties disappeared in the bed linens again.

~ 3 ~

I thumped over in my lonely bed the following morning and fumbled around on my bedside table, the warning signs of a rare hangover already threatening my Sunday. The kink in my neck relaxed after a few seconds of stretching, but the hint of a headache demanded early intervention. I gobbled two ibuprofen pills with gulps of leftover bottled water from last night's feeble hydration attempt. After a few sighs at my ceiling, I curled into a ball facing the wall and listened for sounds of life from the adjacent bedrooms. Sweet silence settled in, gracing me with additional time to sleep and dream.

What was that old saying from my pre-med days?

The best cure for a hangover is an orgasm.

I fuckin' wish.

Only minutes later, or so it seemed, the mattress squeaked and shifted near my hip as an intruder crawled into bed with me. I waited with little hope for a stiff peen to brush against my ass. No such luck.

"Callie? Are you up?"

"Well, I am now."

Shay made herself comfortable against my headboard and released a dramatic sigh. "I can't stop thinking about last night."

"What time is it?" I grumbled. "Go talk to Mia."

Shay continued without breaking stride. "I think we need to get on the same page before we hear from the guys."

"You're fuckin' nuts."

"Callie!"

When I returned no attention, she yanked hard on my bedhead hair.

"I'll fucking stab you, Shay."

"Come on. Just wake the fuck up already." I rolled to my back with an icy glare, but Shay kept pleading against my will. "What are we gonna say to them?"

I rubbed the foggy glaze from my eyes and offered a one-shoulder shrug. Hell, I hadn't been awake long enough to process any coherent thoughts, but Shay's uncharacteristic spazzing forced my mind to clock in. "Maybe this wasn't such a good idea. I mean, I was all about fucking around last night, but—"

"I want in!" Mia hustled through my open door with a bright smile and hopped on the foot of the bed, then jerked back my white comforter and slid her smooth legs underneath. "What did I miss?"

Shay nodded in my direction. "Callie sounds like she has buyer's remorse."

I rolled my eyes. "Oh, stop it."

"I don't know what to think either," Mia said as she examined her split ends. "That shit was wild, though. Sharing and all that? Like a fuckin' fantasy."

I sat up and scooted back against the headboard beside my uninvited friend, finally accepting that I was awake for the day. Fuck, one of them could have at least gifted me with fresh coffee in exchange for squatting in my space. "I never expected things to go that far," I admitted honestly, "but I don't feel as weird about it as I thought I would."

"I'm in the same lane," Shay said. "I had fun, and it seemed like they did, too."

"So, we're cool?" Mia asked with raised brows. "Nothing weird to cover between the three of us?"

"Not for me," I said, and Shay agreed. Hell, I'd enjoyed having the three men draped all over my body, but truth be told? I didn't mind them entertaining my friends while waiting for a turn with me. We were equals in this equation.

"Good." Mia shifted to her knees and bounced with giddiness. "Should we just call them?"

Call them? Already? What the fuck had happened to my usual "morning after" girls? This wasn't our first dance, but both were acting as if we'd frenched our grade school boyfriends for the first time. I admittedly was the resident overthinker of this trio, but even I knew with little contemplation that we should ease up on the effort, at least for now. *Guys 101.*

"Meh." I cringed. "I don't know about all that."

"Don't we wanna see them, though?"

"Yes!" Shay sat up straighter and snatched my cell from the nightstand. "Let's call!"

"No, no, no." I shook my wild mess of blond hair. "Put that away. We'll look thirsty as hell."

She laughed and waved my phone before my eyes. "We *are* thirsty as hell, Callie."

"And it's just the guys," Mia said with a casual shrug. "I don't feel the need to fake indifference."

"I think it will freak them out."

Shay frowned at me. "Seriously?"

"Let them come to us," I suggested as I smoothed the blanket over my lap. "You know how desperate they are, especially after they tasted a sample. They won't be able to help themselves."

Shay caved with a slump. "You're right. We shouldn't do anything that we normally wouldn't."

"Exactly." I grinned and nudged her shoulder. "If we don't want things to change, we shouldn't change things."

"That was hella deep, girl."

"Except for changing that whole 'making out' thing," Mia added with a giggle. "I hope we mix in more of that."

Someone suddenly pounded at the front door and scared the fuck out of us, but we hit a full frenzy when we heard Judge yelling for us to open up. We looked at each other in panic mode, then I assumed control. "Go get dressed, both of you!"

"Just get me something of yours!" Shay whisper-yelled in my face.

"I can't get up until you leave!" I winced, then my eyes darted low to my bare cooch, resting warm and toasty under the comforter. Screw the jokes that would follow. Last night's breathless self-satisfaction was worth it.

"Again?" Mia tipped her head back and laughed. "What the fuck, Callie?"

Shay's jaw dropped. "I'm not sure if I'm repulsed or intrigued."

Most of the time, the guys would quickly knock and roll right in, but we locked the door while we slept, and the pounding was growing impatient.

After our erotic exploration last night, I expected our boys to play it cool for a respectable period, then maybe tease in our group texts or flaunt extra flirting when we studied. This sudden morning visit whipped even more chaos into the already unhinged weekend. Fuck, I hadn't had time to give any of this thorough thought, aside from the tipsy visions of getting fuckin' railed as I strummed myself.

"Go! Hurry!" I shoved both of my besties on the shoulder, so they finally bolted from my bed and turned in opposite directions in the hallway. I wiggled into running shorts and a crew neck sweatshirt, then met Mia in the bathroom.

"Hair, face, or teeth?" she squealed. "What's my priority? *Fuck!*"

"Teeth!" I insisted.

We brushed quickly side by side, finishing before Shay even joined us, then we hauled ass to the living room where the relentless knocking continued. I heard my phone ringing in the bedroom but decided to leave it. One of them, likely Evan, was obviously getting huffy.

"Okay. Let's collect ourselves," I said as I smoothed my wild strays. "I'll piss around with the dishwasher. You answer the door."

Mia nodded. "Okay. Act casual."

"Right." I loaded last night's dirty silverware, knowing that Mia would fuck up the whole "casual" plan with some smartass slip.

Judge grinned with that gorgeous smile as soon as he stepped inside. "Good morning!"

"We brought replenishments!" Decker raised two paper bags at his sides, displaying those thick, flexed biceps.

"What took you so long?" Evan complained as he scanned the room for evidence of our delay. "I just tried to call."

I greeted them with a flirty smile and bumped the dishwasher closed with my hip. "Aww, did you miss us already?"

All three mumbled versions of "maybe" as they unloaded the surprise breakfast delivery. Each appeared bright-eyed, freshly showered, and puffy from a possible morning workout. My mind drifted with memories of hard muscles and hot mouths.

"We were still in bed when you knocked. Callie's bed, actually."

Here we go.

Decker raised curious brows for Mia. "Callie's bed? Nice." I rolled my eyes and started the dishwasher cycle. I guess this was our version of "acting casual."

"And she was naked again, as usual," Mia continued the taunt. "At least on the bottom."

"As usual?" I laughed. "I think you mean twice."

"You were all in Callie's bed, and she was naked again?" Evan asked. "Why, exactly?"

Mia shot me a wicked grin. "She's just naughty like that."

This fuckin' girl.

Our prissy Shay, polished perfectly from head to toe, glided from the hallway as if she'd been awake for hours. She batted her made-up lashes at the boys and twirled her pigtails around her fingers. I loved her, but I hated her.

"Hey, guys!"

"Hey! We got a bunch of random stuff at Sunrise Bakery. Donuts, muffins, croissants..." Decker counted off breakfast items.

Judge laughed and pointed to his contribution on the counter. "Don't forget this cardboard box of coffee, which is just fucking wrong in theory."

Evan pulled out a dining room chair and gestured like a restaurant host. "Have a seat, girls. We'll set you up."

Mia eyed him with skepticism. "Really?"

Decker grabbed the paper bags of baked goodies. "We insist."

Hmm.

We parked at the small table and waited for service as the guys shot us casual grins and prepared our buffet. Sure, they were sweethearts on an average day, but no way they would plan this without an agenda. What could they possibly have to announce with this elaborate display?

"What the fuck is going on?" Shay mouthed to us. Mia and I offered only shrugs of equal confusion in response.

"Your coffee, ladies." Judge beamed as he delivered our steamy addiction. Evan emptied a paper bag in the middle of the table, and little creamers of different colors rolled between us. I grabbed a blue French Vanilla.

Mia cocked her head, eyes shifting between our benefactors. "They even got our cups right. Definitely fuckin' sus."

Judge *had* assigned the correct cups. Mia added a caramel creamer, then sipped from her Gemini mug. Shay tapped freshly manicured fingers along her curved replica of the periodic table. I watched ribbons of sweet cream swirl inside my beach scene and traced fingertips over the mantra printed in the warm sand.

The ocean is calling and I must go.

"*And* your breakfast is served." Deck parked a cookie sheet of various baked goods in the center of the table and tossed arms to his sides with pride.

Hell, if they were going through all this trouble, why not eat? I snagged a chocolate chip muffin and relaxed back into my chair. "This is so thoughtful, boys. Thank you!"

Shay smiled. "Just what we needed."

Evan tugged two bar stools closer to the food. Judge backed into a seat and got right down to the unspoken business.

"So, who wants to talk about last night?"

"Hit it." Mia smiled over her cherished cup.

Deck slid into the empty chair beside me at the table and sipped. "Well, for starters, did you have fun?"

Shay jumped in on our behalf. "Sure. I think we all did." Mia and I nodded along as we chewed.

Deck stayed on topic. "Any regrets?"

"I wish you guys would've stayed over," Mia sighed.

"Same, Mia. Same," Judge agreed under his breath.

I needed the male perspective. "What do you guys think?"

"I'm worried about things being weird," Evan said as he rubbed the back of his neck. "I just don't know."

I let that valid concern settle in my chest. Of course, our first instincts were panic and suspicion when they showed up unannounced, but as our eyes met around the table, I found the same respect that had bonded us from the beginning.

"Do you think this is weird?" Shay asked softly.

"No, but if our crazy nights escalate, we could fuck things up," Evan challenged her.

"True, I guess."

Judge's shoulders sank and he looked down at his coffee cup. "I worried this morning that we'd taken advantage of you," he confessed. "Made me sick."

What?

"You didn't," I quickly assured him. "I promise, it's not like that."

Mia shook her head, too. "No way, Judge. We were drunk, but not *that* drunk."

Shay smiled to herself and ripped off another bite of jelly donut. "I remember everything I did…with each of you."

"Right," I agreed wholeheartedly. "The beer loosened me up, but I was all in. *My* choice."

Relief flooded Judge's face. "It's just that nights like that…"

Decker finished the fleeting thought. "Nights like that don't just happen. Not without jealousy or embarrassment."

"Well, it happened," Mia said. "I'm not jealous at all. It was kinda hot watching you fuck around with my girls." I couldn't appreciate my free-spirited friend more than I did at that moment. Validation swelled in my chest.

"Come on." Evan wasn't buying it. "I just find that impossible to believe."

I repositioned in my seat as her bold admission encouraged mine. "I'm with Mia. I loved watching you guys grinding on my girls. Super fucking hot."

Shay laughed and gestured with her mug to the space behind me. "Especially Callie and Deck against that wall. *Damn.*"

A slight pink rushed to Deck's cheeks. "You saw that?"

"Hell yes, I did." She fanned herself with a napkin. "Christ, you two were on fire over there."

I swallowed a drink and pretended to examine my new pink polish as heat moistened my shorts. I'd been mesmerized by all the other couples in action, but I hadn't fully processed my instant arousal at being watched myself.

"So, what now?" Mia asked. The guys exchanged mischievous glances, then Decker nodded for Judge to take the mic.

Uh-huh. I knew it.

"So, we did some talking this morning…" Judge hesitated and looked to his counterparts for reassurance.

Shay blinked up at him on the tall stool. "And?"

"…and we agreed that the three of us wanna sleep with the three of you. For real."

"Sleep with?" Mia chuckled under her breath. I pressed my lips together to stifle an immature giggle.

Judge smirked down at her before continuing. "But we're not ready to take it that far and risk the friendship we have."

Evan nodded and took a quick drink. "We just don't think it's worth it." I sipped my coffee and added another vanilla creamer. This entire speech was quite disappointing.

"So, that's it?" Shay asked with resignation.

Decker cleared his throat to garner our attention. "Not exactly."

The guys glanced at each other again as Judge shifted uncomfortably on his stool. Evan shook his head at his lap. "Good luck with that, bro," he mumbled. "No fucking way."

Mia threw her hands up. "What's with all the weird fuckin' eye contact? Someone spill it, for fuck's sake!"

"Okay, okay." Decker shifted forward with authority and interlaced fingers over the table. "Now, we've all talked about wanting some casual sex, but that's the problem. With us, it wouldn't be casual. Agreed?" My female half nodded along. "But what if we could fuck regularly, within this group, but avoid the awkwardness the next day?"

Shay rolled her pretty eyes across from me. "Impossible."

"Maybe," he challenged, grinning with boyish charm, "or maybe we could pull it off."

Hmm.

Judge jumped in. "What if we planned nights here where we all hooked up, but we didn't know who we slept with?"

I shook my head with a laugh. "That makes no fuckin' sense."

Evan joined the case after we'd absorbed the initial shock. "What if you could be waiting in a bedroom, then one of us rolled in? Boom. *Magic.*"

Mia doubted the possibility, too. "Um, I think I'd know which of you were on top of me."

Decker nodded and sipped. "That's fair. Let's take it one obstacle at a time."

"First of all, you look different." Shay tossed a palm. "Hair, obviously."

Evan waved it off. "Easily fixed with a trip to the barber."

"And I know I got my own feel over here," Judge noted as he rubbed his buzz cut, "but if we're all tight enough, you won't notice the difference."

Mia's eyes widened and swerved to Deck's dark, tousled locks. "You guys would cut your hair like Judge? Get the fuck out."

"For this chance?" Deck deepened his voice and licked his lips. "In a fucking heartbeat."

Shay glanced at Evan's sexy shag. "You can't be serious."

"Hair grows back," Evan assured her. "It's nothing."

"Okay, fine," she continued. "You're different sizes."

Mia's mouth dropped in shock. "You've seen their cocks?"

This girl.

"No, duh. I mean their bodies."

Judge shook his head. "Not really. If so, it wouldn't be obvious to you in a dark room."

I eyed each guy carefully but decided that I needed visual evidence. "Line up and prove it."

They hopped right up and stripped off their shirts with no hesitation, revealing hard, muscular chests and trim, tight abs that I hadn't fully appreciated during the flexing contest last night. Hell, if this didn't work out, the encore show alone was worth it.

Mia scanned each ripple and ridge. "Hmm."

Evan gestured to his firm physique, then nodded to the others. "See? And we're all within an inch of each other height-wise."

"You measured?"

"We actually did."

Decker added more support for the cause. "Judge is wider through the shoulders, but only slightly."

Shay cocked her head with surprise. "You really *can't* tell." She was onto something, for sure. All three guys flexed with stacked abs and puffy pecs. I noticed only scarce chest hair, not nearly enough to distinguish individuals in the dark. Mia teased that they could continue the meeting topless, but they simply laughed and returned to their fully clothed positions.

Shay was buying in. "Okay, so you cut your hair to the same length. Your bodies wouldn't be discernable. I'm getting it."

Hold up.

"We're missing the most obvious giveaway," I said. "The voices."

Decker smirked at me and lowered his tone. "No talking. No sound."

"Come on," I scoffed with skepticism.

"No way!" Mia laughed and crossed her arms over her tits. "You guys couldn't do it."

"The hell I couldn't," Deck said.

"Trust me," Judge added, "we all fuckin' could."

"I'm not a big talker in bed," Evan told us. "No loss there."

"Wait. So, no background music or anything?" Shay asked, her pretty face scrunched with confusion.

Judge shook his head. "Too many variables with tunes in the rooms. Best to keep it simple."

"But we could play it from the living room."

"Sounds like you're looking for some cover," Evan said, shooting her an arrogant, amused grin. "You worried about controlling yourself?"

Shay rolled her eyes and waved him off, but I noticed the creeping pink on her cheeks. Hell, I had the same concerns. I wasn't exactly the quiet type once the peen was in place.

"Just fuck noises and sexy breaths?" Mia giggled with a shrug. "I'm up for the challenge."

As the guys exchanged satisfied smiles, I imagined how each would sound as they railed me, their rugged rasps amplified in the shadowy silence. I shifted in my chair and stretched an aroused ache from my neck.

We sat quietly, staring at our creamy coffee and considering this potential plan, our naturally analytical med school minds likely approaching each scientific and logistical hurdle. Our boys had presented this elaborate scheme so smoothly that it took a couple of minutes for the next round of doubt to play out.

I shook my head at my muffin crumbs. "No. It still won't work."

"Why not?" Deck asked, fully prepared to fight for it.

"You'd know which of us you were fucking," I insisted.

"How?"

"Your hair is all about the same length," Evan argued. "Your bodies are practically identical."

Shay paused us with a palm. "Wait. My boobs are bigger. Just a little, but they are. I borrowed this hot bra from Callie last week, and the girls were pinched."

"Which bra?" I asked.

She gestured to her nips. "That white one with the silver trim."

"Oh, I *love* that one."

Evan scoffed over our banter. "Shay, you really think we would know your tits from theirs? In the dark?"

"I'd like to think so."

"We wouldn't," Deck laughed. "Trust me."

Mia offered up the real thing. "Should we show our goods so you can compare?"

Wow, Mia. Wow.

Judge perked right up. "Yeah, you absolutely should, if you feel comfortable, that is."

"I guess we *should* be sure," Evan said with cheesy, acceptable sarcasm. Deck simply raised his open palm with an invitation.

Shay shook her head with a laugh as she stood. "You guys are fucking tools, but I'll flash my tits for ya anyway."

Hell, I would've let them see much more than that last night. Plus, this fuck-buddy plan was quite intriguing, so I was willing to step it up. I stood along the wall in a sweet little lineup with my girls, and we jerked up our shirts to display our small racks. Mia and Shay had seen my boobs plenty of times over the years as we borrowed clothes and readied ourselves for wild nights, but I wanted the guys to appreciate what I offered underneath. Their eager eyes roamed from nipple to nipple as they evaluated every anatomical detail.

Decker collapsed back in his chair and raked fingers through his dark hair. "Fuck, you're all so hot."

"Okay, okay. That's enough." I dropped my chin to cover my natural blush after the breathy compliment, then we returned to our seats and waited impatiently for the analysis.

"You girls are so cool with all this. It's fuckin' wild." Judge shook his head in disbelief. "We thought you'd wanna kill us."

"And, just to clear it up," Evan said after a sip, "you're all similar enough. Perky and round."

For a moment, the remarkable transparency of this conversation left me shaking my head as I gazed at the scattering of coffee creamers. Christ, do things like this ever happen in real life? Shay's simple sleepwear suggestion last night had created this alternate universe of fantasy, and I sure as fuck was enjoying my visit.

I drummed my fingertips on the tabletop. "We'd have to mix up the rooms."

Judge nodded. "Yep. Every time."

"Right. You couldn't see what room we entered, and we couldn't see what room you exited," Mia reasoned.

Deck gestured with his mug. "Timing would be crucial, for sure."

Another period of silence passed, our suddenly shy eyes dancing around the table with thoughts of the forbidding fucking. We refilled our coffee quietly, minds cranking through an extra shift to make this work. I surveyed the thoughtful gazes, firm muscles, and confident lips of our appetizing visitors. I couldn't believe they'd devised this entire blueprint for us, specifically for our pussies, all as an effort to protect our friendship. It was kind of endearing in a slightly fucked up way.

"There *is* one more thing," Deck noted, raising his eyebrows between the boys with a slight wince of his shoulders.

"Oh, fuck," Judge laughed and turned to a cringing Evan. "We almost forgot."

"Forgot what?" I pried.

Deck took a slow breath of confidence. "We need to talk about how each of you, um, tend to your garden."

~ 4 ~

Well, shit was getting real now.

"Tend to our garden?" Shay shook her head in disbelief. "How fuckin' quaint."

"It matters, though," Evan insisted.

"You just need us all to look the same?" Mia asked, hovering on the verge of investment.

Deck shrugged and shifted in his chair. "More like *feel* the same."

"Like the same design," I clarified.

"Exactly."

Hmm.

Shay grinned right at me. "Speaking of gardens, Callie doesn't have much hair down there. Just a cute little patch."

I choked mid-drink on my coffee. *These crazy fuckin' girls.*

Mia nodded with amusement. "That's true. We both saw it yesterday." The guys swiveled to me with wide-eyed fascination. My girls knew that I low-key loved the attention.

"It's not as intriguing as you think," I explained with an eye roll, hoping that my nonchalant words overpowered my blush. "They were both in my room when I hopped out of bed. I forgot I wasn't wearing panties."

Decker chewed his lower lip and shifted his focus to Shay. "You got a good look?"

They're just gonna talk about my pussy between bites of pastry?

She nodded. "A few seconds' worth. I know I have more down there than she does. Mine's like a little landing strip."

"That's fine." Judge stretched beefy arms over his head with a half yawn. "So, you three just pick a palette that works and roll with it."

Mia held up a palm. "Well, not so fast."

"You object?"

She shook her head. "Not to looking the same. Not at all. I just..."

"Oh," I giggled as she peeked over at me. "That's right."

Judge looked between us for more detail. "What? What's right?"

"I don't have hair down there," Mia confessed. You could've heard a pin drop. Evan and Judge stared slack-jawed as if she'd climbed on the table and stripped. Decker was about to sip his coffee, but he stopped the cup in mid-air on the flight to his mouth. "What? It's not a big deal. I just prefer to be bare." She ignored the dramatic reactions and chowed down on her glazed donut without a care in the world.

"Believe me, I love all brands," Judge said after a hard swallow, "but bare is next level."

Decker leaned forward in his chair again. "It's completely smooth? Like porn smooth?"

Mia nodded as she chewed. Hell, I couldn't fault him for the specific interest. After all, I enjoyed some smooth-pussied smut on occasion.

"I've always wanted to do that," Shay admitted after a drink. "I just never had the guts."

"Same," I said. Mia had tried to convince us both to take the plunge in the past, claiming that the thrill was next fucking level, but we'd chickened out every time. This could be just the nudge I needed.

Judge was all about the logistics. "So, do you shave it? How often?"

Fuckin' boys.

"Oh, hell no," Mia chuckled and waved him off. "My hairdresser waxes it for me. She takes excellent care of my puss."

Well, damn. Maybe it was time for excellent care of my puss, too. "Will she still do ours?"

"Sure."

"Well, now we have to make this work," Deck mumbled.

Shay smacked his arm. "Oh, *now* we do?"

"Come on, Shay," Deck consoled with a knee pat. "I mean, no offense to your landing strip, cause I'm sure it's sexy as fuck, but the thought of you all smooth against me?"

Evan shifted on the barstool and made a slight package adjustment. "I'm gonna have to step out if this line of questioning continues."

"I wanna try it," Shay ignored him and piped up. "For the record, though, I like my cooch, too. She's just as good."

"It's your call," Mia said with a shrug. "I'm sure you're perfect under there, but like I've told ya before, I've fucked with and without hair. Bare is so much better."

The vivid explanation left a dull ache between my legs. "You can really tell the difference?"

She nodded and sipped. "It's so much more sensitive."

The brazen, cocky smirks flashing on the guys' faces proved to be all too fuckin' cute for Shay. "And what about *your* 'gardens'?" she sassed with theatric finger quotes. "You coming to the salon with us?"

A collective gasp from the shocked, sexy men sucked the air from the space. Deck instinctively placed a slow, protective hand over his balls like I was already warming the wax beside the leftover donuts. Judge's adorable features twitched into pure terror at the mere notion of upgrading his sac. Evan hopped up from his stool so quickly that it almost toppled over behind him.

"Absolutely fuckin' not," he refused with a defiant palm push. "Next topic." We giggled innocently with no intention of insisting on real manscaping. I had no interest in ball action, hair or not, but these hypocritical reactions were something to see.

Judge tried to soften the blow. "Look, it's different for us guys..."

"*Right*," we replied in unison, sarcasm pouring from our amused lips.

Deck, inarguably the smartest brain of the manly bunch, appeared stumped for the first time since we'd met. He stared with stunned eyes at nothing in particular, and I'm pretty sure that a bead of sweat was forming at his temple. Luckily for the boys, we had our own braniac to step in for the save.

"I'll tell ya what," Shay offered with mock sympathy as she cleaned up her chaos, "if you don't wanna groom your groins, we should at least get a peek at what we're expected to work with here."

Brilliant.

My buzzed brain had assumed that they were all packing heat during the dance party, but I wouldn't mind a closer inspection just to be sure. I mean, hell, why not at this point?

"A peek at what, exactly?" Judge asked, his nose crinkled with confusion. "You wanna see our nuts?"

For fuck's sake.

The caffeine had trickled south and the urge to pee almost consumed my fascination. But my entertained ass wasn't going anywhere, though, especially not since we'd successfully turned the tables.

Mia jumped in full force. "At least a puff of pubes," she explained. "You know we'll be smooth, but we gotta be sure that none of you stand out."

I couldn't argue with her logic, but the irony of today's developments hit me sideways, and I chewed my lip to will away the humor. Hell, only an hour ago, I'd been concerned about calling them too quickly. Now, we were contemplating a full-blown pubic hair evaluation as they sipped from our spare mugs.

"Fine," Deck conceded with a lazy grin in my direction. "The girls have a valid point. Let's show 'em some fuzz so we can move on."

This next-level lineup would be something to fuckin' see. I exchanged wide-eyed excitement with the girls while our guests positioned themselves along the wall. Evan, clearly relieved that his sac was safe from the shears, grinned from ear to ear and lowered his slinky shorts to his love line with no prompting. I selfishly gestured for him to lift the hem of his tee so I could appreciate the full scope of that angled path underneath. The other guys followed suit, shifting their weight anxiously and displaying their carved abs as we tried to contain our thirst. Christ, how in the hell did we get so lucky?

I was no pube expert, but the three tufts of dick decoration seemed similar in thickness and style, at least visually. I was much more interested in the brains and bodies attached to those macho gardens, so I left the potential impact of the fur to be sorted by the others. Mia stepped before Judge and glanced down at his lowered waistband before licking her lips.

"Satisfied?" Judge grinned as he tightened his muscular core with an arrogant flex. *Fuck.* He looked good.

"You know what I'm gonna ask," she said with a sexy smirk. "I hope it's not offensive, but it's been a while since I enjoyed some chocolate."

Ahh. We're getting hella deep here.

"Not at all," he laughed and gestured to his boys with a head nod, "but I'm pretty sure my patch feels just like theirs."

Mia smiled seductively and stepped closer with a teasing shrug. "Well, there's an easy way to find out."

This sudden, palpable tension between them drew the attention of every eye in the room. I clenched my bare thighs together, hoping to curb both the dull throb downtown and the frustration of my full bladder. They stood close enough to kiss and, if Mia dove off the deep end, I was fully prepared to climb one of the remaining stacks of sex beside me.

"Just how far do you wanna take this?" Judge taunted, gazing at her short shorts with suggestive eyes and wiggling his long fingers. "I'm game if you are."

Well, damn.

Mia tipped her head back with a throaty laugh, then shoved him in the center of his thick chest. The heavy vibe shifted to light humor as we settled back into our seats, content that the man bushes wouldn't hinder our progress.

Decker exhaled beside me. "Where did you girls come from? You're like fuckin' aliens or something."

"Right?" Judge chuckled with a slight head shake. "We had no idea."

I finished my last drink with a flaunt. "You've just been working up the wrong women."

"Trust me," Evan laughed from his perch, "we fuckin' realize that now."

"Girls like to fuck, too," Shay said. "You think we have any more time or tolerance for a relationship than you do?"

I laughed in agreement. "We don't."

"Nope." Mia licked coffee from her lips. "But we definitely have needs."

"And we're here to fulfill those needs," Judge offered with attractive arrogance. "I hope."

Evan motioned for us to continue. "Let's keep going."

"Are you all socked or snipped?" Shay asked. The guys confirmed their clipped tips, and we moved on. Hell, that was easy.

I looked between my potential fuck partners for additional speed bumps. "Facial hair."

Decker stroked his scruffy jawline. "I usually shave mine when it warms up in the spring. I'll just lose it early."

I imagined the scratch of that beard against my pending smooth slit and immediately spoke up. "What if we want the facial hair?"

Evan rubbed his clean-shaven chin. "I mean, I can grow mine out. Will take some time, though."

"What do you girls prefer?" Judge asked, leaving the decision to us. "I give zero fucks either way."

"I love it, especially considering my situation down there," Mia said, her eyes darting to her puss.

Shay squirmed in her seat. "Right. That could get interesting, for sure."

"Maybe Judge and Decker can trim theirs to some light stubble, then Evan can catch up quicker," I suggested. The guys agreed with no gripes, willing to match like triplets just to get in our pants. I lost my thoughts in a daydream of manly scruff, wet lips, and a smooth cooch, crossing my legs tightly together under the table until Shay spoke up.

"We should all go get tested. You know, just to be safe." Our medically inclined crew offered no objections.

"Well, I'll just throw this out there," Judge presented with a hint of embarrassment. "What about your periods? Are you all on the same days?" I held back a laugh.

"We all have an IUD, right?" Mia confirmed. "We should be good."

"Right. I don't have periods at all now," I explained. "And fuck remembering a pill every day with our schedules."

"Same here," Shay said. "That's why I got mine. Hell, even *I* was missing doses."

Mia fingered her mug and glanced around the table. "Does anyone like toys?"

I wasn't sure where the boys stood, but I'd never explored the world of pleasure devices. Mia had bragged about her stash in the past, but hell, I'd only had tame fucks before and never asked her for the details. I was a bit intimidated by the thought, but my sexually curious side waited for the other responses.

"Sure." Evan grinned with a deviant smile. "I'm down with props."

"Maybe," Deck hesitated. "Elaborate."

"Nothing too heavy. Maybe a vibrator. Cuffs would be too tough to deal with in the dark."

Oh.

Judge took his turn with the subtle junk adjustment. "Yeah. I'm good with that."

Shay shot me with a sheepish smile. She'd admired Mia's wild ways with the same inexperienced eyes as I had before. At least we were cruising in the same lane together.

"What else?" Deck asked.

Hmm.

"If we all test negative, are we using condoms?" I glanced around the table to no immediate answers. This may be a topic for debate.

Mia scanned all our pondering faces. "Well, first, can we agree that we won't be fucking outside of this circle?" We offered an enthusiastic chorus of approval. Hell, why would we need to fuck anyone else?

"And that's gotta hold up," Shay added with authority. "No dragging any randoms back to your apartment. It's us or nothing."

"Well, the goes the same for you," Judge said. "Don't be bringing any fuck boys home."

Decker chewed on his lower lip in thought. "And I think we should agree that if one of us meets someone for real and we want out, we're all out."

Evan nodded. "Right. It doesn't work without all of us."

I agreed along with the girls. I hadn't had decent dick in too long, and I was more than ready to be fucked by the men at this table. I lacked the time and desire to look for love just like the others. No issue there.

Deck circled back. "So, condoms?"

"Do we need them if we're loyal?" Mia asked.

Judge spoke up. "I lean towards yes."

"Why?" Deck asked.

He tossed palms. "I don't know, man. I've just always worn one."

"Is it a trust thing?" Shay asked. "And there's no wrong answer here, but we need to be on the same page."

I didn't want Judge to feel awkward in any way, so I offered a sympathetic smile. "It's a giant leap of faith. I get it."

"Okay, think of it this way," Shay said. "Would you still wear one if you and I were in a monogamous relationship?"

"I mean, I guess not," Judge conceded. "Not if you weren't gonna get pregnant."

"So, it *is* a trust thing."

"Maybe it is," he answered with a shrug. "Hell, I don't know."

"This will feel like a real relationship," Deck said. "I think, anyway."

"Not much experience in that department?" Mia teased.

Deck flashed a charming grin. "You could say that."

"I'm okay with no condom if I see papers," I explained, "but if anyone feels uncomfortable, I'm fine either way. No pressure."

Evan stood from the stool to stretch, giving us another glimpse of his layers of muscle. "We have time to decide, so let's table that for later," he suggested through a yawn. This planned presentation had clearly taken priority over sleep.

"You guys thought of this whole scenario." Shay glanced between the boys. "Did we cover your syllabus?" They nodded with smug grins, seemingly satisfied with this initial planning meeting.

"We'll have some logistics to work out, like blacking out the rooms and stuff like that, but we made good progress." Evan laughed and tossed palms. "Hell, I expected to be slapped across the face, so, all things considered, this went well."

Decker collected our empty coffee cups and stacked them in the sink, then turned to the table and smirked. "We need a code word."

Judge nodded with enthusiasm. "Yeah! This operation is definitely code word worthy."

"Fucking three hot chicks in this orchestrated plan?" Evan laughed. "Yeah, I'd say that's worthy."

"And we're keeping all this secret, right?" Shay asked around the room. "Because you know what the talk would be."

"I hear ya," Deck agreed. "Let's just keep it here. We can always pretend to be dating if anyone catches on."

"Good. So, back to the code word," Mia giggled. "That feels so official."

I scoped the space for inspiration, and the idea clicked when I glanced at our dark hallway. "Let's call it Three Doors," I suggested. "That's normal enough."

"Three Doors!" Mia's smile brightened even more. "It's perfect!"

"Anyone up for some Three Doors tonight?" Evan asked, giving the new name a test run.

Decker snickered under his breath. "I fuckin' wish."

"Me, too," I sighed dramatically. "Grow your shit quick, Evan."

Judge crossed his arms over his broad chest. "So, what do we do in the meantime? While we're waiting, I mean."

"I like Hour of Power. We could fuck around with that on the weekends until Evan hits puberty," Shay joked.

He shot her a cocky smirk and stroked his smooth chin. "Just wait until it grows in. Maybe you'll be the first to enjoy it."

"Touché."

Mia rubbed her hands together with giddy excitement. "Can we all shop for toys together?"

"Sure," Evan agreed. "Next weekend?"

"Yeah. I can't be messing with this shit during the week," Judge said. "I fuckin' wish, though."

"So, it's class all day, studying all night, and then sexy time every weekend."

Decker leaned on the bar with a mischievous smile. "If we pull this off, it will be tough to wait between sessions."

"Maybe, but this semester is already bending us over," Shay said. "We need to stay on point." Both Shay and Decker could likely ace each class in their sleep, but I appreciated the dedication to our bigger goals. Nobody needed to exercise extra discipline more than I did.

The remarkable breakfast came to a natural close. Judge and Evan returned their stools to the bar, and Deck bagged the remaining baked goods. I wanted them to stay all day, but I had papers to write and sections to study. I guess space was a good thing for now.

Fuck. Was I missing them already?

Shay batted flirty lashes and toyed with her black pigtails. "Goodbye kisses? Same as last night?"

Evan stepped closer to her with that beach boy swagger. "You just love kisses, don't you?" He interrupted her eager nod with curled fingers around the back of her neck.

Here we go.

Decker offered open arms. "Come here, Mia."

Judge extended both hands and tugged me in against his towering body. His sensual, soft lips wrapped over mine, then his twisting tongue taunted me with slow, sweeping laps. As soon as his palms cupped my ass, I dove in deeper, crushing my round breasts against his chest and dragging fingertips through his short beard. After only a few seconds, we found ourselves frenching hard as we explored this deep, newly discovered desire. My pussy moistened with just the hint of the action to come as he explored my every curve. I felt no shame in taking advantage of my assigned time and making my girls wait for their turns, but a naughty, hidden side of my soul was desperate to peek as each matchup groped and licked. We finally broke for breath, only to find the other four finished and waiting.

Shay fanned herself and blasted me. "Damn, Callie. Just take his pants off right here. We'll watch."

"Hell, I'm down," I laughed.

"I don't think so." Evan approached aggressively, and my heart fluttered as he backed me against the table's edge. I lost track of the others when our tongues collided in a wet, hot mess, both of us moaning as we shared steamy air between our lips. He held me high, palming my ribs with his warm hands, and my nipples hardened as his thumbs massaged with demanding, hungry strokes.

Motherfuck.

Decker was waiting patiently for me when Evan eventually shifted away. He stepped into my space and placed a gentle hand on my hip. "You like slow kisses?" he whispered, his fingers toying under the hem of my sweatshirt.

Fucking fuck.

Breathe.

"I think I'll like all your kisses, Deck," I flirted as my cheeks pinked.

He lowered his mouth to mine and teased me with his steady, winding tongue, but I immediately demanded more. I tried to deepen our dive, digging my nails into his tee-shirt and gently clawing at his pecs, but unlike his sidekicks, he resisted.

What the fuck?

"You don't wanna kiss me?" I blinked up with an awkward cringe.

Deck pulled back those smirking lips, then lightly laughed at the frustration flashing across my face. He released my waist, pushed my blond hair to the side, and left a seductive whisper against my ear.

"Kissing is one thing, Callie," he said, exaggerating each raspy word, "but I absolutely cannot wait to fuck you."

God.

He blew a hot puff against my jawline, then turned back to the group with a smug grin. "You guys ready?"

I stood there, subtly catching my breath and tingling in all the right places, the wild combination of all three kisses coursing through my veins.

"You okay, Callie? You look a little flushed."

Fucking Shay.

"I'm fine." I blew her off with a wave. "Just taking it all in."

Mia continued the loving roast. "She's gonna run in her room and throw off her panties again as soon as you guys leave."

I finally had the perfect reply after my hurried primp session this morning. "That would be true, but I'm not wearing any." The guys swiveled to my blushing face. Evan whistled under his breath, and Deck chewed on his lower lip, both scanning my shorts for confirmation.

Judge simply shook his head at our antics. "You girls are too much."

~ • ~

"I need to write my paper, but fuck, I can't think straight." I crashed back against the sofa with a bewildered sigh, wishing I could hear the analysis taking place a few floors below. "This is unbelievable."

"So, is it gonna work?" Shay asked as she parked next to me.

"Probably not, but we have to try for it to fail." Mia shrugged over us. "At least we'll get pounded for one night."

I fidgeted with the hem of my sweatshirt and sighed. "They're our closest friends. What about the fallout if this goes south?"

"The risk is there," Shay said, "but we trust them. That counts for something."

"And we all want fucked," Mia reasoned with tossed palms. "It's better than some random."

"True, I guess."

Shay's brows furrowed at me with concern. "Hold up. Are you having second thoughts?"

"After all that? Hell no! You know how my mind works. I'm just flooded over here."

In more ways than one.

"Well, let's hit a hotter topic." She crossed a leg underneath her ass and lowered her voice like the guys were in the next room. "Who do you think is the best kisser?"

Mia answered right away. "Evan. He takes control and I fuckin' love that."

Shay nodded. "I love how Evan touches me, too. But Judge? With that tongue? Like *fuck*."

I recalled each man sliding curious hands all over my body as my lips danced with theirs. Hell, I found myself surprised that my buds even considered a contender at this point. "I don't have a favorite kiss at all," I admitted honestly.

"How can't you?" Shay asked.

"It's not like we've kissed them enough to distinguish," I said nonchalantly. "They're all fuckin' fire. That's all I know."

"Well, no matter what happens, we have to stick together. If anything messes with this," Mia explained, motioning with a circling finger, "we end it."

I nodded. "Absolutely."

Shay jokingly dismissed us. "I'd give at least one of you up for really good dick. Maybe even both." I scowled and smacked her perfect fucking pigtail with a throw pillow. "Okay, okay," she laughed and batted me away. "We come first."

Mia checked her cell screen and sighed. "Time to hit the books, ladies."

I shuffled to the kitchen for a bottle of apple juice and then assumed the position at my bedroom desk. Before I typed even the first word of my paper, Shay cracked the door and poked her head inside.

"Yes, dear?" I smiled.

"Make sure you set an alarm."

"Alarm? For what?"

Shay covered her giggling mouth. "Your finger fuck breaks. Don't want ya to lose track of time."

This girl.

I sarcastically flipped my blond hair from my shoulder. "You're *obsessed* with me."

She shrugged with a sneaky grin. "Maybe I'd like to watch at some point. I could learn a thing or two since you seem to be an expert."

I lovingly rolled my eyes. "Get the fuck out."

~ 5 ~

Despite my sporadic, dirty daydreaming, I managed to finish all of one paper and most of another in just a few hours. I straightened my bedroom, tucked away all my laundry, and even cleaned the kitchen while the other girls worked behind closed doors. Remnants of our morning meeting lay discarded in our trash bin. The crushed box of coffee nearly breached the bag, and the colored creamer containers revealed our various tastes. I replayed the earlier conversation as I rested against the counter and wondered about the male perspective a few floors below.

I considered Deck's suggestion that our arrangement would feel like a real relationship. Fuck, I hadn't stumbled down that path since high school. I'd fucked around on *my* terms in undergrad and rarely spent a weekend night alone, but loyalty was neither offered nor expected by the brazen boys on campus. And hell, not by me either. Of course, I didn't deliver my entire menu to every partner, not to shame those who did, but I'd shared the occasional midnight snack.

Evan, Judge, and Decker had seemed like the typical cocky coeds when they'd first approached us in the fall, with their bold advances and dazzling smiles. I figured that my girls and I would get pounded by the hunky neighbors to relieve the pressure of our demanding medical program, then we'd move on just as we had before. Who knew that the guys would collectively offer so much more than their initial impressions implied?

Within weeks of our tipsy introductions at the otherwise lame mixer, compounded with a few incidental encounters on campus, we found our trios naturally gravitating toward each other. Our solemn solo study nights blossomed into valuable group grind sessions. Makeshift meals morphed into "family" affairs around our cluttered coffee table. Our sexy sixsome developed a genuine friendship as we bonded over the painstaking hardships of being rookies. Sure, my lusty eyes often wandered from the books to the beef, but I, like the others, hadn't considered making real moves and jacking up the group groove.

I needed dick, though. Could this really work?

I had to admit, our handsome classmates had shown us nothing but respect from the beginning. In fact, of all the men I'd rolled with in the past, these three were top-fucking-notch, especially after getting to know them better over the last several months. Judge's cocky flirtations at the start had been but a shell protecting the sweet, sensitive guy inside. Evan's surfer boy smoothness was only a cover for the amped, energetic flirt of the clique. Quiet, impenetrable Decker was nowhere to be found now, with a confident, thoughtful brainiac stealing the show instead. Evan, Judge, and Deck had invested in us, not only as female friends but as counterparts and equals. That notion provided not only the comfort to agree to this Three Doors game but also the mild anxiety over the potential failure.

Sexual tension often seasoned our nights together regardless of the agenda, but we covered it with shallow jokes mocking our lack of action, including complaints about cramped fingers from strumming and sore forearms from stroking. Mia had teased once that her favorite vibrator had submitted a vacation request, to which Evan had countered with his lonely desire to fuck a warm burrito from the food truck on the corner. Flirty eyes shifted from one delicious body to another as we hovered over our takeout meals and laborious studies, but we kept our boundaries in check out of respect for the friendship.

Until last night, anyway.

I shrugged off my rambling thoughts and turned back to the quiet kitchen, finding myself missing my neighbors in an unfamiliar way. I brushed fingertips over my soft lips and licked the memories of their kisses, my body aching to feel strong, trusted arms around me again. They'd offered a teasing sampler, but I hungered for the entire entrée.

Mia invaded my horny fantasies when she shuffled into the kitchen with a loud yawn. I snapped back to the present and noticed the absent hum of the dishwasher, so I decided to unload as we did.

"Tired?"

She shot me a groggy grin. "No, I just woke up."

"You've been sleeping this whole time?"

Mia laughed. "Not the *whole* time. I finished my paper, so I studied for the embryology exam and then grabbed a power nap. Fuck that class, by the way."

I nodded as I returned clean silverware to the drawer. "It confuses the hell out of me."

"I'm counting on Shay to coach me. I suck at it."

"Counting on me for what?" Shay asked as she joined us from her cave.

"Embryology."

She rested elbows on the bar and picked at her nails. "Oh, yeah. That's Wednesday, right?"

"Yep. Gonna be up late Tuesday," I groaned, adding my ocean mug to the collection in the cabinet.

Mia peeled a banana from a basket on the bar and grinned before shoving it between her lips. "Think the guys will come up to study?"

"They always have," Shay figured. "Don't know why they wouldn't."

I closed the last drawer and sighed. "I have a confession, girls." Both motioned for me to continue. "I've been flustered all day. I can't stop thinking about them."

"Glad it's not just me," Mia mumbled as she chewed.

"Same," Shay said. "I miss them already."

"They're just a couple of floors down, ya know," Mia reminded us with a wicked grin.

True.

"You think we should rush them?"

She nodded with enthusiasm. "Abso-fucking-lutely."

Shay was skeptical. "But shouldn't we play it cool after today? Remember your doubt this morning, Callie?"

"Well, yeah," I laughed. "But things have changed with this Three Doors business. I think we should follow our instincts."

Mia giggled beside me. "My instinct is to feel a big dick against me."

"Right?" I fell in with her. "A big dick or three."

Shay needed little convincing. "Okay, okay. Let's see if they're home."

I grabbed my phone from the bar and dropped a quick text as the girls peeked over my shoulders.

```
Callie: hey
 Judge: hey pretty lady
Callie: what's up
  Deck: watching basketball
Callie: no hot women up on our guys, right?
 Judge: lol nope, just us
Callie: studying for embryo with us this week?
  Deck: you know it
```

Shay smiled. "Quick showers and let's hit it."

"We should wear something sneaky or sexy," Mia said, brushing wrinkles from her lounge clothes. "Or maybe both."

"Let's wear all black," Shay giggled. "Like robbers."

"Yes!" Mia clapped. "Let's go steal some shaft!"

This girl.

"Leggings and sports bras?" Shay suggested.

"Sold."

We rinsed off one by one, then popped into our bedrooms to slide into our disguises. I yanked a modest, stretchy bra over my head and was just stepping into my leggings when Shay shuffled in with palms hiding her bare nipples.

"So, yeah, I forgot that I don't own a sports bra."

I laughed. "Well, you know where I keep the goods. Help yourself like always."

Shay thanked me, then fished through my top drawer and tugged a borrowed bra over her bouncy boobs. We nudged each other for prime position before my full-length mirror. "Am I good?"

"Super hot," I assured her. It was true. My girl was a fuckin' knockout.

"Let's freshen up before we chicken out."

We reconvened in the bathroom, creating a chaotic scene of flowy hair as we dried our long locks. I brushed my teeth and watched Mia dig through her toiletry drawer. She sprayed a quick puff of divine perfume on her tits, then passed the pink bottle.

"We'll need to wear the same stuff on Three Doors days," I reasoned, placing strategic splashes along my neck and cleavage. "Lotion and deodorant, too."

Shay raised her eyebrows in the mirror. "I never thought of that, but you're right."

"We'll make a bang basket for all of our sex day goodies," Mia giggled.

I wasn't sure just how the night would evolve, but I was already feeling anxious flutters of anticipation. The entire operation felt like an odd first date mixed with a filthy booty call. I bent at the waist and ran my fingers through my thick hair, then popped up as Shay fluffed her own. "Anything else?"

Mia flashed devilish eyes in the big mirror. "Okay, hear me out. I'm thinking that we could take this to the next level."

Damn, my chick was making moves.

"How?"

"Do you guys still have those sleep masks from the Christmas baskets I made you?" Shay and I nodded with curiosity. Masks? Where the fuck was she going with this? "Good. Go grab them, and I'll explain on the way."

~ • ~

We giggled like school girls skipping class as we glided down the hallway, passing a few curious faces on our joyride. We bounced down the steps of the enclosed stairwell and paused at the third-floor landing, then looked to our mastermind for the next instructions.

"Okay, this may sound crazy," Mia warned, "but it could break the Three Doors ice."

My heart rate hopped. "Nice. Lay it on me."

She slung arms over our shoulders and huddled us up as we listened. "So, I'm thinking that we pop in and surprise them. Exchange hellos and all that. Then, we pair up, mask each guy, and switch around as we make out."

"Mia!" Shay's jaw dropped with amused disbelief. "That's just filthy!"

Mia frowned with genuine disappointment. "Too much?"

"Oh, no," she laughed. "I think it's hot as fuck. Let's do it."

I shook my head at our crazy-ass ways. "They're gonna fuckin' die."

~ • ~

The male, mirrored version of our apartment fell right by the stairwell, so we didn't have far to creep. Mia turned back to us as we positioned at the door. "Should we knock?" she whisper-yelled.

"Let's just try opening it first."

Shay interrupted just before Mia's bold hand brushed the doorknob. "Wait. Before we get all hot and heavy, think we can get a shot from them? I'm a little nervous."

"Really?"

"I am, too," I whispered.

Mia enjoyed a stifled laugh at our amateur asses but agreed to take it slow once inside. She turned the handle quietly like a cautious intruder, then peeked through the slight crack.

"Can you see them?"

Mia nodded. "Yeah. All three on the sectional."

Shay poked her in the ass. "Say something!"

"Anyone home?"

"Mia?" Evan called from inside. "What the hell?"

She suddenly opened the door wide and exposed our sultry invasion. Shay and I waved sheepishly as the eye masks dangled at our sides. All three guys jumped up in shock and rushed to meet us, with Judge and Decker appearing in bare-chested glory. *Delicious.*

Judge scanned us from head to toe. "Well, this is one hell of a surprise."

Decker was all smiles. "Come in!"

"Is everything okay?" Evan asked with confused concern.

"We just couldn't stop thinking about you," Shay spilled as we passed through the threshold. While I usually appreciated her blunt approach, my cheeks and chest reddened as our blatant thirst was exposed.

Mia seamlessly stepped in for the save. "*And* we wanted to say thanks for breakfast."

Deck raked a hand through his messy hair and shot a grin at Evan before admiring our attire. "Those matching outfits are something else."

"We tried to be sneaky," I laughed. Fuck, I sounded like such a dork.

Judge licked those tempting lips. "Well, mission accomplished. Make yourselves at home."

Mia charmed our hosts with a flirtatious smile. "Could we bother you for a drink?"

"Any special requests?" Evan asked.

"What are you drinking?"

He pointed to the trusty gray cooler that rested in place of a coffee table. "Just beer."

I cocked an amused brow. "Easy access?"

"We're super lazy, remember?"

Judge offered to load the liquor and coaxed us to make ourselves comfortable, so we wandered deeper into the apartment with Deck and Evan in tow. We'd spent nearly no time in their manly, no-frills residence before, with the guys always squatting at our place upstairs. These bare walls, fluffless furnishings, and clean countertops implied maturity and simplicity, in glaring contrast to the frat houses I'd partied at before. Well, aside from the beer-stocked centerpiece, of course. The girls and I sat side by side on one strip of the sectional as basketball announcers relayed play-by-play coverage on the big screen. Butterflies bounced lightly in my belly, but Mia palmed my jittery knee, and I exhaled some anxious energy.

Judge called out from the kitchen. "You want shots? Or regular cups?"

"Just pass the bottle," Shay said.

Good call.

Evan and Decker parked adjacent to us, speechless but for expletives muttered at our bold ways. Shay took a heavy gulp from the liquor Judge offered, winced like a rookie, and then passed it to me. I loved this brand, so I took the sharp burn much easier and licked the intense flavor from my lips. Mia took the short sip of a seasoned pro and rested the remainder on the cooler.

Judge parked on the sectional arm with warm brown eyes roaming between us. "So, you missed us?"

I returned his sexy grin. "We did. We really did."

"Well, if it's any consolation," Evan confessed quietly, "we talked about our arrangement all afternoon."

Mia shifted slightly beside me. "Seriously?"

Decker pressed his palms into his thighs and rubbed. "Hard to think about anything else, to be honest."

"What about your papers for patho?" Shay pried like a skeptical mom.

Judge laughed. "We got our work done before the game like good boys."

The alcohol hit me just right as we slipped into silence after the warm reception. My earlier angst transformed into a desperate desire to feel hands and lips on my body again. Warmth settled in my pelvis as I admired the chiseled muscles and boyish grins.

Decker tossed an inviting palm. "So, girls, what can we do for you?"

Oh, Deck. So many things.

Shay assumed control, apparently experiencing that same transition from apprehension to lust. "Well, first, let's turn out these lights."

Evan jumped right up. "You got it."

"And you guys get comfortable for us," Mia suggested in a soft, sultry voice.

We stood as Evan darkened the room and lowered the volume on the television. Our victims found comfy spots on the sectional, glancing at each other with bright-eyed anticipation, with Judge on one end and Decker on the other. Evan returned and parked in the middle at the bend.

"You have me curious, girls," Deck admitted as he rubbed the back of his neck and met my eyes. "And excited."

"Really fuckin' excited," Evan mumbled and adjusted his balls.

Even before the guys touched me, my pussy ached with burning, wet need as I stood before their intense gazes. Although we'd laid loose plans for how this entire event would go down, I looked to my partners for our next move.

Mia stepped before Judge and bent forward, tits practically dangling in his face. "Mind if I put this on you?" she asked, brushing the dark eye mask against his scruffy jaw.

Judge flashed those dimples. "Be my guest."

I slinked over to Evan and stepped between his spread knees. His crystal eyes roamed over my slim curves, and his clenched fingers resisted the temptation to touch me before the bell. I inched his blue tee-shirt over his head and tossed it aside, dragging my fresh nails over his rippled chest, then I slipped the black eye mask over his sandy hair.

"Do you like that?" I whispered.

"You have no fuckin' idea, Callie."

"Your turn," Shay said softly beside me. She bowed to slide the blindfold over Decker's face, ruffling his hair even more and blocking his view of her slightly larger breasts.

"Are you boys ready for a Three Doors teaser?" Mia asked.

"I fuckin' am," Evan answered eagerly, repositioning that stacked body against the blue cushions.

"No noise," Shay reminded us. "We need practice."

Decker's earlier confidence in his discipline now wavered. "I'll try, but no promises."

Mia motioned to rotate clockwise, so I slowly backed away from Evan and posted up in front of Judge. He cocked his head and listened, cracking his knuckles with expectation. My heart pounded in my ears as I took one last glance around the dim room. There was something so thrilling about the guys having no clue what we were about to do or, more specifically, which girl would be doing it. This wasn't time for emotion, but I was touched that they trusted us so blindly and so willingly.

I admired Judge's carved body and wide, welcoming stance. I tried to assess his shaft size in the loose gym shorts, but the shadows obscured my view. He was still wearing that sweet, sexy smile, and I just couldn't fuckin' wait any longer.

I crawled directly onto his lap, straddling him, and he guided me down to his groin with hungry hands on my ass. Wet warmth rushed between my legs as his long cock raked against my center. I licked his alluring lips with a flirty tease, then he parted mine with his hot tongue. Instinct replaced my earlier uncertainty. As our kiss deepened, I rocked my hips into a slow, grinding rhythm and rotated my tight pussy against Judge's length. He met my need, angling his thick tip until it tapped directly into my damp bottoms. A moan threatened to escape my throat as he pulled on my ass for more, but I fought to keep silent for the sake of the game.

I left his lips behind and took time sliding my wet tongue from his jawline to his firm chest, inhaling his delicious scent as I frenched his warm skin. I savored his tight nipple, teasing it with my teeth as his thighs stiffened beneath me. Just as I drifted lower to his abs, I caught a flicker of movement from the corner of my eye. The girls signaled another rotation, with Mia peeling from Deck's embrace as Shay stood from Evan's lap.

I kissed my way north over Judge's sculpted pecs and found his panting lips waiting for mine. After one last brush of our tongues, I raised my moist center from his steel. He held fast to my hips, silently begging me not to leave, but I wiggled free from his grasp and tiptoed to the opposite corner of the couch.

I spent a few selfish seconds watching Deck catch his breath. That rippled olive torso heaved as he palmed the cushion and waited for his next round. The display of blind excitement was so fucking scorching that my lungs burned along with his. I slid onto his lap, bridal style, deciding at the last second to scope the other participants and possibly pick up some moves.

Deck slipped a dominant hand between my thighs as I wiggled against his hard shaft. His length felt thick and ready to fuck from Mia's performance, so I positioned myself until he tucked tightly against my ass. With nothing but thin layers between us, he pumped his hips and grinded his stiff cock forcefully between my round cheeks.

Every nerve of my exposed skin tingled and burned as our urgent lips opened for each other. Deck ravaged me with a deep, merciless kiss as he palmed the back of my neck, blazing heat from his firm body warming my wet core. Overwhelming arousal pooled between my legs as our tongues twisted, so I wrestled my mouth away for silent gasps of calming air. He used that momentary opportunity to slide his fingertips to my soaking pussy, so I opened my knees eagerly, begging without words for him to stimulate me even more. He thumbed my juicy clit through the paper-thin leggings as his fingers ripped at my waistband. *Christ*, I wanted to fuck him so bad as I writhed against his hand and over his cock.

I hoped to find Deck as amped as I was when I blinked open my eyes. I caught him chewing his lip with a mischievous smirk as he controlled my body with slow circles and fiery friction. The eerie blue light of the TV screensaver highlighted the movements of the others in action. Mia was riding Evan beside us like it was her job. She leaned over his buff chest, one hand gripping the back of the couch and the other scratching at his rounded shoulder. Her pussy rolled hard against his groin with deep, relentless cycles as he ripped at her brown waves and pawed at her perfect ass. Shay was circling on Judge's cock as she faced me from the other corner, her delicate fingers fondling her own nipples as he guided the tempo of her hips from behind. Her striking dark eyes flashed to my face from across the space, and I flushed with more sticky excitement under Deck's busy thumb.

Aside from my drunken wall bang with Deck and the couple of chorus line kisses with the boys, I'd never "performed" in front of an audience, so to speak. I didn't expect the rush of erotic energy unleashing deep within my mind and body. I slipped my fingers over Deck's as he rubbed my thirsty clit with slick, rapid strums, forcing his thumb deeper in my folds.

"Fuck," he gasped, barely over a breath against my ear.

Just as I smothered his disobedient lips with my free hand, I noticed Shay surface from Judge's lap as she turned to kiss him. I slid off Deck's cock, despite his desperate gropes at my waist, and left him suffering, throbbing, and breathless again.

I stepped to the center of the couch before a clearly struggling Evan. He crashed back against the cushions with his hand down his shorts, shamelessly stroking himself with vigorous pumps. I smiled to myself and stifled a laugh, then dipped over that defined body and smashed into his lips. He drove his tongue deep against mine and swirled as if he were devouring a delectable dessert. I palmed his manly nipples and dragged nails over his pecs as he continued to stroke his full length before me.

Not yet, Evan.

I yanked his selfish hand from his package, and he countered with wetter, more aggressive frenching that ripped the breath from my ribs. I jerked away abruptly as he tried to drive, dropped to my knees between his legs, and lowered my face to his cock. He shifted in surprise as I slid wandering hands under his slinky shorts and swirled my warm tongue over his ripped abs.

Of course, we weren't advancing the agenda to a blow job level tonight, but I felt unhinged with Evan and ready to amplify the electricity humming through my core. His shaft was sprung inside the shiny fabric, so I wrapped my mouth around his thickness from the outside. As soon as I tightened my naughty lips, he tangled fingers in my long hair and tugged.

Evan was a little rough. I liked it.

I felt emboldened by his advances and found his round, swollen tip with my tongue, then squeezed my mouth against his rigid rim and massaged. After only a few seconds of my mock oral, Evan had enough of our wild evening. In one unexpected motion, he jumped up, knocking me on my ass, and threw off the eye mask. His bewildered baby blues scanned my shocked face.

"Jesus Christ, Callie!" he cried, bolting down the hall at full speed. I covered my naughty mouth, but I couldn't contain the whimpers of amusement.

Evan's outburst had halted the entire operation. Mia and Shay stood from their partners and quickly backed away towards the TV, scolding me with narrowed eyes of disapproval as I draped an arm across my belly and fuckin' lost it. Decker and Judge, now realizing the party was over, peeled back their masks and looked around with frantic confusion.

"What the hell happened? Where did Evan go?" an exasperated Judge asked.

"To beat off," I answered with a giggle.

He peeked at his stiffy, then glanced toward the hallway. "Well, fuck it. If he's allowed, I'm allowed." We swiveled to a dumbfounded Deck, who simply shrugged, hopped from his seat, and hauled ass behind him.

"Callie, come on!"

"It wasn't my fault, Shay!"

"*Right.*"

"Hey, he was ready to explode when I got over here," I defended myself.

"He *was* pretty worked up," Mia said with a shrug. "I'm sure we all played a part."

Shay sighed as she adjusted my bra over her tits. "Should we stay or go?"

"I'm staying," I answered. "I want some real-time reactions."

"Did any of them go in the bathroom?"

Shay peeked in the hallway. "No. All three bedroom doors are closed."

"Let's put ourselves back together before they finish."

"Good idea."

We took turns peeing, smoothed our strays, and swished with blue mouthwash we found under the sink. My cheeks and chest showed splotchy red remnants of the sordid affair.

"So?" Mia eyed us in the mirror.

"That was, by far, the craziest fucking thing I've ever done," Shay whispered.

"I feel weird, but not in a bad way," I explained. "Like a combination of dirty and empowered." We heard movement from just behind one of the bedroom doors, so we hustled back to the living room to act casual before we were busted.

"Well, I guess we'll see what happens next." Mia giggled.

I grabbed the bottle of liquor and took one last shot, my eyes darting anxiously to the hallway as we waited for their impressions.

~ 6 ~

We made comfortable moves on one side of the big sectional as we waited. I stretched out between my girls, intertwining my bare feet with Shay's while Mia absentmindedly played with my hair in her lap. I strained to hear the muffled voices from the hallway once the bedroom doors opened and the boys huddled out of view, but I had no idea what to expect. On the surface, I probably should've suffered some level of shame for offering my body to multiple men on the same night but, strangely enough, I didn't. I felt no shame at all. Although I'd never experienced anything like this whole sharing stuff before, I felt safer in this space than I expected.

Eventually, the guys joined us after relieving themselves and parked in a line on the other sectional side. I couldn't help but notice how each beamed with that irresistible post-come glow. We exchanged sheepish smiles of disbelief, and heat rose to my cheeks as each gorgeous grin took a turn landing on me.

Judge leaned forward and split the silence. "Girls..."

"Yes?" Mia asked innocently when he offered nothing more.

Decker shook his head. "That was..."

"Intense," Evan finished his thought.

"Unexpected," Deck added.

"Confusing." Judge rubbed the back of his head and peered up at us.

Shay eyed me with a sly smirk, then turned back to our victims. "Amazing?"

"Well, obviously," Evan mumbled.

Judge laughed and called him right the fuck out. "We *all* know how amazing it was for you, man." I cringed with mock guilt and covered my giggling mouth.

Evan tossed defensive palms. "Callie had her lips wrapped around my cock. I think I deserve a pass here."

"You gonna be that quick every time?" Shay teased.

"If I have all of you in one night? Yes. Yes, I will be."

I cut to the chase. "Now, for the real question. Could any of you tell us apart?"

"No. I thought maybe I would, but in the heat of the moment, no," Deck answered. "Full truth."

"I couldn't," Judge said. "That's for damned sure."

"I had my ideas, but I was way off," Evan laughed.

Mia raised her brows. "You had ideas?"

"Yeah. I figured Shay had her head in my lap. I was shocked to see Callie's blond hair around my rod."

Nice.

"So, I guess that means it works," I said with a cheeky smile, "at least on our end."

Judge stood and paced before us. He always looked fuckin' adorable when he was flustered, but this bare-chested brand was admittedly hotter than the struggling student version on study nights. "Are we gonna glaze over what just happened?"

Mia continued to caress my waves as we watched the scene unfold, and I found my eyes growing heavy. Fuck, I loved having someone play with my hair.

Judge gestured to our female side of the sectional. "And look at them right now! Just laying there like that!"

Shay stuck out her bottom lip. "You want us to leave?"

"No. Fuck."

"What's wrong, Judge?" I asked sincerely.

"Mia, you have to stop with the hair," Deck groaned. "It's too much."

Mia laughed. "What?"

He fell back on the cushion and glanced at his groin. "Fuck. I'm getting hard again."

"Girls, you don't even realize." Evan raked fingers through his mane and shifted in his seat.

I rolled my eyes. "Will someone decipher the bro code for me?"

"I mean, we were all practically fucking!" Judge threw arms to his sides with theatrical frustration, and I tried not to laugh.

"And?"

"Multiple people…" Evan added.

"…in front of each other," Decker chimed in. "That's the biggest thing."

Mia twisted my locks through her delicate fingers. "You say that like it's a bad thing. I thought it was hot."

Evan rubbed his eyes as if he were clearing a mirage. "I just don't know what to fuckin' say."

Christ, I was feeling guilty. "I'm sorry if we made you uncomfortable," I mumbled. "That wasn't our intention."

Shay joined in my apology. "Not at all. Our bad, guys."

Judge held palms up in another level of panic. "No, no, no—"

"It's not that," Evan cut him off.

"Don't apologize," Deck insisted. "We're not uncomfortable. No way."

Mia shifted underneath me. "Okay. So, what is it?"

He scanned our expectant faces. "It's unbelievable. That's what it is."

Evan raised skeptical eyebrows. "I just have a hard time buying that you're all cool with this. For real."

Shay offered consolation on our behalf. "We're good. Promise."

Judge relaxed a bit and parked back in his seat. "You girls liked it? Really?" he asked, the hint of a happy dimple appearing on one side.

"Hell yes," I said. "I can't fuckin' wait for the main event."

"So, we were blindfolded obviously, but did you girls watch each other?" Deck asked.

I exchanged naughty smirks with my partners in crime. "I did," I confessed.

"Me, too."

"Yep."

Hearing my best friends admit that they'd scoped my moves sent an unexpected shiver down my shoulders. Maybe we should scrap the game and do this every weekend instead.

Judge shook his head with awe. "Am I dreaming?"

Shay was quick with the wit. "You'd be inside me if you were."

Evan turned to Deck and rolled his eyes. "I can't with these chicks, man."

"Tell me about how you watched, what you liked…"

"I thought you didn't wanna get hard again," I challenged Deck with a glance at his groin.

"I changed my mind."

"We can't," Shay interrupted, shooting down our flirty exchange. "You'd know who did what, and that defeats the purpose."

"You'll just have to wonder, boys," Mia giggled above me.

Judge was clearly intrigued. "Do you get off watching each other?"

Hmm.

"I like watching everyone get excited," Mia answered matter-of-factly. She'd paused playing with my blond tangles, but I nudged her to continue, so she did.

"Oh, come on. You don't get hot?" Evan asked. "At all?"

I tugged at my bottom lip with thoughtful consideration of an explanation. I'd been friends with Mia and Shay since our undergrad days, and I never once found myself sexually attracted to either of them. Both were objectively beautiful, head to toe, but my mind had never strayed beyond admiration and appreciation for our remarkable friendship. Hell, I'd witnessed them lock lips with randoms at parties, grind sultry bodies when we hit the clubs, and wake up naked in our tiny dorm room. I'd never felt a single ache downtown during any of it. I'd been all about peen during every scene and, as far as I knew, Shay and Mia were, too.

That being said, watching them seduce our shared shafts awakened unexpected sparks inside. While I wasn't exactly scaling the fence to sample from their gardens, I noticed the smooth curves of their bodies more as they rubbed against our boys. I shifted on the sectional cushion with visions of Shay's dark eyes meeting mine as she rode Judge's lap. I thought of Mia's nails scoring Evan's buff shoulder as she brought him to his brink. This particular combo of six just hit different.

"*You* make us hot," Shay jumped in, interrupting my internal evaluation. "All three of you. Whether we're dancing with you or bouncing on your cock, we get hot being around you. All of you."

Judge looked up in thought. "So, if you saw some fine ass chick up on me at a club, you'd like it?"

"Well, that's completely different," Shay scoffed.

"That makes no sense."

"I'd be jealous," I admitted with full fuckin' truth. "Not necessarily emotionally, but physically, for sure."

Decker raised his eyebrows. "But you're not jealous now?"

Shay explained it best. "I'll share with my girls, but not with some random pussy at the bar."

Exactly.

"I'd get hot if I saw you out," Mia added with a sweet smile, "but Callie and Shay add something extra spicy."

Judge tugged at that sexy bottom lip with his teeth. "You don't have to worry about us chasing. We have more than we need right here."

I was thirsty for the flip side, though. "Would you guys be jealous if you found us with other men?"

"I don't even wanna fuckin' think about it," Deck growled as Evan and Judge mumbled similar sentiments.

"You have nothing to worry about either," Mia assured them as she brushed strands from my face. "We're stacked right here with you."

"So," Evan said, his face flashing with leftover lust, "can we explore more this weekend?"

"Who knows what the Hour of Power will bring?" I shot him a flirty grin.

Shay broke the bad news. "We gotta go for now, though. You know how it is."

Decker scowled. "Fuckin' Mondays."

Our adorable hosts escorted us to the door like the gentleman they were and thanked us for the surprise visit. Since we'd already sucked face and the hour had grown late, we passed on the group groping and elaborate kisses, enjoying soft, sensitive smooches from each guy instead before strolling to the elevator.

~ • ~

Once we returned to our apartment and locked up, we hovered around the bar, chugging bottles of water and comparing notes.

"I'm not surprised Evan had to yank it," Mia laughed. "I thought he was gonna squirt in his shorts."

I nodded through a drink. "That bulge is the real fuckin' deal."

"I'll be honest," Shay admitted, "I could've juiced if I kept going with Judge. He's got fuckin' rhythm."

"Deck was fingering me over my leggings," I sighed. "I would've let him slide in tonight. No doubt."

"Right?" Mia tipped her head back and moaned. "God, Deck and those hands. *Fuck. Me.*" Seconds passed as we shared cheesy grins and shrugs. This was quite the fuckin' ride.

"So? Everyone feeling good?" Shay checked.

"Yeah. Just don't know how to top it this weekend."

"No worries." I bumped Mia's hip. "Maybe the sex shop will inspire us."

"Well, no matter what," Shay reminded us with her professional voice, "we need to stay on task this week with classes."

"Right." Mia yawned. "I gotta get to bed."

I finished the last of my water and nodded. "Let's go."

~ • ~

I renamed our group chat "Three Doors" the following day. My last afternoon class released early, so I decided to slip over to the student health clinic for my STD testing. The others declined as our schedules varied with different class sections, but Decker offered to tag along. He met me at the Sunrise Bakery and smiled brightly as soon as our eyes connected.

"Hey!" Although the late winter wind whipped against the windows, he slid into the booth across from me with no shield but a black hoodie.

"Hi! Thanks for the escort!" I returned his sunny greeting.

"My pleasure."

"Aren't you freezing?"

"Real men don't get cold, Callie."

This fuckin' guy.

"*Right*," I said with a humored eye roll. Deck man-giggled and scanned the dining room. Other students hovered over laptops, sipped from steaming cups, and munched on baked delicacies. "So, having a good day?" I asked.

He blinked back to me and subtly sucked his bottom lip. "I am now."

Redness rushed to my cheeks, and I adjusted my plaid scarf as a distraction. It may have been chilly outside, but Deck was bringing the fuckin' heat, and I liked it. "Are you flirting with me?" I asked with a playful bat of my lashes.

He slightly cocked his head and blessed me with a boyish grin. "Maybe. Is it working?"

Yes.

"I'm not sure yet. Keep it up."

His usually pensive eyes sparkled with amusement. "You're something else, Callie."

Damn.

"Want some coffee before we go?" I offered. "My treat."

"How about hot chocolate instead?"

I crinkled my nose. "I suppose. I'll be right back."

~ • ~

We walked side-by-side down the busy campus streets. Those passing could've naturally assumed that we were a young couple spending the sunny but blustery day together. According to our loose group definition, I guess that wasn't much of a stretch. I glanced up at his tall frame, watching the gusts manhandle his thick, dark hair, and I could almost feel his firm fingers playing between my legs.

Fuck.

Deck caught me daydreaming and shot me a smile. "So, what's going on in that head of yours?"

How do I answer that? I acknowledged that I was riding a fine line here. My girls and I had never spent significant time with any of the guys individually. Of course, we were all close friends, but no pair more than the other. I had to admit, though, I was looking at Deck differently as we strolled alone along the sidewalk. His earlier flirtations, innocent though they may have been, seasoned my lustful images from the evening before. My fluttering heart and cautious mind battled over how to approach this.

Do I shrug off his question and keep things neutral?

Do I open up and inch closer to him?

Oh, what the hell.

"Just thinking about last night," I admitted as I watched cracks pass in the concrete.

Deck wanted more. "Care to elaborate?"

"I can't. Really."

"Because it 'defeats the purpose,' right?" he mocked, mimicking Shay's shrill voice of authority.

I had to laugh. "Exactly."

"So, this is awkward for you, I take it," he said with sympathy.

"Awkward is a bit harsh. Let's just say that I understand why we can't be fucking face to face." We passed a few eclectic shops with window dressings of extravagant dream catchers, colorful tapestries, and shiny beaded curtains. Deck hadn't responded yet, so I continued. "I mean, I'm looking at you and thinking of exactly what I did with you. If I'm being real, it's kinda hard to concentrate."

He looked quite fuckin' satisfied with my response. "I must've been good," he bragged with an adorable, arrogant grin. "*Really* good."

My cheeks warmed despite the crisp afternoon air. "You were fantastic."

"Well, thank you," Deck said, eyeing me with a bit more depth than usual. "I have a different take on all this, though."

What the hell was he about to say? A shiver rushed beneath my coat and down my spine. Had to be the wind, right? *Right*. "Okay. Lay it on me."

"When I think about everything I did last night," he reflected, rubbing his stubbly chin, "and to know that at least some of it was with you? Well, it lights a fuckin' fire inside me for more."

An instinctive ache throbbed in my lower pelvis. That shameless revelation was so fucking unexpected. How in the hell do I interpret that? "Oh-okay," I stuttered.

We stepped up to the glass clinic door and Decker paused, his hand resting on the stainless steel handle before us. He leaned close enough for a sudden kiss, and I'm positive he enjoyed my sharp inhale as our eyes met inches apart.

"I know you want the other guys, too, Callie. And that's okay. I sure as hell won't be holding back with the other girls." Deck paused for my heart to squeak through a few weak beats. "But I can't control who I'm thinking of, regardless of whose pussy I'm touching."

My jaw dropped as he opened the door in front of me. A swoosh of warm air greeted us and he nudged my shoulder.

"After you."

~ • ~

The conversation turned lighter on the walk back to the student apartment complex, but the natural lapses provided ample opportunity for my brain to clock in for overtime.

This flirtatious day hadn't changed a thing, right? I mean, Deck hadn't hesitated to flatter me with his lustful thoughts, but he clearly acknowledged that we both enjoyed other interests within this Three Doors circle. Judge and Evan usually played the roles of outspoken flirters while he preferred suggestive glances and soft-spoken teases instead. So, what changed today?

I let that simmer as we quietly approached our building. Deck's bold admission could've just been an effort to equal the awkwardness after my shaky analysis of last night. Wasn't that the point of this entire operation? To avoid these messy next-day exchanges? Deck had been one of the masterminds behind this agenda, so I could see him relieving some of my apprehension by admitting his perceptions, too.

I resigned to that conclusion. Decker was simply helping me navigate these foreign waters with a sexy brand of consolation. I couldn't help but smile as I shuffled along the sidewalk beside his lanky strides.

"After the embryology exam, we should focus on patho. I think it will be early next week." He jammed his hands in his hoodie pocket and lowered his face from the wind. *Not cold, my ass.*

"I still need to write up my lab from Friday."

"Me, too," he said. "Maybe we can hit that Wednesday night."

Fuck. I wish we'd be hitting something else Wednesday night.

My stomach rumbled inside my puffy coat. "I wonder if the rest of the crew planned for dinner. I need food while I cram."

"I could make a sausage joke, but I won't," he teased, then glanced over at me with naughty eyes.

"You're starting to sound like Judge," I laughed.

"Do I kiss like him, too?"

My heart flopped between my ribs at the implication of jealousy, which would certainly be incompatible with the game, but Deck didn't seem to intend the question in that way as he strolled carelessly beside me. "I haven't kissed you guys much yet, but Judge sets a high bar so far."

A surprised smirk stretched across his lips. "Well, don't fuckin' mention that to him. I'll never hear the end of it."

I watched the weak sun as it lowered behind the trees, leaving a chill that even Decker had to feel. "Honestly? You're all pretty good."

"I'm hella intrigued by it," he said. "You know, the dynamic between each of us..."

"We should write a Three Doors thesis," I joked.

"We could be revolutionizing casual sex for the next generation."

I had to laugh. "Right? We're fuckin' pioneers."

"It's groundbreaking research," he added with a grin.

"Well, that's yet to be seen."

"You have doubts?" Deck unlocked the glass door of the complex with his student ID and ushered me inside towards the elevators.

I sighed. "Doubts about wanting to do it? Not at all. Doubts about the success? Yes."

He rolled playful eyes. "Oh, it'll work. Trust me."

Fuck, that trademark confidence stroked my arousal in all the right places. A light sexual tension followed us into the empty elevator and thickened as the door closed. I wondered if I would've felt the same heat in my panties if Judge or Evan had been alone with me instead.

Decker stood slightly in front of me, so I tipped my head to the side to check out his tight ass in the perfectly draped gym pants. I shrugged off a tingle of lust just as I noticed his hand hovering over the red "STOP" button on the elevator panel. He smiled down at me with suggestive eyes.

"So, Callie," Deck whispered, "should we?"

Christ.

I had to admit that I considered jumping him before logic stepped in for the assist, but I decided to call his bluff simply to see his reaction. I surveyed his threads from top to bottom, making sure he noticed my thirst, and I remembered how fuckin' ripped he was under that hoodie. "Oh yeah. Let's do it," I whispered with pretend seduction.

His eyebrows jumped in shock. "Really?"

"No, Deck," I laughed. "If you want me, you'll have to wait."

His dark gaze drifted lower to my lips. "Wait my turn, you mean."

Damn. He had me there.

My heart slammed between my ribs. "That's the plan, remember? *Your plan?*"

The elevator glided to a stop, and the doors split to the empty hallway before us. Deck stepped over the threshold and turned with a sexy smile. "See you later."

"Sounds good." I swallowed hard. "Thanks for the company."

Our eyes remained locked as the silver doors crept closed.

~ • ~

I rode up two more levels to my floor with that last vision of Decker etched in my mind. Shay was emptying her bookbag on the dining room table as I strolled inside our girly sanctuary.

"Hi!"

"Hey, girl! Did you get your test?"

I nodded. "Is Mia home yet?"

"She's changing."

I slipped from my coat, and my stomach rumbled again. "I'm hella hungry. What are we doing for dinner?"

"Pizza, I think."

I laughed lightly to myself. "Let's order one with sausage, okay?"

~ 7 ~

"You're up, Evan." I waved a large handwritten index card.

He rubbed his hands together in anticipation. "Hit it."

We'd been using this method to review since the fall semester, making bullet point notes for a single topic on each card, then crashing around our coffee table and firing questions around the room. Our crew had gathered tonight like any other study night, with no mention of our dirty deeds from the evening before. We were staying on task so far, especially considering the temptations we'd prompted with our flirty escapade. Hell, maybe this *could* work.

"Okay. Ductus Arteriosus. Go."

"A normal artery in the fetus connecting the aorta and the main pulmonary artery."

"Mia, what is the purpose?"

"It allows blood to bypass the undeveloped lungs of the fetus."

"Deck, what happens after birth?"

"It naturally closes as the baby breathes with functioning lungs."

"Shay, what is the danger if it fails to close?"

"Significant lung damage."

"Last one! Judge, how is it detected?"

"Suspected on physical exam and auscultation, but echo is preferred to confirm."

"Five for fuckin' five!" I squealed, tossing the index card to the used pile in the middle of the table.

"I need a pee break before the next round." Shay hopped up from the sofa and slipped down the hallway.

"I think it's time for more coffee," Decker requested through a yawn, raising his brows in my direction. Our quick kiss hello had lasted longer than the others after our day together, but nobody seemed to notice. I sure as fuck hadn't minded.

"I'm glad I got the industrial size," I sighed over my notebook. "We fuckin' need it this section."

"Speaking of industrial size," Deck mouthed from our big blue chair with a nod to his junk. I rolled my eyes playfully but couldn't deny that I peeked between his legs.

"I'll start a new pot this time," Evan offered, shockingly relieving me of my duties.

Mia cocked her head with a smirk as she stood. "Do you even know how to make coffee?"

"Give me some credit, woman," he chuckled as he strolled to the kitchen.

I eased up from the floor and stretched. I'd been tucked against the sofa, curling my legs under the table, and my hips were aching from the cramped position. At least, I think that's why they were sore, but it could've been all the dry fucking from the night before.

Mia unwound into a goofy dance. "We're killing it tonight! I'm so proud of us!"

"Me, too," Judge laughed as he watched her chest bounce in the tiny green top. "I haven't pictured you girls naked once. Until now, anyway."

"Does that usually happen?" I eyed him with a smirk.

"Yeah, and it was happening long before this past weekend."

Well, damn.

Decker grinned at me and tossed a palm. "It's a delicate balance now."

"You know what would help?" Evan stood at the edge of the kitchen with crossed arms and smiled between us as the coffee brewed. "You could make yourselves a little less attractive for these work sessions."

"Oh, come on," I laughed and glanced down at my comfy clothes.

"That's a great idea," Judge added, gesturing to Shay as she returned. "Take this one, for example."

She cocked a brow and whipped her black hair into a loose bun. "Come again?"

Judge held out his palm as if he were a tour guide and Shay was the featured exhibit. "Have you seen her ass in these silky pants? And do we need to be subjected to the torture of this cleavage? Is that really necessary?"

Shay scoffed and surveyed her rack. "What's wrong with my clothes?"

"The boys think they could concentrate on the material easier if we covered up more," I explained with a dramatic eye roll.

She puffed her perky tits and waved them off. "Get the fuck out with that."

"I know, right?"

"That's such a dick thing to say," Mia scolded with a headshake. "Control your fuckin' selves."

Evan threw his beefy arms up in defeat. "Relax! I wasn't serious. Believe me, the last thing I want you to do is cover up. In fact, take a little off."

"Don't fuck this up, man," Deck laughed from his perch. "I kinda like looking at tits while I recite random embryology facts."

"Maybe next time we'll surprise you with bikinis." Shay dipped over Judge's lap and batted her lashes with mock seduction. "What will ya do then?"

Judge cleared his throat as his eyes darted away from her boobs. "Fail. Fail whatever the fuck I'm studying."

This guy.

"Everyone ready for the next interrogation?" I asked, loving our antics but knowing that we needed to get back to business.

The guys delivered our coffee like thoughtful boyfriends. Judge handed me my ocean mug dressed with the perfect amount of cream and slid in next to me on the floor. I thanked him with a warm smile and inhaled the steam from the sweet caffeine.

"Is this seat taken?"

"I hope it is now," I flirted.

He shot me his dimpled grin and sipped from the borrowed cup. "Maybe some of your smarts will rub off on me."

I'd like to rub something off on you.

"Not in this class." I shook my head with a light laugh at my expense. "You should probably park by Shay. This is her wheelhouse."

"Nah. I'm good right here with you."

Nice.

I missed my next question when we jumped back into the lesson. Mia had chosen the card about a challenging heart defect called Tetralogy of Fallot, and I completely bombed it. "*Fuck!*" I groaned and slumped against sofa. "Why can't I get that one?"

"I understand exactly what you're jacking up," Shay said. "Let me go over it with you."

Judge jumped in from beside me. "I could use another look at that one, too."

Although Judge and I were undoubtedly the weakest scholars of the crew, the others never hesitated to pause our process and break down the difficult lessons. Shay and Mia had helped me countless times before our study group became a sixsome, but having Judge nearby provided much-appreciated validation. I felt more confident in the classroom knowing that I wasn't facing my struggles alone.

Shay grabbed the large whiteboard and dry erase marker we kept off to the side for these scenarios, then she explained my mistake with a professor's ease and patience. We watched her sketch an elaborate diagram of the diseased heart, labeling each abnormal part as she covered the defects.

"Right!" I nodded as she pointed with the tip of her marker. "I see it now!"

"Just know these main four components of the diagnosis, and don't forget the surgical fix. It's complex."

"That was so much more helpful than lecture," Mia said. "Seriously."

Shay beamed with pride. "Thanks, guys! I love this embryo stuff."

I flipped through my old school notebook to add Shay's hints, preferring handwritten notes over digital because I could never type quickly enough, and Judge huddled closer with a peek over my pencil. I grinned at my paper, his sultry trademark scent teasing my breath.

"See? I told ya," I giggled. "You picked the wrong girl tonight."

Judge's wide hand suddenly slid over my smooth leg under the table, gently rubbing my bare thigh with consolation. The intimate contact was unexpected, but as his fingertips wandered under my boxers to my instantly eager pussy, my heart thundered with unrestrained approval. His solemn face revealed nothing to the room, and that intentional secrecy rang my bell so fucking hard that I decided to encourage him. I widened my knees with an invitation as my pelvis throbbed for more.

Judge's flirtatious brown eyes met my baby blues. We silently acknowledged the hidden yet deliberate and provocative action under the table. He licked those luscious lips and my breath snagged.

"Are you ready to move on, Callie?" Shay asked thoughtfully as she parked the whiteboard. "We can wait a minute if you need to."

I scribbled the last of my notes and looked up with a cheesy grin.

Mastering my weakness? Check.

Secret touching? Score.

"No, I'm good now. I appreciate it."

Judge recognized that we both needed to focus, so he didn't overplay his hand, literally or figuratively. He left thick fingers lingering on my inner thigh as we continued with the tough lesson, but if we both showed a thorough knowledge of the material, he let his fingertips dance under the hem of my revealing shorts. During the last index card of questions, he boldly brushed my lace panties directly over my thirsty clit, forcing moist desire to dampen my folds even more. I felt him watching my reaction and bit hard on my bottom lip as he played with my pussy.

Evan looked up from his laptop. "I think that's it. We covered both chapters."

Decker stood and stretched. "I feel fuckin' smarter already."

"We should run through the cards again tomorrow," Shay mumbled, "just to be safe."

"Definitely," I agreed, trying with little success to ignore the agony between my legs when Judge slipped away. "I wanna be able to sketch a T.O.F. heart just like you did."

My deviant companion stood and helped me up from the floor by taking both of my hands in his. I moaned like a feeble grandma as he pulled me to standing.

"Damn, old woman…"

"I know! I don't mind sitting on the floor so I can use the table to write, but I get stiff after a while."

"Me, too," Judge whispered, tightening those sexy lips to stifle a laugh.

This guy.

"Nothing a hot bubble bath won't cure, I hope," I sassed back with a seductive smirk.

Judge's view roamed over my body with no shame. "More like a cold shower for me."

Heat radiated between us, and I couldn't tear my eyes from his smile. My nipples tightened beneath my sweatshirt as I imagined those perfect lips sucking my pink skin.

"You're bad," I mouthed as everyone else gathered their things.

"And you're wet," he breathed back.

My cheeks flared. "Because of you."

Evan broke the spell between us with an announcement. "Light kisses tonight, ladies. I need sleep."

"Me, too," Mia agreed. "No tongue during the week."

"We need that rule," Shay said. "I hate it, but we need it."

"Well, if nothing else, holding back will enhance our weekends," Deck agreed as he loaded his backpack.

Judge grinned down at me. "Like we need enhancing."

Fuck.

We shifted around the room and offered sweet goodnight smooches. Judge returned to kiss me after the others and, although the rule was quite clear to all of us, he let his warm tongue trail teasingly over mine before pulling back with a slight moan. Christ, I wanted him to fucking rail me on the spot.

~ • ~

Just what the hell was happening here?

I tossed and turned alone in bed later that night, my battered brain juggling both the daunting embryology lesson and the complicated, confusing events of the day. Decker had been flirty earlier, and Judge had been overly physical, both making individual moves in my direction. Plus, I hadn't fuckin' discouraged either of them, so I was just as guilty. This clearly blurred the lines of what our group had agreed upon.

Who was I kidding? What fucking lines? Just last night, hot tongues had twisted down my throat and heavy hands had explored my inviting curves, the anticipation of Three Doors surging through each of us as every day passed. Was it surprising that we would naturally grow closer throughout this? How could we not?

I rolled onto my back and stared at the ceiling. I could be overthinking it, as usual. After all, maybe I wasn't the only chick receiving extra attention. Maybe Decker had whispered seductively to Mia and Shay out of earshot. Perhaps Judge had teasingly touched both girls in the moments I'd missed. I considered our recent group encounters, and nothing seemed off. I hadn't noticed any guy playing favorites.

Is that what was happening? Playing favorites?

I supposed that I could simply ask my girls. Hell, maybe Shay and Mia were both getting side action, too, and they were staring into the dark, restlessly resisting sleep like me. How would I feel about that? Although my selfish side enjoyed being the surprising center of attention, I wanted my friends to thrive on this ride just as much as I was. This was about all of us, right?

But what if the focused flirtations *were* only for me? I'd shared every painstaking detail of my life with my best friends to this point, but hesitation crept into my conscience. If I confessed, they could be hurt or offended. I could cause major problems within our circle and potentially jeopardize the entire game for what could be nothing of consequence. And *fuck*, I wanted to see this through.

I let it go, convincing myself that I was overreacting. I pledged to stay true to the agreement and blow off any attempted side action from this point on. Flirting was harmless. A stolen touch here and there was to be expected. It wasn't like either had coaxed me into a closet and fucked me on the down-low.

Christ, if only.

I promised my ceiling that I would pay closer attention tomorrow. If Decker was sweet-talking or Judge was getting handsy, I would notice. And, of course, I couldn't forget about Evan, who had emerged as the wild card in this stack. I tried to recall a time when he'd shown preference to me like the others, but nothing specific came to mind. Evan had been hot for all three of us from day one, or so it seemed, and a big part of me hoped he didn't join this whole "Club Callie" thing. I had a weak spot for my fellow blond from the beginning that I didn't want to admit, and if he came knocking with that beautiful body, I might not be able to resist.

~ • ~

Detective Callie was on the case during our study session the next night. I kept my eyes and ears on alert for any side bets, but my amateur investigation yielded evidence from neither Judge nor Deck. Evan behaved properly, too, offering nothing but open compliments and the usual sexual innuendos for all three of us.

Hmm.

We worked like proper students for the rest of the uneventful week, keeping our tongues and everything else to ourselves. Decker, Mia, and I finished our lab report after the impossible embryology exam, while the others started writing up index cards for the patho test next week. We shared laughs over meals on the nights we studied and spent quiet evenings apart when we didn't. The remaining four in our clan found time to get tested at the clinic, and Evan's baby face showed an alluring layer of blond stubble that was starting to take shape.

The simple days were a subtle reminder of the friendly conditions before Three Doors. When Friday night arrived, we all declined group time, each suffering from the expected exhaustion and craving the extra hours of quiet. Our trios retired to our own apartments and, speaking for the female half of the crew, we were snoozing before a streaming series by nine.

But Saturday? Well, Saturday was a different story altogether.

~ 8 ~

>Evan: TIME TO GO SHOPPING!
>Deck: Wake up!

My phone dinged with notifications entirely too fuckin' early for a weekend morning. I initially rolled away with groggy defiance and slumped against the wall, but it chirped again, and my curiosity conquered my fatigue. I blinked awake and held the screen above my face.

>Evan: answer or we'll just keep bugging you

You gotta be fucking kidding me. And *we* were concerned about appearing too thirsty?

>Deck: wear something cute
>Judge: are you girls in Callie's bed
>Evan: send pics
>Shay: shut the fuck up

I figured this wouldn't die down anytime soon. My phone vibrated relentlessly in between my fingers before I could even reply.

>Judge: hi Shay
>Deck: so, you ARE in Callie's bed
>Evan: nice, but still waiting on a pic
>Mia: I'm going down on Callie
>Mia: you guys are interrupting

I laughed out loud in my bed. I could just picture the guys hovered over their screens at the kitchen counter, guzzling protein shakes and trying to determine if that could possibly be true.

```
Evan: are you jacking with us or no
Deck: we could come up, if you want
```

Hmm.

I heard movement from both side walls as the girls crawled out of bed. Shay whipped open my door and shook her head with amusement.

"I'm gonna get my shower. You guys got this?"

Mia yawned beside her. "Yeah, but send another text in a minute to stall them while we set up."

"Set up?" I asked with confusion.

Mia climbed on the foot of my bed and waved her phone, then peeked under my fluffy comforter with a cocked brow. "Just checking," she giggled.

"Oh, shut up with that," I laughed. "You wanna fake a pic?"

"Yeah. Lay back and look like you're getting off."

Hell, this could be fun. I'd never seen my fuck face firsthand, but I was hella intrigued about shipping the ultimate tease before our sex toy shopping adventure. I propped myself up against my pillow, pushed a strap of my pink tank from my bare shoulder to reveal a hint of cleavage, and then I puffed my messy hair into a just-fucked look. I heard the notification of Shay's stall text and a few reply dings after.

"Impressive." Mia grinned, then she waved me on with encouragement. "Now, do something with your hands, but not too much." I had a feeling that this wasn't Mia's first dirty directing gig, but I didn't ask.

I figured I should make this as realistic as possible, so I summoned some outside inspiration. *Hmm. Which scene with the potential peen had pushed my biggest buttons so far?* One vivid memory stood tall above them all, so I envisioned that very moment as warm tingles stirred in my belly. I twisted my light locks between my clenched fingers and snagged my lower lip between my teeth.

"Fucking perfect," she laughed and motioned to my cell. "Now get one of me."

We were both cracking up as we repositioned for the kill shot. I couldn't deny the cheap thrill that crept up my spine when Mia eased my knees apart and covered my panties with a comforter corner. She lined up at just the right angle and height between my thighs, effortlessly appearing as if she were coming up for air from my puss.

"Mess up your hair," I instructed. "I'm a hair grabber."

"Noted." She shook her head until long brown layers fell unevenly to one side, then licked her lips until they glistened with my fake juice.

"Nice touch." I snapped the seductive scene, then we checked our texts right after and belly laughed in a clump on my disheveled bed.

```
Shay: leave them alone, they're busy
Judge: wait what
Evan: why aren't you in there?
Deck: receipts?
```

Mia nudged my leg. "Ship the pic of me."

I clicked send, then reviewed our fake evidence again. Mia looked stunning with her lusty morning eyes and smooth, sunny complexion. My stems didn't look too bad either. I'd even draped one over her shoulder for added effect.

```
Deck: well, fuck me
Evan: that's not fucking real
```

We paused for what we assumed would be enough time for Mia to dive back in and for me to climax, then shipped my final pose. A ridiculous sense of pride kicked in when I viewed the finished product. Of course, I lacked Mia's natural beauty, but I had to admit, I looked kinda hot in my peak-pleasure position. My ratty strands spilled over the pillow perfectly, and the light tank revealed just a faint outline of nip. We waited impatiently for a response. Nothing.

"Interesting turn of events," she said as she sprawled across my legs.

Hmm.

"I wonder what they're doing."

```
Judge: no FUCKING way
```

Ahh, here we go.

```
Evan: did you just finish?
Deck: are you still in bed?
```

Mia laughed out loud at her screen. "They're such fucking tools."

"I know, but they're *our* tools now."

Right on cue, we heard pounding at the front door a few minutes later. I swear, these men hit the next fucking level. Shivers of excitement rushed over my skin at the thought of them dropping everything and racing to see us. I hadn't been gifted with dedication like that in, well, forever. The very vibe of these guys was so adorable and addictive that I didn't mind sharing the ample wealth with my best friends. Sure, the immediate purpose was simply to dip their sticks, but I knew that underneath that macho, primal hunger, Deck, Judge, and Evan actually cared. The feeling was almost euphoric.

"Well, now what?"

"I guess I'll answer it," Mia said as she slid from my mattress. "Stay in here and play along."

I snuggled in deeper under my bed linens, fully prepared to take part in this Saturday morning show. My partner-in-crime answered the door with an enthusiastic greeting, and I heard the guys' psyched voices almost immediately. At the last minute, I decided to wiggle from my panties and toss them to the floor.

"Mia, come on!" Deck whined. "What was that?"

"Hey, you asked for receipts."

Evan jumped in. "Where's Shay?"

"In the shower."

"Where's Callie?" Hell, even Judge had made the trip.

"In bed. Recovering."

I covered my giggling lips.

"She is not," Evan doubted.

"Go look for yourself. Middle room."

Time for my spotlight

All three guys crowded brawny bodies in my doorway, nudging past each other for front row seats. I usually wouldn't want them to see me in such disarray, but I was fully invested in this role and the potential antics after.

"Good morning!" I stretched my arms and sighed dramatically, selling my satisfaction like a seasoned porn star.

Judge cleared his throat. "Um, hey, Callie. What's up?"

Don't laugh.

"Nothing now. Just relaxing."

Evan scanned my room, his view landing on my makeshift prop. "Are those your panties?" Three sets of eager eyes focused on my floor, then swerved to me with disbelief. Guys were *so* gullible.

"Oh, yeah! I guess they are! Mia's a fuckin' animal."

Decker's dark, curious gaze melted into sizzling heat. "So, you have nothing on under there?"

"This tank top." I thumbed a pink spaghetti strap and snapped it.

Shay peeked in from her quick morning shower, her black locks dripping over her cheeks. I realized that we'd leveled up the comfort with the boys since her prissy ass hadn't applied one smear of makeup. She shot us a bright-eyed smile and tightened the belt of her elegant robe. "Well? How was it?"

Eyes darted between us.

"She's *so* good," I replied with a theatrical moan. "I can't believe we didn't do this sooner."

"Ugh, I know. She can wake me up any day. Oh, and the shower is free when you're ready." I heard the closing click of Shay's bedroom door and guessed that she was likely pressed against it listening. All three boys stood dumbfounded.

"But you girls don't mess like that, right?" Deck asked, cocking his head with doubt.

Evan shifted his weight with frustration. "Did she really lick you?"

These fuckin' guys.

"What do you think?"

"I mean, I wanna believe it," Judge muttered.

I laughed and sat up. "Um, do you mind? I need a shower." I pointed to my cooch region for added effect. "You get it."

"Oh, you want us to step out?"

"Please." They pouted with scorn, then stepped one by one into the hallway.

"Callie, are you getting in now?" Mia called.

I took her cue to deepen the tease. "Whenever you're ready!"

"Okay! I'll be right in!"

"Get the fuck out with that, Mia!" Judge moaned. "Can't we just stay?"

I couldn't act to save my life, so I finally caved. I lost it laughing and Mia joined in as she rounded the corner from her room.

"I fuckin' knew it," Evan bitched.

"*Right.*" Mia rolled her eyes as they convened in front of my open door. "You guys would believe anything."

"That's so wrong."

Decker laughed at himself. "I ran up the stairs in bare feet, for fuck's sake."

"We just couldn't resist." I smiled at the faces peeking in.

"So, nothing happened?"

Shay had emerged, fully dressed, and patted a sulking Judge on the shoulder. "We're all about our boys."

"Are those really your panties, though?" Evan hit me with flirty eyes. "You're naked under there?"

"I tried to tell ya," Mia cackled. "She's *always* naked under there."

"That part is true, but now I need to get up for real. Go home."

~ • ~

Not long later, we shuffled together to the parking garage and slid into Evan's fancy SUV, then cruised to a freaky little sex shop right off the interstate. The boys were still worked up, mumbling grumbles about our fake morning fantasy and shooting us disappointed smirks. I parked in the middle seat next to Judge and batted my lashes innocently.

"I can't believe you girls did that," he groaned.

"You went all out," Deck complained from the back bench. "Hell, even Shay joined in."

"Those pictures were hella convincing," Evan praised in the rearview mirror. "Fuckin' art."

Mia spoke up. "Speaking of pictures, I think it's time for a witnessed delete."

"I knew that was fuckin' coming," Judge muttered and retrieved his cell.

"Not that we don't trust you," I explained as I patted his knee, "but we have reps to protect. You understand."

Decker held his phone in front of his face and stared. "It kills me to hit this button. Let me take one last look."

Mia took no prisoners. "Delete them. Now. Both the message and the download, which I know damned well you all have."

We glided into the parking lot of the enthralling establishment, and Evan threw the vehicle into park. I leaned over the back of his seat and poked his muscled shoulder. "You, too, mister. Cough it up."

He obliged, then man-giggled in the mirror. "Hell, maybe I'll see that scene for real one day."

~ • ~

The toy shop had just opened and we were the only car in the customer lot. We piled out with purpose and entered single file through the tinted front door. As a novice, I'd heard of joints like this but had never stepped inside one before. My eyes darted with bashful interest to the colorful containers and wild walls. A middle-aged male clerk offered us a flat, obligatory greeting from behind the checkout counter.

"Welcome to The Basement. Can I help you find anything?'"

"We're just browsing." Shay smiled like an innocent princess. "Thank you!"

"*Sure*," he replied, then he returned to scrolling through his computer screen.

I strolled through the front aisles of daring devices, and I felt a bit overwhelmed as my heart picked up the pace. I tucked my hands in my jacket pockets and hugged myself as my eyes wandered over a variety of elaborate collars and chains. Were the guys really into all this stuff?

Judge fingered a feathered thing beside me. "I'm not even sure what some of this is for."

"I'm with you." I relaxed in relief. "This is Mia's world."

"True." Mia shrugged casually. "I can't deny that I'm kinky."

He raised intrigued brows. "Well, why don't you show me some of your favorites?"

Her smile shined with pride. "I'd love to."

"I'm coming with," Shay insisted as she linked her arm through Mia's. "I have so much to learn."

I decided to stick with the somewhat familiar, thanks to both common knowledge and porn, so I wandered alone through a side aisle of countless vibrators. A rocket-shaped purple option caught my eye, so I sheepishly removed it from the rack for inspection. I wide-eyed the thick, curved tip and flipped the box to the back for more detail. I was engrossed in the elaborate description of vibration patterns when I felt a light brush against my ass.

"You like that one?"

Evan.

He crowded against my backside and peeked over my shoulder. I took a slow, controlled breath, the essence of his assertiveness sending a hot, damp thrill to my panties.

"I honestly don't know much about these," I confessed in a whisper. "I'm pretty basic."

Evan innocently palmed my hip with hesitation, then changed gears, slowly and brazenly snaking his fingers under my warm layers. His teasing touch danced over the front of my slender waist and tickled above my zipper.

Well, welcome to Club Callie.

He inched his lips through my blond hair as I tried to fake nonchalance. "Toys can be fun," he murmured, "but I bet we wouldn't need any."

Collect yourself, Callie.

Breathe.

"I'm not even sure how to use this stuff with a partner," I admitted. I had some ideas from watching smut, but my plain preferences showed little more than the actresses pleasuring themselves before someone rolled in and railed them with real peen.

Evan's raspy voice tickled my ear. "Well, the first way is obvious. I could just pump it inside you and watch you go crazy."

Jesus Christ.

I closed my thighs tightly together as moist flames gathered south of his leisurely strokes. Desperation clenched between my ribs at the mere thought of those fingers fucking my wetness. Evan noticed.

"Oh, you liked that," he exhaled.

I nodded, still facing forward as his bold hand wandered higher. I urgently scanned the room from my vertically challenged view. Deck was hamming it up against the clerk's counter with his back to us while the others were living large in the bondage section. The rack height kept Evan's naughty touches from the public eye, or so I hoped. My content cooch was more than comfortable with this individual attention, but my heart and mind hadn't quite caught up.

Evan sensed my concern and paused his tease above my jeans. "They can't see. I checked," he assured me, confirming that he had planned this otherwise surprising moment between us.

I swallowed hard with a nod of approval. Fuck, my body begged both of us for more.

"Now, back to business," he continued with a throaty rasp against my ear. "I could also use it to enhance your pleasure in other areas." His fingertips made a slow, smooth trip north to skim my tightened nipple, trapping the breath in my chest, then he sauntered mercilessly downstairs. He trailed a finger against my trembling pussy, coaxing my clit over my tight jeans, then he returned slowly to his starting position on my hip.

"You're killing me." My heart thundered behind my breasts as my senses overloaded with his every move. *Could he hear it? Feel it?* Christ, this agonizing, public slow dance almost sent me spiraling.

"Oh, I'm not finished yet," he laughed lightly and continued the game with no shame. "If I had my choice, I'd use it on you right here." He grinded his heavy cock against my ass, shifting with sweet friction between my cheeks until my weakened knees nearly buckled.

"Evan," I whimpered.

He grew even bolder after hearing my lips surrender his name. His rough, wet tongue swept against my earlobe with a thrilling confession.

"I can't wait much longer to fuck you, Callie."

I shrugged one shoulder against his kiss, the gentle scratch of his stubble revealing that we wouldn't be waiting much longer at all. He stepped away with no warning, and I sucked in a sharp recovery breath.

"Did Callie pick a vibrator?" Shay's approaching voice snapped me right back to reality.

Get yourself together, Callie.

"I think she did," Evan chuckled.

"Yay! Lemme see!" Mia chirped as I held up the forgotten toy in my hand.

Judge laughed. "It's fuckin' purple."

"Maybe I like purple." I grinned, simultaneously defending my abrupt choice and attempting to deflect from my obvious arousal.

Mia took the vibe package from my hands and gave it a once-over. "Oh, that's a nice one. We'll get three."

"You sure you like this one best, Callie?" No one noticed, but Evan's suddenly subtle eyes darted down to his groin, then back up to meet mine. A cocky smile stretched across his lips.

I returned the tease. "I haven't tried it yet, so I'm not so sure."

He laughed and shook his head. "*Right.*"

With her arms full of the purple rocket vibrators, Mia captained us to the front of the store. Decker met us with a sneaky grin in the kinky candy department.

"Just what have you been doing up here?" Shay pried. "Did you even look around?"

"I was just chatting with this Joe guy and thinking of ideas for Hour of Power tonight."

"And the verdict?"

"Wait, what are those, Mia?" Deck asked, eyeing the freaky pile against her tits.

Mia grinned and raised the goods. "Our matching vibrators."

Evan gestured to me with a nod, then shot Deck a wide smile. "Callie picked them out for us."

"Oh, did she now?" Decker met my eyes with heated amusement.

"I did," I bragged, blushing under their scrutiny.

Deck seemed satisfied with the selections, then he huddled us up in front of the edible panty section. "So, I have an idea," he whispered. "It could be fun, but it's a gamble."

"Go on," Shay coaxed.

"First, to get in the mood, we play an innocent game of Spin the Bottle."

Mia giggled. "You think we need help getting ready to fuck? Read the room, Deck." My girl was entirely too much, and I fuckin' loved her for it.

"And after?" Evan asked.

"Porn. We watch porn together."

Oh.

"You think we could all curb ourselves? Not take it too far? I mean, if any of us fuck, it's game over." I reminded everyone of the harsh truth. Three Doors was on the line.

"Bring it on," Shay challenged like a hardass. "I have nerves of steel."

"And I'm the queen of control," Mia laughed.

Crazy fuckin' liars.

A hopeful and excited Deck looked directly at me for final consent. I was already dripping from Evan's advances, and now I had to face that simmering gaze. Could I trust myself to stop if the opportunity to fuck presented itself on one of these gorgeous platters?

I rolled my eyes with mock reluctance. "Fine, but there better be at least a little chick action."

"I think we can manage that."

Evan smirked with sarcasm. "We'll try our best to get through it."

"Let's get outta here," Shay said with a glance at her cell. "It's barely noon, I'm already hot and bothered."

"Fuck streaming something," Judge laughed, looking around the store before his eyes settled in the back corner. "I think they stash the movies behind that curtain over there. Let's grab some hardware instead."

"Old school." Mia grinned. "I like it."

Eagerness rushed through me as I followed the others to the restricted section. Deck held the dark drapes aside as the girls passed through and flashed me a sultry smile.

"It's about to be a wild night, Callie. You ready?"

~ 9 ~

"I hope this porn is super fuckin' cheesy," Shay laughed in the bathroom mirror later as we primped for the much-anticipated evening.

I ready to unwind after spending the afternoon alone and cramming my brain to capacity. "I'm sure 'Don't Tell The Doctor' has a thrilling plotline," I giggled.

She shrugged. "Not that it matters with the boys around. Porn is just icing on the dick."

"I know it'll be fun," I sighed, "but I have concerns." All three men had toyed with the game's unwritten rules, each showering me with dirty intentions and advancing our individual relationships. Deck's way with words still lingered against my lustful lips, and Judge's deviant touch still tempted my soft skin. And, after my earlier antics with Evan, I feared that my need to fuck would triumph over any remaining logic.

"Think we'll go too far?" Mia asked, widening her eyes to protect her wet lashes.

I'd passed on the heavy makeup for the date and instead spent extra time curling my hair. I sighed as the wand heated a strand by my cheek and decided to explain my rambling thoughts, steering clear of the bigger underlying apprehension about my side action. Theories whipped up by my overactive mind might sour this special scenario, and I didn't want to spoil the fun for my girls.

"Well, I felt freaky around Deck after the robber night at their place. We walked to the clinic together, and I couldn't think of anything but his fingers inside me."

Mia smeared a shimmery cream blush on her cheekbones. "Did he act weird with you?"

"No, but he didn't know which session I delivered," I explained. "He had no reason to feel weird facing me. I, on the other hand…"

"True." Mia nodded in the mirror. "I get ya."

Shay cut right to the chase. "So, you think if we mess around in the open tonight, this entire game is pointless and we should just fuck?"

"Basically. Maybe. Hell, I don't know."

Mia rested her hip against the white sink. "All this foreplay is hella annoying. I'm ready to do it."

"We have to wait for the rest of the test results," Shay reminded her. "Hang in there for just a few more days."

"Oh, I understand." Mia waved her off with a laugh. "I'm just horny."

"I still like the idea of fucking all of them sooner rather than later," I said, slipping my fingers through a hot curl. "But that next day concern is real. I felt it firsthand."

"We kiss them in the open," Shay said as she applied a subtle silver shadow. "No issues yet, I guess."

"Right, but sex is different."

"Hell, I joke about getting it, but even *I* think things would go downhill fast," Mia admitted. "Three Doors is the way to go."

"So, where do we draw the line?" I whined.

"I say we take whatever we can get, as long as the bigger plan is protected." We reluctantly agreed with Shay and posed with her before the bright mirror. "Well, how do we look?"

We looked fuckin' good. Shay enjoyed an extensive, elegant lingerie collection and, staying on point with the matching theme, she'd suggested that we show off identical babydoll negligees in different shades. We'd chosen our favorite fabric colors, with Mia's pale green complimenting her golden glow and Shay's soft yellow gracing her black locks. The sky-blue satin I'd selected flowed over my slim curves and amplified the speckles in my light eyes. I rarely wore anything fancy, especially sleepwear, but I had to admit, I felt like a million bucks.

"I fucking love these." Shay shimmied beside me. "I had to have one in every color."

I pointed to our reflection with a laugh. "Are the tits gonna be an issue?" The cold, silky colors had left our nipples standing at attention, presented as six little soldiers in a formation line.

"Nah." Mia grinned and adjusted her straps, then she hugged us both by the hips. "We look perfect."

~ • ~

The guys had decided to host, which both blew our fuckin' minds and piqued our intrigue, so we slipped into our robes and headed for the stairwell. Luckily, the residential hallways were dead on Saturday nights, and we could sneak downstairs undetected. I'm sure the security cameras found our relaxed attire somewhat bizarre, but we owned it, waving shamelessly to the black ceiling lens as we turned the corner.

After the first knock, Evan welcomed us with open arms while Judge and Deck waited just inside the threshold. My heart stuttered as their plan partially unfolded. Our thoughtful trio of irresistible men wore matching pajama sets, similar to the setup Judge had displayed before. But the biggest shockers were the fresh, tight haircuts and closely trimmed facial hair. Fuck, they'd been busy.

"Wow!" Mia squealed and clapped. "Look at you!"

"We wanted to surprise you." Deck grinned with a bashful glow. I absorbed every inch of his muscular body, the thin, dark turquoise cotton draped perfectly over his tall frame and revealing hints of the glorious ridges inside. I'd embraced his thick, messy hair before, but there was something about this cleaner cut version that hit right, too. Those smokey, seductive eyes pierced deeper without shaggy strands providing cover.

Evan admittedly wasn't a fan of the matching threads, but I found his dedication to this grand scheme absolutely adorable. He shot me a charming grin. "Big change, isn't it?"

"Kinda," I flirted with a slow lip lick, "but I like it." Although his stacks of muscle matched Deck's, the navy-colored sleep set drew the darker hues of blue from Evan's sparkling eyes. With that moppy blond mess trimmed away, I could fully appreciate the layer of golden stubble that had teased my neck during earlier perversions. He stroked his jawline with a sly smirk as he scoped my bare legs, and I imagined the potential of tempting tickles between my squirming thighs.

"I think we got it pretty close," Judge laughed, arrogantly adjusting the lapel of his slate gray set and nodding to his two almost twins. "Just had to polish these guys up a bit."

Already the most stylish of the three, Judge didn't have far to leap in achieving the perfect polished look, but tonight, his warm brown eyes glowed with an extra helping of shine. Pride? Excitement? Arousal?

"I can't believe the way you match." Shay beamed. "I fuckin' love it!"

Evan gave us a runway spin on his heels. "Hey, you suggested that I make more of an effort."

Mia licked her glossy lips. "Well, it worked. You look hot."

"When did you get these outfits?" I asked, fingering the cuff of Deck's buttoned top. "And the haircuts?"

"After we dropped you off earlier," Decker explained as he smiled down at me. "Judge convinced us that we needed more swag to impress you."

Aww.

Shay, Mia, and I causally removed our cushy robes as we offered more praise, then hooked them beside the front door. Judge hit us with a low whistle.

"Speaking of matching, *damn*, girls."

Decker eyed Mia's round ass as it peeked from her green slip. "Like three sexy presents, all wrapped up just for us."

"I hope you brought the extra shot glasses," Evan chuckled. "I'm sprung already."

Mia passed him a small gift bag from our apartment. "As requested."

Our sweet hosts had seriously prepared for dirty movie night. They'd pushed the big cooler back by the bookshelf, leaving the floor open in front of the television. I noticed three neatly folded blankets in various shades of gray resting in the sectional bend and on both ends. Anticipation bubbled in my chest.

"Someone cleaned up," Shay laughed as she scanned the welcomed changes. "And it looks like you guys are expecting more couch action."

Judge pocketed his hands in the thin bottoms and rocked on his heels. "*Hoping* for more couch action, you could say."

"Do we have assigned seats?" I flirted, twisting a curl around my finger.

Deck shot me a smirk and pointed to his groin. "Your seat is right here, Callie."

Fuck. Me.

"Are these blankets for us?" Mia raised her eyebrows and swept fingers over the soft fleece. Judge nodded with a guilty grin beside me. "Well, that's very thoughtful," she said.

He made no effort to hide their filthy intentions. "We plan to keep you warmed up, but just in case we want privacy..."

~ • ~

Our crew crashed on the sectional over cold beers and random chatter about class. I curled between Evan and Shay on one side and relaxed as much as my desperate downtown would allow. The guys drifted into basketball banter and I almost fuckin' yawned with boredom. We'd been playing this small talk game for months since we met, and there was no need for it now. *It's dick time.*

"Ready to roll?" Judge asked after the last sip of his drink.

"Fuck yes!" Mia sat up straighter beside him. "I haven't played in forever."

Evan set the ground rules. "Can we agree that the guys aren't kissing, Shay?"

"Why are you asking me?" Shay laughed and palmed the space between her tits. "I'm not in charge."

"Because you said you liked it."

"Oh, I love it! But if something makes you uncomfortable, absolutely not."

"I'm not kissing a dude and especially not these fucks," Judge snickered and hooked a thumb at his boys.

Decker brushed off his shoulder and faked disappointment. "No? Not even in my fancy threads?"

Mia patted his knee. "Don't worry, Deck. We can't wait to kiss you."

True.

"Are you girls getting down together?" Evan asked with a sliver of hope. "I mean, whatever you want, of course..."

Well, that was a loaded fuckin' question, at least for me. I'd never kissed a chick before and hadn't even considered it when the bottle game was first suggested. The prospect of tasting feminine lips had never appealed to me, but after watching the way my girls worked up these specific guys, I had to admit that the proposal seemed enticing. I'm not sure if attraction developed in different layers since I'd always desired dick, but this sixsome sparked something primal inside me. Flutters of arousal, curiosity, and angst combined in my belly as eyes shifted around the room, the crew waiting for someone to speak up.

Hell, it was only a kiss, right?

But what if I said that I wanted to try it, but my girlfriends hesitated or resisted?

Daredevil Mia sliced through the light tension. "I'm down if my girls are."

Shay smiled sheepishly beside me. "I'm in."

Wow.

"Why not?" My pulse pounded in my ears and relief warmed my chest. "Let's do it."

We wrapped our smooth, bare legs in the borrowed blankets and gathered in a circle on the floor. Judge crashed next to Shay and slumped back against the sectional across from me, allowing the perfect line of sight between his wide, bent knees.

"See something you like, Callie?" He smirked when he caught me peeking for peen.

"Maybe."

"Well, maybe you can get a closer look later."

Well, fuck.

Judge apparently came to play, but I did, too.

"What if I'd like to do more than look?" I countered with my sexiest smile.

"Get in fuckin' line, girl," Mia laughed with a feeble attempt to smack me.

"Pretty sure the line starts behind me," I sassed back.

Deck raised his brows at our pretend catfight. "Damn. Claws are fuckin' out tonight."

Evan placed an empty amber bottle in the center of the circle and dropped by my other side. "You saved me a seat?" he teased.

I patted the sliver of rug between us. "Yeah, but you're too far away."

Shay interrupted my flirtatious appetizers and offered to go first. She leaned forward and gave the bottle a smooth spin, allowing the guys one hell of a view of the round assets beneath her slinky slip. The glass rim eventually slowed between Deck's knees, and their lips met in a slow, sensual greeting.

"Aww, that was so cute," Mia swooned as Shay fanned her flushed cheeks.

Decker proudly beamed at the reaction to his opening round, then gave the bottle a quick whirl. It initially landed on Evan, but his second attempt pointed right at my cooch.

If fuckin' only.

"My turn," I flirted beside him with a shy smile, a slight ache already acting up between my legs.

Decker lowered into my space with no words and slipped his hand softly against the back of my neck, coaxing my waiting lips closer to his. He paused over me with a dark, heated gaze, then twisted his tongue in merciless, meticulous waves over mine. I clenched the collar of his fancy teal top and begged for more as intense throbs of need pounded in my pussy. He sadly freed his hot mouth as the crew bitched and groaned at our lengthy indulgence, then he looked directly into my lustful eyes.

"Sorry, everyone. Callie just tastes so fuckin' good."

I inhaled a breath of composure. Fuck, that man could kiss, and I mean *kiss*. I'd mentioned Judge's high bar on our clinic walk, but Deck may have just vaulted the fuck over it. Obviously, we'd all enjoyed embraces with each other before, but this simple game and the porn plans after seemed to spark a stronger brand of confidence within the crew.

Speaking of Judge, my turn sent a spin landing directly on him. I raised to my knees and crept on all fours to reach him, giving Decker and Evan a racy preview of my ass peeking from under the blue hem. Judge met me halfway with that skilled tongue and licked away the previous kiss. His swirling sweeps summoned fantasies of his hot breath warming my wet center his lips sucking hard on my slick clit. Different fingertips suddenly traced up the back of my right thigh to my cheeks, and I moaned uncontrollably into Judge's mouth.

Evan.

Fuck.

"A little bonus there?" Shay laughed as I departed from my oral fantasyland.

Evan shot me a sexy smirk as I returned to my seat. "I guess I couldn't help myself."

"Somebody kiss me, damn it!" Mia sniffed and kicked free from her cover.

"Done. Screw that fuckin' bottle." Despite leaving my lips only seconds before, Judge crashed against her surprised mouth and ravaged her, taking her to a much deeper place than during our turn. Their palpable passion mesmerized me as they lapped at each other and stroked that leftover, undeniable tension from the pube lineup.

"Now, that's more like it," Shay mouthed to me.

No fuckin' kidding.

Mia's round settled on Shay, and I think the entire group gasped with a collective breath of anticipation. Both eagerly angled to the middle with quiet, girly giggles, their two sets of brown eyes alive with curiosity as they brushed breaths. Unspoken desire blossomed between their long, silky strands as they tasted each other for the first time. I watched in awe with the boys, enthralled by delicate tongues sliding in and out of their perfectly pouty lips. I found myself nibbling my own with eager hunger until they finally broke free.

"Fuck me," Deck muttered under his breath and shifted beside me.

"I know, man." Judge stared at my beautiful friends as Evan audibly exhaled on my other side.

Shay wiped Mia's leftovers from her bottom lip with a dainty finger and gazed across the circle. "I'm not spinning. Let's go."

Evan didn't hesitate when she remained in position on her knees. He crawled completely over the forgotten bottle and grabbed her sultry hips with both hands. Their open mouths collided into a wild mess of muffled moans and twisting tongues as wandering fingers explored the fancy sleepwear.

Mia cheered. "Yes! That's how you take what you want!"

Evan eventually crawled back with a cocky grin.

"Having fun?" I laughed.

"*Fuck*, this is unreal."

~ • ~

Deck suggested we start the Hour of Power before the next round, so we slammed five minutes' worth of shots before playing again. I felt the hot tingles from both the satisfying buzz of the beer and the sticky arousal of the smooches. When Shay's spin landed on me, my needy pussy ached with excitement against all my previous tendencies. I'd watched the way she sucked on Mia's puffy lips, not to mention the stunned, mouthwatering reaction of our guys, so I was more than ready to try this feminine flavor for myself.

Decker was parked between us, so I leaned across his lap for my kiss, hoping for his raw, effortless appeal to add another enthralling layer to my first taste. Shay met me from the other side and we hovered over his stiff shaft.

"Girls," he growled under his breath.

Mia giggled. "Lucky guy."

Despite my recent battle with constant arousal, the shy girl inside me blushed with anxiety, letting the now experienced Shay take the lead. Her tender lips tasted warm, wet, and smooth as they wrapped into mine, frenching me with a flair that I'd never felt. The sweet perfume we'd shared seasoned my senses as her black hair tickled my heaving chest below.

Deck used his prime seating to play, too, tangling his fingers in my curls and easing me deeper into her. Our curious tongues lapped with a new thirst, and a soft whimper escaped my throat as pulses of fresh but familiar heat danced between my thighs. Shay slowly pulled back, then we caught our breath and took our next shots with sly smiles for each other. Pink warmth spread across my cheeks and chest as Deck's eyes shifted between us.

"That was fucking unreal," he mumbled.

"Tell me about it," Shay sighed with bliss, "and that moan, girl. *Damn.*"

"I guess I need to work on this whole 'staying quiet' thing," I giggled.

"I wish you didn't have to." Deck met my blue eyes and spilled his secret for only me as the others chatted away around us. "I kinda liked it."

God.

After a few more shots and laughs, I gave the bottle another twirl and found Mia's eyes wide with excitement at the other end of the spin. I realized only seconds after our mouths brushed that Mia was a dirty fuckin' kisser. She nipped at my tingly lips and clawed at my blue gown as we hovered over Evan's groin together. The shy girl inside stepped aside, allowing the tipsy tease to take over my body. I bunched her loose chestnut locks between my fingers and taunted her with massaging swirls of my tongue. Evan slipped his hand under my hem and grabbed extra skin again, drawing a loud gasp from my lungs as he tickled my panties low between my legs.

Evan's next turn with the bottle finally landed in my direction. Fuck, I'd been waiting for that delicious mouth all night. We grinned at each other before slowly tilting in with restraint, but our mutual yearning unleashed as soon as our mouths barely touched. His rough, wet tongue forced my lips apart with drip-worthy dominance, and waves of throbbing heat crashed between my legs. My heart rate skyrocketed as the audience watched our lust unfold.

Decker adjusted his steel with no shame after we finally finished. "I don't know about anyone else, but I'm ready for the movie."

Judge raised his eyebrows and urged Deck to zip it. "I think we're watching a better live-action flick right now, man."

Shay fumbled with the forgotten gray fleece. "I'm ready to cuddle up, though."

"I wanna get comfortable, too," I agreed, hoping that one of these naughty men would take care of my selfish needs once we dimmed the lights.

I knew I couldn't pick a dick, so I made the first move. I scooped up my assigned blanket and secured the middle bend where I'd mocked a blow job before, leaving the fate of my pussy up for grabs. Shay preferred her space on the floor, so she simply scooted against the side of the sectional and covered her bare legs. Mia hopped up beside me and sprawled out on the opposite end, then we beamed up at the boys with batted lashes.

Decker admired our welcoming snuggle moves and stroked his freshly trimmed chin. "Excuse us for a minute to confer, girls."

"Confer?" Shay laughed. "About what?"

Judge man-giggled. "We're just gonna step in the hall and talk about you."

"Oh. Okay, then."

Were the guys about to sneak off to the shadows, huddling in those sleek, matching sets while they argued over which cooch to claim? I stifled a tipsy giggle. *Fuck, what are we doing?*

"So, how is this going down?" Mia whisper-yelled as soon as they stepped out.

"Hell, I know as much as you do," I mouthed.

"I mean, are you getting nasty or not?"

I shrugged. "Not too nasty, I guess."

"Just let things take their natural course," Shay advised from the floor.

"I'm fuckin' someone, then."

"Mia!" I laughed under my breath. "No, you're fuckin' not!"

"Watch me," she threatened with a goofy grin.

"Big picture, remember? It's just a week," Shay said, then she shushed us when we heard shuffling.

Our delectable trio strolled back in with smug, sinful smiles as we waited impatiently for the verdict. Deck cued up the dirty doctors while Judge collected empty cans and hit the lights. Evan returned his cooler to the coffee table space and refilled our shot glasses. All three had to assume that we were dying for the delivery, so they took their sweet fuckin' time planning before finally perfecting the vibe.

"Can we get you anything before we settle in?" Deck offered. We each kindly declined with the implication that we needed only warm bodies and hard dicks. I was bursting through my satin seams to see how this scene would be handled.

Judge approached my sectional space with a suggestive smile. "Best seat in the house, right here." *Had he fought for me in particular?*

"You're welcome to join me," I offered. The beer buzz hit me in all the proper places, and I wanted to rip his cute little pajamas off.

He shadowed me with those strapping muscles and placed both palms on the couch beside my shoulders, trapping me between his powerful arms. "And just where would you like me?"

Mmm, Judge.

I spread my legs slightly and lifted my hem to reveal the white lace panties underneath. "In here," I whispered.

Judge inhaled sharply and growled my name before tonguing me much deeper than during our game embrace. I clawed at his waistband and urged his hot body even closer, but he pulled away and crashed on the cushion beside me.

We took another group shot over the cooler, then the others paired off, as well. Decker aimed the remote, then stretched his lanky legs around Shay as she relaxed back into his pecs. Mia crawled over Evan's lap, drawing her knees up under the blanket and resting her head sweetly on his shoulder. I curled into Judge's open arm against his supple gray threads, then he covered our waists and cuddled me closer. Had a stranger peeked in, they would've assumed that three lovely couples had passed on the nightlife in town and stayed in to enjoy a romantic comedy.

Fuck that.

I'd enjoyed my fair share of cellphone porn over the years, especially during my dry spells with no specific dick to inspire me, so my eyes lit up as the opening scene flashed on the screen. Two scantily clad nurses met up in a hospital room, most likely some seedy director's garage, and eventually started going at it after the typical awkward dialogue. I was pleasantly surprised to find that the producer had secured an authentic hospital bed, but random mock medical gear filled the rest of the setting. The actresses, both blond and busty, had squeezed into the cheapest, tiniest nurse uniforms known to man, similar to those Joe probably sold at The Basement.

The beautiful models ripped at buttons and straps until their big tits bounced free. Judge shifted in his seat as we watched them maul each other in a frenzy, their shiny hair flying and red lipstick smearing.

"Watching you kiss the other girls drove me fuckin' wild," he whispered against my ear, gliding his fingers up my smooth thigh under the blanket.

God.

"It turned me on, too." Redness rushed to my cheeks as the nearly naked women panted and whimpered on the big screen. Judge refilled our shot glasses and we swallowed two more gulps, then he returned to his sensuous ways and frenched me with sultry lips. The cold beer flavored our warm tongues, and I sucked every sour drop.

The nurses, all buttoned back up, began the next scene by rifling through paperwork at a makeshift workstation. They hovered together, big breasts rubbing over the counter until the decent-looking male lead entered in a generic white coat. The girls dramatically jumped apart as he glared with suspicious eyes.

"Uh-oh," Judge man-giggled in the dark.

I slid my hands all over his tight torso. "You're *way* hotter than he is."

"Ya think?"

"Fuck yes."

After three more shots, Judge tucked his fingers between my bare thighs and cradled me closer as I scanned the space for the latest developments. Evan and Mia were kissing deeply but quietly beside us. Decker's arms draped low around Shay's waist as she rocked back against his thick chest. The flickering screen cast a dirty, cinematic glow over the sexy couples, adding sensual highlights to each as we made our daring moves.

The flick cut to the naughty nurses, alone again, in the same patient room setting as the opener. One blond sprawled over the tidy bed while the other ravaged her hard nipples with a swirling, wet tongue. The doctor abruptly entered from the side and unexpectedly scolded them for their forbidden lust, muttering ridiculous excuses about hospital property and on-the-clock hours.

"Oh, they are in troub-le," I tipsy-giggled.

Judge chuckled beside me and eased his hand even higher now, his brave fingers tempting the moist skin near my damp lace. He nosed my curls aside and puckered behind my ear with velvety, open lips. Shivers trickled down my spine, and I scratched at his rippled abs with approval.

The shocked nurses begged the doctor not to report their forbidden foreplay, but he scoffed in their faces and turned to leave. They whined and pleaded, offering anything to keep their sacred jobs. The actor paused theatrically and glanced over his shoulder.

"Anything?"

"Yes, we'll do anything!"

He slowly removed his white coat as the funky background music began and spoke of some cheap, rehearsed sex ultimatum. The prettier nurse nodded gratefully and dropped to her knees to unbuckle his slacks. The other sweetly kissed his cheek, then joined her secret lover in a dual blowjob. They dragged thankful, wet tongues over his impressive length until one swallowed his swollen tip.

I squirmed in my seat with thoughts of choking on a hard cock, slightly changing the angle of my hips as Judge's hand wandered higher against my thirsty folds. Christ, this scene-by-scene tease was stoking the simmering embers inside me. "That punishment isn't so bad," I whispered.

"I'd love to feel your lips around me like that." Judge's hushed confession shipped an agonizing throb directly to my core, and I inched my impatient pelvis into his waiting fingertips. He finally rubbed my tight slit through the thin fabric, and I gasped with hot, eager breath against his neck.

Judge stroked the slow burn between my legs as the nurses now performed on demand for the blackmailing doctor. The doc chilled in the corner of the patient room during one scene, jerking off selfishly as he watched the beauties finger fuck each other. Later, he stretched on his back while one sexy model rode his hard length, and the other grinded her wet pussy on his wide tongue. Hell, the prick was getting his money's worth.

I checked on my girls during a lagging part of the plot. Mia had turned entirely away from the screen and was now slow humping Evan's groin in the dim television light. His dark, unbuttoned pajama shirt spilled open to the sides as she lapped at his chiseled pecs. He groped her ass with grabby fingers and tipped his chin to the ceiling, eyes clenched shut in overwhelming pleasure.

She better still have her fuckin' panties on.

Shay was writhing back against Deck's chest, his visible fingers massaging her round breast and thumbing her nipple over the shimmery yellow satin. He slanted his open lips against her neck and sucked with passion along her delicate jawline. I'm pretty sure I knew where his other hand was buried.

Fuckin' get some, Shay.

The porn performances paled when compared to the natural heat building before me in the room. Inspired by the sultry sighs from my best friends' whimpering lips, I palmed Judge's hardened cock as he continued to toy with my swollen clit under the covers. With a gentle hip thrust, I silently gave my polite partner permission to dive deeper. Judge met my eyes for consent, then edged his fingertips inside my panties and strummed my juicy center.

Finally.

I willed away the urge to binge fuck Judge's hand and focused on the big screen. My deepest, wettest spots hadn't been stroked by strange fingers in entirely too fuckin' long, and there would be no muffling my moans of delight if he tapped that trigger.

The dickhead doctor brought a better-looking friend during the next abrupt interruption and explained his amendment to the unwritten contract, insisting that the buddy now be included. The frustrated nurses eventually submitted to the agreement and stripped away their skimpy white skirts. The new pairs fucked side by side over the edge of the hospital bed, with both blonds being railed hard from behind by giant, heavy cocks.

Judge apparently enjoyed that scene, and he sucked on my neck with hungry, snarling lips as he continued to toy with my pining pussy. I recognized the need to slow things down, but I craved this contact too much, desperately wanting to come close to crossing the bigger line. I swept nimble fingertips under Judge's loose, low waistband and taunted his swollen, sticky tip.

Christ, he was ready to go.

My naturally nosy ass thirsted for the end of the story, so I continued to watch as we worked each other with skilled hands. The poor nurses huddled alone again, tired of pleasing the greedy bastards and contemplating walking the fuck out. They consoled each other, which led to some realistic kissing, but once more, Dr. Dick interrupted.

"How dare you pleasure each other without me?!"

The nurses were fuckin' over it, and I internally cheered as they threatened to expose his shady ass. The doc haughtily laughed and challenged them both to turn him in, producing an ancient flip phone from his white coat pocket and daring them to summon the big boss.

A fuckin' flip phone?

I'd been so enthralled with the on-screen argument that I didn't complain when Judge paused to pour a fresh shot. We both slowed our seduction as he dumped two drinks down my throat and licked my soaked lips. He swallowed his share from the same glass, tossed it aside, and circled the cool, damp tip of his tongue against my ear. The big boss's arrival stole my attention and, much to the surprise of my tipsy mind, she was a beautiful, busty blond, too.

"It's on," I whispered.

Judge's gritty breath tickled my neck. "Oh, I know."

Our blanket-covered buildup had paced with the porn plot so far, so I stroked his rigid cock with swift fingers in anticipation of the final scene on screen. He picked up the pace between my legs, coaxing me with a thick, curved finger as I grinded my wetness against his palm.

After a fiery, convincing exchange, the sultry boss dismissed the prick with little fanfare, then she turned to the two lusty lovers and promptly forgave them for their indiscretions. She gently explained that there was certainly nothing wrong with some stress relief when the workload was slow. The nurses embraced with a relieved kiss and gushed about keeping their jobs, asking gleefully how they could show appreciation. Boss Lady puckered her red lips with a sly smile and slowly unbuttoned her crisp black blouse.

"Well, there is ONE way."

My discipline had reached its breaking point as the three striking actresses tore into each other, so I shifted completely over Judge's pelvis and straddled him on my knees with no warning. He read the room as I rocked my desperate hips against him, stretching my lace with his big hand and forcing two thick fingers inside my tight, dripping walls. My body jerked with pleasure as he fucked me with deep, unbearable pumps. I arched my back, moaning shamelessly as he slithered his wet mouth over my chest and tongued my hard nipple through the thin satin.

"Guys, the movie is over."

What the fuck, Evan?

"Ignore him, please," I begged with a whisper as Judge's fingers instinctively slowed.

"I can't, Callie."

"*Fuck*, please..."

Instead of a toe-curling climax, Judge offered only a consolation smile. He eased his hand from my wetness, leaving my building crest to crash without release. Mia and Shay bitched around me, apparently falling victim to the same evil deeds.

"Are you kidding me right now, Deck?"

"Evan! Why did you fuckin' stop?"

I awkwardly slid from Judge's lap and adjusted my soaked panties as shame flushed over my face. We shared painful, silent glances of frustration and confusion when all three men disappeared into the bathroom without explanation. We listened to running water and muffled discussion for a minute, then both girls hopped from their spots and plopped down next to me in the middle. When the guys appeared again and lined up in front of the rolling credits, they each still looked fucking gorgeous, and that pissed me off even more.

"Don't be mad," Decker pleaded as he held up a palm. "Please..."

Evan jumped in for the assist. "You girls know why we can't fuck tonight."

"We already considered it," Judge added with a soft smile in my direction. "Trust me."

The three of us sat side by side on the couch, obviously feeling dejected and rejected. None of this fucking bro speech was helping the current situation, so Mia shockingly offered to take matters into her own hands.

"Fuck it," she sassed with a shoulder shrug, turning away from the boys to focus on us. "I'll just finish you both off."

Jesus, Mia. I wasn't quite ready for that fuckin' leap.

Deck stroked his chin with a stifled smile. "As much as I don't wanna stop the girl party..."

"Hell, let's not stop them." Evan smirked over at Judge. "Change of plans?"

Judge laughed. "Come on, man."

"Change of plans? What the hell are you talking about?" Shay demanded.

Deck strolled to the corner and retrieved our three black masks from a box on the bookshelf.

"I didn't realize we left those here," I mumbled with surprise. "What's going on?"

Evan laughed and shook his head. "Girls, the movie was just foreplay."

Judge nodded along. "Your unofficial Three Doors experience starts tonight."

What the...

Decker crossed his muscular arms over his chest and grinned arrogantly as he dangled the blindfolds from a single finger. "So, pick a room, but keep the lights off. Sit on the bed and put on your mask. One of us will be right in."

~ 10 ~

Wait, what?
Three Doors?
Tonight?
"If that's okay, of course," Decker added after noticing our shocked faces.
Evan threw up his palms with an assist. "Only if you want to…"
"But we can't—" I began.
"We know," Judge interrupted. "But we can have *some* fun."
Shay shifted beside me as her analytical gears cranked. "All of our rapid tests came back negative from the clinic, right?" We nodded with confirmation around the room. While we still had a couple of days to wait for the blood tests, which the girls and I had lovingly deemed the "free to fuck" results, we'd all been cleared of most sexually transmitted diseases.
"You three gave us a teaser," Decker noted with a grin and a glance at the guys, "and believe me, we haven't stopped thinking about it since."
Wow.
Shay and I were still absorbing the shocking turn of the evening, but Mia abruptly stood and smoothed her green slip.
"I'm in. You two coming?"
I fuckin' hope.
Judge laughed at her thirsty ways. "Damn, Mia. We need to hide in the kitchen first. Can't know what room you go in, remember?"
"Oh, right." Mia's cheeks reddened with a rare blush as she returned to her seat. "Sorry. I'm just excited."
Decker hit us with the logistics. "Since we can't talk, here's how we figured it could work. Keep your mask on at all times. We'll knock, roll in and, um, do our thing…"

Evan chuckled under his breath. "I'll do my thing, alright."

This fuckin' guy.

"...then you can take off the mask once we leave. We'll knock when it's safe to come out."

"Wait," I hesitated and looked between them. "So, we'll be in blindfolds, but you won't? You'll be able to see us, but we can't see you?" The thought alone made me squirm against the cushions as my impatient puss continued to beg for attention.

Evan nodded. "You got it."

"Just a preview of the bigger game," Deck explained with a hint of cockiness. "Kinda like your little sectional surprise for us the other night."

Oh.

Shay followed along beside me. "So, we'll be in the dark for you this time."

"Bingo."

Fuck, we were putting this Three Doors theory to the test tonight. My moist motor kicked into gear again with the thought of one of these striking men finally losing control with my naked body. I looked to my lap and fiddled with my hem to distract from the pink heat creeping up my neck. Was I ready for this level of intensity? It took only a glance up at the stacks of muscle and my eager cooch did the nodding for me.

"*That's* why you got the haircuts today," Shay said. "You planned this."

"Guilty." Evan cringed. "We just couldn't fuckin' wait."

"And I hope you don't feel weird," Judge added, suddenly showing some apprehension. "It's completely cool if it stops here."

Christ, they really cared. My selfish frustration from the earlier edging shifted into adoration and appreciation. Truthfully, any or all of the guys could've tried to get it in before tonight and chalked it up to a one-night stand, but they respected us enough to wait. These elaborate gestures provided glaring evidence of their decency. Had they wanted only cock action, despite their whiny complaints, I was positive that all three of them could have picked up some strange on campus. This effort meant something.

"Are you fuckin' kidding?" I blurted out. "I can't believe you guys planned this! I'm blown away!"

Shay bounced on the sectional beside me. "I'm still wound up, so let's try it."

The guys carried their cheesy grins behind the kitchen wall, and I tiptoed to the dark hallway with my girls, armed with only a sleep mask and filthy intentions. We huddled in front of the restroom and paused to collect ourselves.

"You guys ready for this?" Shay asked.

"Fuck, I was almost there a few minutes ago," I whispered. "Bring it."

Mia cringed with excitement. "And the thought of not knowing which one? I just can't fuckin' take it."

Shay pointed to the first bedroom door off the living room. "I'll take this one. It matches mine," she mouthed. Mia licked her lips with a confident grin and nodded at door number three as she followed suit.

We'd never had a reason to explore the bedrooms of our counterparts before, so I had no clue whose private space I was slinking into. Months ago, as our trios were first becoming friends, I would've thought nothing of seeing their sleep spaces by chance. But now? Now that we'd revealed our collective cravings and this wicked plan was taking shape? Christ, my heart backflipped in my chest as I closed the middle door behind me.

A scant glow from the street-side window cast odd gray highlights over the contents. A framed mattress lined the wall to my right, same as in my room a couple of floors above. Both the nightstand and desk were bare but for a nondescript lamp by the headboard, perhaps intentionally stripped of any identifying items. I considered peeking in the closet or opening a drawer, but then I realized that my discoveries wouldn't matter. The guys could slip through any of the three doors to deliver our desires. Hell, they'd probably giggle like goofy schoolboys about shooting their shots on each other's sheets.

There was no way to know who would step inside and pleasure me, especially after the lengths they'd taken to blend, but one fact stood tall...

...the man who slept in this room wanted to fuck me.

I hesitated as I approached the dark comforter, not knowing if I should toss the nightie or not, but I ultimately left it for him to take off. The slinky fabric left me feeling sexy as it glided over my smooth skin, and I could use that boost of confidence as I waited for the jiggle of the doorknob.

I crawled to my knees facing the door on the strange yet familiar bed and slipped the mask over my blond waves. The instant darkness unexpectedly amplified the intensity of the moment, and my heart raged against my ribs in response. I brushed my hand over the single propped pillow to my side and wondered if the resident of this room ever rested his head and pictured me in his dreams. My deepest core ached at the thought of all three men and their hardened cocks, waiting eagerly in the dark hallway to creep inside and give this game a ride.

I waited with them, for one of them, clenching my thighs together to dull the demanding throb as my busy brain ticked away. After careful consideration, I realized that it didn't matter who joined me in this bed. I wanted all of them. Judge had stroked my pussy exactly how I needed, and my skin still tingled with the stain of his seduction. I massaged my round breasts through the slippery fabric, remembering his hot mouth tugging at my tightened nipple. Evan had taken his share, too, rocking against my ass with his thick shaft as we "shopped" and floating the idea of pumping inside my tightest hole. There was just something about his dominant touch that drove me fuckin' crazy.

Christ, they're dragging this out.

I hadn't been exaggerating when I'd crowned Deck the sexiest of the group. I pictured the mischievous sparkle in his eyes when he toyed with stopping our elevator. How would he have fucked me had I accepted his out-of-bounds invitation? Would he have forced me to all fours and slammed inside me from behind? Or would he have craved my kiss and crushed me against the wall?

I rubbed the luxurious lingerie over my bare thighs, drawing from the well of my deepest, darkest fantasies. I fingered myself frequently back in my bed, most often to Judge, Deck, and Evan ravishing my body at the same time. Hell, they spoke and moved in perfect sync as friends, but the thought of their naked bodies sharing me? Licking me? Filling me?

Fuck. I'm about to do this myself.

I rocked my hips in a slow circle, and warm, early juice slid between my folds.

What would be the harm in a quick, superficial strum?

My fingertips had just breached the edge of my panties when the door clicked open and closed with no warning. I jerked my fuckin' hand from my cooch like I'd been caught in the cookie jar.

Fuck, who is it?

The silence screamed in my ears until my thumping heart interrupted. The black mask blinded me to his reactions but enhanced my other senses as he waited to make his move. Shivers raced down my chest and hardened my nipples. The faint smell of the blue bathroom soap tickled my nose. The sour shots still tasted bitter on my dry tongue.

Why isn't he coming closer?

Oh.

He's watching me.

I'd been so distracted by my body's reactions that I'd forgotten my status as the only masked participant in the room. He could see me…my every labored breath, my every eager quiver, my every exposed inch. Fuck, I finally understood the guys' jerk happy responses when we crashed them. This was fucking exhilarating.

There was no creak over the solid floor, but somehow I sensed him approaching the bed. I instinctively reached into the darkness beyond the mask but felt nothing.

Please.

That good burn ignited between my thighs again as he destroyed me with this delay. I cocked my head and slowly licked my lips, hoping to hear just one sigh of anticipation. Seconds dragged like years as he dangled my patience from a twisted, agonizing string. My discipline had been tested earlier, but I now found myself ready to rip the blindfold from my hungry eyes and willingly spread my legs for my man, regardless of who the fuck he was…

…but then he touched me.

Big, warm hands finally covered my restless fingers, calming me without a single spoken word. After my few ragged breaths of relief, he gently guided me from the mattress and tilted my chin to his for my first anonymous kiss. My mind ran in circles as I tried to decipher the identity of the tongue lapping between my lips. Judge loved to lick. Evan was aggressive. Deck preferred it paced. Hell, this current action revealed nothing. I'd kissed the guys with genuine passion on only a handful of occasions and, frankly, I assumed that their individual styles would provide a hint.

Fuck, was I wrong.

As our bodies drifted closer and his fingertips tightened under my curls, I realized he was probably feeling anxious, too, and depending on primal instinct rather than any trademark methods. None of the men had enjoyed us completely alone, with no distractions or rotations to deter from the tension, so this likely meant as much to him as it did to me.

As I relaxed into his embrace, I closed the impossible case. I didn't want to ruin this incredible experience by clouding my mind with a fruitless mission. Whoever stood before me was someone that I cared for, trusted, and desired. That was enough for me.

I'd rarely found ways to quiet my excessive thoughts before, but his roaming touch provided quite the roadmap. I melted into the moment, clawing at his cotton shirt as our sweet, welcoming kiss flaunted a deeper fire. He scraped gentle teeth against my bottom lip, perhaps with a promise of passion yet to come, then he stepped away from our sizzling space. In one quick gesture, he slipped the blue satin from over my head to expose my bare breasts and soaked lace for the first time. I had no way to gauge his reaction from behind the blindfold, but the lapse in action implied that he was admiring my assets. My cheeks flushed when facing the elevated vulnerability, but I couldn't deny feeling incredibly sexy under his watch.

As I waited for his next move, I considered the submissive stance that this wild ride required. I'd never trusted a man with this level of control, and the mask shielded my usual strengths. Friends and lovers alike had always called me a tease and believe me, I loved the label. But I couldn't rely on flirty eyes or whispered words with Three Doors. Tonight, I was at his mercy and his mercy alone.

Suddenly, his wet tongue trailed over my lower pelvis near my panties. My startled hands twitched at my sides and I almost jumped back, but the need to urge him closer crushed my instinct to resist. I shifted my hips forward for more, but his warm mouth abruptly left my shivering skin. My breath hitched and my lungs burned.

Fuck. Why did he stop?

One of these unbelievable men had lips within inches of my thirsty pussy. I'd never experienced earth-shattering oral, but as his teeth suddenly snagged my skimpy bottoms, I hoped to the heavens that tonight would be the night. Our makeshift team of wiggling hips and fingertips inched my lace to the floor, then I stood practically dripping before him. I thought he may pause to inspect my most private part from afar, but he decided to take a closer peek instead. I muffled a moan and clenched fists at my sides as he coaxed my knees apart and taunted my shivering skin.

The carefully planned facial hair scratched at my shivers as he frenched along my upper thigh. I almost forfeited the mystery for the other players by screaming to the ceiling when he abandoned me again, only to feel his wide, wet lick on the other side seconds later. My damp nerve endings tingled with cool chills as his kisses lingered between breaks, and every muscle tensed as I waited for more. Soft puffs of hot breath rushed over my tight slit and nearly sent me spiraling, but when his nose brushed my tuft of fur with a slight sniff, I realized that I'd arrived at the edge of my discipline cliff. I palmed his fresh haircut and forced his scorching mouth closer to my mound, but he abruptly stood from my hold.

I parked any remaining hesitation and reached through the darkness to find his firm frame. My blind fingertips brushed layers of naked, tight ab muscles, so I instinctively explored farther south over his body. Much to my disappointment, those fancy fuckin' pajama pants still rested low on his hips. I urgently clawed at the waistband, dying to get a grip on that bare dick, but he batted my nosy hands away. When I evaded his defenses and tried harder, he simply lifted me like a rag doll and tossed me gently back on the bed before leaving me hanging again.

Fuck, this cat-and-mouse chase was undeniably the most electrifying moment of my life. He was watching my every reaction. He knew exactly the impact he was having on my desperate body. I writhed against the strange pillow and sighed with breathtaking frustration as I waited in my personal darkness for his next mesmerizing move. After seconds with no response and jonesing for more stimulation, I cupped my heaving breasts and thumbed my swollen nips, launching my waves of arousal again and hoping that I could convince him to come captain my crests.

The lonely storm didn't last. The mattress caved beside me, and he pushed my hands aside, then he smothered my pink nipple with his hot, wet mouth like a starving fuckin' animal. His bare leg brushed over mine and I thought he was finally naked, too. But as he shifted those hips over my arched body, the tickle of boxers disappointed my aching pussy. He grinded that steel shaft aggressively against my drenched slit, dragging merciless friction over my plump clit, then he ravaged my neck until our tongues finally met again.

My heart soared as our desperate lips opened for each other, pouring months of unspoken yearning and painstaking patience into the blistering breath we shared. I hadn't realized just how madly I needed to kiss one of them like this. Unhinged. Unforgiving. Uninterrupted. I'd never experienced a passion so hypnotic as our mouths twisted into a wet, mysterious mess. He enhanced my every steamy storybook need with thirsty tugs at my blond strands, needy nibbles on my bottom lip, and sensual sucks of my delicate tongue. As our bodies absorbed and reflected the mutual longing, our embrace felt like something we'd waited for our entire lives...

...which was an odd fucking feeling since I didn't know who he was.

But he knew who I was.

Christ, the pressure of the moment became too overwhelming to bear. I jerked my chin from his, desperate to gasp sweet breaths of relief, but my seducer didn't yield any ground. After a silent snarl against my jawline, he claimed even more space, swirling his tongue relentlessly across my collarbone and sweeping his parted lips between my round tits. I whimpered through clenched teeth as his swollen cock angled against my wetness again, but he was quick to cover my blatant violation with a cupped palm.

Just like I had done to Decker.

Was that a hint?

Fucking stop it, Callie!

I licked his bossy hand and shook it from my face, the display of authority sending unexpected surges south. I fought underneath his crushing weight and tried to take control, aggressively pumping my bare pussy into his boxers and screaming silently for him to put me out of my wonderful misery. Christ, I had never wanted to fuck so badly in my life.

As if he felt pity for my pathetic attempts at taking charge, he rolled to my side and shoved my thighs apart, then pumped a curved finger inside my wet hole. The first thrusts provided only a cruel tease of what his cock could do, so I tightened my walls and rocked my pelvis into his palm with a promise of what I could deliver if he caved. The boxers stayed in place, but a second finger joined the show, providing more filling and friction as I jerked my hips to the ceiling. This magic man knew exactly how to work those fuckin' strokes, beckoning me with curved, come hither drags against my deepest, hottest spot. I choked myself with my hand to stifle my cries as intense throbs burned my core.

At that point, after hours of seemingly endless teasing, I needed to climax more than I needed to breathe.

I could've submitted at that very moment. I could've relaxed into the ripples of pleasure pooling around his hand and let him witness me completely coming undone, but I didn't. Those skilled fingers felt delicious as I squeezed them inside me, but against every urging of logic and with confirmation of my earlier concerns, I wanted that cock.

And I wanted it fuckin' bad.

I curled my flat belly into a crunch and fumbled in my blindness for a brush of those bottoms, certain that I could convince him to break all these fuckin' rules with me, but he edged just out of reach. He mocked me again, probably while wearing an arrogant fucking grin, and thumbed my puffy clit with slow, sensational circles as he watched me squirm. I dropped my knees wider and invited that iron cock to flee from the boxers and take me, but he still made no moves to undress.

Fuck this man and his discipline.

The enticing anonymity may have hampered my ability to lure him in directly, but I had one more tool in my arsenal. Although I was confined behind the blindfold, the streetlights outside provided just enough brightness for my victim to bear witness. I floated fingers into the dark again, this time with a higher target, and turned his alluring scruff to my lips with a last-ditch attempt. Once his downtown toying slowed and I knew my words would be his only focus, I mouthed my final plea…silently, slowly, and deliberately.

"Fuck me."

A sharp inhale tightened his jaw in my palms.

"Please, fuck me so hard. *Please.*"

His hand instantly recoiled from my wetness. His heavy body grazed my breasts as he crawled over me and left me alone on the bed again.

Fuck, was he leaving?

Had I made him uncomfortable?

I'd appreciated the efforts these amazing men had taken to secure this time with us, their respect and thoughtfulness taking center stage, and my selfish fuckin' ass had ruined everything. My shoulders slumped in defeat for not only me but for the entire crew.

Without warning, he grabbed my hips, turning me in his direction and pulling me aggressively to the edge of the bed. My short legs dangled helplessly over the side until he pinned them back with pure fucking dominance, displaying my glistening, aching pussy on his personal platter. For the first time during this intense encounter, he shelved the teasing temptation, licking wide laps through my sticky folds and curling the tip of his tongue around my throbbing clit. The unexpected, intimate contact nearly sprung me from my submissive position. I clawed at the rumpled linens to my left and groped aimlessly in the dark to the right.

There was no fucking way I could be quiet through this.

Likely inspired by my thrashing reaction, he pinned my pelvis to the mattress under his heavy palm and put his pussy expertise to the test. I flailed on the comforter as he sucked my folds through hot, massaging lips and darted inside my clenched hole with a fast, flickering tongue.

I finally brushed the pillow off to my side and shoved it between my teeth, gritting silently through the swells of a rushing climax. His grinding mouth slathered through my wetness to pulsing my center, and he flicked my tortured clit with firm strokes. Every fucking nerve in my body fired with painful, pleasurable flames, and I flooded his sweet lips with my hot, juicy finish. I lost control, gagging myself with the pillow's corner as I cried out with no shame.

He softened his masterful mouth and escorted me from my high with gentle sucking, showing tender aftercare until my knees stopped quivering. After a delicate kiss on my pubic line, he disappeared again, leaving me breathless as I closed my legs and stared into the blindfold. My intrusive brain nudged me to start the analysis, but I had no fucking idea what to think. I just laid there, raw and exposed, feeling completely fulfilled but also strikingly empty without the comfort of his touch.

Were we finished?
What about his needs?
Would he say goodbye?

The warmth of his body hovered over me once more as he returned with a slow, tantalizing kiss. I tasted my pleasure as I licked lovingly at his lips and a deep throb stirred low as I selfishly craved being indulged again. This sensual, comforting brand of embrace mirrored our first, capping the end of the experience with the same respect that had started it. My suspicions were confirmed seconds later when he stepped from my skin for the last time.

Suddenly feeling shy, I shifted deeper on the bed, covered my nude body with the loosened linens, and turned away from the hallway. I waited for the door to open as expected, but he didn't leave. I cocked my head and listened for his reasoning, hearing hushed panting and faint skin slapping.

Oh.

He was jacking off.

Fuck.

After a minute of listening to the intriguing sounds, I sensed him gathering his pajama uniform and sliding out the door. I waited for a few heart cycles, then ripped off my sleep mask in a frenzy. Once my eyes adjusted through countless blinks, I switched on the bedside table lamp and sat disoriented on the borrowed bed. I'd lost my sense of time and had no clue how long I'd been in here.

Were the others finished?

I scooped up my discarded negligee, located my lace panties, and dressed quickly in the anonymous room. We'd left the comforter quite a mess for the usual resident, so I tried to make the space look presentable again. A mirror reflected on the back of the bedroom door, so I stepped before it and stared at my dim reflection. My mind began to wander before I'd barely taken a breath, but it didn't make it far. My heart pushed past the crowded thoughts and dropped five flights in my chest as someone knocked on the door.

~ 11 ~

After allowing a couple of minutes for my heart to restart while the knocker walked away, I crept through the bedroom door and rushed directly to the bathroom without diverting my eyes. I needed another minute to compose myself before facing anyone, including my girlfriends. I flipped on the harsh light and glimpsed at my reflection in the big mirror before darting to the toilet. Hell, maybe I wasn't even ready to face myself.

As warm pee trickled from my recovering cooch, I stared at the boring white shower curtain and finally let my brain lead the way. For starters, I couldn't blame shame for tightening the nervous knots in my belly. I had a fuckin' blast with the boys and, despite the brutal battering my discipline had endured, I wanted more. No doubt about that.

No, my hesitation blossomed from another level of uncertainty. After that incredible experience, I had no closure. Sure, we'd rehash the generals as a group, but what about my specific partner? Was he happy to find me waiting on the bed? Did he enjoy himself, or was he uncomfortable in any way?

I felt leftover guilt that he stroked himself in the corner rather than enjoying my mouth or my hands, but that was because of his silent insistence. He'd resisted all my advances, regardless of his rock-hard enthusiasm, and heaven knows that I tried all the tricks. Maybe he feared that once he unleashed his peen near my pussy, he'd cross every imaginable line and could never look at me the same again.

Which, of course, was the whole point of the game.

Fuck, I felt so many versions of dirty. I cleaned my downtown with extra toilet paper, giggling to myself that only therapy could wash this feeling away, then I stood before the bright mirror for the post-preview evaluation.

Thank goodness that I'd passed on the heavy makeup since the bit I wore had smeared around my eyes. I found nothing in the manly bathroom gentle enough to scrub, so I did my best to polish my face and accepted that the smudges would have to stay. Rosy blotches stretched from my neck to my cheekbones with my trademark pattern of arousal. I fingered my smooth skin and traced remnant trails of his wet mouth and warm tongue, wondering just whose lips had left their mark. After swishing with the nearly empty bottle of blue mouthwash, I stared back at the short, messy blond chick in front of me.

And ya know what? I liked her.

I would need to evaluate my role much more than that simple assessment, but I'd save that for another time. I didn't want to keep my girls waiting even longer than they already had, but I especially didn't want to keep *him* waiting, whoever he was.

I finally opened the door to face the proverbial music, finding my friends emitting safe, serene vibes as they chilled in the living room. Shay chugged a bottle of water and passed it to Judge. Deck lightly stroked Mia's shoulder as she curled on his lap. Evan, the only solo soldier, jumped up from the sectional and smiled at my late entrance.

"Sorry I took so long," I apologized with a cringe.

Mia grinned from across the room. "You're fine, girl. No hurry."

Judge pulled Shay closer against his chest, and my mind erupted with a rush of rambling thoughts. *How did this cuddle pairing happen? Was it significant? Did the girls or guys choose? If the guys decided, was it based on who they'd just fucked with? Or did they intentionally mix it up?*

Evan spoke up and unknowingly saved me from falling overboard. "You want some water? Or something else?"

"Water would be great. Thank you." I parked in the empty spot he left and smoothed one of the gray blankets over my legs. All eyes landed on me.

"So?" Mia blinked with expectation.

"So..." I echoed.

"How are you feeling?" Judge asked.

Oh, so we're breaking this down? Right now? Did I have to go first?

"Wait," I hesitated, "how long have you girls been out here?"

"Not long at all. I was just sitting down when you ran in the bathroom."

"And you were already in there when I came out," Shay added.

I was a bit confused by the logistics. "You haven't been out here waiting?"

"No, Callie," Evan explained as he joined me on the cushions. I took a quick drink of the offered water as he continued. "The guys all came out at different times. Once we freshened up, we knocked on all three doors." I guess that worked. Emerging one by one would put each of us face to face with the guy who just rocked our world. "After the knock, then we just waited in the kitchen until you all came out. We stepped away so we wouldn't know who left each room."

"Right." I nodded over my refreshing bottle. "I don't know what I was thinking."

"Does that make sense?" Deck popped in for the assist. "Everything is still a secret. I know what room the other guys went into, but not which girl was in there. Just like you don't know what room we each covered."

Thankfully, my patient peeps already knew that I sometimes required another round of explanation. "You didn't see me come out?"

Judge shook his head. "Nope. We were already waiting in the kitchen. The girls told us you slipped into the bathroom, so we parked out here to wait."

It finally clicked. Damn, I had some clever fuckin' friends.

Shay still looked like a rock star as she stood from Judge's embrace and smoothed her yellow lingerie. "Speaking of the bathroom, I need a minute. Save the good stuff until I get back."

Mia swatted Shay's ass as she maneuvered around the cooler table. "Make it quick. I'm next."

Evan snaked his long arm behind my waist, so I snuggled against his hard muscles in those navy pajamas. Despite the usual primal arousal that sparked inside whenever he was near, I longed for a different brand of comfort, and he provided it. My earlier uncertainty calmed as he kissed the top of my hair and softly stroked my hip.

"What a night," Deck sighed.

"One of the best nights of my life," Mia said as she shifted on his lap.

Judge laughed and shook his head. "Only *one* of the best? Damn, woman."

"I think this is gonna be addictive," Evan murmured against my ear.

It already fuckin' is.

A comfortable silence settled as we waited for Shay to finish primping. As soon as she returned, Mia hopped up and shot me wild, wide eyes as she walked past. Evan rested his head on mine, and I glanced subtly around the room, wondering just what *my* mystery guy was thinking.

This chill vibe provided some sanity after the entire week of crossing lines. Separating sex from emotion had been easy in the past because I'd spent those few dirty nights with men I had no intention of vibing with long term. I'd dabbled in casual dating through college and couldn't define any actual one-night stands, but I'd never bonded with any boys beyond the basics. Deck, Judge, and Evan were different somehow.

On the one hand, until I started hanging with this unique group, I'd never enjoyed a genuine friendship with the opposite sex. My high school boyfriend was a possessive prick, basically beating friendly "rivals" away with a mouthy stick. I had acquaintances in undergrad, of course, but I'd never clicked with them on that deeper level as I had with these guys.

On the other hand, I was hopelessly attracted to all three of our gorgeous hosts and felt no regrets about exploring this sexual realm with each of them. Three Doors filled the void between those friend and lover contradictions, allowing these men to work my body to a frenzy by night and still listen to me ramble over my school books the next day.

Decker was right. This *did* feel like a relationship….an unconventional, incredible relationship.

"*And* I'm back!" Mia cat-walked down the hallway with a beautiful smile, sashaying those hips in her green negligee. "You need more mouthwash, by the way."

As soon as she relaxed into Decker's arms again, Judge jumped in with both feet. "So, I'll start. I know the guys were at an advantage tonight, but it was fuckin' incredible."

Aww.

"Same for me," Evan added. "From the game to the movie, it was the perfect night. Hell, the perfect day, really."

Mia flashed him a flirty smile. "Did we even watch the movie?"

Evan man-giggled against me. "Well, not much, but it sounded hot." We all laughed. Hell, it was starting to feel like a standard study night.

"So much better than anything I imagined," Deck admitted with a charming grin. "And when I think about next weekend? *Fuck*." Much to my relief, the other guys mumbled agreement with not one hint of disappointment. Of course, my overthinking mind had tortured me without cause again.

"So, what was it like for you?" Evan asked with a slight nudge against my shoulder.

"Amazing," Shay said. "Like the fulfillment of a fantasy I never knew I wanted."

"Same here," I added as my body settled back to baseline. "It was thrilling not knowing who was touching me."

"Exactly," Mia agreed. "But I could also relax knowing that it was one of you." So true. This would never work with anyone else.

"Well, boys," Judge laughed with a bicep flex, "I think we did a good job."

Mia raised her brows. "My guy sure as fuck did. Like *wow*."

I caught the boys slipping adorable, cocky grins over our heads and considered how the conversation may turn after we left them alone. "Will you be comparing notes?"

"Sure." Our female half tossed an orchestra of bitchy moans in Deck's direction. "Notes, not names," he assured us with a grin. "Promise."

"You, too?" Shay blinked up at Judge.

He scoffed at the implication. "Of course. We don't wanna fuck this up."

"Well, thank you." I smiled with an appreciative blush.

Evan patted my hip until I joined our blue eyes. "We care about you, ya know," he convinced me. "This isn't just the average dip for any of us."

Christ, these men.

Shay stretched into a yawn beside Judge. "We'll all be in the dark next time. Let's hope we can pull it off."

I toyed with Evan's stretchy waistband under the blanket, mesmerized by the memory of scruff buried between my legs. "I can't wait. Seriously."

"So, our other test results should come this week," Mia reminded us of the busy agenda, "and I'll schedule our waxes."

Deck nodded. "And we'll need to figure out the logistics in your rooms."

"And go to class, study for patho, and take that fuckin' exam," Shay groaned.

"We're wearing the same perfume and deodorant on Three Doors nights," I added. "You guys may want to, too."

"We already took care of that," Deck laughed. Come to think of it, I'd been within a breath of all three men and hadn't noticed any alluring aromas, not even from the style king himself.

"Yeah, we skipped the heavy scents tonight," Evan said. "We can match it up next time if you want. Who smells best?"

"Judge!" we answered in confident unison, followed by a round of ridiculous giggles as he boasted over the scoffs.

"So, we'll study on Monday and Tuesday," Shay rattled off our final schedule, "then exam and chill on Wednesday. Window treatments and wax on Thursday. Room check on Friday."

"And finally fuck our brains out on Saturday!" Mia squealed with excitement.

Evan shook his head beside me. "You're fuckin' crazy."

She shipped him an air kiss. "And you love *every* second of it."

Our generous hosts tried to persuade us to spend the night, promising a clean group crash on the sectional and even hand-delivered breakfast, but we declined, citing the need for girl time and actual sleep. We did, however, accept the offered goodnight kisses. Knowing that I had been with one of them made me long for the other two in a jacked-up way, as if my secret someone already stacked some advantage and the others needed to catch up. Of course, I couldn't pinpoint who had serviced my station, so my feelings made no fuckin' sense.

Hell, none of this did, but it worked.

My chest rattled with a second rumble of anticipation. One of these men would approach me after having sucked on my wet pussy. He'd watched as I shamelessly begged him to fuck me. He'd kissed me like I'd never been kissed. Would I be able to tell which guy had made my heart hammer and my face flush? Would I know which of the three pleasured himself in the dark while I listened?

In another first, we inadvertently passed on the lineup style of departure and migrated to different corners of the living space to share our goodbyes. Maybe we all held private whispers on our tongues, feeling the deviant and delightful highlights of the night while also recognizing the connective and impactful result. I shrugged into my robe in the kitchen while Shay paused by the dining room table and Mia lingered near the sectional. It didn't take long for our fellow medical students to catch on.

Judge strolled up to me with pocketed hands and sympathetic eyes. His fingers had sampled my wet agony after the naughty nurse movie, but considering the unforgettable indiscretions behind closed doors, I had no reason to complain now. Hell, maybe he had been the one to relieve me, after all.

"Am I forgiven?" he asked with a sheepish smile, changing gears from his cocky demeanor.

I fumbled with his buttons and met his warm gaze. "Oh, I was so mad at you," I teased.

"I didn't wanna stop, Callie." He cupped my chin in both hands. "I never wanna stop with you."

I fell victim to his endless charm and offered my pouty lips for his penance. His skilled tongue swept sensual waves over mine, leaving further confusion and arousal in its wake. Was that admission a nod to my begging behind closed doors? Had he tasted my dripping wetness with this sweet mouth?

Deck sauntered into the kitchen next to claim his round with my lips. His relaxed, rippled body exuded calmness and confidence, but that gaze reflected intensity and intention. The addictive combination sent my heart to a full fuckin' skip.

"Callie."

"Decker."

Those dark bedroom eyes roamed over my curves as he cornered me against the cool counter. He tugged on the sides of my open robe, drawing me closer with sweltering authority, then a slight grin curled the corners of his lips. Was that an ache between my legs?

Jesus, girl. Lock it up down there.

"You're not last," I whispered my diversion, blinking up at him through my smeared makeup.

Deck slipped eager hands inside my cover and rubbed his wide palms over my satin-covered hips. "I couldn't wait this time," he rasped. "Not one more fuckin' second."

Hell, I couldn't wait, either. I fingered his sexy stubble, then guided his parted lips to mine as I melted against his firm frame. Muffled moans escaped his throat as his aggressive tongue possessed my breaths. His urgency was so uncharacteristic, and my train wreck of a mind veered even farther off the tracks. Was this a continuation of our pitch-black passion from earlier? Or was he missing his share after barely touching me all evening?

By the time Evan stepped close for my finale, Judge and Deck had left me simmering inside my sleepwear. I swept my tongue over my top lip and prepared my weakened will for his demanding moves, but fate stole the last laugh. My futile attempts to piece together the night suffered another setback when Evan played the sweetheart role.

"You haven't left yet, but I already miss you," he confessed with a charming smile. Christ, he was simply mouthwatering.

"You'll see me Monday when we study," I reminded him, shifting my weight and edging deeper into the palpable spark between us.

"True," Evan whispered, "but you won't be dressed like this." His frisky fingers grazed my soft nipple, then his hands drifted lower to my ass. Electricity pulsed under his palms as he explored my slim curves, then he covered my needy mouth with his. I clutched at his chest and ripped at the cotton as his imposter of a tongue lapped delicate licks between my lips, this tantalizing kiss mimicking the same comfort that he'd provided when we cuddled on the sofa.

This game was starting to mind fuck me.

The guys were switching roles right before my eyes, leaving me a clueless clusterfuck as their initial methods faded. How foolish was I to think that I could solve this case by relying on the style of a simple kiss? And why did I want to solve anything? My heart had played fuckin' hopscotch as the mystery man seduced me beyond the blindfold. Shouldn't I just let it ride?

~ • ~

Shay, Mia, and I relaxed against the back wall of the elevator, sharing blissful sighs and bemused glances on the short trip to our crib. A swaying drunk who'd barged through behind us stole peeks at our matching bodies as he fished for a potential booty call. After passing the fourth floor, he gave up the individual chase and dangled bait for all three.

"You're all so hot. Hell, I thought I was dreaming." He grinned and balanced against the wall. "Single?"

We shook our heads with a confident, collective no, and my chest swelled with unexpected pride. Fuck, it felt unbelievable to be all in with our binge-worthy men.

Although part of me craved a decompression chat session when we finally shuffled through our door, my bewildered brain and body begged for some downtime after the long, remarkable day. My girls agreed over yawns to save the analysis for breakfast, then we hugged goodnight and closed our doors behind us.

~ • ~

After interruption-free snoozing and refreshing showers the next morning, we met in the kitchen to enjoy our caffeine fix with a side of girly gossip. Shay hoisted herself up on the kitchen counter as Mia danced around joyfully and waited for her toast to brown.

"Girls, we struck gold, didn't we?" Mia gushed.

"It sure as fuck feels like it," I laughed.

"Okay, let's start with us," she said, meeting both of our eyes. "Do either of you feel weird about our kisses?" After the boys delivered their stunning announcement, the preview had taken precedence over any prior feminine flirtations. I still found my best friends beautiful by the morning light, but my mind was hyper-focused on the three tempting dicks downstairs.

"It was fun," I acknowledged, dumping an obscene amount of creamer in my coffee. "I don't feel weird."

"Neither do I," Shay said, "and, if I may say, you're both fantastic kissers."

"Aww, thanks!" I grinned and raised my drink.

Mia giggled as she hot-handed her breakfast from the toaster. "I loved it, too, and you know the boys were salivating."

"Hell, that was half the fun."

"So, about the boys, what happened on your end?" Shay pried.

"I won't lie," I caved. "I tried to get my guy to fuck me, but he wasn't having it."

Mia waved me off. "I did, too, girl. It wasn't just you."

"Well, my so-called 'nerves of steel' buckled hard," Shay laughed at herself. "I was fuckin' begging for it."

Mia slathered strawberry jelly on her toast. "We ended up having a sixty-nine session instead," she offered nonchalantly.

Shay gasped. "Shut. Up."

She took a giant bite, and a bit of fruit dribbled from the side of her mouth. "What?"

"I pawed at my guy's cock like it was fuckin' water in a desert!" I complained. "He shut me down every time!"

Shay piped up from her perch. "My guy did, too! He didn't even take his pants off!"

Harsh.

Mia offered her a consolation knee pat. "Did you at least get oral?"

"Yeah," Shay said, "but I rode him for a while before that. My hips are hella sore."

Mia's eyes widened with realization. "Wait, you're telling me that neither of you even touched bare peen?"

Shay cringed. "I didn't."

"I mean, I was half-stroking Judge on the couch during the movie, but that's about it."

"You guys got fuckin' robbed," Mia laughed. "I was all up in there."

Shay rolled her amused eyes at the flaunt and turned to me. "Did you get oral, too?"

"Yeah. It was perfect."

Mia finished chewing and cut to the chase. "Okay. The moment of truth. Do either of you know who worked you up? Be real."

"I really don't," I answered honestly as I rinsed my ocean mug. "Nothing to report here."

"Me, neither. I tried to figure it out but gave up once we got deep."

"Damn," Mia bitched. "I was hoping one of you figured it out to narrow down my choices."

I cocked my brow. "Did you want someone in particular?"

She shook her head before shoving in another messy bite. "Not at all."

"I didn't care, either." Shay slid from her seat with a shrug. "I was on fire, and it wouldn't have mattered."

"Same here." I gazed aimlessly into the living room. "I don't have a favorite."

Or did I?

~ 12 ~

Monday morning arrived like an evil, tortuous bitch. After hunching over my books hour after hour on Sunday, saving my sexy fantasies for only the bed, I'd wrestled with my sheets all night during dreams of demanding dicks. I woke to my annoying alarm with my modest panties already damp, my thighs clenched with thirst for one of them to slide inside. I glanced at the digits in the corner of my cell and decided to spend a few minutes strumming for relief under my comforter. To hell with hair and makeup today.

The boys lingered in my lustful daydreams as I tried to concentrate in class. *Lips, cocks, fingers, tongues*. Sure, I was focused on advanced anatomy, just not on the dumbass skeletal system my instructor was rambling about. My heart pounded with panic during embryology lecture when my poised prof returned my most recent struggle exam. He paused at my desk, glared with stern eyes through his wire-rimmed glasses, and dangled my test between two pinched fingertips. I swallowed hard and forced a hesitant, mildly flirtatious smile. *Damn, that mascara could've helped today.*

"I'm not sure what you've been doing with your time outside of the classroom, Callie..." he flatly warned.

Oh, sweet baby Jesus. Had I fucking bombed it?

"...but, whatever it is, keep it up. It's working."

This motherfucker.

He coyly placed the packet face up in front of me, and I caught the red A-minus boldly scribbled across the top by my name. Relief and pride choked me right there in the middle of the classroom. Embryology had sabotaged my mind from every direction, and this was the first stellar grade I'd secured all semester. A congratulatory fuck from one of the guys would've been icing on the cake.

Patience, Callie.

~ • ~

Despite my shaky start, Monday night's study session with the sixsome was pretty uneventful. We stuck to business like proper students, beginning with burgers and index cards, then ending with yawns and coffee-flavored kisses.

I enjoyed some incognito attention, though, when Judge flashed me a subtle lip lick between questions and Deck stirred my juices with a seductive wink. Evan's baby blues were buried in the books for most of the night, so that was the extent of Club Callie's agenda for the evening. Hell, that was perfectly fine with me. I needed nothing deeper to dwell on.

The guys unloaded their junk on the coffee table for round two on Tuesday, claiming their preferred positions as if they lived here. I smiled to myself as they bluntly bickered about basketball as if Mia, Shay, and I didn't exist. How would we have paired if they'd sacked up at the beginning and asked us on dates like normal neighbors? Would those initial impressions and attractions still hold true?

I pretended to mess with my school supplies at the dining room table and studied the specifications of each handsome squatter. Evan scoffed with a skeptical head shake as Judge counted off some kinda list on his fingers. Deck stood by with crossed arms over his carved chest, raising dark, amused brows when Evan mimicked a jump shot under duress. I pinched my lips together with a laugh as Judge threw up a mock block, simply enjoying how comfortable each felt being himself around us.

The clattering of cookware interrupted the amateur commentary. The boys dramatically paused mid convo and turned with apprehension to the kitchen.

Oh, here we go.

"So, uh, what's the plan for food?" Judge asked calmly.

"We're cooking," Mia called as she wrestled a frying pan from a lower cabinet.

Record scratch.

"You're what?" Evan choked on a laugh. All three abandoned their belongings and crept to the dining room to investigate. Shay rolled her eyes beside me.

"Cooking," Mia repeated, then she smiled like a happy housewife. "Just a quick bite so we can get to it."

Judge cocked his head with concern. "But why are you doing that?"

"Are we being punished for something?" Deck asked.

"Seriously?" Evan tried to backpedal with tossed palms.

"It's not that we don't appreciate the effort—"

"Right," Deck quickly added.

Mia pointed at them with a clean spatula as her fiery side made a rare, humorous appearance. "We're making a taco bar. I'm part Mexican, for fuck's sake. How hard could it be?"

"Well, in fairness, you did fuck up macaroni and cheese," Judge laughed under his breath.

"From a box," Deck chuckled beside him.

"Look, that was *one* time."

"And don't forget those 'cookies' you made us for Christmas," Evan man-giggled with air quotes.

"Hey," Shay pouted with a weak, whiny defense, "those were edible!"

Decker shook his head. "I think I broke a tooth."

These fuckin' guys.

Mia continued with her dinner prep. "I'm tired of the takeout garbage we munch all the time. We're gonna be up late and I need actual food."

"So do we, girl," Judge mumbled. "That's why we're concerned."

Mia laughed with a gasp and frisbee-tossed a tortilla at his head from across the room.

"Okay, okay. You win." He swerved from the attack and fished his cell from his pocket. "Just give me a second to save the poison control number…"

~ • ~

We bragged over the home-cooked meal about mastering our exams, with the entire group nailing surprising scores despite the challenging material. The guys muttered humble, gruff apologies as they polished off the fresh fare we'd provided, then offered to straighten up the kitchen as repentance. After eventually downing the last of our frosty beer and exchanging the cans for coffee mugs, we transferred to our workspace in the living room, feeling determined to slaughter another lesson.

"Who has the section for renal failure? I need to cover renovascular hypertension again," Shay asked as she shuffled through our index cards.

"I have it right here." Evan waved the handwritten material. "I'll set it off to the side."

"I gotta cover the standard lab values for that," Judge noted without looking up from his laptop.

"What about renal artery stenosis?" Deck asked as he thumbed through his stack.

"I have it." Mia fished a notecard from her established pile. "It's with renal vein thrombosis."

After the first hour, I had to admit, we were killing it. I didn't expect to sharpen my study skills and improve my grades after this Three Doors business, but without realizing it, that's exactly what was happening. Despite the potential for distractions, the crew remained hardcore about class, providing me with just the discipline I needed. I forced myself to compartmentalize, knowing that we reserved the weekends for fucking, regardless of how my pussy tried to lure my mind from the books to the buff boys before me. Around three in the morning, long after chugging the last few drops of caffeine, we finally called it quits.

Evan crashed back on the sofa and displayed that delicious body. "Just a few more days now, girls. You ready for us?"

"Born ready." Mia flashed a flirty smile and stretched. "You guys?"

"I'll show you just how ready I am, Mia," Judge teased.

"I'm gonna bury myself in my bed," I moaned through a yawn from my spot on the floor.

"Well, you can't go to sleep without a goodnight kiss," Deck mused as he approached with an outstretched hand. Christ, that dark, sleepy grin forced a rejuvenating thump between my ribs.

"Or three." Evan tugged his lip through his perfect teeth as I stood and straightened my bottoms.

As Mia and Shay nonchalantly gathered their study supplies, Judge's warm brown eyes landed on me, too, and my cheeks flushed under the weight of all three sinful gazes. We may have saved the salacious intent until after we closed the lessons for the night, but tension thickened with each passing goodbye as we approached the weekend. One by one, each man caressed my soft skin and emptied longing between my lips, tormenting me with hints of the sensations to come.

~ • ~

I woke on Wednesday with pure adrenaline coursing through my veins, desperate to pour my knowledge into the exam before I forgot everything I'd studied. I marched into that fuckin' classroom, conquered page after page, and felt overly confident in my thorough answers for the first time all semester. After killing the remaining classes of the day, I fled campus in the early evening, already basking in a weekend-level glow. Mia and Shay met me at Sunrise for a fancy coffee to go, and we took the leisurely way home. February had gifted us with unseasonable sun, so we sipped and spilled in the remaining shine of the day.

"I can finally think straight," Mia groaned.

"I know. I'm so fuckin' relieved."

"This may be my best semester ever." I beamed after a delicious sip of creamy caramel goodness. "Hell, if I'd only known…"

Mia and Shay laughed with agreement on both sides as we strolled. "We haven't changed methods," Shay noted, "but there's something about settling our sex lives that clears the clutter."

Mia nodded and gestured to a weathered wooden bench around the corner from our complex. We tossed our bags together on one end, then parked hip to hip in the sinking rays to continue the breakdown. "I love how the guys are just as dedicated as we are," she explained. "They're all in with school, with our friendship…"

"Right?" I agreed over my warm cup. "Nothing like the fuck boys we used to mess with."

Shay tucked a black strand behind her ear and shifted to face us. "I gotta admit, though, I still lay in bed at night trying to comprehend how all of this is working."

Mia bumped me with a giggle. "Hell, I don't. I just let it ride."

I cracked a smile. Between Shay's analytical side and Mia's carefree vibe, my besties couldn't be more different. I caught a young woman at the bus stop across the street balancing on one foot as she traded her business heels for some beige ballet flats. I could practically hear her sigh of satisfaction through the light traffic, and I felt an odd, unexpected parallel in the context of this time with my girls. During my freshman year in college, after finally walking away from a relationship that wrecked me, I was left with only a few class acquaintances on the new campus and not nearly enough confidence to expand my horizons. I'd been wallowing in my discomfort and barely breaching the dating world when Mia and Shay unexpectedly appeared in my life to provide the ultimate relief.

They became my own ballet flats.

"Earth to Callie," Shay laughed and nudged me.

"Sorry! What did I miss?"

"We're contemplating some trio time," Mia sighed to the dusky sky. "Maybe a little more play before the big day."

"We could just text them later," Shay said. "I know we don't hang during the week if we're not studying, but maybe we could make an exception if they want."

God, that sounded *so* good. "I'm down. I could use a deep, hard kiss to celebrate."

Mia laughed. "And I could use a deep, hard dicking to celebrate."

Well, that, too.

We trashed our empties in a street corner bin and hauled our goods to the complex door. Shay swiped her student ID card through the scanner, and we strolled to our apartment with boys on the brain. I paused when we passed the resident post boxes.

"Wait. Have you checked your mail this week?"

Shay furrowed puzzled brows. "No, why?"

"The test results!" Mia gasped. "How in the fuck did we forget?"

"You know the guys forgot, too," Shay added with a headshake. "They would've already been poking at us."

Sure enough, we each found results from the campus clinic waiting in our mail cubbies. We ripped open the blue envelopes as we stepped into the elevator and checked the forms line by line for pussy clearance. I didn't expect any surprises but still felt relieved to see my permission to screw right there in black and white. We lapsed into a ridiculous dance performance to celebrate our negative results, grinding and giggling like we were half-naked at the club. During the joyful chaos, we forgot about the couple holding hands along the back wall. They eyed us with confusion until Mia spilled our success.

"See, we couldn't have sex with our boyfriends without these papers—"

"And we've been waiting so patiently," I added with a wave of my results.

"Uh, congratulations?" The random girl cringed at our indiscretion.

Shay laughed with a prissy shrug. "Why, thank you!"

As we stepped through the doors into our home hallway, we heard the dejected boyfriend ask, "Why don't you get that excited about sex with me?"

~ • ~

```
    Shay: hey
    Evan: helllllo Shay
    Deck: hey
   Callie: did you guys check for test results?
    Evan: fuck
     Mia: we'd like to
   Judge: nice
    Deck: completely forgot with the exam
    Shay: we're gonna get comfy
    Shay: grab your results and come up
   Judge: consider it done
```

~ • ~

"So?"

"Good to go!"

"Same."

"I'm good, too."

Our sixsome shuffled the notifications between our eager hands and compared notes, confirming that we were indeed free to get it the fuck on when the weekend finally arrived. We tossed the papers in the air like party confetti and eyed each other with renewed interest.

Mia unexpectedly jumped into Judge's muscled arms and he swung her around as she cheered, then he lowered her ass on the dining room table. Evan beckoned me with a sexy head nod, then effortlessly parked me on the kitchen side of the bar.

"Happy, Callie?" he asked with that hint of mischief I'd grown to love.

"Oh, you have no idea," I exhaled as he stepped closer and nudged my knees open wide. *Fuck*, his big bulge was so close.

Decker scooped Shay up bridal style through her prissy giggles and lowered her over the arm of the cozy couch. Clearly, the girls and I weren't the only ones craving more contact.

"So, how do we celebrate?" I questioned with shameless excitement.

"I think the guys should rotate. Above the clothes only," Shay dictated from over the back of the couch. "That means you, Mia."

"What the fuck?"

"Too much access now and the mystery will be ruined this weekend," she explained matter-of-factly. "Control yourself."

"Well, you're no fuckin' fun," Mia giggled.

"But I'm fun," Judge rasped over her, rubbing his hand near her cooch and demanding her undivided attention. Mia scooted her ass to the table's edge and looped her arms around his neck, drawing him closer to her sultry brown eyes and perky tits. Judge tucked her legs around the waist of his gym pants and dove in for a taste. I watched intensely as they twirled tongues between their wet, open lips. She clawed at the back of his shoulders with need as he shifted his pelvis with slow thrusts directly against her center. *Christ*, they were both so fuckin' sexy, better than any on-screen combination. My mouth watered as they ravaged each other, my core warming with moist lust underneath my leggings. I imagined his heavy, rigid cock dragging through her wetness, and my chest ached with desperation.

Evan suddenly palmed my flushed cheeks and interrupted my staring, confronting me with curious eyes as he tilted my chin to his. "You like watching them?"

Fuck yes.

"Maybe," I whispered with a pinch of embarrassment.

Evan scanned my hesitant lips, then growled through gritted teeth as that trademark aggression rushed back to center stage. "God, you make me so fucking hot."

"Touch me," I whimpered, my pulse practically cracking my ribs.

Evan slid splayed fingers over my hips and jerked my throbbing folds closer to his groin, then paused over me with heavy breaths. After a few agonizing seconds, he devoured my willing lips with an animalistic kiss. His scorching, demanding tongue choked me with hunger, and I offered full approval, dragging my manicure down his cut biceps and rocking my damp slit close for that sweet friction. As soon as he felt my pussy pleading with permission, he pinched my braless nipples through my skin-tight tee, squeezing both of my small tits and massaging as our tongues continued to dance. My intention to practice silence failed miserably when I moaned passionately into his throat. He nibbled at my cries, scraping his teeth over my lower lip as he crushed my wet clit with his steel.

"I wish I could have this tight pussy tonight," he snarled.

Jesus Christ.

Evan left those words hanging in the humidity between us as his hands trailed away from my writhing body. I missed his touch within a second of his retreat, but I knew Deck or Judge would be trading places to sample my thirst. I clenched my eyes closed and flattened my palms on the countertop behind me, presenting my panting chest and soaked bottoms for the next joyrider. In this wild world of rotating and sharing, I yearned to feel my partner before I saw him, the mystery amplifying my thrill like nothing I'd ever experienced.

The round-two claimant wanted body play before our lips even brushed. Both heavy hands groped my braless breasts and churned, thumbs sliding back and forth over my trembling nipples. I craved that sweltering sting that would leave my pussy crazed and sticky, so I arched my back sharply and practically begged for him to suck me.

"Goddamn," Judge groaned over me.

I blinked just in time to watch him lower to my heaving chest. He peered up at me as he rolled my nipple between his thumb and index finger, then he sucked it hard with luscious lips through the thin fabric of my top. Electrifying pulses jolted south to the deepest ache between my legs.

I found nothing safe to squeeze on the counter, so I clenched my eyes closed and cried out to the ceiling, my body reeling in both pleasure and frustration. Judge's fiery, frolicking kisses swept across my breasts as he feasted, leaving my cotton shirt clinging to my tightened nipples. I wanted him to tear my tee to shreds so I could feel his rough tongue slather over my bare skin.

Although I was expecting Decker to assume control and steal the last minutes of the show, I wasn't prepared for what happened next. Judge was still caressing both mounds, sucking me and kneading me like a man starving, when a third hand brazenly slid up my thigh. I sucked in a harsh breath of disbelief and fluttered open my eyes.

Judge smirked at me, freeing my breast from his sensuous lips as he continued to stroke my other soaked nipple through my shirt. Deck hovered beside him, his fingers creeping closer to my dripping pussy as he eyed my body's reaction with dark hunger.

I felt an incredible surge of wetness downtown as the best friends shockingly explored my body together. The closest I'd ever been to a threesome was Evan copping feels during our bottle spinning game, but this contact seemed so much more intense and intentional. Both willingly left space for the other as they stood mesmerized by my squirms and sighs, sharing as they summoned my pending peak. I'd never desired to be objectified, but I found myself more than willing to be used for whatever kink they were conveying.

I caught a flash of movement to my side and glanced, finding Evan grinding against Mia's ass as he bent her over the dining room table. She scratched at the surface, cheek flattened on the wood facing away from me, as he destroyed her will from all directions. Thick fingers of one hand tangled in her streaky brown locks while the others reached around her slim hip for prime pussy access. I noticed the stretch of his shirt straining over his chiseled biceps as he dragged his cock between her round cheeks.

But Evan was watching me.

His crystal eyes shimmered under our ceiling light, observing every second of his friends manhandling my body.

"Judge, let's go! I'm dying here," Shay whined from the sofa.

Christ, I'd selfishly forgotten all about Shay. I snapped back to reality at the sound of her voice, breaking the lustful blue contact with my fellow blond. Decker's fingertips tapped lightly over my leggings at the top of my thigh, as if he were now waiting impatiently for his solo ride. Each flutter of his touch sent a ripple of anticipation over my flushed skin.

"I'll take it from here," he demanded, dismissing Judge and invoking possession over the last round.

Fuck.

I was barely breathing as Judge stepped away. Deck slipped both chiseled arms behind my arched back and pulled me abruptly to his thick chest. Our hearts bumped together through slam after slam as our lustful eyes aligned. "You're all mine now," he whispered.

Before I could respond, though it was doubtful that I could form words anyway, he curled a firm thumb directly against my throbbing clit and arrogantly watched me unravel as he played. My legs trembled as he circled with deep pressure, the friction from my wet panties sparking swells underneath his skilled strokes. I gasped in broken breaths against his parted lips before he finally smothered my hot mouth with his. I practically strangled his neck and tried to kiss him back, but my tongue slipped in and out with sloppy enthusiasm as he beckoned me to my brink.

I needed air. I couldn't function. I couldn't think. I was about to come utterly un-fucking-done in front of Deck. Face to face. Eye to eye. I wrestled away from the passionate embrace and rested my chin on his shoulder, panting as he picked up the pace with my pussy. He urgently tugged at my long strands, never slowing the strums of his thumb, so I shifted back against the strength of his arm. I watched him scan the room, then he fixed his focus back on me.

"The others aren't finished yet," Deck mouthed.

I couldn't look away from his captivating eyes to monitor my friends, so I hung my trust on his every word.

"Do you want me to make you come, Callie?"

God, yes.

I abandoned all sense of logic. Deck's dirty request enhanced his naughty fingers, and a throb of burning need rocked me to my selfish core as he rubbed some more. There was no chance that I could end this evening without letting this crest spill. Fuck the consequences.

"Please," I begged under my breath.

Deck cocked an arrogant brow. "Tell me," he demanded, that raspy voice scraping away at my limited inhibitions.

Christ.

"Make me come, Deck. *Fuck, please.*"

He licked his lips with cocky satisfaction and dropped his mouth against my ear. "I wanna watch you get off, but you have to be quiet so nobody knows." He mercilessly rolled his thumb over my slick clit and let his tongue drift against my earlobe. "If you can't be quiet, just kiss me."

I felt like a nasty, seductive slut sharing this secret with him. I nodded weakly, knowing full well that I would fail my mission. He tugged at my blond waves again, tipping my shoulders back and my chin up, then he mercilessly frenched my blushing neck. His hot lips tempted my trigger spots, his tongue twisting behind my ear and dragging over my jawline as he fingered me with rapid bursts. I fucked his strokes with shameless thrusts as the peak gathered strength in my pelvis. Christ, I was about to come.

Hard.

With Deck.

In my fuckin' kitchen.

I palmed his stubble with both hands and jerked his mouth aggressively to mine as moans threatened to creep from my throat. I weakened with pleasure as our tongues drove passionate laps together, but he steadied with me a reassuring hand on my back and quieted me with a punishing kiss. I whimpered into him as the agonizing orgasm flooded my pussy with a hot, wet mess inside my already soaked leggings. Wave after wave pulsed through my entire body, curling my toes and stealing my breath.

When my tensed muscles finally relaxed, and Deck was sure that I'd finished, he shifted both hands to my thighs and softened his control, escorting me down from my high with a soft, comforting kiss. Slow and steady Decker was back, so I let him lead the way until voices in the room alerted us to pull apart.

What the fuck did we just do?

~ 13 ~

Deck and I turned together to face our friends, his perfectly prickly stubble brushing my crimson cheek. I silently caught my breath, touching my fingertips to my parted, puffy lips with self-induced shock and shame.

"Damn."

"I know."

Evan and Mia both sounded dumbfounded as they adjusted themselves in the dining room. Evan tucked his obvious erection deeper into his gym pants as Mia straightened her green crop top over her perky chest. Judge helped Shay up from the beige sofa and wiped remnants of a glistening kiss from her bottom lip. Deck lifted me from the bar countertop and gently lowered me to the wooden floor, then he slipped his arm around my waist and pulled me closer.

Although I usually carried the clusterfuck card on behalf of my girls, we were all looking fuckin' rough. Thin shirts clung wet and wrinkled over their hard nipples, matching the soaked spots gracing my tee. Rough, manly fingers had wrecked our long locks, leaving us facing each other with frayed, frizzy messes. Though my satisfied pussy was returning to baseline, I shifted my hips and casually tried to hide the darkened patch in my leggings. The guys had accepted the assignment, committing crimes of passion over our clothes, but they each left a moist trail of evidence behind.

Mia smiled with rosy cheeks. "Um, Callie?"

"Yeah?"

She gestured to my chest with a circling finger. "I think you have a little situation there."

"So do you," I said with a stifled smile. "And, Shay, too."

We reflexively palmed our tits, but Deck graciously stepped in for the save. "Why don't we step out and give you girls some privacy? We'll run down to our apartment for a few and be right back."

"I could use some fuckin' privacy about now," Evan mumbled.

Judge darted to the door. "Me, too. Let's go."

"Fifteen minutes," Deck promised.

I dashed to the bathroom the second the knob latched behind them and flipped on the fluorescent light. Shay and Mia practically pummeled me as they vied for valuable mirror space. *Fuck*, I'd creamed all over my panties, and I would need to decide quickly if I should share that tidbit with my besties. This wasn't like preview night, when we are all hidden in the tipsy dark, wound up from tonguing each other and watching porn together. I'd just juiced on my kitchen counter with sober Deck supervising my secret satisfaction.

We'd tried to keep the coming on the down-low, but for how long could we hide it? Was Deck leaking to the guys that I'd come unglued?

"Fuck," Shay groaned. "I looked like I pissed myself!"

"Well, guess the whole 'over the clothes' thing was taken pretty literally," Mia laughed as she pointed to her hardened nips.

I loosened my leggings from my cooch and tried to salvage my image to no avail. "Let's just go change, at least until we have time to shower. I'm fuckin' drenched over here."

We scurried to our spaces, and I used the few minutes alone to sort my scattered thoughts. Would my girls be pissed that I'd succumbed to impulse? Would my stingy achievement jack up the master plan? Deck seemed all too eager to finish me off, so maybe I hadn't fucked up too terribly.

Decker.

Christ, what the hell would we say to each other?

I snaked out of my dirty threads and yanked a warm blue hoodie over my mangled mane, then hopped into comfy pajama pants. Shay, Mia, and I reconvened in the living room to sort our responses before the boys shuffled back up the stairs.

Shay spoke up first as she settled in her seat. "So, yeah, that was intense."

"I'm not surprised." Mia shrugged and fingered her satin black bottoms. "We've all been fuckin' salivating for each other."

"Could you guys hear me?" I asked with a slight cringe to test the waters. Hell, maybe they already assumed I'd finished.

"I could." Shay grinned and tucked an ankle under her ass. "It was hot, though."

"I could, too," Mia laughed. "And Shay with those prissy fuckin' whimpers. You both need work on the quiet thing."

We shared sympathetic scoffs that spilled into laughter. Hell, I supposed it was time to clear this up. "Decker got me off," I confessed with a hard swallow.

"Nice." Mia beamed with no concern. "Evan, took care of me, too." A tall glass of warm relief emptied between my ribs.

"Same," Shay sighed and adjusted her tits in her soft white nightgown. "I'm relieved it wasn't just me. Judge was on fuckin' fire."

"I mean, I know we've gone pretty far in front of each other," I explained. "This was different, though. Unexpected."

"Well, we're sober, for one," Shay added.

"Right. With the lights on—"

"And it's a fucking Wednesday!" Mia laughed. "What the fuck?"

We collapsed against the cushions with giggles and smirked at each other in disbelief. Never in a million years could I have imagined us willfully sharing a man. Hell, now we were sharing three. We steadied ourselves into serious mode before our naughty neighbors returned.

"I feel kinda weird," Shay admitted as she chewed anxiously on her bottom lip. "I don't know why. It's not shame, but it's close."

Mia met her with softened eyes. "Are you okay?"

Shay nodded. "I just didn't expect to face them like this. It's not bad, exactly. I need to process it."

"I'm a little nervous to talk to them," I confessed. Mia slipped a hand over my bouncing knee. "I'm just not sure what to say now."

"I don't feel awkward," Mia said, "but I hate that you guys feel that way, and I wanna help."

"You don't? Really?" I stared in awe at my bold, beautiful friend. Maybe her wise, wild ways could calm the fluttering in my gut.

"It's just sex," she explained with a one-shoulder shrug. "I might've been freaked weeks ago, but we've come so far since then."

"I guess you're right."

Mia continued with a light laugh. "Think about it. I sucked one of their big dicks on Saturday night, then the dude was right back to studying with me on Monday, as planned."

I couldn't help but smile. "You're better at this than I am."

Shay still seemed anxious as she hugged a throw pillow over her belly. "What do you think they're gonna say?"

"Look, we just need to talk to them like we always do," Mia consoled us. "Maybe this crossed a line. We need to address it."

"It's on me, though. Decker asked if he could take things that far, and I pushed for it." I tucked my hands in my hoodie pocket and slumped.

Shay jumped right in at my defense. "It's on all of us, Callie. We're in this together."

A casual knock interrupted from the front door, and we instinctively turned to greet our guests. Judge's cheeky smile met us through the crack and Mia waved them in. Evan and Deck circled the sofa, and Judge squeezed next to Shay in our oversized blue chair. While I still hadn't deciphered the post-preview night cuddling, this pairing was definitely planned.

Evan scooted close to Mia and grinned. "Well, *I* feel better."

Fuckin' dork.

Decker snuggled in beside me and rubbed the knee of my pajama pants, then possessively left his fingers in place. "You look cute," he flirted under his breath.

I blushed with sudden shyness and looked down at my lap. "Thank you."

Judge slipped his arm around Shay's waist. "Wow. That's all I can say. Wow."

"Not too bad for a weeknight," Mia laughed, her playful nature slicing through the unspoken tension.

Decker scanned the room to meet each of our eyes until landing on me last. "How are you girls feeling?"

"Awkward," I answered honestly. I didn't want to kill the attempts at a relaxed vibe but covering my reaction would serve no purpose here.

Judge puckered his bottom lip with sympathy. "Oh, Callie..."

"I feel the same way," Shay added beside him. "Maybe this was too much out in the open."

"No mask. No blanket. No door," I said. "We just went for it. Face to face."

"I get it," Evan said. "Tonight definitely hit different."

"Well, I feel good." Mia casually draped her legs over Evan's lap. "But I think we should clear the air so everyone is on the same page."

"What about you guys?" Shay asked.

"I understand why you're feeling weird," Judge conceded thoughtfully. "You left it *all* out there in front of us."

"Exactly," Evan agreed. "I don't know how I would feel in your shoes."

Decker stroked my thigh with a slow thumb. "I think the anticipation has been building all week, and it just spilled over as soon as we got our hands on each other."

"Believe me, when we walked up here with our results, I didn't expect to be dry humping Shay on the sofa before dinner." Judge laughed lightly and shook his head at his lap.

Evan met my eyes with concern. "Do you feel weird with us here now?"

"It's helping to talk about it." I couldn't quite explain the innate comfort I felt with these men, even after they'd taken turns with my body. Each momentary panic wilted away whenever we gathered in this circle, and I'd never encountered ease like this. Their deep, gentle voices of patience and authentic expressions of understanding seemed to soothe my busy brain and wringing hands.

"What about you, Shay?" Deck asked sweetly.

"I'm okay. I think it would've been hella awkward tomorrow if you hadn't come right back."

Facts.

"The last thing we want is to make you uncomfortable," Evan said.

"I wanted it all." Mia flashed a radiant smile. "No regrets here."

"I wanted it, too." Shay blushed into Judge's chest. "I got jumpy right after, but I can't deny how much fun I had."

"Me, too," I said quietly as Deck squeezed my knee. "I wanted every fucking second."

Evan chuckled under his breath. "Even that threesome action, Callie?"

Shay perked up. "Threesome?"

Mia's head turned on a quick swivel. "Get. Out."

I shrugged through another round of heat burning my cheeks. "You'd have to check with your boys on that. I was an innocent bystander." *Not that I minded.*

"Well, I was having fun with Callie," Judge laughed and hooked a thumb in our direction, "then *this* guy walked over and wouldn't fuckin' wait his turn, so he got up in there, too."

"*Couldn't* wait," Deck corrected him.

Fuck.

Shay fanned herself. "That's fucking hot. I've never been jealous until now."

"How did I miss this?" Mia bitched.

Evan shook his head down at her and laughed. "I was distracting you with my giant rod."

Yes, you certainly were.

"Can I get a little reenactment?" Mia joked.

Christ, I hope so.

I played along. "Not tonight anyway, but who knows?"

"Well, fuck." Judge shot Deck a cocky smirk. "That sounds promising."

Shay shifted in her seat. "So, this entire night seems contrary to why we wanted Three Doors to begin with."

My wise friend was right. We risked the full fuck level whenever we groped each other, and tonight may have altered our course completely. But we still couldn't just jump in and start fucking each other regularly, could we? Isn't that when these "friends with benefits" arrangements became messy? Even if our bond allowed us to curb the awkwardness, jealousy would naturally appear at some point. Plus, I got off on the whole mystery of the game.

"I mean, so much is exposed now," Shay continued. "What's the point of all the prep?"

Evan jumped in. "Well, I still wanna do it."

Mia nodded. "Oh, we're fuckin' doing it."

"I want it, too," I spoke up. "I think my reasoning has changed, though."

"How?" Deck asked.

"Well, before, I wanted everything in secret to prevent damage to our friendship."

"And now?"

I swallowed hard and offered my confession. "Now, I want it because it's fucking hot."

Shay laughed lightly. "I guess you're right. That's reason enough."

Mischief flashed over Mia's beautiful face. "I hope I'm not being too forward in saying this." Fuck, was that even possible in this setting now? "I can't wait to feel one of you inside of me."

Evan stared down at her with widened blue eyes. "Well, damn, Mia."

"What?"

"Can we make a promise to each other?" I asked. "No more making out until Saturday. Because if anything comes even close to what happened tonight, I can't be so sure I'll stop." Christ, I was putting myself out there, displaying my desperation to get fucked with a Mia-level flaunt.

"Well, that's tempting," Deck mumbled under his breath beside me.

Jesus.

I smiled through the shivers as we all agreed to keep our privates in our pants. I couldn't help but give each mesmerizing man another inspection as we prepared to part. Judge thoughtfully straightened the cushions and I scoped his cute ass in those loose joggers. Deck stood and yawned with muscled arms over his head, revealing peeks of the godlike physique underneath his tee. Evan offered kind hands and flirty eyes as he pulled Mia up from her seat. Fuck, they were *hot*. Like next-level hot. How in the hell did I stumble into this scenario?

Deck rubbed his tight abs over the waistband of his loungers. "You girls want dinner?"

Shay shook her head. "Nah. Thanks, though."

"I need a shower more than food right now," Mia said.

Same.

"I think we'll bail on the curtain shopping tomorrow. We're gonna catch the game," Evan said.

"So, we'll see you Friday?" I smiled.

"Definitely."

Judge let those dimples shine. "How about a group hug?"

"You're so cheesy sometimes," Mia giggled. Let's be honest. We were all pretty fuckin' cheesy.

I squeezed in between Evan's hard body and Shay's soft curves, realizing that my small circle of two best girlfriends was suddenly becoming so much more. We committed enviable, lustful, dirty deeds on these wild nights together, but the respect, trust, and appreciation that followed had to be one in a million. And, speaking for myself, this relationship was filling a void that I never knew existed.

~ • ~

"Mia, be straight," Shay whispered in a deadly serious tone the next evening. "How much is my cooch gonna hurt during this?"

"Oh, it will be agonizing the first time."

Her pretty mouth dropped. "Seriously?"

"Hey, you wanted it straight."

We parked in plush purple chairs at the front of Mia's preferred salon, waiting for the stylist to call us for our planned pussy primping. I trusted her promise that the result would be worth the hassle, but the anticipation was amplifying my apprehension.

"I just wanna get it over with," I groaned, recrossing my legs defensively for the hundredth time.

Shay rolled her eyes. "It won't hurt you as much. You barely have hair."

"Well, I'm sure it won't be sunshine for either of us," I snapped.

Mia rolled her eyes at our whiny antics. "It will be Saturday night, though. Just fuckin' trust me."

Ruby, the alleged muff magician, eventually called my name first and ushered me to a room in the back. I watched her scarlet, poker-straight ponytail swing between her shoulders and wondered if she'd dyed it to match her name.

I sheepishly stripped from the waist down and climbed on the cot as she instructed, my heart rate pounding in defense of my privates. I loved my cooch, but I was about to torture the fuck out of her to secure my mystery peen. Ruby had obviously seen countless pussies, but I still felt self-conscious as I sprawled bare before her. She made small talk as she spread the sticky wax over my slit with a thick popsicle stick, then she patted the paper over my precious folds and smiled up at me.

"So, you're good friends with Mia?"

"She's one of my best friends," I explained. "Actually, we're rooooom — *Jesus Christ!*" Ruby ripped away my fur as I was mid-sentence. *That crazy bitch.*

"Oh, you're roommates? Are you in school together?"

I wasn't falling for that fuckin' trick again. "Are you gonna tear that paper away again with no warnnnnn — *fuck, Ruby!*"

She continued her evil process indifferently with a faint giggle. "You don't have much hair. We're almost done." She added another unexpected tear the second she finished her last syllable.

"I can't believe," I panted and wiped my watering eyes, "that I'm paying you for this."

Ruby offered a deep, genuine laugh. "Oh, honey, you just wait."

~ • ~

We rode to the department store together in Mia's little black sedan after our three rounds in Ruby's torture chamber. The last step of this Three Doors mission required purchasing the perfect window coverings to drape our rooms in adequate darkness.

Two more fuckin' days.

Shay scoffed from the backseat. "Well, that was hell."

"I feel all squirmy," I said, shifting in the passenger seat, "and kinda wet." Truth be told, my garden felt fuckin' fantastic after the initial sting subsided.

"That's the good part," Mia laughed as she whipped around a corner.

"She got all up near my ass, too," Shay added. "It was hella weird."

"Well, yeah." Mia shook her head at our amateur ways. "You don't want a beautiful, smooth pussy with random ass hairs hanging there."

This fuckin' girl.

"You have a way with words. You know that, Mia?"

"That's what my mom tells me."

~ • ~

We were browsing through the drapery department for the perfect window treatment options when a silver-haired clerk approached us.

"Hi! My name is Deb. Can I help you find something in particular? Redecorating your rooms?"

Mia grinned. "You could say that."

"We're looking for blackout curtains. Do you sell those?" Shay asked.

Deb smiled warmly. "Of course. Let me show you."

We followed her to a display near the back and thumbed through the sample selections hanging from a tall rack. Mia held a dark panel up to the harsh department store lighting.

"Oooh. These are money. Completely opaque."

"That brand is one of our best sellers." Deb beamed with pride.

"We need to make sure no light can come through. No sunlight, moonlight, street light," Shay specified, listing restrictions on her fingers. "We need absolute darkness."

The suspicious sales rep glanced between us. "Well, those should certainly do the trick."

We followed her to the checkout counter after deciding on matching black sets, then she scanned Mia's package as we fished debit cards from our wallets.

"I feel like I must ask." Deb eyed our faces with concern and lowered her voice as she leaned over the counter. "You're not doing anything illegal, right, girls?"

"Maybe in some states," Shay muttered under her breath. I choked on a laugh and tried to kick her in the shin.

Mia blinked up with those big, innocent brown eyes. "Not at all, Deb. We're medical students."

Deb looked relieved and nodded, accepting the bullshit "lack of sleep" implication as a perfectly reasonable explanation. She bagged our goodies and wished us good luck, promising that the curtains would be a dream when we finally fell into bed.

Well, I certainly fuckin' hope so, Deb.

~ • ~

Friday evening, we practically ran home from campus to begin our weekend. Shay, Mia, and I shared a bottle of sweet white wine and danced around the living room to some of our favorite chick ballads from undergrad. Mia chugged her last drink and offered to pour more.

"Someone's getting laid tomorrow!" Shay sang into her wine glass microphone. "It's me!"

"And me!"

"And me!" Mia smacked her ass repeatedly as she returned with a fresh bottle.

"We are *such* fucking dorks," I laughed and sipped my refill.

"But we're 'young and upcoming, brilliant, future doctor' kinda dorks!" Shay squealed.

"Cheers to that!"

"And 'about to get fucked by the three sweetest, hottest guys in the world' kinda dorks!" Mia bumped our hips with a wild wiggle, the sloshing alcohol nearly spilling from her glass.

The nostalgic song closed with the final notes, and we stood before each other, laughing and buzzing as the next tune began. I held up my drink for a toast, meeting their beautiful, tipsy eyes. "And, most importantly, we're the 'best friends sharing the most incredible experience of our lives' kinda dorks."

"Aww," Shay gushed and palmed her chest. "We are."

Mia cocked her head and smiled sweetly. "I just love you girls." We clinked glasses and danced away, waxed pussies and all.

~ • ~

After the sun finally set, leaving our apartment decorated with early darkness, we decided to chuck the wine and finalize our fuck venues. Decker called from the front door as soon as I climbed up on my desk chair.

"We're in our rooms!" I yelled with an overdose of enthusiasm, bubbling with excitement inside to see them again. *And maybe touch them again.* "Come on back!"

I heard the guys laughing and approaching in the hallway. Shay had just slipped into the restroom after their trademark knock, probably to primp for the dicks, so all three stopped right at my open door.

Judge whistled. "Nice view."

I balanced my short ass as best I could, trying with outstretched arms to reach the curtain rod high above my head. I peeked over my shoulder and wobbled a bit, but Evan rushed up and steadied my bare legs with care.

Decker laughed. "Are you drunk?"

"No. We just had some wine and danced."

"Interesting," Judge chuckled with that charming grin.

I rolled my eyes and waggled a finger. "Not *that* kind of dancing. We talked about fucking you, though, if that counts." Deck and Judge raised quick, matching brows before mumbling to each other.

"You guys check on the others before someone falls," Evan said before looking up at me. "You good?"

I nodded. *Fuck, were we about to share some alone time again?*

Evan huddled up the boys, then they shared secret laughs and sauntered off in different directions. He closed my door behind him and approached, then turned with second thoughts and clicked the lock into place.

"Callie, Callie, Callie," he sighed and shook his head up at me.

Oh, those crystal blue eyes. That dazzling, flirty smile. Those shredded, puffy muscles. I tipsy giggled and palmed my mouth. This was about to be trouble.

"Look at you," he growled, humming with hunger under his breath.

I checked out my curves from my perch on the chair as Evan held my hand. My black tank top had inched up to reveal a sliver of belly, and my plaid sleep shorts barely covered my perky ass. I'm sure the girls were wearing their best sleepwear in anticipation of the visit, but I was comfortable in my plain gear. "I think I look good," I bragged with the help of my buzz.

"Yes, you certainly do," Evan whispered, blinking up at me with shameless lust. He slowly circled in front of me and placed his wide hands on my hips, his thumbs tickling my bare skin above the elastic band. Tingles rushed south, and I rolled my neck in an aroused stretch. "You want me to do it?" he offered.

"Yes," I moaned, waiting for fingers to breach my panties, then I jerked back to reality. "Wait. What are we talking about?"

"The curtains."

"Oh, no!" I assured him, laughing inside at my horny diversion. "I totally got this. Just don't let me fall."

"Never," he promised.

Aww.

I freed the curtains and Evan helped me jump to the floor, then I replaced the old sheer white panels with the new heavy black set and tried to climb back up on my chair. He grabbed my ass and boosted me high, then steadied me again as I locked the rod in place. "So much better," I noted, admiring my work with my hands on my hips. I arranged the drapes evenly on both sides and felt Evan's thumbs grazing over my thighs under the hem of my shorts. Fuck, I was getting moist. Between the wine, the fresh wax, and his confident touch, it sure as hell didn't take much tonight.

"Evan?"

"Callie?"

"You're getting dangerously close to my garden," I giggled with a flirtatious twirl of my blond curls, then I cocked my head in mock thought. "Well, I guess it's not much of a garden anymore."

"Jesus," he exhaled. "You're killing me."

I considered jumping into his brawny arms, possibly causing a tempting tumble back onto my bed, but I hopped down with his help on my best behavior and surveyed my enhanced space. The room was considerably darker, despite the bright overhead light above us.

"I'll be damned. Deb was right."

"Who's Deb?"

"The saleslady," I explained. "They *do* work."

Evan palmed my lower back and coaxed me toward my bedroom door. "Wanna see how well?"

A deep ache of wet anticipation rippled between my legs as I crossed my blue rug behind him. He pulled me close, then switched off the lights with no warning and covered us in complete darkness. My heart rate soared as the blind mystery of his next moves settled in the silence. I waited for something, *anything*, batting my eyes with a fruitless adjustment as breaths locked in my lungs. Finally, he intertwined his fingers with mine and hugged me close against his steel frame. I raised my lips and whispered into the pitch-black between us.

"You're so bad, Evan."

"Let's be bad together, Callie."

I couldn't see even his silhouette, but I could feel his heavy, hardening cock brushing against my pelvis through his thin bottoms. He brazenly slid his palms over my ass and rocked my newly smooth pussy against his impressive length. I waited with a combination of guilt and desperation, worried but hoping that his dominant mouth would find my parted lips. I rested my nails on his rippled pecs, finding his excited breaths mimicking the same desire that stirred inside my panties. A loud, evil knock on the door interrupted the seductive moment.

"You two better not be fucking in there!" Mia shouted. I exhaled frustration in the space between us as my pussy pulsed with unquenched thirst.

"To be continued," Evan whispered with a warm breath against my lips, "I hope."

~ 14 ~

I woke with a bright smile already plastered on my face.
Fucking finally.

"Get up, girls!" I squealed. "It's Three Doors Day!" I hopped from under my comforter with uncharacteristic, early morning enthusiasm and rounded the hallway corner to the kitchen, finding my dazzling friends wide awake.

"We've been up, you lazy fuck," Shay laughed. "We made your coffee, but do you want cereal?"

"Thanks, but I'm just having a banana." I snatched my simple breakfast from the bar basket and rubbed my belly. "No food babies for me today."

Mia cracked a naughty grin. "Oh, I'm in. I need fuel for later." She mock-fucked one of our barstools from behind and we lost it laughing.

"When are they coming over?" Shay asked as she popped a bagel in the toaster.

"Judge said around eight." I filled my ocean mug from the glorious pot of fresh caffeine. "That gives us plenty of time for some cramming and prepping."

"After we're finished studying, we need to clean our rooms, shave, pick out outfits..." Mia listed on her fingers.

"I think we should stick to Shay's matching things we wore before," I said before sliding my lips over the banana tip. *Hmm. Maybe I'll be able to give some head tonight.*

"Does it matter?" Shay laughed. "Won't we just get naked once we're in the room?"

"Nah," Mia giggled, then she leaned in to snatch a snarling bite of my fruity breakfast. "I want my man to *r-r-rip* it off."

I swallowed my serving with a smile and imagined big, wandering hands sliding the silky satin over my body again. "Same. So much same."

Shay laughed and shook her head at us. "That's fine, but no 'ripping' my good stuff." She turned to the fridge and glanced over her shoulder. "And, once again, that means you, Mia."

Mia rolled playful eyes in my direction, then slapped Shay square on that bubbly ass. "I hope you get dicked hardest tonight, babe. You fuckin' need it."

~ • ~

The guys hadn't checked in by the time we finished our food, but we didn't need the distraction. After our usual day with noses buried in the books, we busied ourselves with tidying up the apartment and dashing downstairs to launder our bed linens in the same fragrant, floral fabric softener. We each freshened up our bedrooms, clearing the clutter from our corners, dressers, and desks. I wasn't sure yet where I'd be enjoying my secret shaft, but I wanted the space to feel comfortable for whoever ended up fucking in my room. We decided to leave the vibrators for later antics, hoping that the new cooch styles and anticipation alone would enhance the natural cock experience. Hell, that was more than fine with me.

Early in the evening, we each prepped with the same shampoo, conditioner, and body wash, then sat in the living room sharing soft pink nail polish to cover our fingers and toes. We hung the pastel lingerie from the shower rod and hovered around the mirror to choose a hairstyle.

"Wanna wear it straight?" Shay asked as she lifted her black locks into a potential ponytail. "That would make it the hardest to tell us apart."

"Good call." I smiled, smoothing my blond streaks over my shoulders. "And let's leave it down."

We thought of all the possible details, or at least we hoped. We shared my deodorant and Mia's light perfume, then fixed our faces with matching makeup. As we stood hip to hip before our reflections, I noticed how our unique features augmented our short, similar statures. Mia's golden body and flecked amber eyes glowed under the bright light with her shimmery brown locks. In contrast, Shay's sultry, ebony eyes popped against her creamy, flawless complexion and black strands. My rosy cheeks, sandy strays, and baby blues paled in direct comparison, but together, we became one hell of a tempting team.

Shay called out as soon as we shuffled to our bedrooms for the final dressing. "Wait, girls! Take off your jewelry!"

"On it!" Mia yelled.

I slipped the slinky satin over my freshly ironed hair, then loosened the basic silver hoops from my ears. I gazed at the independent woman standing in the mirror before me and took a slow, deep breath. Hell, I'd played with men before, but this experience was about to drag my desire off the charts.

Three of my closest friends desperately wanted my body. They wanted to fuck me in the dark. They wanted to share me and share my girlfriends.

And I was about to let them.

~ • ~

We lit aromatic candles throughout the living room and relaxed on the couch as we anticipated their arrival, tucking soft legs beneath our bottoms and smoothing the sexy nightgowns over our knees. Fuck, if nothing else, we looked ready.

"Nervous?" I asked quietly, praying that the butterflies in my belly had neighbors nearby.

"Kinda."

"Me, too," Mia whispered.

"You are?" "Yeah. Not about the fucking, though. I just want it all to work out."

This girl.

I smiled. "Well, we'll have fun no matter what."

Knock, knock, knock.

"Oh, fuck! They're here!" Mia yelped and jumped up from her cushion. We followed her to the front door, and she whipped it open before our boys could roll in on their own. Evan, Decker, and Judge stood waiting for us, each holding a ribboned bouquet of pastel flowers. My heart ricocheted in my chest at the simplicity of their sweetness.

Shay beamed. "Come in!"

Our brilliant boys had the same idea as we did, strolling inside wearing their matching pajamas from porn night. Each guy presented the lovely gift to the initial girl they encountered.

"These are for you, Callie," Judge offered with a sheepish smile, reminding me of being asked to slow dance for the first time in my teenage days.

I inhaled the soft spring scent. "That's so nice of you! They're beautiful!"

He fingered a blond strand as it fell over my cheek. "*You're* beautiful," he whispered. "I'm loving this look."

Christ, was I already blushing?

"Thank you, and you know I love these." I tugged on his gray pajama shirt and gave him a sultry smooch on the lips.

"Would you like a drink?"

"Maybe I should," I confessed with quiet comfort. "I'm pretty nervous."

Judge leaned close, his hallmark scent piquing my senses. "Don't tell my boys, but I am, too." I laughed, suddenly feeling a bit more relaxed under his boyish charm.

Shay filled three tall drinking glasses with fresh water, then arranged the bouquets on the dining room table and surveyed our gifts. "Guys, this is too much."

"We know tonight isn't just any other night," Evan admitted with unusual shyness as he shuffled his feet. "It isn't for us either."

And that's exactly why this entire operation had a chance of working. Never once had these men treated us like a casual fuck from the corner bar. Although the adventures behind closed doors would be the highlight of the night, our endearing friendship graced the evening with serenity and tenderness. I'd seen their desire directly. I'd felt the hungry groping and lustful lapping when they held me in their arms. But in these meaningful moments between, Decker, Evan, and Judge knew just how to make a woman feel appreciated.

Deck pulled his bottom lip through his teeth and surveyed my body in the blue satin before finally finding my eyes. I shook my head at his guilty grin, but inside, I felt honored to be one of the objects of his attention. "What would you like to drink?" he offered.

"Wine, please. We have a few bottles for us to share."

"Sounds great."

"Let's sit in the living room and go over everything," Judge suggested.

We crashed on our plush furniture to discuss the crucial details. Words couldn't describe the war brewing inside my mind. As I looked at the magnificent men around me, I felt the uncanny comfort they garnered whenever we gathered. But one of them was about to slide deep into my precious pussy and deliver a dark euphoria like I'd never experienced. I curled my legs beneath me on the couch beside Mia and gulped from my goblet of sweet red. This was no time for sipping.

"So, are we all on the same page?" Evan asked.

"I think so, but I'm wondering about something," Shay said. "Let's say I'm in a room waiting for you. I'm gonna see you when you open the door. You'll see me, too."

"Funny you mention that," Evan said. "I thought of that today, and Judge suggested we use these." Each guy fished one of our sleep masks from the chest pocket of his swanky pajamas.

Mia cocked her head. "How will that work?"

"You could each wait on the bed, facing away from the door," Judge explained. "We'll wear the eye mask inside so we don't see you, then close the door behind us. We'll pocket the mask once we're in the dark."

Hmm.

"I think that will work," I said after a minute of consideration.

"Then we just stay until you knock?"

"That's right."

"Did you bring condoms?" Mia asked.

"We brought some in case you wanted them," Deck answered. "Your call."

"Judge, have you decided? We're all in if you want," Shay assured him.

"I'm good without," he said with a shrug. "You girls have protection, and the papers are enough for me."

With the technicalities out of the way, our thoughtful boys waited patiently and quietly until the girls and I were ready to leap. Although I was eager to lock in for what would surely be a wild, winding trip, I saw no harm in taking a few minutes to consider the final destination. Sex was sex, but tonight, friendship and fantasy would collide. The blurred boundaries, precise plans, and passionate practice would be put to the ultimate test. As I scoped each potential partner, their tempting bodies displayed like trophies on our comfy furniture, I knew these men were worthy of all the work.

A minute passed before Shay inhaled a deep breath and scooted forward in her seat. "Okay. I think I'm ready."

Deck, Evan, and Judge checked us individually with both eyes and words for positive consent or lingering doubt.

"Mia?"

"Let's do it."

"Callie?"

Since they couldn't yet feel the assuring hum of my heart or the wicked heat of my wetness, I offered the most confident smile I possibly could. "Let's go."

~ • ~

After all three sexy pajama sets disappeared behind the partial kitchen wall, I gathered with my girls in the dim hallway, our matching satin shimmering in the light of the living room candles. Mia grabbed both of our nervous hands and squeezed with encouragement, then gestured with a head nod to the bedroom doors and shrugged with uncertainty. We didn't discuss this choice beforehand, leaving our fuck location decision to the very last minute. Shay stepped away from our huddle and stood before her own space, then tossed a palm and mouthed, "Is this okay?"

I hadn't given much thought to whose soft sheets I'd be tangled in, but since we were venturing into uncharted territory, I sympathized with Shay's preference for familiar surroundings, at least for this first time. I nodded and stepped before my own silver knob, then Mia followed suit beside me. We swapped eager smiles and blown kisses, then swept inside our secret spots.

The deep darkness, though expected, still surprised me as I quietly closed my door and extinguished the faint flickers of the flames outside. With no sense of when he'd join me, I darted directly to my perfectly made mattress and climbed on the ruffled comforter, then smoothed my long locks behind my back. I turned to face the corner opposite of the hall and waited with my hands resting on my freshly shaved thighs, just as Judge had instructed.

Each ticking second wreaked havoc on my brain and body. I stared into the nothingness, relishing in the same addictive thrill of the sleep mask, and acknowledged each sensation and sentiment. My heart thrashed against my lungs with doubled strength rather than speed, rumbling between my ribs with constant reminders to breathe. My muscles tensed in suspense, preparing for unknown hands to fumble and fondle over each inch of my smooth skin. My moist pussy tightened and twitched, longing to be stroked, sucked, and screwed into shameless submission. I fingered the delicate hem of my negligee, letting my pink nails drag low between my legs, my amped nerve endings tingling under my gentle touch alone.

Fuck. Come on.

Judge, Decker, and Evan had provided so many sweet, sexy moments, but also filthy, forbidden flirtations that drove me fuckin' wild with need for this very night. I stretched my neck and rolled my face to the blackened ceiling, envisioning each of their cocky, captivating smiles and strapping, swollen muscles. I heard all three deep, distinctive voices whispering naughty intentions in my ears and shivered with the swoon of each delicious kiss. Although I was undeniably willing to fuck them all, to ride on any of their thick, steel cocks until I dripped down my thighs, I couldn't deny that nagging nudge in my chest whenever one man moved to the front of my mind.

I knew exactly who I wanted to fuck me tonight.

The click of the knob startled me to sit up straight. The wispy candlelight crept across the blank wall before me, then shadows of his silhouette fell over me as he stepped inside. The door latched closed behind him and I was left in the dark again, but this time, I wasn't alone.

Knowing that he couldn't see me provided some level of relief for my naturally shy side. My shoulders heaved with frenzied, silent gasps to protect the game, and I gnawed at my bottom lip as I expected that first electrifying contact. He crossed the room with painfully slow steps, then his fingertips brushed blindly over my bare shoulder. I let him explore, his touch trailing through my hair and tracing enticing paths along my neck. A deep, impatient pang of desperation cramped low in my pelvis, and I turned into his hovering frame, seeing nothing but darkness as planned. I clenched his muscled forearm, guiding him closer and navigating his ripples until I found that scratchy scruff. He joined my journey for an opening kiss and cupped my jawline in his palms, edging us together until we could taste each other's breaths. We tilted our chins in a clumsy dance as our parted lips finally touched.

Hesitation melted in the hidden heatwave between us. My thirsty tongue sparred for space as he took me with unleashed fervor, our mouths dipping and twisting into each other like starving wildlife. Any effort to identify my man disappeared as my remaining senses fell victim to his primal ways. I tasted the fever on his hungry lips as I listened to our wet passion smearing. I sensed the anguish of his touch as he snaked curious hands over my curves. I inhaled the alluring scent of Judge's trademark aroma drifting from his pecs, accepting that the trio had shared his stylish spray tonight. Sight was an afterthought as each moment of this blind madness sent throb after agonizing throb to my demanding pussy.

I craved his naked skin crushing mine and clawed at the waistband under his buttoned sleep top. He ripped his lips away and stepped from my grip, so I hoped like hell that he was undressing. In those few lonely seconds, I tossed the idea of him removing my gown, whipping it over my head and chucking it near the foot of the bed. I waited, nearly bare but for my black thong, as I fought to silence my labored gasps.

When he reached for me again, his fingertips brushed across my naked breasts, then traced over my abs as he traveled downtown. He yanked my remaining cover from my wiggling hips and steadied me as we eased it over my knees.

With our skin exposed and no barriers to slow the next steps, the mattress sank under his weight as he climbed on the comforter with me. I kept my fingertips close as he shifted and positioned, not wanting to lose another second of contact with this mysterious man again.

He glided palms around my hips to my round cheeks as we joined on our knees, turning me slightly and urging me closer. With no words spoken, we paused the frenzy to appreciate the sensual, meaningful moment that both of our bare bodies aligned. Our naked forms fell flush together from the chest down, my little tits tucked against the tight ripples of his torso. His thickened cock rested at full, mouthwatering length against my flushed belly as his hands roamed curiously over my curves. I dragged my pink nails softly over the ridges of his rounded shoulders and chiseled back, landing at the top of his perfect ass.

The war inside my mind continued, but the battleground shifted. This was no longer about flowers or friendship. I found myself conflicted, enjoying the heightened temptation as his lazy hands savored every inch of my skin but also wishing for him to force my legs apart and hammer me with that swollen, anonymous shaft. *Is he taking things slow just for me? Should I let this happen naturally, or should I pounce?*

As if he'd heard my brain debating, my sexy shadow of a man dropped warm lips to my neck and frenched me with a twisting tongue, dipping deep enough to drag his length across my aching pussy. Shivers sparked down my spine as I experienced two first-time sensations simultaneously: the exhilaration of his thick, smooth cock taunting my bare folds and the undeniable triumph of the priceless bikini wax.

He rocked his fur against my pelvis, teasing me with hesitant, gentle thrusts as he nipped and nibbled behind my ear. My soaked slit clenched with need in response, and I found myself finished with the foreplay.

Our entry kiss had been thrilling. Fingering would've been amazing, and oral alone could bring me to my brink, as previously noted. I'm sure that I would've enjoyed every second that any part of his body played with mine.

But tonight, I wanted to fuck.

I tracked my fingertips across his hip and over the muscular path to his pelvis, then abruptly wrapped my fingers around his throbbing thickness. I angled his length straight down with no warning, circling the puffy tip over my clit before sliding it through my dripping center and coating him with my early juice. *Christ, I needed him inside me.*

His parted lips paused under my jawline and he left lingering hands splayed over my ass, signaling some unexpected hesitation. Maybe he couldn't interpret what my body was silently screaming in the dark. I'd given him permission to skip the opening credits, but his finger was hovering over the fast-forward button.

Fuck it.

I dropped his dick and pushed aggressively on his solid frame until he buckled back on the mattress near my pillows, then I straddled him and took the fuckin' wheel. My moist pussy glided over his muscular abs as I leaned forward to palm his pecs, and his chest heaved underneath me with surprised breaths of desire.

God, his excitement alone drove me fuckin' wild.

I ushered his hand to my scorching slit and he needed no further instruction. His fingertips drifted as he explored my new smoothness, then he primed me even more, pumping two thick fingers through my sticky wetness. My body jerked over him as he fucked me with slow, forceful thrusts, and I stifled a moan through gritted teeth.

When he'd tapped my trigger spot enough to stir the rumbles of a climax, I reached for his heavy shaft. He shifted his weight underneath me with anticipation, assisting me at just the right angle for his rim to part my slick folds. I lowered my tight, hot opening, slowly sinking over his length, and arched my back until he filled me completely. A harsh breath of exhilaration escaped from my lips. *Fuck*, he was longer than I expected, feeling much bigger in my pussy than in my palm, but I absorbed every glorious inch.

Let's fuckin' ride.

I felt unhinged in the dark, letting my bare body shamelessly take exactly what it wanted. Adrenaline fueled my hips as I rocked over his steel cock with relentless, rapid thrusts. His rigid rim dragged tight against my wet walls as I selfishly fondled my aroused nipples. He clawed at my thighs for control, grinding his groin heavily into mine as we fell into an erotic rhythm. His naughty fingers found my slick center and strummed my clit with juicy friction as I bounced. My legs jerked and twitched as I prepared to drip all over his perfect dick, the mystery and darkness enhancing the experience more than I ever imagined possible. I tipped my head back into the void and sank teeth into my bottom lip as unbearable waves of an early climax crested.

My discipline nearly cracked as I clenched down on his throbbing thickness, squeezing him mercilessly as my soaked slit spasmed in agonizing pleasure. I swallowed a scream as I rushed over my edge, the pledge of silence practically strangling me.

We both slowed through the aftershocks of my finish, but the stretched, swollen shaft resting inside reminded me that this ride wasn't over just yet. He abruptly curled into a crunch and palmed my waist, then lifted my aching center from his length. As soon as we were separated, he crawled over me with raging dominance and effortlessly flipped me to my stomach, then pulled back hard on my hips until my face dragged against the bed linens. I felt like a plaything in his powerful hands as he positioned my tight ass against his pelvis, his hungry cock primed to plow my pussy exactly how he wanted. He'd humored me to this point, allowing me to manipulate his magnificent body to service my desperate needs.

Not anymore.

The blackened room hadn't allowed me much anticipation of his moves, but as his firm tip offered a courtesy tap against my recovering cooch, it wasn't rocket science to assume what was coming next. I urgently scratched at my white comforter until I gathered enough slack to bite, then I shoved it between my panting lips. In the last seconds before he assumed the driver's seat, I noticed the faint scent of the floral fabric softener wafting through my muffled breaths.

Fuck, this is crazy.

In one magic motion, he palmed my ass and drove that stiff cock inside me from behind with a heavy thrust, forcing the air from my lungs and snarling my teeth in the sheets. I arched my back hard as he relentlessly railed me, his length slamming through my clenched wetness over and over. His hands left no sensual touches on my smooth skin as he blatantly used my tight, hot pussy to summon his pleasure. No, this was *his* show now. The opening scene had been all about me. *My needs. My desires. My finish.* This second act was all about him.

This mysterious partner, one who casually raided my fridge and selflessly helped me master my studies, delivered the hardest fuck I had ever felt in my life. My petite body flailed underneath his watch, my small breasts bouncing and my short legs trembling. After a few quick minutes of absolute pounding, he threw weight behind his final pump and smacked my ass hard with an open palm, timing his punishment perfectly as his hot, wet load shot deep against my tingling target. I'd never been spanked during sex before, and the unexpected, breathtaking thrill left me choking on my comforter.

He slowed his pace as he spilled his last drops, then eased gently from my slickness. I fell from his grip in an exhausted slump on the bed, my pussy feeling raw, sore, and possibly bruised. My invasive mind tried to interrupt my satisfaction with rambling theories of which friend had fucked me, but I forced myself to focus on when this exhilarating evening would end.

How would we say goodbye?

He smoothed my now tangled hair over my back with slow, sweet strokes, then he shifted to the edge of the bed and guided me through the darkness to his lap. I swept my fingers up his neck and searched his stubble, meeting his warm lips in the scarce space between our faces. We kissed passionately like seasoned lovers, our tongues twirling in a blissful embrace, then our foreheads found rest together through our shared breaths. In the unexpected moment of tenderness, I wondered aimlessly whose beautiful eyes were only inches from mine.

We stood hand in hand, but as I started to step away for his retreat, he coaxed me back against his firm chest. He unexpectedly brushed soft lips over my temple, then he slipped into the dark like an escaping thief. I climbed on the comforter so he could gather his fancy sleepwear and waited for the creeping candlelight again as he dressed. When the door eventually opened and closed minutes later, I released an overdue sigh into my cupped hands.

I reflected on the ripples of his muscles, the brush of his scruff, and the taste of his lips, but not one clear identity floated into view. After all the chatter, the buildup, and the worry, Three Doors had worked, at least for me. Had I given him any unintentional hints? Had he remembered the flavor of my kiss or the path of my curves?

Knowing right where my silver lamp was parked, even in the dark, I flicked the switch and recovered my borrowed blue gown from the foot of the bed. I scanned the dim surroundings for my black thong, finding that he had hurled it across the room by my closed closet door. I laughed to myself and appreciated that my secret lover had been just as thirsty as I was. Like Evan had said, this wasn't any other night. *Not by far.* Maybe my partner had hidden under his bed linens, too, stroking that delicious cock in nights past with visions of the wild girls from upstairs. *Hell, maybe even with visions of me.*

I had to admit, the boys' planned preview aided the post-fuck process. I felt much more comfortable and confident with the logistics in order, so I took my precious time gathering myself. I used the bath towel from my earlier shower to wipe my dripping pussy clean, then stood before my mirror and attempted to polish my look. Satisfied with my meager efforts, I crashed back on the mattress and waited impatiently with my busy brain.

What was he thinking right now? Did he like how my puss felt around him? Did he have fun? Would he want me again if he could choose me?

Fuck, this is taking forever.

Had we finished first? What about Mia and Shay? Were their fucks as amazing as mine? Had we really fuckin' pulled this off?

~ • ~

Knock, knock, knock.

Finally.

I jumped up from my sprawl on the bed and rushed to the door, then palmed the knob and waited for a few minutes until I heard a movement in the hallway. I found Mia and Shay both emerging from their bedrooms at the same time, so I motioned for them to join me in the bathroom and yelled an all clear to the boys. It took a second for my eyes to adjust in the bright light, but as I surveyed my best friends for signs of satisfaction, I realized that they'd both likely had quite different experiences.

Mia looked like she'd been through a war as she rushed to the toilet for the customary post-peen pee. Her brown, streaky strands clumped in damp sections around her neck, and her once pretty makeup was smeared under her eyes like she'd been crying. Shay appeared barely touched, her sleek black hair keeping its smooth shine and only faint wrinkles appearing in her yellow satin.

"My God," Mia moaned as she palmed her rosy cheeks.

I cocked a curious brow. "That good?"

"I need a minute here."

This girl.

"How about you?" Shay asked, whipping a hairbrush from her assigned toiletry drawer.

"Amazing, but I'm sore as fuck." I loaded my toothbrush with minty paste and gestured with the tube. "You?"

Shay cringed in the mirror. "Please, don't think I'm a super-bitch, but it was just okay."

My jaw dropped with shock. "You're fucking kidding."

"I wish. It was all vanilla missionary stuff."

"Why didn't you just take over?"

"I mean, I could have. I don't know."

"Did you get off?" I pressed as my nosy instincts kicked in. "Give me something, girl."

"Oh, yeah. It wasn't terrible. It was just boring. The dark room and anonymity helped it along." Shay shifted past a dazed Mia to pee next.

"So, it was like pizza," I laughed. "I mean, there's bad pizza, but hell, it's still pizza."

"Right. You get it."

"I can form words now," Mia informed us through her trance. She palmed the bathroom counter and stared at her reflection. "I don't know who that was, but I think I'm in love with him. The things we did...*fuck*." I couldn't imagine the mystery methods that had stolen the soul of our most deviant crew member, but one of our boys knew how to *bring it*.

I shuffled for my turn to squat as my girls freshened up further, staring at the tile as my bladder emptied. My guy had kinda landed right in the middle of those wildly different ways. Had the friend I'd been mildly craving been a bore with Shay or a pro with Mia?

Or had he been perfect with me?

~ • ~

We stepped together from the shadows of the hallway to find our guys relaxing in our living room, bare-chested and gorgeous in the soft candlelight. Judge relaxed on one end of the sofa with his warm eyes roaming between us. Evan parked on the beige loveseat, anxiously resting his elbows on his knees and hanging on our every movement. Deck was comfortably sprawled out in the big blue chair with a leg draped over the arm, scanning us with a sultry gaze. My recovering heart suddenly slammed against my ribs in anticipation of the conversation to come.

Although I didn't know which of these three phenomenal men had fucked me tonight, I had already drawn one conclusion...

...I wanted him to fuck me again.

~ 15 ~

"Hi, girls." Deck shot us a lazy, charming grin.

"Well, hey, boys." Shay presented an awkward, prissy wave as I simply stood there like a tool.

See? We're so fuckin' cheesy.

Mia, still recovering from her Three Doors hypnosis, crashed flat on her back at Deck's feet and smiled at the ceiling. "I'm just gonna lay right here," she sighed.

"Are you okay?" Evan furrowed his brows with concern.

"Oh, I'm *better* than okay."

Judge flashed me a warm smile and patted the sofa cushion beside him with a thoughtful invitation. I settled in and scooted close while Shay snuggled up into Evan's open arm on the loveseat. Deck laughed lightly at Mia's seductive stretch and tossed his palms with no partner.

"You girls feeling good?" Judge asked as he nudged my shoulder.

"Amazing, actually," I admitted quietly. "It was unbelievable." I glanced up at Shay and waited for her polite reaction, knowing that she wouldn't embarrass her less than thrilling lover.

"I'm great," she fibbed with convincing authority. "It was a blast." That's my girl. All class.

"I'm sure you *all* know I loved it." Mia sat upright and backed between Deck's knees against the blue chair, suddenly interested in the analysis. "What did you guys think?"

"I'll be brutally honest," Evan confessed, shaking his head in disbelief. "The thought of one of you behind that door waiting to fuck me?" He paused and took a breath. "It's the hardest I've ever been in my life."

Wow.

"I really couldn't tell who was with me." Judge rubbed a palm along the back of his neck as his eyes crept around the room. "I'm sitting here now, looking at all three of you and wondering which girl…" He trailed off into a light chuckle.

Our attention shifted in Decker's direction. "It was intense," he told us.

Mia swatted his knee with frustration. "That's it?"

Decker laughed, displaying a rare, bashful side as his dark eyes darted to his lap. "I mean, you're all amazing women. I just fucked one of you, and I'm blown away. Just blown away."

After hearing that my favorite guys had been sexually satisfied, relief settled in my chest. I wouldn't have doubted my seductive skills nearly as much under ordinary circumstances. I'd made a man moan my name on occasion, and I could give a decent blow job when I put forth the effort. This scene, though? When the pleasure indicators were secret and silenced? Fuck, I needed the reassurance.

"So, none of you had any suspicions?" Shay asked. "Be straight with us."

"None," Judge confirmed with a palm oath. "I swear."

"I didn't," Evan said with a shrug. "And I'm still fuckin' surprised there weren't any snags."

"I had no idea," Deck added. "Still kinda shocked myself."

Mia repositioned on the floor and gave us a brief glimpse of her thong-covered cooch. "Well, I sure as fuck didn't know, but great job, buddy."

Shay laughed and shook her head. "I had no clue, either."

All eyes landed on me. "Oh, I was lost, too, but it was super hot in the dark like that."

Decker tossed pleased palms of pride. "Sounds like the plan worked perfectly."

So far, so good.

"Let's cut to the chase," Mia said. "Is this an every weekend thing?"

"Fuck, I hope so," Judge chuckled.

Although I'd suffered a moment of worry before we sat for the summary, I found my footing again as the crew registered simple, positive reactions. "I need it," I boldly confessed. "I need it like a fuckin' drug. No going back now."

Deck raised brows at my sudden spill. "Same here," he agreed. "Totally addicted."

"Let me just say," Mia added, schooling each guy with serious eyes, "my man brought it this week. Like fuckin' rocked me. So, pack your A-game, boys."

"No fuckin' pressure or anything, right?" Evan laughed.

"So, Saturday?"

"Saturday it is."

~ • ~

Well, we held out until Wednesday.

I was daydreaming about a steamy bubble bath when I heard Judge calling out from behind me on my walk home. I turned with a surprised smile and waited on the corner as he trotted to catch up. Those deep dimples framed a wider smirk than usual. Something was up.

"I'd know that tight little ass anywhere," he teased as he reached my side.

"Oh, yeah?" I said with a flirty grin. "Even in the dark?" He laughed and crossed the street with me to the housing complex. "Are you done for the day? I thought you and Shay had a late lab."

Judge stopped abruptly in front of the entrance. "Haven't you checked your phone?"

"No. I came straight from an advisor meeting. Is everything okay?"

He swiped his ID through the lock and held the glass door for me. "Oh, Callie."

"What?"

"Just check your phone. I'm gonna take the stairs. I need to grab a shower."

"Now?"

"Yes, now," he chuckled.

"Well, okay then."

Judge glanced around the empty lobby, then he abruptly dipped in for a quick, delicious kiss. I blushed with a shrug against his stubbly cheek and beamed up at him. "See you later, girl," he whispered.

I called out to him with confusion when he suddenly hauled ass to the stairwell. "See me later?" I whipped out my phone and scrolled through the texts that I'd missed from earlier.

Oh. Fuck yes.

```
Evan: girls?
Shay: I'm here
 Mia: yes?
Evan: how was your day?
Shay: awesome, my lab got canceled
 Mia: yay! you'll be home early!
Evan: we miss you
Shay: aww
 Mia: wanna come over later?
Evan: yes, please
Shay: dinner?
Evan: not exactly
 Mia: oh
Shay: we need to check with the others
Deck: I'm in
Shay: have you been reading this whole time?
Deck: yeah, I'm sitting here next to him
 Mia: fuckin' creeper!
 Mia: why didn't you say anything?
Deck: just waiting for Evan to close the deal
Judge: I'm headed to the library, but I'm in
Evan: why hasn't Callie answered?
 Mia: in a meeting
Deck: I guess we'll see
```

I'm not sure which responded quicker, my heart rate or my fingers.

```
Callie: I'm in, getting in the elevator now
  Mia: ohhhh yeahhhh
 Deck: it's on
 Shay: what time
 Deck: 7?
  Mia: it's a go
```

I rushed through the apartment door to find a freshly showered Mia dancing in her robe and Shay already opening a bottle of white. I slung my bag on the dining room table, stripped from my winter coat, and joined the sex celebration. "Girls!" I shrieked with a happy clap. "We're gettin' laid tonight!"

Mia laughed. "I knew we wouldn't be able to wait all week."

"I need a shower," Shay said as she sniffed her hair. I'm sure it smelled like sunshine, but she was being extra.

"I need to shave again," I groaned. "Hurry the fuck up."

Mia toasted us with a shrug. "And I'll just sit here and drink."

"You can't get too drunk!" Shay warned with a laugh. "We may be getting weeknight peen, but we still have to study and that alarm rings early."

"I won't get wasted," Mia assured us, "but I need just enough to relax in case I want anal."

Jesus, Mia.

"We may have a problem," Shay cringed.

"With my hypothetical anal sex?" I held my belly with a hard laugh. Mia was fuckin' ridiculous.

"Oh my God. No. Get fucked however you want, but the nightgowns aren't clean."

"So, we'll just wait naked this time," Mia proposed. "Robber outfits until we hit it."

"Sounds like a plan."

~ • ~

Our guys arrived promptly at seven o'clock and greeted us each with fresh, minty kisses as they stepped inside. We'd all be slurping on each other in a few minutes, so I didn't mind the quick hello. I sipped on my wine, peering over the rim of my goblet at each hunky neighbor and already excited about which would provide me with secret peen. Evan had worn *those* khakis today, and I followed the outline of his shaft as we chatted in the dining room.

Judge held up a navy duffle bag. "We brought our pajama bottoms. Too many curious eyes in the hallway."

Mia nodded to the bathroom door. "Go for it."

Evan eyed our not-so-revealing sex attire for the evening. "Where are those dress things you wear?"

Dress things.

"Dirty." Shay broke the bad news and pointed to her tits. "This will have to do."

Decker smirked between us and licked his lips. "I have some fond memories of those outfits. No complaints here."

We offered the boys beer and chatted casually about classes until Judge emerged from the hallway wearing nothing but those gray cotton pants. His chest and arm muscles swelled with seduction, so I took a long gulp and admired each dark ridge and ripple.

"I have an idea. Not sure how it will go over." He rested against the bar and tossed a palm. "Since we have class tomorrow and can't stay late, how about Three Doors quickies?"

Hmm.

My impatient side had always been a fan of the fast fuck. This could be hot.

Evan raised brows. "I like it."

"Hell, I'll take a quickie," Mia tipsy laughed. "I need to work on a paper before bed anyway."

"As much as I love the full version, I'm in," I said.

Shay bumped my hip with hers. "Even microwave pizza is still pizza, right, Callie?"

I choked on my wine as a giggle erupted. "And we fucking *love* pizza."

"I won't ask," Deck laughed as Evan shuffled away to change.

Mia pinched our beefy blond hard on the ass as he passed. "Make it quick, mister!"

"I'll light the candles," I offered. "I liked that."

Decker smiled at me. "Me, too."

~ • ~

I was already feeling warm and fuzzy from the wine as I stripped in my blackened bedroom. I'd enjoyed fucking in my own bed, so I stuck with it during the brief pre-game hallway huddle, as did my teammates. We had no clue how our dicks were choosing doors, but I hoped that the skilled shaft from the weekend drew number two. Not that it mattered. I was about to be fuckin' hammered, so I couldn't go wrong.

Did I prefer the same peen as before? Or would I be sampling a new flavor?

As long as that new flavor isn't fucking vanilla.

I giggled silently at myself as I climbed on the bed wearing nothing but a smile. Let's be honest, I was positive that I couldn't identify any length in the lineup. Other than my bare tip teasing with Judge during the porn, all my cock contact had been hindered by clothing or disguised by darkness.

I rested on my knees over my soft comforter and shivered in my lonely room. My pink nipples tightened as a chill tickled my naked skin, so I tucked my palms around my tiny tits and rocked my anxious hips. The guys didn't realize that we would already be bare, so that thought warmed my cooch up a bit as I waited.

Fuck, the boys had initiated this unexpected round tonight. Had they been daydreaming of our slick, smooth pussies during class? Did Evan and Deck mumble to each other on their walk home, suggesting secret sex under their breath as they strolled to their apartment?

Minutes passed, and my busy-bodied brain tried to decipher the delay as my greedy hands threatened to travel south. Perhaps they were performing final primps in our bathroom or getting an early start with a few swift strokes. Hell, at this point, maybe our men were making sandwiches and indulging in some intentional, mind-fucking agony.

Christ, I loathed it, but I loved it.

I released a heavy sigh and dipped my fingertips downtown, feeling my plump clit already slick with anticipation. My tensed muscles loosened as I rubbed my achy center with slow, selfish circles. Gratifying sparks pulsed underneath my fingers, tempting me to spread my knees wider and bring myself to the brink before my boy brought the real burn. I stretched my shivering neck and strummed, pleasuring myself in the darkness as I imagined a hot, twisting tongue tapping through my wetness. I shifted on the mattress as a potential peak lingered low, then candlelight suddenly flooded the wall before me. It disappeared with the closing click of the door, and I sucked in a harsh breath.

Showtime.

My senses found strength again in the seconds between us. I listened through light shuffling as he presumably dropped his fancy bottoms. The community cologne greeted me as he approached, and my cool skin tingled as I waited for the landing of his first touch. My heart slammed with the urge to prompt this play, my wet hand still resting anxiously between my thighs, but I forced myself to relinquish control and let him lead the way.

Thick fingertips brushed my bare back just after the creak of the mattress, and my entire body quivered in response. Realizing that I'd stripped off my sports bra, his curiosity immediately slipped lower to my exposed ass. He groped both cheeks with surprise, forcing my pelvis to thrust forward against my palm, so I dragged my fingers one last time over my aching clit.

That's right. I'm ready. Let's go.

He urgently tangled my hair around his fist, then yanked hard and high, presenting my neck for his puckered lips. Wet, wild kisses slathered below my ear and under my jaw, leaving me breathless and squirming uncontrollably under his command. His hairy legs straddled my calves behind me and he circled my body with strong arms, trapping me with an implicit warning to hold still for his entertainment. His swelling shaft lay cushioned against the top of my ass as his wide hands surveyed my curves. One reached high to my breast, massaging my thickened nipple with pinching fingers while the other slithered low between my moist, eager folds.

This guy was fuckin' on it.

My smooth pussy clenched as he dropped merciless pressure against my primed clit, nearly compelling waves of the climax I'd already launched. I rolled my head back against his carved chest and slung my arms around his neck, displaying my entire tight body for his lustful enjoyment. I longed for him to take whatever he wanted and ravage me until I unraveled in pretty pieces between his palms.

He accepted my invitation, snatching my earlobe between his snarling teeth as he exploited my exposure again. He switched positions with effortless slides over my stomach, his hand now slick with my warm juice as he tweaked my other hard nipple. The filthy, wet sensation shipped painstaking throbs to my core, enhanced even more as he continued to fuck my soaked slit with rapid strokes. I writhed against his firm frame for release, fumbling until I found his parted lips over my shoulder, then I forced my fingers in against his rough tongue.

I wanted him to taste the damp desperation on my fingerprints. I needed him to realize that I'd been so hungry for his big cock, I'd indulged in my own dirty deeds as I waited in the dark.

Was that his first sample of my goods?

He sucked the moist pleasure from my hand, lapping with insatiable thirst as I thrust my demanding pussy against his finger friction. I preferred to come all over the steel shaft begging against my ass, but as ripple after ripple edged me closer to my crest, I didn't give one fuck where I finished. I clenched my inner walls and clawed the back of his buzzed hair in preparation to explode, but my partner slowed and left me hanging by a delicate thread over my climax cliff.

I wanted to scream in frantic frustration, interrupting every studying student in the building as my lungs bitched for release. He suddenly grabbed my hips with primal need and jerked me through the darkness, throwing his legs over the edge of my bed and escorting me to his lap.

Oh, he wanted me to ride. No problem.

I swung my bent knee over his thighs with blind trust, facing him in the pitch black of the room, and he clutched my ass cheeks to keep me from toppling over. As soon as his swollen tip breached my wet, aching pussy, he tightened his grip and yanked down, forcing that demanding cock deep inside my tensed hole. He pumped his pelvis hard to fill me, his thickness stretching my slick walls until I almost cried out with pure fucking pleasure. I tipped my chin to the ceiling and gnawed at my bottom lip, my heart thundering between my ribs and pounding in my ears.

He used the opportunity of my arched back to lick hot, wide laps over my left nipple, savoring the sweet juices that he'd smeared over my pink skin. I flailed again between his muscular arms with no fuckin' discipline, that swollen shaft grinding deep in my desperate pussy, but he hardened his hands and jerked my hips forward with a demand for attention.

No more warnings.

I dangled aimlessly over his thighs, far too short for my feet to touch the floor from his lap, so I clutched his rugged shoulders and clung for dear life. I had no leverage, left completely powerless to his rhythm and pace. As if I were nothing more than a weightless toy, he bounced my burning slit over his throbbing tip, sliding in deep over and over to meet his greedy needs first. I squeezed the head of his thrusting cock inside my wetness, feeling so overwhelmed by *his* thirst that I found myself craving his sinful spill.

We exchanged humid breaths, our sloppy tongues and sticky lips brushing against each other as we panted silently through mutual pleasure. Tap after relentless tap, his firm ridge raked over my trigger spot, dragging my euphoria along with his. He stiffened underneath me through sudden, slow thrusts, then he raised his groin from the mattress and shoved that long shaft in as tightly and deeply as it would fit. His last drag emptied a splash of wet heat exploding against my aching center.

Fuck! Not yet!

As my smooth pussy pooled with his pleasure, I bucked weakly against his buried cock to alert him to continue. I swallowed whimpers as he taunted me inside and tickled my core through our dripping juices. His buff shoulders shook lightly underneath my fingers, and my mouth dropped in the darkness between us.

He was laughing at me.

Fucking laughing.

And as sick and twisted as it was, it drove me wild.

I tiptoed fingertips from his shoulder to his face until that stubbled chin scratched my palm, then I grabbed with both hands and yanked forward, jamming my demanding tongue down his throat like a fuckin' boss. I dominated his surprised lips, completely covering his mouth with mine and choking him with the frustrations of my unresolved hunger.

Yeah. Laugh at me now.

He must've sensed that I wasn't letting this go. One of his big palms slid north from my bare hip, stopping between my shoulders, then he pushed me back to rest against his flexed forearm. I ripped my slick mouth aggressively from his and angled my hips so he could slide out through our dripping mess, then I placed my sacred trust in the hands of this mystery man once more.

I rested back against the safety of his arm, my naked body on invisible display before him, and opened my knees wide with an invitation. I offered my tight, throbbing pussy again with a slight pump, and prayed that he would somehow relieve me this time. The delayed finish clawed for escape deep in my pelvis, and puffs of sweet oxygen hitched inside my chest.

The dramatic level of vulnerability twisted my gut with erotic flutters. As he paused over me in the shadows, I pictured the sexy smirks of all three addictive men, wondering which one had taunted me as his cum trickled between my thighs. This friend had dangled my delight all fucking night, and now I submitted to his clutches like a coveted possession. And, at that moment, I didn't mind being owned.

His teasing touch brushed painfully past my throbbing clit, then he forced two curved fingers inside my slippery slit and fucked me again with full force, knuckling my wet nerves as he pumped in and out. He tugged fingertips directly against my tightened trigger like he'd designed the fucking map, my back arching sharply at this unexpected show of pussy expertise.

My helpless legs quivered and jerked as my mind abandoned all sense of pride, allowing his skilled strokes to coax the climax that his dick didn't deliver with the quick ride. I hugged each unbearable thrust until a deep, excruciating crest flooded me in fresh waves.

My arms fell limply at my sides as my wet walls weakened and, unable to release the cry muffled in my throat, I dug nails into my palms with complete exhilaration. With a smug sense of arrogance, he painted my juicy finish over my bare folds as I hung there, smearing stickiness over every tight inch of my cooch and silently bragging that he'd finally completed the job. Hell, I almost laughed, too.

When he urged me forward with that wide hand between my shoulders, I hoped for the same level of sensual aftercare that my first anonymous fuck had furnished. Our lips naturally navigated within the recovery breaths, and we kissed with slow, flirtatious appreciation until our heart rates tumbled back to baseline.

God, it was such an incredible ending.

We parted ways as planned, and I shifted onto my bunched comforter to face away from him. A giddy grin stretched across my flushed cheeks as I waited for him to dress, my patient brain waiting eagerly for a moment of focus to consider the playful antics. As soon as the door clicked closed, my loose analysis took shape.

This freestyle fun had been so different from my first experience. Both unhinged nights had littered my reflections with both intrigue and enthusiasm. Hell, I wasn't sure how much weight to throw behind the theory of each potential partner. After we'd all dipped our toes in these erotic waters over the weekend, there was no telling which tools each experienced man had hidden in those sexy pajamas. All I acknowledged was that I couldn't fucking wait for my next roll of the dice...

...and maybe ending up in the arms of my favorite without even knowing.

~ • ~

The notification knock arrived quicker than expected. *Fuck, we must've taken the longest.* I was still positioning my black sports bra over my perky nips as I peeked out my bedroom door several minutes later. Shay and Mia were already lingering in the bathroom threshold, so I stepped quickly through the dim candlelight and joined them inside. Mia signaled to the boys that we were good, then she switched on the bright overhead lights and closed the door behind us. We batted lashes at each other as we adjusted our vision.

"Well?" I asked Shay with hope as I rushed to pee.

She smiled radiantly in the mirror. "It was amazing."

"Mine, too," Mia sighed dreamily. "Totally blew my mind."

Interesting.

I wiped my privates and wiggled back into my leggings. "I had a great time, too. Fuckin' loved it."

"Did you get anal?" Shay teased as she fixed one of Mia's wild strays.

"No. Maybe Saturday, though."

I cracked up and shook my head. "Well, it's important to have goals, Mia."

She lowered her voice and coaxed us closer. "So, wait a minute. No one got Mr. Vanilla?"

"Hell no! Not tonight!" Shay whisper-yelled.

"Definitely not me."

Mia doubled over and lost it laughing until we just had to join in. "There's just three guys out there, right?"

~ • ~

Our boys were nosing through the kitchen when we joined them. Evan buried his head deep in the fridge as Judge and Decker scoured the cabinets for scraps. They'd already changed back into their school clothes while we'd been jacking around in the bathroom, but I still scoped their tight tees and perfect asses with thirst. I loved the bare-chested look, but we had things to do.

Fucking Wednesday.

"Good luck, guys!" Shay laughed as she sashayed through the space. "We haven't been to the store."

Decker raised brows at our giddy smiles. "Well, you're all bubbly as fuck."

"Just what were you laughing at in there?" Judge asked.

"Oh, girl stuff," I teased with an eye roll, my cheeks retaining their post-peen pink.

"Anyone want a water?" Evan offered, raising his golden stubble from behind the fridge door. We all accepted and settled in for the presumably quick discussion. *Would my guy leave any subtle hints?*

Mia hoisted herself up onto the bar and took a drink. "Time for your therapy, people. Tell Mia all about it."

Judge raised a mock toast. "I feel exhilarated. Fucking awesome."

Evan smiled arrogantly. "Short, sweet, and sexy...just like whoever was in that room with me."

"It was faster but still fantastic," Deck added, crossing his ripped arms over his chest with a naughty smirk. "You girls up for another round tonight?"

"I fuckin' wish," I sighed as I met his eyes.

"I'm loving this too damned much for my own good," Mia said, swinging her legs with a guilty grin.

"I kinda like this weeknight thing," I giggled. "Too bad we have so much fucking work to do."

Evan nodded through his drink. "I hear ya. As soon as my last class ended today, it was all I could think about."

Shay yawned with a glance at the microwave clock. "Speaking of class, it's time to get to it."

"Goodbye kisses?" Judge flashed a darling smile.

I drifted into the dining room for a semi-private farewell, parking my water on the table and letting my mind check out until I opened the books. Although I'd moved past the prospect of discovering which dick had spilled inside me, I longed to listen to each man's whispered words and taste the desire still seasoning their tongues.

Evan's baby blues twinkled as he joined me near the front door, and my pussy instinctively sparked with raw heat. My eyes darted directly to his groin and back. *Was he the one who just finger fucked me until I saw stars?*

"Did you have fun tonight?" he asked softly, snaking an arm around my bare waist.

"Yes." I blinked long lashes up at his inviting smile. "I hope he did, too."

"I'm sure he did, Callie. Look at you."

"Stop." Red embarrassment rushed to my cheeks under his gaze.

"I can't," he rasped with a slow lick of his lips. "I think you're perfect."

His brazen compliment threw me entirely off guard. He scanned my shock, then covered my surprised mouth with his, wrapping his tongue passionately around mine until my knees weakened with ignited lust.

Judge claimed his turn the second Evan stepped back to switch. He gently fingered the blond strands cascading over my naked shoulders, and I shrugged away sparks of tempting tingles.

"I'm looking forward to Saturday," he admitted before lowering his voice barely above a breath. "I have some things I'd like to do to you."

Christ, he was so fucking smooth.

"Oh, I can think of some ways you could use those lips," I teased seductively.

Judge cocked a sexy brow. "Well, let's start with this."

When that delicious mouth met mine, I looped my arms around his neck and urged our sultry french kiss even deeper. I craved that swirling tongue over my smooth skin, and I wanted him to know just how welcome he was.

Decker sauntered over as soon as I was free and smirked down at me before his hands landed. "You're glowing," he whispered with a gorgeous grin.

I swallowed hard as those dark eyes pierced through me. "I am?"

"You are." He suddenly swept me into an entrancing embrace, then he swayed my hips as if we were slow dancing to non-existent music.

"I guess the night shows on my face." I beamed up at him through my blush. "I had an incredible time."

"And I hope I was the one who gave it to you." Deck kissed me with that leisurely, determined tongue, lapping up the remains of the other goodbyes as we finished the silent song.

~ • ~

After finally closing my notebook for the night, I slept like an exhausted rock and felt surprisingly refreshed on Thursday morning. Hell, I guess all this fucking was the perfect form of cardio, providing much more entertainment than an hour at the gym. Classes throughout the day proved quite interesting, despite the competition with my erotic nights. I assisted the professor and my classmates in dissecting a newly donated human cadaver in my fascinating anatomy lab. My watchful instructor glowed with pride and patted me on the back after I carefully extracted the femoral nerve from the surrounding thigh tissues. Joy sprung in my heart to the skip of my step as I left the science center and stepped into the cool breeze outside.

I met the girls at a café near the medical arts building late that afternoon. Succulent homemade chicken noodle soup warmed my belly even more than the sun spilling over my window seat. We rehashed our busy days, comparing notes from our different class sections and developing a loose study schedule for the upcoming week. Shay and I were bragging about our cadaver skills when Mia interrupted.

"Oh, look! The boys!"

Evan, Judge, and Deck were jogging across the street, hamming it up with bright, boyish smiles and long, lanky strides. Something clicked about seeing the three of them together, their not-so-innocent grins and apparent inside jokes sparking a simmer for the days before our nefarious nights. I loved the individual attention behind closed doors, absolutely fucking loved it, but restlessness for more prompted me to speak my mind.

"Girls, I need to talk," I mumbled as I stared. My best friends immediately stammered over each other with concern.

"Are you okay?"

"Tell us."

I took a deep breath and returned my eyes to the table. "Let me start off by saying that I absolutely love Three Doors…"

Mia shot Shay a side-eye. "This doesn't sound good."

"No, it doesn't."

"It's good," I reassured them. "I'm all in. But something is missing."

Mia cocked her head with a puzzled frown. "Like what?"

"Like the group excitement we had before. Spin the Bottle, Hour of Power, dirty dancing, porn night," I explained, listing our naughty sex acts on my fingers. Although I voiced it vaguely, I missed the watching. I missed my crew members being sucked and seduced as my mouth watered with desire from across the room. I missed scoping perfect bodies grinding and listening to parted lips whimpering, all while being ushered to the edge by my own irresistible partner.

"I'm not bored," I continued. "I'm getting fucked better than I ever have, and it's thrilling when I'm in there, but…"

Shay nodded. "I see what you mean."

"Am I crazy?"

"No, not at all." Mia grinned over her half-eaten salad. "Group foreplay is fire."

"I liked all that stuff, too," Shay said with a wave of her spoon. "Maybe I didn't even realize that I missed it until you brought it up."

Mia leaned in with those big, eager eyes. "So, what do we do? What's the fix?"

Hmm.

I'd noticed an intriguing ad online during my last porn scroll, back when self-satisfaction was my only viable option, but I hadn't given it any real consideration until now. I cringed and sank into my sweater, then I decided to try it. "I *maybe* have an idea to spark things up again, but you might not go along with it."

Shay narrowed suspicious eyes. "Why wouldn't we?"

"It's filthy."

"All that stuff was filthy," Mia chuckled.

"No," I elaborated, shaking my head, "I mean physically filthy. Disgusting. Dirty. Like 'wear old clothes' kinda nasty."

Both raised intrigued, perfectly arched brows, so I pushed my lukewarm soup aside and described the potential plan under the hum of the busy dining room. When I finished relaying my blueprint for the boys, Shay fell back in her seat and gawked at me with shock.

"You're serious?" She scowled with a prissy crinkle of her button nose.

"I'm all in," Mia giggled beside her. "I'm so fucking down."

I laughed out loud at my beautiful best friends, expecting both those responses practically verbatim. "One more thing," I added with a satisfied smirk. "I wanna do it tomorrow night."

~ 16 ~

"But I wanna look cute," Shay bitched, sifting through hangers of designer threads and shaking her head at the closet. "You know I don't have any old jeans."

Because of course.

After we'd crammed in the last bit of studying we could swallow for the week and, despite some reluctance from my fussy friend, we were finally prepping for our filthy Friday adventure. A few quick texts confirmed that our guys were in for the evening, likely crashed on their sectional, watching whatever sport they could summon on the screen. I kept my proverbial fingers crossed and hoped our excursion would spark that group fire again, even if just for the night.

"Wear leggings, you fuckin' whiner," Mia laughed from her seat on Shay's perfectly made bed.

"No way. Not thick enough."

I rolled my eyes behind Shay's back and fiddled with my flyaways in her full-length mirror. "We're taking towels, remember?"

"Speaking of, "Shay said, palming her hips and turning to us with a smirk, "towels aren't gonna work. I need something like plastic wrap."

Hmm.

"Okay, maybe you're onto something there," I agreed.

"Shay, listen," Mia lectured, slicing through the space with an authoritative chop, "you gotta get past this fuckin' apprehension before we leave."

"I know. I'm excited, but I'm just concerned, too."

"Stop being such a snob," I roasted with love and gestured to my tattered denim. "Think of the endgame here. You'll be fine."

A pretty smile tugged at her cheeks after my nudge to the master plan. "Can I wear some of yours?"

"Oh, I'd be fuckin' honored," I giggled with a chest palm, swerving from her ass swat as she left for my room.

Shay's ridiculous, uppity ways often forced our loving groans, but she made a solid point about the towel option. Something plastic would be much more hygienic, all things considered, so I stood in the hallway as my girls finished up and chewed my bottom lip with careful consideration. *Fuck, that's it!* I whipped open the bathroom vanity cabinet, plucked three scented trash bags from under the sink, and then folded them into tight squares.

"Okay, I'm ready!" Shay met us in the dining room minutes later as she smoothed palms over her final selections. Even in my worn, ratty jeans and a faded pink sweatshirt, she still looked like a million bucks.

"Shove these in your pockets," I directed, then I passed our "protection" to my sidekicks.

Shay cringed, of course, then she unfolded her bag in the overhead light and inspected it for rips. "I hope there isn't random jick on the floor."

Mia laughed and adjusted her long locks over her gray zip-up, looking effortlessly stunning, as usual. "Hell, I feel dirty already, and I love it."

I sucked in an anxious breath and checked the time. "Well, let's go see if our boys will love it, too."

~ • ~

We trotted down the stairwell and huddled once more at the front door of our sexy targets. I'm confident that the security guards assumed we were psycho ex-girlfriends at this point, but hell, at least we were fully dressed for this visit. Sure, we could've just planned this escapade in advance, but since we all got off of the element of surprise, why not make it interesting?

"We don't have much time," Shay whisper-yelled.

"Right. We gotta be quick."

Mia knocked on the door and opened it slowly. "Guys?"

I heard muffled voices, then Judge greeted us with a shocked yet excited smile. "Wow! Hi!"

"Hi! Can we come in?" Shay asked, toying flirtatiously with her shiny hair.

Judge grinned and gestured for us to enter. "Always."

Aww.

We filed past the kitchen with purpose, the faint smell of pizza seasoning the air, finding Evan asleep on the couch and Deck stretched out in nothing but navy boxers. I peeped the access panel in the front and swallowed. Hard.

"What's happening, girls?" he asked with a sleepy smile. He rubbed his dark, groggy eyes but thankfully made no effort to hide the hints of his impressive package.

Judge looked us over and stroked his scruffy chin. "You didn't dress for Three Doors, not that I'm opposed…"

"Nope. Not tonight." I grinned and glanced down at my rather rugged attire, noticing a grass stain on my purple crewneck.

"We're here to steal you," Mia giggled.

"Come again?" Judge laughed, pausing the basketball game on the big screen.

She stepped up and poked his chest with fake authority. "Get dressed. Both of you. And bring the masks."

Decker looked confused, blinking his thick lashes as if he were waking from a dream. "Wait. What time is it?"

"Around eleven."

"What about that one?" Judge nodded to his snoozing roommate and our eyes followed. Evan lay sprawled across a straight stretch of the blue sectional, snoring softly through his parted lips. *Fucking adorable.*

"I got it," Shay announced confidently with a cocky hair flip. She climbed over Evan's lap and straddled his red gym shorts in those skin-tight jeans, then she rocked her pussy a few times over his nap-hardened wood.

"*This* is the content I needed," I whispered with an elbow to Mia's ribs.

"Right?" she giggled and watched our girl move. "It's working already."

Shay moaned dramatically and grinded directly into the sleeping prince's shaft. "*Oh, Evan. Yes!*"

Judge released a low-toned whistle beside us and shook his head. "Is it too late for me to fall asleep, too?"

This fuckin' guy.

Evan reached for her hips with groping fingers and smiled in his sleep, leaving us to stifle a collective laugh.

"You feel *so* good," Shay whimpered over him, rivaling the acting skills of our naughty nurses.

One bright blue eye cracked open, then he surveyed his surroundings with bewilderment as we anticipated his reaction. In textbook Evan fashion, he simply curled into a crunch and pulled a shocked Shay down to his grinning lips. She let him.

We are all so fucked up.

I stared at the sensual tease with the remaining thirsty crew members, watching their lustful tongues twist with hunger, but I regretfully had to interject once my girl tried to remove Evan's shirt. "Shay, come on. No time for that."

"I'll be quick."

"Shay!" Mia snapped with a spirited laugh.

"I'm joking. Chill." She tossed palms with mock defense and slinked from her show, leaving a groggy Evan in her wake. He glanced around the room in a daze, then sat upright and adjusted his balls.

"What's going on?"

"The girls are kidnapping us," Deck answered with a chuckle.

Evan didn't hesitate. "Cool. Where we goin'?"

That's the spirit.

"It's a surprise," I told him. "Get dressed cause we can't be late."

"And nothing too fancy," Mia added.

Deck, Evan, and Judge left us with unprompted cheek pecks, like the sweethearts they were, before disappearing to the hallway with muffled, manly mumbles. Of course, my nosy instincts kicked in, and I intentionally eavesdropped for any apprehension. I flattened my back against the living room wall out of view and covered my mouth with a finger to shush my girls.

"Christ, how fuckin' cute are they with this shit?"

"Dude, I'm lost."

"So are we."

"Shay can ride a rod, though."

"True."

"Hell, I'm up for whatever they bring."

"Me, too. Literally."

"What's with the jeans?"

Smiling at the excitement in their voices and satisfied that we hadn't overstepped at this late hour, I motioned for my girls to join me in the kitchen while we waited. We turned the tables, poking around in cryptic cabinets and drawers, finding nothing more than nearly empty cereal boxes and a couple of random screwdrivers.

"Wonder what's in here," Shay whispered as her fingers lingered on the refrigerator handle. "Any guesses?"

"Milk, for sure," I guessed, knowing that a tub of protein mix was surely stashed somewhere.

"Staged beer for the cooler," Mia added.

"And I'll go with leftover pizza." Shay whipped open the fridge door and we scanned the cold interior, finding all three of our predictions and nothing else.

"Oh. My. God." I clutched my belly and fuckin' lost it.

Shay shook her head and checked the expiration date on the milk jug. "No wonder they're always at our crib."

We heard rustling in the hallway, so Mia shoved the door closed. Evan popped out looking fine as fuck in those dark jeans.

"Ready to go!"

"You got the masks?" Shay reminded him.

Deck joined seconds later and tugged a navy hoodie over his bare shoulders. "Check."

"Let's roll."

~ • ~

"Blindfolds on," Mia instructed after we piled into my black crossover.

I chauffeured my curious crew through dimly lit streets on the outskirts of town to the address I'd found online. I was hella jealous of the group groping that was likely occurring in the back seat, especially with all the heavy breathing and whispered whimpers filling the cabin. I peeked in my rearview mirror a few times for the show, but I noticed nothing but shadows.

"Was this your idea?" Evan chilled in the front beside me, tilting his blond whiskers in my general direction. He looked so innocent sitting there, but I knew better.

"It *was* my idea," I bragged with a bright smile he couldn't see.

"Nice. I'm fuckin' amped."

Feeling emboldened by his enthusiasm, I found his big hand in the dashboard light and guided it across my lap, sliding his fingers between my thighs and shifting my hips against his touch. He bit his lower lip with a mutter and stroked me lightly below my zipper, forcing a flow of moist heat to my relaxed pussy.

The parking lot was mostly dark, with only a few other cars in the spaces, so I stationed my ride near the safety of the front entrance lights. The entire scene looked super fuckin' shady, just as I had hoped.

"We're here!" Shay announced.

"Masks off?"

"Not yet."

"We'll tell you when."

Once we helped our dates from their seats, Mia took Judge's hand, Shay guided Deck, and I tugged Evan along beside me. We paused in front of the disheveled brick building, exchanging hopeful, impatient grins as the guys blindly scanned the surroundings.

"Okay! Masks off!" I squealed.

We watched with intrigue as our boys yanked free from the blindfolds and blinked at our destination with disbelief, the mysterious signage casting a crimson glow over their widened eyes.

"What the…"

"No fucking way…"

"You gotta be kidding…"

Although several letters had burned out, the place showing much more wear in person than on the website, the red neon sign was clearly legible.

"The Back Door Theatre?" Judge asked in awe.

I glowed with pride as my plan unfolded. "Have any of you been here?"

Deck shook his head and stared. "No, but we've heard about it."

Evan grinned down at me. "Are you sure about this?"

"Positive. Let's go. The show starts at midnight."

We swapped partners with no planning before passing through the front doors to the shady lobby. Shay and Judge casually intertwined fingers as they giggled over a raunchy display poster. Evan and Mia were already tonguing hard as they slow-walked ahead. Decker slid a possessive arm around my waist and escorted me inside.

The wild reviews online had served no justice. Conflicting shades of red coated every sleazy surface. Tacky and stained scarlet carpet. Grimy and smudged cherry wallpaper. A cracked and peeling burgundy ceiling. Hell, I couldn't have produced a seedier scene had I written a fuckin' script. Pure perfection.

"Wow," Deck mumbled under his breath, his gorgeous, awestruck smile swiveling between the colors. "Classy joint."

"Fuck, I hope not," I laughed and bumped his hip with mine.

An attractive middle-aged man in a metallic red bow tie parked his paperback as Decker and I approached the small ticket counter. "Welcome to The Back Door!" Bow Tie welcomed us with a toothy smile and theatrical arms.

Deck matched his warm greeting. "Thank you, sir!"

"We need six tickets for the show, please," I said.

"We have two main features every week. Which would you like?"

Well, damn. I hadn't taken the time to pick a title. "What are my choices?"

Decker slowly slid behind me and lowered his head to my shoulder, that alluring shadow of scruff teasing my neck and distracting me from the task at hand. His thick, tight body hugged my curves, and I shivered with arousal under my old sweatshirt.

"We have two fantastic options tonight." Bow Tie beamed. "The first is 'Anal at the Aquarium' and the other is 'Two Chicks, One Dick.'"

"Oh, honey," Deck moaned with amusing enthusiasm before I could even utter a response. "I've always wanted to do it in an aquarium." He rocked against my ass with that heavy shaft, and his tempting fingers danced at my frayed waistline.

Fuck.

I willed myself to fumble along through the humorous but seductive tease. "But baby," I whined, playing directly into Deck's compelling lead, "you know how I love watching two women together."

Deck suddenly sucked in a harsh breath, then he snagged my earlobe between his teeth with a gritty growl of my name. Despite this little charade, there was nothing fucking fake about it. A dull, warm ache pounded inside my panties as fire rushed to my cheeks.

"You can't go wrong with either choice," Bow Tie interrupted, pausing our promising opening act.

I swallowed my desire and opted for the opinions of the others, but I found both pairs interlocked on opposite sides of the lobby and completely distracted by each other's tempting bodies. Fuck, I guess Deck and I were making the executive decision on behalf of our sixsome.

"Please?" I coaxed, covering his wandering hands with mine as they lingered on my belly.

Deck shook his head at Bow Tie with mock disappointment. "Whatever she wants, I suppose."

"We'll have six for 'Two Chicks, One Dick,' please!" I pinched my lips together after I repeated the risqué movie title, blushing at the mere thought of what my parents would think of their once wholesome daughter.

Bow Tie clicked away with his ancient mouse and produced six old-school paper tickets. Deck offered to pay the way for the crew, but I insisted on presenting my debit card instead. My idea, my treat. Our host grinned with cocked head nostalgia as he slid the stubs across the red countertop.

"You kids help me keep the lights on, ya know. Thanks for coming."

"Aww, you're welcome! We're super excited!" I told him honestly.

"Is it busy in there?" Deck asked.

"Oh, not too bad. Most people chose the anal special tonight," Bow Tie informed us matter-of-factly, adding in a slight shrug. "You know how it is."

"Of course." Decker nodded with convincing seriousness.

"Don't tell Mia we passed on that one," I giggled under my breath as we beckoned for our deviant friends. "She'll never fuckin' forgive me."

~ • ~

Deck and I held swinging hands between our hips as we ushered our pack down a shadowed hallway to the right, then we rolled together into the screening room. Bow Tie had already dimmed the lights, but I could distinguish rows of red, tattered cushions lining the seating area before the large blank screen. The place looked acceptably clean upon my initial inspection of the floor.

"Back row at The Back Door!" Mia laughed from behind me.

We scaled the slight incline of the ramp to the back of the theater. I noticed dark silhouettes of other presumed porn lovers scattered throughout the sketchy space. Most huddled in pairs, but a few singles and one interesting trio had also declined the aquarium option.

"I'm gonna check it out before we commit," Shay whispered. "I don't wanna sit in dried juices or anything." Judge shifted his hips into the last row, with Shay apprehensively scooting along behind, both surveying the seats with the flashlight on her phone. They were about halfway down the aisle when they both turned around abruptly and shook their heads no.

"What's wrong?" Deck whisper-yelled as they returned.

"There's a giant wet spot on one seat and a used condom on another," Shay bitched, offering me a stern glare in the shadows.

I shrugged. "Well, I guess we know why it was empty."

"Shut that fuckin' light off!"

We all swiveled with surprise to the shadowed figures parked in the positions below.

"You shouldn't sit in the back row! Are you fucking new here?"

"Just find a fucking seat already and shut up!"

Decker chuckled down at me with a deep cringe. "Tough crowd."

"Let's just check another area," Judge offered.

We found the third row from the back somewhat acceptable, with no visible body fluids spilled and the nearest dickhead patron several rows down. Judge boldly entered first again, squatting a few seats from the side wall, followed by Shay, Decker, me, Evan, and Mia. As I gave my seat one last inspection before sitting, I noticed no armrests, not even the optional fold-up style. The ratty chairs sat crammed together with wide-open access to the cushions on either side. Hell, I guess the spiffy owner wasn't expecting people to sip from jumbo sodas and munch on buckets of popcorn. Bow Tie knew exactly what we were here for...

...and he was right.

We finally settled just as the pre-porn advertisements flickered on the screen. Deck palmed my hand over his thigh, stroking my soft skin with a gentle thumb. Evan rested his fingers near my knee to the other side, his mischievous eyes sparkling as the commercials flashed before us. My heart rate ticked up several notches as both men claimed space on my body, adding in a few thumps that I could feel pulsing deep in my jeans. Although my girls and I had strategized over the grand finale last night as we readied ourselves for bed, we hadn't planned any of this filler material. I couldn't guess what to expect, but fuck, I was ready.

Evan turned to me with a flirtatious grin. "Just what did you get us into tonight?" he whispered.

"We may have some plans for you guys," I teased under my breath. "We'll see."

"Look, it's Joe!" Deck noted as a new promotion popped up on the screen. Our friendly neighborhood sex clerk appeared in his vivid showroom, explaining that The Basement had just received a shipment of top-of-the-line anal beads. I smirked to my left, finding Mia sprung in her seat beside Evan as she drooled over every word.

After a couple of quick videos showcasing a local liquor store and, oddly enough, a retirement community, the already low lights darkened even more around us. Decker squeezed my hand and cuddled closer, his warm breath shipping tingles down my spine.

"I definitely wanna retire somewhere that advertises in here," he joked.

I giggled at his flirty nonsense as the filthy show began.

~ • ~

The no context fucking started from the opening scene, so I was immediately both disappointed and intrigued by the lack of a backstory. A tall, beefy man was fuckin' railing a curvy redhead from behind within seconds of the title flash. The camera panned to reveal the sultry siren bent forward over a humming washing machine, her plump ass rocking, giant tits bouncing, and bare pelvis slamming. The male lead seemed attractive enough from the side, with ripples of rich, brown muscle flexing as he pumped, but the hammering didn't allow for much determination of dick quality.

I was evaluating the laundry room detail, deciding if the washer was *actually* running, when Evan dipped his sneaky fingers to my inner thigh and squeezed. I turned at the request for attention, finding Mia's pink manicure groping at the back of his neck and shoulders as they mauled each other. Evan's thumb kneaded near my pussy, tempting me through his own arousal at the hands of my best friend. A blazing thrill rushed to my skimpy panties with his desire for me to watch, so I guided his hand higher and gave him silent permission to explore.

Despite the steam being created beside me, Shay's muffled whimpering coaxed me to scrutinize the action on my other side. She faced away from me, Judge's hungry hands tangled in the dark strands down her back as their bodies rocked with natural rhythm. I pulled my bottom lip through my teeth, watching his fingertips curl in desperation as she slid a bold leg onto his lap. A primal growl from the stacked stud on screen yanked me from my voyeuristic fetish, flushing my cheeks with a shameful pink and forcing my baby blues to sway. Under the shifting lights of the freaky film, I found my partner's deep brown eyes fixated on only me.

A cocky smirk curled the corners of Deck's lips as if he'd been waiting patiently for my focus, allowing my kinky indulgence to trump his own aroused anticipation. The seductive moment hung with heat in the stuffy air between us, our gazes drifting over each other's shadowed faces. Invigorated by the prickly tension, I freed my fingers from his and dragged my hand up the inner seam of his jeans, finding his long, thickened cock bulging against his zipper.

Christ, he felt so big.

I rubbed slow, tempting strokes through the denim and left my eyes locked on his, my damp pussy aching as I waited for his reaction to my ambitious advances. He scooted his ass forward on the cushion, eagerly stretching to give me easier access to his shaft, so I thumbed his rigid tip with deeper pressure. He released a haughty sigh through grinding teeth, then he grabbed the back of my neck and forced my mouth to his.

Demanding Decker clocked in for duty, benching the disciplined tease as he choked me with his hot, thrusting tongue. Both hands raked through my hair and tugged at my tangles, forcing my gasps against his dominant lips. He grinded his needy cock against my palm, pumping his pelvis desperately as we listened to the redhead moan through a breathy climax. I heard the change of scene on the big screen, but when I tried to tilt my chin for a natural, nosy peek, Deck wasn't fuckin' having it.

He aggressively cupped my jawline and snarled greedy teeth against my mouth, then drove his rough tongue inside for another agonizing round. The arrogant exercise of complete control left me clawing at his steel, begging for him to bend me over the row and fuck me in front of our friends until I couldn't breathe.

I blindly fumbled with Deck's button below, then jerked his zipper open over his boxers. Just as I grazed the fluff of his pubic hair, Evan tugged at the hem of my sweatshirt from behind. I ripped my panting lips from the kiss and threw a glance over my shoulder, finding my blond counterpart's hungry, hooded eyes burning with lustful blue flames.

That blistering appeal pulsed deep in my pussy, my body nearly igniting as I stoked one friend's cock while another demanded my attention. In my few heartbeats of hesitation, Evan twisted my purple top inside his fist and yanked me closer, then he buried his wet tongue between my lips and claimed the territory that Deck had just tasted.

I scratched at Evan's hoodie as our mutual primal appeal blazed between us. Whimpers choked my throat as I emptied remnants of my previous kiss into his. His determined hand drifted north, snaking under my sweatshirt, ripping at my lace bra, and pinching my tightened nipples. Just when I thought this clothed, public pleasure could reach no higher peak, Deck's dominant grip wrenched my clenched thighs apart and massaged my throbbing clit mercilessly through my jeans. The slick friction sent me spiraling between the competing fingers of the best friends, and I cried weakly into the dark jaws of the theater, only to find an enthralled Mia watching every move over Evan's shoulder.

As I broke for breaths of relief, she shifted to her knees in the worn, red seat and licked Evan's scruff, dragging nails down over his panting pecs and cupping his swollen package with a dominant squeeze. Just as Evan turned to meet her feisty mouth again, the noise of another scene change sounded on the forgotten screen. I sucked sweet oxygen to calm my burning lungs and blinked through the flickers to catch up. The rugged male lead had cornered a scrawny blond against the refrigerator, thrusting deep into her smooth, tight pussy as she writhed naked against the stainless steel. I rocked my soaked slit into Deck's firm fingers, imagining a huge, hardened dick stretching me through my sticky juices.

Hold up. Who was this blond chick? Was there some appliance kink involved? What the hell was happening?

Decker's earlier selfishness had clearly caused me to miss critical elements of the plot. As if my seductive sidekick had read my crazy mind and decided to plead for penance, Deck skillfully popped my button and forced down my zipper. His finger eased inside my panties and swirled over my plump clit, our aroused gazes locking as my hips reflexively jerked into his palm. His fingertip dove deeper as he watched my squirming body, dragging through my dripping pleasure and stroking my soft folds.

Shay wrapped a delicate hand around his neck and steered his scruffy chin to hers for a wet, tongue-twisting kiss, then navigated his boxer access and teased his heavy cock with nimble fingers. Judge appeared over her shoulder and sucked her earlobe between his sensual lips, his warm, sexy eyes meeting mine as he groped her perky tits from behind.

Christ, just kill me.

We were in way fuckin' deeper than we'd ever been, Judge and Deck's cocky flaunt of a potential threesome now seeming somewhat amateur in comparison. Each member of our secret society had flung themselves over this captivating cliff with no hesitation, humping and licking each other in these stained seats like we'd never been pleasured before. Although Three Doors may have quenched our collective thirsts for both friendship and fucking, this primal craving for group action coursed through not only my veins.

With Decker occupied now, both his mouth and his cock being handled by my girlfriend to the right, I turned to check on the wild things to my left. Mia had reclaimed Evan in my absence, riding his thigh with slow pussy thrusts as they gagged each other with a suffocating kiss. The eerie cinema lights danced over their delicious bodies in the dark as I stared at their soaked lips. Moisture glistened between their muffled gasps, and I wondered if she could taste me on his tongue.

Despite the dirty deeds around me, I wasn't left lonely as the scandalous scenes continued on the big screen. Deck's fingers still danced inside my panties with promise, so I sank back into my tattered chair and watched the arousing actors. Our hovering hunk was standing before both the busty redhead and the slim blond as they huddled together in a cheap living room setting. The models rested hip to hip on an ugly plaid couch, completely naked and listening to the male lead with eager breathlessness.

Fuck. Had the chicks been making out and I missed it?

The guy puffed his brawn and gave a compelling speech about adoring both of them, explaining that he loved being their roommate and fucking them both, but he was having difficulty choosing just one.

Roommates? Nice.

Deck interrupted my preference for the porn plot again, this time panting beside me with loud, laboring breaths to the ceiling. I glanced at his darkened lap to find Shay slowly stroking his full, bare length as it sprung from his boxers. She met my eyes and nodded slightly to prompt the planned conclusion of the erotic evening, so I turned to Mia and tugged on her gray sweatshirt. She left Evan's lips with a wide, wet grin of approval.

I pulled Deck's dirty hand from my panties and, even as he perched on the peak of his pleasure, he resisted my efforts to part ways. He dragged firm fingertips hard over my puffy clit, leaving me seriously and selfishly considering the abandonment of my original plan. I composed myself through a few skipped beats as I zipped my jeans, then I snatched the folded trash bag from my back pocket and slid from my red seat. Deck watched my every move with dark, puzzled eyes.

Shay, Mia, and I had strolled into this seductive scenario with full intentions of sucking some shaft, leaving our peen partners to chance until we naturally paired off within the theater. As both of my besties mimicked my moves in front of their somewhat assigned guys, I clumsily arranged my plastic barrier on the floor before a shocked Decker and dropped with sexy submission between his thighs.

While we paused with anticipation before our next deviant step, I surveyed our three delicious men as the flickers of the forgotten movie flashed across their stunned faces. There was something incredibly perverse about these best friends, side by side with no lingering pride, waiting anxiously for these public blow jobs.

Decker abruptly curled over me and cupped my cheeks, kissing me with sensual softness. I parted my lips along his sharp jawline, trailing sweet smooches up his neck and tickling his ear with a warm, moist breath. "I can't wait to taste you," I whispered. "I've waited so long for this."

"Callie..."

I discovered Deck's long cock rigid and ready to fuck when I returned to his lap. I thumbed the round tip, swirling his early stickiness and meeting his smoldering eyes again. A wicked thought crossed my mind as Shay and Mia tempted the other boys from my peripheral vision.

"I want you to watch the other girls," I mouthed up to him. "Watch them lick and suck your friends as I make you come."

"*Fuck*," Deck mumbled under his breath.

As if the pleasure gods had offered a timely gift, the screen heated up with obvious oral behind me. One of the leading ladies gagged and moaned, the male star's deep voice begging her to suck harder and faster. Practically in unison and within unexplained chick sync, Mia, Shay, and I lowered our faces to our presented groins and sucked the three throbbing cocks between our thirsty lips.

I dragged my hot, wet tongue under Deck's impressive length, lapping with lust as I palmed the base of his thickness with slight strokes. When I reached his curved ridge, I swallowed him whole, letting his smooth, stretched skin ride inside my mouth. Christ, I hadn't tasted a bare shaft in so long, finding myself bobbing and blowing with unbridled enthusiasm as he shifted with exhilaration before me. When I nearly choked as his pulsing tip breached the edge of my throat, I licked my way back to breath and pumped him with rapid thrusts.

As I swept my saliva under his rim, rubbing firm friction along the underside with my wide tongue, I peeked up to see if Deck was following my illicit instructions. Much to my satisfaction, his smokey eyes were narrowed to our side as Mia's shimmering locks bounced in Evan's lap. Deck rubbed clenched fists into his thighs, then he turned back to catch me watching his hunger with excited eyes over his steel.

He suddenly thrust his hips forward with dominance, driving his cock over my heated tongue and forcing me to choke on every inch above my fist. I swallowed the urge to gag and lowered my head to his will, my blond waves falling over my cheeks as I let him fuck my slick, tightened lips. My soaked pussy clenched deep inside my jeans as the need to be fucked nearly dizzied me with desire.

When I raised my eyes again, beating hard as I puffed on his thickened tip, I found Deck gazing lustfully at Shay as she slathered sultry kisses near Judge's heavy sac. I picked up my pace, gliding over his round ridge and dipping quickly to join my jacking fingers with my sliding lips. Deck suddenly grabbed two fistfuls of my hair, then he urgently rocked his cock with rapid jerks over my tongue. He tugged wildly at my strands until his fingertips trailed across my temples, then he fell back into the seat and unloaded his steamy, sticky finish directly down my throat. I swallowed over and over, the salty juice smearing between my lips as I watched him unravel above me. That dark scruff tipped to the ceiling, and his muscular shoulders shuddered inside his sweatshirt as I lapped up every drop from his tip.

Once Deck was spent, I wiped the job from my tingling mouth, feeling prideful that I'd remembered enough sucking skills to make him spill. He blinked with disbelief and found my flushed cheeks grinning in the darkness. The looming porn dialogue momentarily distracted us as the three horny roommates organized a fuck schedule for each partnership. The big guy announced that on weekends, they would all screw each other. Our amused eyes twinkled in the highlights as we stifled ironic laughs together.

Decker tucked his recovering package in his boxers as Mia helped Evan adjust beside us. I gave his marvelous member a final love pat of appreciation, and he offered me a humored smirk, then he opened his arms wide with an invitation.

Shay was still going strong beside me, so I climbed up on Deck's thighs with eagerness to watch Judge finish. My once reluctant friend now darted over his groin with no shame, her black strands hiding the intensity as her gorgeous partner groaned under his breath above her. I heard her whimper through a rough choke, but Judge finally tipped his head back over the seat and released a throaty sigh as he exploded through his peak.

Deck tucked a gentle hand around my bare waist under my top and cuddled me closer to his buff chest. The rolling light of the film credits caught the pleased glint in his eyes as he gazed at my lips. His stubble scratched at my jawline as he inched his way through my waves to my ear.

"That was unbelievable, Callie," he whispered.

"Well, believe it," I gushed as he tickled my earlobe with a sweet kiss. "I'm right here."

~ • ~

We waited until the other porn patrons retreated before gathering our handy trash bags and heading for the exit. Bow Tie looked up from his book again with a bright smile as our naughty crew returned to the red lobby, all six of us holding hands like the kinkiest but proudest fuckin' group in town.

"Thanks for dropping by!" he called. "We have a Wednesday lunchtime special each week if you're interested!"

"Hell, embryology isn't that important, is it?" Deck joked under his breath.

"Thank you, sir!" I responded with a wave. I laughed to myself as we strolled to the exit, wondering just what crossed the owner's undoubtedly wicked mind as he witnessed his customers crawling from the shadows.

Our sixsome stepped out into the chilly night together with no words yet spoken about the impact of our crazy fuckin' field trip. Judge climbed in the front seat with me, then he swept in with those soft lips and kissed my cheek as I started the engine. "I loved watching you tonight," he breathed against my neck. "I sat too far away to enjoy that sexy body of yours."

"I liked watching you, too," I swooned, our eyes meeting in the glow of the dashboard lights. "You're fuckin' fire when you get off, ya know."

Those adorable dimples made an appearance as he shot me a cocky smile. "Callie, you're literally killing me."

~ 17 ~

I stretched into a glorious yawn after dreaming of redheads, bow ties, and dirty jeans.

And maybe of a certain special someone.

"We're fucking nuts," Shay groaned over her chemistry mug when we assembled for breakfast. "Who does this? Who in the fuck behaves this way?"

I rammed a spoonful of sugary cereal between my lips as we reflected on our oral antics and, apparently, our general lifestyle choices. I'd already battered my brain with the analysis after our girly bedtime hug last night.

Did I crawl under my comforter feeling filthy? Yes.

Did I bury my shameful face in the blankets for thriving during this group action? Yes.

Did I crave the lust of all three men while my heart whispered the name of only one? Yes.

Did I finger myself to a delayed finish with guilty fantasies of all my friends? Yes.

Was I happy despite all of it? Yes.

"Look, we're having fun," Mia countered Shay's concern as she offered to refresh our coffee. "That was the whole point, right?"

"Plus, we're safe, and we're doing well in school," I added, convincing myself, too, as I raised my ocean mug for a refill.

Mia spilled more of my steamy addiction to the brim and nodded along.

"I know," Shay sighed. "I think I'm just hungry."

Mia sashayed back to the kitchen, poured Shay a bowl of colorful cereal, and then smirked as she placed it on the table. "You didn't seem too worried when Judge's cock was choking you."

Good point.

"That's true." Shay shrugged and dug into her gifted breakfast. "Totally worth it."

Mia turned to me with a charming grin over her cup. "So, how was Decker?"

I gulped down a fruity bite with memories of having my throat fucked. "Thick. Long. Not gonna lie, I struggled at times."

"Evan's stacked, too," Mia said. "He'd drag my sweet spot with no trouble."

I gestured with my milky spoon. "Hell, maybe he already has."

Mia laughed, raising her caffeine with a mock toast. "Touché, Callie. Tou-fucking-ché."

Shay's cell buzzed beside her bowl, and she tapped the screen as she chewed. "It's them," she said, cupping her chin to catch a milk dribble. "Grab your phones."

```
  Deck: good morning, girls
Callie: hey!
 Judge: what's up?
   Mia: probably Evan
  Evan: bingo
 Judge: wanted to say thanks for last night
   Mia: you mean the porn or the pucker?
  Deck: there was porn?
  Shay: smooth
Callie: both were our pleasure
  Shay: what are you guys doing today?
  Evan: study, gym, beer run
 Judge: what about you?
Callie: study, laundry, clean
   Mia: Shay and I are making a grocery trip later
 Judge: or we could just stick to takeout
   Mia: ha fucking ha
  Deck: what time tonight?
  Shay: 8:00 works
  Evan: we'll be there
 Judge: in our studly threads
  Evan: Christ
Callie: have a good day!
```

~ • ~

The girls and I separated for our solo study sessions earlier than usual. The upcoming, high-volume gastroenterology exam had us all rattled, so we cut our breezy Saturday morning coffee break short in favor of extra time with the material. I rustled through every handwritten line of my notes, jotting in the margins with helpful details from my textbook and highlighting crucial definitions to commit to memory. After determining which sections I'd mastered, I made a separate list of the components that challenged me most, then I zoned in until I felt more comfortable with the concepts.

Although some elements took me longer to grasp than the average student, I'd proven my place over the years by learning what methods worked best for my mind and applying them over double the time. Behind closed doors, I'm sure that Shay and Mia could shut their books much sooner than I did, likely switching to a streaming series or chatting with loved ones back home while I continued to grind. Both respected my space, though, leaving me to my priorities with no pressure and emerging from their bedrooms only after I did.

In the late afternoon, my phone vibrated on the bar after I rinsed the last of our breakfast bowls. I figured that my mom was checking in for a chat or that the girls were requesting any overlooked grocery items, so surprise brightened my eyes when I saw the name of one of my boys instead.

```
   Guy: hey
Callie: hey there
   Guy: you still studying?
Callie: nope, just cleaning
Callie: girls are at the store
   Guy: can I borrow some laundry soap?
   Guy: didn't realize we were out
Callie: sure
Callie: I thought you were all going to the gym
   Guy: I decided to hang back
   Guy: have stuff to do
Callie: gotcha
Callie: we have plenty, though
Callie: come on up
```

Minutes later, I had just stripped the soft white sheets from my mattress when the front door opened after a light knock. Although I realized that the guys washed their own clothes, I smiled at the picture of him sorting his seductive boxers and hauling a full laundry basket on his hip.

"Callie?"

"I'm back here!"

He appeared in my bedroom doorway looking fine as fuck, those rugged muscles slightly distorting the logo on his undergrad tee. I shot him a cheeky grin as he approached, then I pointed in the direction of the kitchen. "The soap is in the—" I tried to explain, but his lips interrupted my instructions.

Holy...

Before I could process a coherent thought, we were devouring each other in the middle of my room. I instinctively tongued him back with equal urgency as his bold hands slid possessively over my body. He whimpered my name in the fevered breaths between our lips, our mouths twisting with passion and, in my case, confusion.

I scanned his handsome face with disbelief. "What is this? What's happening?"

"*Fuck*," he rasped, fingering my long ponytail as it hung down my back, "I just can't stop thinking about you." He drove his tongue wildly between my shocked lips again and cupped my round ass cheeks in both hands, lifting me against his tight torso and dragging my surprised pussy over his cock. I looped my arms over his neck and tightened my legs around his waist, letting him spin me into euphoria as we ravaged each other. Although I'd been tasting his kiss for weeks now, I felt like this was my first full flavor, elation ripping my insides to shreds as we emptied our unspoken emotions.

He eventually backed my bare thighs against my desk, so I raked my arm behind me to make room for our meshed bodies, carelessly tipping a pen cup and hearing the contents spill to the floor. I lost myself in this forbidden ecstasy and curled my back into a sharp arch as his hot mouth swept over my flushed skin. He frenched my exposed collarbone over the straps of my tank top, then he trailed that tempting tongue to the silky spot between my braless breasts.

His stone cock grinded into my clit with frustrating friction, so I clawed at his low riding waistband, fully prepared to let him fuck me on top of my school books. I'd always assumed that he'd be amazing in bed, but the rules of the game had prevented me from confirming it.

The game. Right.

My body was on fire, but my mind abruptly extinguished the flames. I palmed his heavy pecs and pushed him away, then I scanned his flustered face. "We have to stop. We can't do this."

"Callie, just hear me out," he pleaded with panting lips. "*Please.*"

I read his distress and nodded as I caught my breath. My brain bounced from agonizing arousal to guilt-ridden apprehension, but either way, I needed to pause and hear what he had to say.

"I think something is happening between us," he confessed, "and it's something much more than Three Doors."

My heart rioted inside my ribs, his whispered words splintering the secrets I'd saved only for my dreams. In the lonely shadows of my bedroom and under the cozy protection of my comforter, my fantasies often drifted to him long after my best friends hugged me goodnight.

"Maybe this was just physical at first, but it's more now," he continued, holding intense eye contact. "I *know* you feel it, too."

I held the confirmation on my tongue as we stared at each other. Over time, I'd kept my preference to myself for countless reasons within the frame of the game, and my logical conscience bellowed the reasoned list to my racing heart. *Your friends want him, too. You're not willing to give up the other men. You'd ruin this experience for everyone. You don't know that he feels the same way. What if he prefers one of your girls instead?*

I tried to look anywhere but in his eyes as gnawing guilt crippled my swelling confidence, but he cupped my chin and held my hesitant lips hostage just inches from his.

"Callie..."

Christ.

"I've wanted it to be you fucking me," I exhaled under his spell. "I think about you while I'm waiting for the door to open."

"I fucking knew it," he growled through gritted teeth.

Our crazed fingers clawed at inconvenient articles of clothing as we lunged for each other again. I snaked palms underneath his tee-shirt and dragged nails down the ridges of his abs, then I followed the defined path below his waistband to his angular pelvis. He ripped my spaghetti straps down over my shoulders, exposing my shallow cleavage, then he worshiped my heaving breasts with massaging hands. My aching, wet walls clenched as I groped at the damp tip of his cock, and I wondered if he'd ever pounded my pussy before.

Fuck.

Three Doors.

We were about to throw it all away.

"Wait," I gasped up at him. His rippled chest rested over me, and his bedroom eyes searched my face for the source of the intermission. I swallowed a lump of emotion in my throat and offered my transparent truth. "I still want the other guys, too," I admitted, then I followed up with as much explanation as I could muster at the moment. "It's not the same as with you. It's just physical with them." I paused for a breath and held his gaze. "I want you so bad, but I still love how they both kiss me and touch me. I'm so, so sorry."

A lightning bolt of fear struck my already anxious nerves when he abruptly backed away. I covered my trembling lips, hoping to the heavens that I hadn't hurt him with my shameful selfishness. He towered just out of reach before me, perhaps accepting this conversation's need for space as his eyes softened with sympathy.

"I see Mia and Shay in the same way," he spilled, dumping sweet relief over my panicked heart. "I have fun with them and they turn me on, but it's nothing like what I feel for you."

The fire of desire ignited in my wet pussy again as he took a slow step forward between my thighs, the next words rolling intently from his tongue.

"Callie, it's not even fucking close."

I choked back the urge to kiss him as my emboldened brain demanded more. "Why now?" I questioned him desperately, my wringing hands longing to touch him but knowing that we needed this moment of clarity to continue. "Why are you telling me this now?"

"Look, our whole situation is fucked up," he explained with a slight head shake of exasperation. "I want you for myself, but I love watching you with my friends. You get so hot when they touch you, and I fuckin' love it. I can't help it."

As offensive as that explanation would've sounded outside of this room, I understood exactly what he was trying to convey. "It's okay," I assured him, taking his hands in mine and slowly stroking his knuckles. "I feel the same way when you're with the girls." I held hope that he'd elaborate about the timing of his shocking visit, but I didn't press as his gears grinded through the answers.

"I know you get it, Callie, but at the movie last night, something different snapped inside me."

I blinked up at him in confusion. "What do you mean?"

His scrutiny slowly roamed over my breasts to the damp spot developing downtown, then he met my eyes again. He dragged his bottom lip through frustrated teeth, then he finally admitted to the only carnal sin that could threaten Three Doors for good.

"I was so fucking jealous, I almost couldn't take it."

Jealous?

What the fuck?

Arousal trumped logic once more as my heart practically ruptured behind my ribs. I grabbed a fistful of his tee and jerked him closer until we both tumbled back over my scattered notebooks. He crushed me with that hard, hefty body, rocking his muscles into my curves as we choked on the confessions still seasoning our lips. We mumbled through our frenzied kisses, our fiery tongues lapping at each other as we found a successful balance between sucking and spilling.

"I kept thinking about the game tonight," he gasped. "And I couldn't take the chance...of you fucking...one of my friends again."

Christ, my head spiraled with thoughts of our oblivious roommates, and I panted as he palmed the wall behind me for leverage. "This game, our friends..." I echoed, my voice fading into his breaths.

"We might love playing with them," he growled, nuzzling against my neck and nibbling the blushing skin under my jaw, "but I'm not sharing you tonight."

His twisted, arrogant brand of selective possessiveness flooded my throbbing pussy with even more sticky heat. "So, what do we do?" I pleaded, drawing his steel shaft closer as I locked my legs around his tight ass. He raised his stubble from my neck and hovered over my lips.

"Just let *me* fuck you during the game," he whispered.

Despite the lustful pang in my pelvis that urged me to accept, I let the realization of his shocking request settle in my chest. I whimpered his name with obvious uncertainty and prepared to present logical opposition, but he buried his hot mouth against my ear and continued the convincing case.

"All I want, even if it's just this *one* time," he begged, teasing my earlobe with the tip of his swirling tongue, "is to know that it's *you* waiting for me. Tell me which door."

My blissful heart collapsed as his implied proposal met spoken reality. "No. That's not right," I stressed as he continued his sensual torture, his wandering lips delivering blow after blow to my weakened will.

"*Fuck*, I want you so bad." He exhaled blistering breaths over the wet trails left by his tongue. "*Please.*"

My body and heart wrestled with my mind, trying to level both pleasure and emotion with consequence. But before I even considered a decision, I needed him to recognize and respect my anguish. I shrugged away his temptation, and he shifted over me with a guilty grin, surely knowing exactly how his merciless moves were affecting me.

"I just don't know." I palmed his cheeks and forced seriousness between us. "It's so unfair to the others. I'll feel fuckin' terrible."

"And I'll feel bad, too," he admitted with sincere eyes, "but not nearly as bad as knowing someone else could be fucking you. I can't do it anymore, Callie." He brushed his loving lips over mine. "Especially not now."

Not now.

His weighty words forced the impact of this forbidden encounter to the forefront. This man, this astonishing man, had swept me off my feet and dismissed each barrier to us being together that had haunted my conscience. He unknowingly wagered this blind bet for both of us and, in surrendering to his fearless heart above all else, he allowed me to surrender, too. Regardless of what happened during Three Doors tonight, everything would change after today.

I palmed his thick chest over the college emblem and welcomed the revealing rate of his pulse. A bashful smile tugged at the corners of his lips as my touch alone exposed his deeper vulnerabilities. I slid my fingertips under the shadow of his scruff and cocked a sassy brow.

"Any more convincing evidence?" I whispered, slowly rocking my pussy into his groin and tempting another scandalous round.

He raised brows with adorable surprise, then he accepted my sultry challenge by delivering a mortal wound to my resistance. "We can both keep messing with the group," he taunted, driving that stiff shaft directly into my throbbing clit and circling with lazy hips. "But after knowing how I feel about you, Callie, do you want me to *fuck* one of your friends?"

That closing argument melted from his lips, flaring unfamiliar jealousy in my chest. He hovered over me as my cheeks flushed from the burn, his striking, satisfied smirk glowing with victory.

"No," I growled with defeat. "I don't."

Just as our insatiable tongues intertwined again, my ringing cell echoed through the apartment from the kitchen. Reality rushed in for an abrupt reminder of our limited time alone, and I pushed him forcefully from my disappointed pussy.

"You have to go. The girls will be back soon."

We raised from my desk together, then he smiled with leftover seduction as he thoughtfully straightened my tank top straps. "So? Which door?"

Well, fuck.

"I'll be in here," I decided with one last sigh, remnants of guilt still snagging inside. "Door number two."

He swept over my blushing cheek with a farewell kiss, then those naughty, arrogant lips sauntered to my ear. "I'll make it happen."

~ 18 ~

"What the hell is up with you tonight?" Shay paused her primping, mascara wand hovering near her lashes, as she scoped me suspiciously in the bathroom mirror. I chugged my white wine from my seat on the sink, tipping my goblet to the ceiling and avoiding her eyes. Needless to say, I was nervous as fuck.

Although I'd agreed to this blatant breaking of the rules and convinced myself that he was worth it, my acting skills left something to be desired. Aside from drinking more than my norm, my dangling legs jittered over the edge of the countertop, and I'd barely uttered any of my giddy pre-cock commentary. My girls could read me like nobody else and would coax even the slightest deception from my shadows. Best to keep it quiet and simple.

"What?" I questioned innocently after licking the last drops from the rim. At least the alcohol provided an excuse for my continuous blush.

Shay shook her head and continued applying her face. "That's your third glass, girl. You're gonna pass out before you even get dicked."

"I just wanted extra tonight. I studied hard today. Suck it."

Mia patted my bare knee with empathy. "It's all good. I get like that."

Shay laughed at her reflection and shot me a sly smirk. "Hell, maybe Callie is getting relaxed for anal, too."

"Callie is absolutely *not* getting relaxed for anal," I insisted, having no intention of losing my ass virginity under these odd sexual circumstances, if ever.

Mia raised her eyebrows at me with humorous hope. "I was right about the smooth puss, though, wasn't I?"

Damn, my girl scored there.

"It's almost time," Shay noted with one final review. "Let's light the candles."

~ • ~

As my girls sipped casually on the beige sofa and gossiped about our professors, I parked alone in the big blue chair and waited for my undercover partner. We hadn't spoken since our tempting tryst, but his lust-laced promise had lingered all evening.

"I'll make it happen."

I fidgeted with my satin hem and blinked low at my lap. My strained brain had tried to calm my concerns throughout the day, focusing mostly on the risky aftermath, but as the night surrounded me, I could think of nothing but fucking him. I pictured the flex of his broad chest as he shadowed me against my desk and felt the tickling taunt of his tongue as he begged for my body. I shifted in my seat and rocked my pussy subtly against the cushion, remembering the pressure of that swollen cock crushing my aching clit.

When our spiffy boys arrived right on time, I hopped up all too eagerly and nearly stumbled over my feet, desperate to look in the eyes of the only person who could sympathize. He flashed me a reassuring grin as soon as our glimpses connected, then we proceeded with the performance on behalf of our crew. Hell, it wasn't entirely an act. We'd both admitted the unquestionable craving of friendly foreplay, despite the affection blooming between us. Plus, I had to admit, his best bros fuckin' sizzled as they stacked beside him.

As we gathered for our greetings, I think we were all still feeling the fire from our erotic experience at The Back Door. The initial hellos exhibited a little more flirtation, our eyes sparkling with arousal and our six bodies gravitating together. Evan approached me first, our baby blues locking in candlelight, then he burrowed a bold hand on my ass under the hem of my slip. I smoothed his navy sleep shirt over his rippled pecs as he tugged me to his groin.

"Are you wet yet?" he taunted with a suggestive smile.

Like a fucking river over here.

"Getting there," I flirted with a bat of my lashes, tickling the firm muscles between his buttons.

"I bet you are, but let me just verify." Evan's heated gaze drifted to my lips to watch my excited breaths, his fingers creeping forward over my hip to brush my damp pussy through my thin thong. My bare legs quivered as I weakly resisted the urge to thrust into his tease.

"Fuck, you feel *so* warm," he rasped over me.

I swallowed a whimper as he continued the featherlike flirt. "Hell, if I wasn't wet before, I am now," I muttered.

What the fuck did I just say?

Evan interrupted the seduction with a light laugh before offering one final whisper. "I can't wait to feel for real."

Deck turned to me after leaving a sultry lick over Shay's lips, then he seized his share with a few lanky strides once he found me alone. He searched the pink flush of my cheeks without a formal hello as I waited for his delicious kiss, but he decided to dine elsewhere instead. He dropped his warm mouth low to my ear, biting and licking my delicate skin like a man possessed. "I can't stop thinking about your pretty mouth around my big cock," he confessed with a burning breath. "Just sucking on me and swallowing me."

My needy pussy throbbed as each nasty word landed against my neck. "I could do that to you every day," I stammered.

What the fuck, Callie?

Heaven fuckin' help me.

Decker lapsed into a goofy giggle, then he grinned down at me. "Are you offering, or are you drunk?"

"Maybe a little of both?" I admitted with a slight cringe.

"Well, you know what they say," he said with an arrogant shrug. "Drunk words are sober thoughts." My wine-soaked mind couldn't argue with that logic, so I just smashed my round tits against his fancy pajamas with a distraction and frenched him deeply with my swirling, sassy tongue.

Judge didn't bother with the pleasantries when I was finally freed for his turn to tease. He moistened those perfect lips with a hungry hum and jerked me flush against his pelvis, his strained dick heavy and thick in the light layers between us. Mia and Shay had left him ready to fuck, but I sure as hell didn't mind their leftovers.

"I could fuckin' devour you," he warned with a whisper.

Oh, God.

"Which part of me?" I asked, tracing a manicured finger over his hidden dimple.

Judge shifted his weight, that hard cock riding against my gown with a twisting, tempting rhythm. "This is what happens when I see you, Callie. Can you feel that?"

I not-so-subtly inched to my toes with hopes of a decent clit grind. *Christ, no more third glasses for me.*

"Fuck, yes," I exhaled into his alluring chest, pinching my lips to curb any more ridiculous, alcohol-induced mumbles.

"Good. I want you to feel it," Judge whispered over me, "and not just like this."

~ • ~

Luckily, my buds offered no apprehension when I shuffled to my bedroom door first and tossed my palms in the dim hallway. We puffed sweet kisses of luck before stepping inside, then I propped my ass properly on my bed, suffering from an odd mix of uncertainty and eagerness as I settled in for the downtime.

With a split-second decision, I scooted down from my warm blankets and wiggled from my soaked panties, then I hopped up again and assumed the pre-fuck position. The dry air hit my slick folds and sent a shiver rushing down my thighs, my early buzz fading with each rapid rumble between my ribs. He better not make me wait long tonight. Neither my brain nor my body could withstand the torment.

I shrugged anxiety from my shoulders with thoughts of his tantalizing welcome. The other guys had sweetened this secret pot between us, and I hoped he'd been watching their hellos, his cock hardening with hunger as his roommates unknowingly seduced me for his use. I hadn't reasoned through the rationale just yet, but their collective desire made me long for him to fuck me even harder. Our friends added fuel to my fire, but only he would get to feel it burn.

My eyes wandered over the nothingness before me. I didn't yet understand the depth of his devotion, so I had no idea what to expect once we shed our romantic inhibitions along with our sexy sleepwear. It had been ages since I'd screwed with sentiment, so I'd forgotten what it felt like to pour more than my body alone into a lover's arms.

Would the spark fizzle since we'd parked the dark anonymity? Or would the cheap thrill of our shared trickery rally our arousal? Would our bodies collide in chaos since the worrying wait was over? Or would we take it slow, appreciating that this wasn't simply another Saturday night romp?

I wanted to fuck him more than the other cocks combined. Hell, maybe I already had and neither of us realized. *What a wild possibility.*

Regardless of the coming attractions, I was gonna kill him for making me wait. Or even better, if his dick ended up pumping between my lips, I would drag my teeth like an amateur. I covered a stifled giggle.

Christ, who was I kidding? I lived for this.

I was silently both cursing and blessing his delay when the door finally clicked open, then closed right away. I expected a surge of pulsing panic, but I felt oddly calm instead. I was officially no longer alone in this treachery as my favorite of the three swooped in to save me. He approached before removing any clothing as if he couldn't fuckin' wait to reach me, and my heart flipped with that sweet, quick burn between my nips.

"Callie?" he whispered in a voice that was barely more than a breath, shielding our secret from the adjoining rooms.

I shifted on the mattress and reached into the black, brushing his arm as it extended into the dark. "I'm right here."

He lowered that considerable frame beside me on the comforter and blindly explored my breasts with hesitant fingertips, his thumbs hovering over the silky fabric and grazing lazy circles against my peaks. There was no doubt that he could feel the paused breath trembling around my heart as my plump nipples tightened under his touch.

As if a delicate pretender had replaced the animal who had attacked me earlier, his lips sank shyly to my collarbone, his warm tongue sampling slivers of my quivering skin. He snagged the nearby spaghetti strap between his teeth and edged it gradually over my shoulder, driving my clenched pussy mad with impatience.

"I'm trying to control myself," he admitted softly as if he could hear my internal ache. He painted tender, wet kisses across my flushed chest and stripped me from my other strap, my back curling into an agonizing arch.

"Why?" I exhaled desperately.

"Because if I take you how I want to, the way I think about as I stroke my cock," he rasped, pausing to taste the blush between my breasts, "you'll wake up everyone in this building."

God.

He seasoned his words with just enough arrogance to make me squirm with suspense. "Try me," I whispered, damp heat pooling between my thighs.

He hissed against my chest, then swirled dirty, lustful kisses north until he found my lips. Our mouths twisted together in the darkness as we emptied shared passion and anticipation into each other. I tasted remnants of sweet mint and sour liquor on his breath. I absorbed the raw hunger and growing urgency of his tongue.

We unbuttoned his sleep shirt with nimble fingers, then I forced it back over his rounded shoulders. I sensed him shrug it from his chest, then the cotton brushed my arm as he tossed it behind me on the bed.

"You'll need that," he warned with a touch of arrogance.

Fuck.

After standing to slip from his remaining threads, he joined me again, now allowing me to feel the scorching sexuality radiating from his bare body. He slipped a hand under my gown to remove my panties, so I leaned back and parted my knees wide, urging his fingers to drift to the smooth wetness between my legs. He inhaled with sharp surprise when he'd found that I'd already stripped, then he brazenly dipped his fingers in my hot slit and whispered over my lips as he played.

"I've thought about tasting your tight, juicy pussy when I fuck myself."

If I'd been standing, I think I would have collapsed.

I brushed through his fur and thumbed his silky, sticky tip, relishing in the pride that tonight, his early excitement was all for me. I stroked him lightly and imagined how appealing he would look had there been light, stiffened to steel with his naughty hand buried under my nightgown. My nerves inflamed when he gathered the lingerie in his damp fingers and whipped it over my blond locks, certain that each incidental brush of our skin would push me over the edge.

He guided me back to the fluffy pillow, then I fumbled for his rumpled shirt beside me, both of us doubting my ability to quiet my cries without assistance. I tucked the familiar scent between my lips, then I braced myself as he teasingly widened my thighs. I clenched my eyes closed and expected his hot mouth to land on my naked pussy, but I nearly choked when the swollen ridge of his shaft breached my soaked hole instead. I gritted teeth at the unexpected fuck and arched abruptly from the bed in surprise, waiting for him to bury that fuckin' cock as deep as he could fit.

"Not yet," he whispered with a smug taunt. He twisted from my juices with a deliberate tease and I gasped with fucking agony into his shirt. His scruffy chin replaced his pelvis as he lowered between my legs, hitching my thighs around his shoulders and cradling me on his elbows. I strangled his sleepwear, my heart fluttering through each moist breath he blew over my bikini line. His wide, warm tongue suddenly flattened against half of my smooth folds, rubbing wet friction against my recent wax, then he left a tantalizing trail over my clit as he frenched his way to the other side.

Nope.

Mia was fucking right about this bare thing being next level, especially knowing which man was behind that mouth. I curled from the mattress in panic mode, but he didn't hesitate to continue the torture as if my unraveling added ammo to his arsenal. He dipped his tongue deeper in my slick slit and traced the lining of my clenched hole, then he wiggled deep inside my walls and dragged my roof with firm licks.

I fell back and squeezed the soft shirt in both hands, shoving it between my lips with a wild, whispered scream. Except for preview night with the boys, my oral experience had consisted of the standard unsatisfying sloppiness. I'd never enjoyed the gratifying sensation of having my precious pussy being courted, and fuck, my guy knew just how to charm with that tongue.

He sucked his way back through my slippery skin, lapping up my moistness, then he used my pleasure to massage my clit over and over in relentless circles. I bucked beneath him and raised in another frenzy, but he took me by surprise, grabbing one of my hands and guiding it south as I crumpled back on the comforter. He pressed my fingertips hard against my throbbing center and prompted me to caress myself through his saliva, then he fucked me lower again with deep, merciless thrusts of his tongue. My heart and lungs slammed against each other as the pressure of a peak hammered at my core, and I had no idea how I would handle falling over the edge.

My pelvis tightened with even more tension as I prepared to flood his mouth with my gushing finish, but he delayed my climax, sweeping through my pussy again and slowing my strums by sucking my dripping fingertips between his puckered lips. My potential explosion persisted as he brashly licked the silky stickiness from my hand, his tongue still tickling my amped clit.

Too fuckin' much.

"Please," I cried under my breath, ripping at his shirt with frustrated fingers. "Fuck me."

As if he'd been waiting all night to hear me beg, he left a lasting kiss against my smoothness, then he shifted to his knees with unspoken dominance. He lifted my weakened legs and rested them along his sculpted chest on either side of his neck. One long arm swept behind my back and raised my thirsty pussy to his love line, his other hand aligning that bulky, stiff cock between us. In the light, I could've appreciated his carved muscles towering and flexing over me just as he drove inside.

His rigid tip screwed through my tight walls as he rolled my hips with his. As if he'd sensed my nearby threshold the second I clenched around his length, he started methodically thrusting that heavy cock against my sweetest spot. He angled our bodies together with every thoughtful pump, ensuring fiery friction against each aching nerve inside my pussy. I fucked him back drag after drag, tap after tap, gliding over his thickened shaft as he selflessly assured my pleasure first. I snaked my free hand in my blond mess and gagged myself on his shirt, my pelvis grinding helplessly to the heavens as he held me high in his arms. I'd never been fucked with such breathless passion.

As my unbearable crest finally crashed in my core and rippled over my flushed skin, I intentionally allowed his shirt to slip a bit from my lips so he could hear me whimpering his name. I dragged my curling toes over the nape of his neck, my legs twitching around his scruff as the climax dismantled my remaining defenses. My sexy spasms triggered his burst soon after, and he forced that pulsing cock deeper through my wet walls with a round of thigh stiffening pumps.

He left a muffled moan over my bare body as he shot his hot, juicy finish deep inside my clenched pussy. I rocked against him through my aftershocks, soaking up every drop as he gasped with exhilaration in the darkness.

I was numb. Numb from the most amazing oral of my life. Numb from his loving attention to my body. Numb from not knowing what would happen when I walked out that door. My heart thundered behind my breasts as he lowered my back, coaxing my mind to step aside and let pure emotion have its moment. The ache of his absence wrecked me as soon as he eased from my warm wetness.

After a scratchy fumble as he searched desperately for my lips, he swallowed me whole with a gripping kiss, crushing me into my comforter under the heat of his glorious body. We exchanged silent sentiment between our breaths, sharing the taste of our secret as our sinful finish dripped between my thighs.

He stayed close when he eventually shifted beside me, hovering with a draped arm over my abs and cupping my lower ribs. Rare tears threatened from the corners of my eyes as the weight of the evening crushed my laboring lungs. I couldn't see even a shadow of his sexy smile, but I felt it coating me with comfort.

"This was…the most incredible night…of my life," he admitted in gasps above me. How could he find the perfect words when I could barely find my breath?

"Mine, too," I managed to mumble. That wasn't simply sex. Not this time. Not with *this* man.

A comfortable silence hung between us until a slight giggle escaped his lips. "Will you let me do it again?"

This fuckin' guy.

I laughed softly, blinked away emotion, and then raked soft nails over his buff bicep. "I'll be begging for it," I promised. "Trust me."

He tiptoed gentle fingertips over the swell of my breast and palmed the pounding in my chest. "Your heart is racing," he whispered near my cheek.

I sucked in a shallow breath and took a giant leap under cover of the darkened room. "I know. It's racing for you."

He growled my name under his breath, then buried his tongue between my lips again, this time leaving me with much more than a temporary goodbye.

~ • ~

"Fuck, how did we get so lucky?" Shay asked, shaking her head in disbelief as she wiggled back into her tiny thong. I traded her places at the sink and lowered to the toilet for my post-climax pee.

"I got off twice tonight," Mia informed us proudly. "Christ, I'm having the best sex of my life, and I don't even know who's been giving it to me."

The shameful burn of a guilty conscience rippled through my chest and spilled into my stomach. I wiped my secret's juices from my puffy pussy and joined my friends at the sink. Both beamed with genuine happiness as I washed my hands, babbling away about our breathtaking boys and giggling with glowing grins. Memories of our undergrad days flashed before my eyes, and I wondered how I'd ever be able to break the news of my betrayal.

"One of us needs to choose a psychiatry residency," Shay laughed. "We're all gonna need help."

"Not me." I grinned at her in the mirror, shaking off the worry, at least for the moment. "I'm fucked up enough as it is."

Christ, that was an understatement.

Once again, we found our dashing dates draped over our comfy furniture, the flickering candlelight accentuating the definition of their bare chests. I let my eyes roam, feasting on his friends first, then I locked lustful gazes with him as I approached.

As he circled a casually appearing arm around my waist and clawed at my hip on the down-low, I knew right then that we would need to tell our friends everything.

Just not tonight.

~ 19 ~

Later that night, after giving sensual goodbye kisses to the guys and lingering seconds longer on his lips, I crashed in my messy bed with only the wall to keep me company. My thighs clenched with memories of the moment he sucked on my soaking fingers between my legs. Instead of floating off into my usual fantasies, I was still on fire for *only* him.

My confused heart found it difficult to tread these rocky waters alone, so I enlisted my mind to assist. I recalled something he'd said when he surprised me after the laundry lie. This did begin as only physical attraction. Over the months since we met, I couldn't deny my warm rush of lust whenever he peeked over his laptop, but my eyes were on the other prizes at the time, too.

I sighed against my pillow and twisted restlessly to my other side. Little by little, I found myself more interested, but not enough to act on it for all the obvious reasons. Our friendship had taken precedent, but since we'd embraced the sexual plunge, I wanted Three Doors just as much. We were both living this life of fantasy with our best friends, so who would I be to wreak havoc over infatuation that may not be mutual?

And, let's be honest, I just loved to fuck. Period.

Over time, I'd developed preference, then hope, and then need. When considering the bigger picture, I likely never would've shared my secret, but something nudged him to take the leap. I couldn't read the map he used to deliver his heart on his sleeve this morning, but our parallel paths unexpectedly crossed the moment his confession left his lips. What did all this mean? And what would happen now?

My brain busied itself with making a mental list of our options. We could acknowledge that the damage to our group relationship may not be worth the risk and try to return things to as they were. Blah. I crinkled my nose just considering that possibility and quickly stashed it at the bottom of the stack. I preferred telling the crew right away, accepting the guilt, and betting the bank on this spark between us, all while hoping that our friends would find our situation endearing or comical. Lastly, we could wait it out as we developed a safer strategy, maybe sneaking in some discreet fucks along the way.

I curled into a ball and sought deeper reasoning under my sheets. That last prospect may be the only path for now. After all, I wanted to be with him again, but how? We'd already cheated at Three Doors once, and I couldn't bring myself to hide the lie for much longer, not from any member of our sixsome, but especially from Mia and Shay. But I also wasn't prepared to play roulette again with my cooch...

...or with his cock.

Not after tonight's sultry scene. No fuckin' way did I want him spilling those skills into someone else. As feared, wretched jealousy had entered the arena, and it would slaughter Three Doors as we knew it. The only question now was when. Even if our refreshing romance never blossomed beyond a bud, this game wouldn't continue.

Why the fuck was I dealing with this alone? I scooped up my phone from the bedside table.

```
Callie: hey
   Guy: hi
Callie: I can't sleep
   Guy: I can't either
Callie: when are we telling them?
   Guy: why don't we give it a day or two?
Callie: why wait? convince me
   Guy: I'll be there in five minutes
Callie: I fuckin' wish
   Guy: How mad will the girls be?
Callie: idk. maybe happy for me
Callie: maybe ready to throat punch me
   Guy: big spread there
Callie: hence our dilemma
   Guy: the guys will be fine
   Guy: sad they can't fuck you anymore, but fine
Callie: but they'll all stop when we tell them
```

```
Guy: meet tomorrow and talk about it together?
Callie: message me when you wake up
Guy: dream of me inside you
Callie: that's a given
```

~ • ~

"Good morning, girls!" Shay beamed with bright eyes as we gathered in the kitchen the next day. I had no clue when to expect his incoming text, but I kept my phone on a virtual leash at my side.

"Smoothies and toast?" Mia offered as she rounded the bar.

"I'm good, thanks." I shuffled directly to the coffeemaker. My cluttered mind had curbed my usual morning hunger, for food anyway, so I settled on a caffeinated fix instead. I loaded the black grounds and filled the water chamber, then faked scrolling through my cell as I waited for his name to appear.

"Smoothies sound great," Shay said. "I'll help."

I was vaguely listening to them discuss our study schedule when my phone brightened with a notification a few minutes later.

```
Guy: I miss you already
Guy: laundry in 5
```

Be still my fuckin' heart.

I swallowed a swoonful sigh to avoid alerting my babbling besties, grateful that he'd left me an obvious opening to slip away. "Not to sound nasty, but I think I'm gonna toss my comforter in the wash again while you guys are eating."

Mia whistled over the hum of the blender, her fruity concoction creating a swirl of pink and white. "Damn, Callie. Was it *that* good?"

"Yes, it was *that* good," I laughed, the natural blush warming my cheeks. Hell, I wasn't lying in that case.

"Will you throw in the lingerie, too?" Shay asked over her shoulder as she fished fresh slices from our bag of wheat bread. "We won't have to worry about it for quickies this week."

My stomach tumbled several flights as I nodded. Fuck, I had forgotten about the Wednesday romps. Our time to sort this situation was even more limited than I'd realized.

~ • ~

After freshening up far too much for a lazy laundry room visit, blissful bubbles of joy popped around my heart as I rode the elevator to my basement rendezvous. I slow-danced with my full basket, swaying my comforter in the small space like a lovesick schoolgirl. Despite all the uncertainty surrounding our situation, seeing him would provide the perfect start to my Sunday.

A few of the washers hummed in use, reminding me of our Back Door beauty getting railed, but the room was free of other residents. I shoved my fluffy cover in the front loader, then tossed our sexy satin and soap on top. Just as I tapped the start button, greedy fingers grabbed my ass cheeks and scared the fuck out of me. I yelped with surprise at his stealthy ways, then whipped around to find him man-giggling behind me. Those groggy morning eyes made me fuckin' melt and I found myself craving a sleepover. Hell, maybe we could all crash together one night.

If we make it through this drama, that is...

"Come with me." He grinned and gestured with a nod to the hall.

I followed him around the corner to an unlabeled door, noticing a few shelves of office gear and cleaning supplies when he switched on the light. Hmm. I lifted a curious brow. "And just how do you know about this closet?"

He shot me a naughty grin and slipped palms on the sliver of my bare waist. "I just scoped it out this morning. I promise."

"But someone could catch us," I whispered.

"Well, we're just talking, aren't we?" His gaze landed on my lips, then his wandering hands drifted over my ass as we scooted closer. I wrapped my arms around his neck and softly kissed his warm, minty mouth. His sleep-stiff shaft was ready for me as it rocked against my running shorts.

"I can think of things I'd rather do." I scowled as his heavy length teased my downtown.

"Same," he sighed. "You good, though?"

"I'm feeling hella guilty this morning. I'm not sure what to do."

"I feel guilty, too," he admitted, then he cracked a bashful smile and lowered his voice. "But you were worth every fucking second."

This man.

"I'm just nervous," I explained. "What if one of the girls is crushing on you? Or what if they get pissed that the game has to end?"

"We can't control how the girls react, Callie. Or the guys. We just need to be honest. If we're all as close as we say, then we'll get through this."

"They're my best friends," I continued as I stared into his assuring eyes. "We agreed that if this interfered with our friendship, we would end it. And now I've basically lied to them, not just about last night, but about these new feelings for you."

He raised his eyebrows with amusement. "You have feelings for me?" I laughed and shoved his solid chest, but he tugged me in closer. "Okay, seriously," he consoled me, "we'll talk to them together. They love you. They'll understand."

I took a deep breath against his broad muscles and blinked up at him, feeling wrapped in a fresh layer of security between his arms. I hesitated to drift off topic, but I couldn't resist as our eyes lingered on each other. "I don't know what this is between us," I quietly confessed.

He brushed soft lips over my forehead. "I don't know either, but let's find out together."

I offered a sassy shrug. "At least I can get some good oral while we figure it out."

"*Good* oral?" he scoffed. "Just good?" He rubbed light, long strokes over my pussy with those tempting fingers. "Sounds like I have some work to do," he whispered seductively.

I initially rocked into his tease, allowing the moist ache to gather strength under his tortuous touch, then I shifted my hips away. "You know we don't have time to fuck. Stop that."

"Okay, okay," he laughed and tossed palms. "We need a plan of attack."

"Our exam is Tuesday, so we'll probably hit quickies on Wednesday."

"So, we wait until after the exam," he proposed with a shrug. "We'll study tomorrow like normal, then tell them Tuesday night."

I chewed my bottom lip with consideration. It would be an agonizing two days of keeping this lie locked behind my lips, especially when facing my best friends, but our studies were far more important than my self-induced shame. Although none of this was ideal, at least we had a time and date arranged to confess our sins. "Okay. I feel better," I conceded with a weak smile.

"Are you sure you wanna stop?" he asked with quiet sincerity, searching my face for hesitation. "If we don't tell them, the game doesn't have to end."

I took a slow breath to soak up the moment, fondling his broad muscles beneath his worn, wrinkled tee and remembering how our bare bodies blended in the dark heat. "Yeah, it does. I can't go back after last night. I just can't."

"Good. I feel the same way," he said, then a smug smile stretched his lips. "Now, back to these feelings you're having..."

~ • ~

"I'm over this section," I whined, slumping my shoulders over my handwritten notes. I'm pretty sure this digestive stuff will be the death of me." I'd spent the entire morning behind closed doors pouring over the material again, juggling in a few of my other classes, too, then I joined my girls in the afternoon to make index cards for the upcoming study session. Mia hopped up during our bitchfest and rummaged through the cabinets for reinforcements.

"And gastro on top of that," Shay groaned beside me and closed her laptop.

"Fuck food. You guys want a beer?" Mia offered from behind the bar.

I tossed my pencil and nodded, feeling desperate for a mental break but also praying that the pause didn't set me up for failure. The heavy lesson had been a blessing in disguise and distracted me from my deceitful deeds, but I hoped that my overworked mind wouldn't search for escape elsewhere.

Mia returned with three frosty bottles, then we mused over memories of less complicated times. I admired both gorgeous smiles and hearty laughs over the rim of my beer.

"I can't believe we were trying to ride the same football player," Shay said. "The fuckin' irony."

"Hell, that's how we met." I grinned with a head nod to Mia. "All thanks to our girl over here."

She giggled and dribbled beer over her chin. "Look, I may have technically won, but it was the worst lay of my fuckin' life."

"And you had to tell us *all* about it," Shay sassed, gesturing between our trio with her amber bottle. "I remember getting this weird text with two random numbers in it."

"Me, too!" I laughed and sat up straighter. "I didn't know many people, so I was like, what the fuck?"

"Well, I knew he'd been working up other girls on the down-low as I tried to land him." Mia rolled her eyes. "Christ, he was such a prick."

"So, you went through his phone," I recalled, shaking my head with amusement.

Mia tossed a casual palm. "I mean, after he flopped his dead fish dick around inside me, I figured it was only fair to warn you."

This girl.

"I still can't fuckin' believe you did that," Shay said. Knowing Mia now, though, I could *totally* believe it.

"Me?" Our feisty friend laughed and palmed her chest. "I'm still shocked that you two met up with my crazy ass! That took balls."

I smiled at the memory and fingered the label of my beer. "I strolled into that restaurant expecting one hell of a catfight. Found my best friends instead."

Mia tucked a throw blanket up over her bare legs. "You girls cracked me up. We definitely bonded."

"Yeah, bonded over comparing cock notes!" I laughed.

Shay tilted her head with emotion. "Aww, we saved each other that night, girls."

"And look at us now!" Mia beamed beside me and raised her drink.

My heart dropped in my chest.

~ • ~

The next day's lectures provided required relief from that nagging voice inside. We discussed bacterial infections of the heart in patho and, since I was mildly interested in cardiology as a career, the guilt took a natural backseat as I listened eagerly to the lesson. I left the class feeling a little lighter, still determined not to let my confession conversation interfere with tomorrow's exam.

My phone buzzed in my jacket pocket as I filed into the busy hallway, so I stepped from the path of my classmates to check the notification. My day brightened even more as soon as I read his text.

```
    Guy: hey sexy
  Callie: hi
    Guy: are you okay?
  Callie: I'm better, had a great class
```

```
Callie: you?
   Guy: I'm good
   Guy: want to meet up?
```

Yes. Yes, I did.

```
Callie: when are you free?
   Guy: now, but not for long
Callie: I'm off for lunch
   Guy: where?
Callie: are we talking, eating, or something else?
   Guy: definitely something else
```

Fuck. An exhilarating wave of excitement rushed through my body at the thought of being in his arms again. I glanced out the window and considered the possible locations for an afternoon railing.

```
Callie: I'm closest to Sunrise
   Guy: on my way
```

I pushed through the glass doors of the science center, the brisk wind energizing my spirit as it whipped my hair into a frenzy. I fruitlessly tried to calm my strays as I strolled to the corner, laughing over the acceptable excuse for my post-sex appearance later. My conscience may have been crushing me more with each step, but my amped pussy assumed control, figuring that the damage was already done. *Why not take advantage of one final, forbidden fuck?*

The Sunrise Bakery buzzed with students needing midday fuel. I scanned the room and didn't find that gorgeous face yet, so I hovered near the counter and pretended to read the menu. A few minutes later, I felt a bold hand squeeze my hip as he whispered against my neck.

"Men's restroom."

God.

He copped a cocky feel of my ass as his hand slid away, my heart rate already launching as I watched him maneuver to the back of the eatery. I sucked in a few control breaths and waited for about thirty seconds, then I followed his footsteps to the brightly lit yellow hallway. At least our local café was immaculately clean, so I wouldn't be needing a trash bag today.

Like that would've mattered.

I paused at the cracked bathroom door, then nudged it open as my pulse hammered in my ears. He abruptly grabbed my fingers, urged me inside, and swiftly clicked the lock behind me. Our eager eyes met for only a glance before we lunged for each other.

"I saw you in the hallway this morning when I left class," he rasped, shoving my jacket aside and grabbing my tits through my tight tee shirt. He buried his scruff under my jaw, tickling and nibbling against my soft skin. "You looked so fuckin' cute."

"Why didn't you say anything?" I snaked hands under his loose sweatshirt and down the waist of his athletic pants, finding his heavy shaft thickening between my palms. He was almost ready to rumble.

"You were busy talking to the professor."

I jerked his bottoms down over his chiseled pelvis and pumped his full length with firm strokes. "You could've—*mmm, fuck that feels good*," I moaned as his thick fingers dipped inside my panties and slid through my sticky folds. "You could've at least said hi."

"You're so wet for me already," he growled against my skin.

I felt unhinged with primal fuckin' lust for his cock as he touched me and teased me. I turned in his arms, bent forward over the black bathroom counter in front of the mirror, and propped my pussy for the taking. My windblown hair dangled over my eyes as I peeked over my shoulder. "Fuck me like this so I can watch."

"Damn," he mumbled under his breath, positioning behind me with purpose. His dominant fingers ripped my leggings to my ankles, then I inched my feet apart just enough for him to tuck in between. He braced with a wide palm flattened against my bare ass, his other hand teasing my warm, wet slit with his throbbing tip. My core burned as I watched his moves in the bright mirror, his lowered eyes locked on his stiff shaft as he twisted through my wetness. He hadn't yet hardened to full strength, but I felt his thickness swelling as I squeezed.

"You're so fucking tight," he whispered through gritted teeth. "Christ, you make me feel so big."

He pushed deeper, filling and stretching my snug walls until his cock was buried inside. My body hitched against the sink as he eased back and thrust forward, dragging over my sweetest spot with his stiff rim. My pussy throbbed harder with every pump, tightening and clinging with each quick tap.

I stared at his bulky frame hovering from behind, his white teeth gnawing intensely at his bottom lip as he squeezed my bare waist. I clawed at the edge of the counter as he drove that thick cock over and over, my tits bouncing near the faucet as he picked up his pace. Fuck, he knew just how to rock those hips.

"Right there," I whimpered, a peak pending as I squirmed beneath him. "Please."

Fingers suddenly tangled in my messy blond locks and jerked my face north as he watched me unwind in the mirror. A hurried, hot climax sparked between my legs, my wet pussy gripping his every inch as I moaned his name to our reflection.

He fuckin' exploded inside me minutes later, crushing me against the counter as his thick juice emptied with one tight pump. I instinctively snatched my jacket collar between my teeth, choking on the desperation to cry out in this public space.

We held a breathless gaze in the mirror before he pulled out. Sudden shyness spread over our smiles as we straightened our appearances back to presentable. "So, same time tomorrow?" He smirked as I adjusted my waistband.

I cracked up laughing. "If I didn't need last-minute cramming during my break, I would." I turned to him and leaned against our makeshift mattress, feeling empowered as his wet spill stirred inside me. "After tomorrow night, though, I'm hoping we can do this without hiding."

He scanned my face, my sincere words sinking in, then he palmed the countertop on either side and trapped me against the sink between his muscles. "I know it may not seem like it right now, but I want the other stuff, too," he confessed, his heartfelt eyes locking on mine. "This is exciting, but I wanna take you to dinner and hold your hand and spend late nights laughing in bed."

His soft words spilled warmth over my racing heart. Although we'd both admitted to wanting more, we hadn't defined what "more" actually meant at this stage. In our jacked-up sequence, friendship and fucking had both taken shape before romance, but damn, he was making up for lost time.

I answered with a kiss of confirmation, sliding my nails along his jawline and coaxing his sweet lips to mine. We poured passion into each other, exchanging both clarity about our intentions and uncertainty of our circumstances, as we savored the little privacy left before returning to the demands of the day. Our twisting tongues danced again as we forgot the clock, but an abrupt knock on the door interrupted our indulgence.

"Just a second!" I called out.

"I bet that confused him."

"Hell, let's have a little fun with it," I giggled.

After one final peck, we opened the door to find a guy around our age scrolling through his phone. He glanced up and back to his cell, then returned to check me from tits to toes, whistling under his breath as a fresh blush reddened my cheeks.

"I know, man." My partner in crime beamed with pride, snaking a possessive arm over my hip. "I know."

"Sorry to keep you waiting," I offered with a bright smile. "I wanted it hard and fast, but he just insisted on taking his time." I hooked a thumb at my cohort and laughed as he defensively pinched my ass on the down-low. Our third wheel stared blankly at my implication.

"Is the coffee good here?" my guy asked. "We've never tried it."

"C-coffee?" the stranger stuttered. "Uh, yeah. It's good."

We thanked him, then stepped to the back of the line with a serious case of the giggles. I peeked over my shoulder to find the customer shaking his head as he closed the door to our fuck room. "So, study session tonight," I said, returning my attention to the stud beside me. "I need a good grade."

"We'll just work like normal," he whispered as he hovered behind me, his hot breath leaving a moist tease behind my ear, "but I'll be watching when the other guys touch you and kiss you. God, I *love* that."

I could've fucked him again with no hesitation, right there against the muffin display.

~ • ~

Shay scrolled through her cell for dinner options later that night. "Are subs okay? I'm over the usuals."

Evan whipped his laptop from his bag and smiled. "I'm good with subs."

Oh, my dirty mind.

Mia slumped into her seat on the sofa and tangled her brown locks into the perfect messy bun. "I hate the gastro system. Why can't we just skip this shit? Literally."

"If we all focus, it won't take long," Shay encouraged us.

Decker booted up his laptop, then stretched into a yawn. "That's the one positive, I guess. We're in this together."

I arranged our index cards and distributed piles to my study partners for the last cram session before this killer exam. "I just really wanna get an A in this class."

Judge smiled with warm sympathy in my direction. "Well, let's get at it."

I assumed my regular position on the floor, but nobody joined to keep me company, which was quite the blessing in disguise after my midday peen distraction. Judge parked next to Mia on the couch, and Evan flipped through his textbook on the loveseat with Shay. Decker was already clicking away from his spot in the big blue chair. Hell, I needed to focus and the group obliged, as usual.

~ • ~

Our sixsome had conquered about a third of the study cards before the food delivery arrived, so we took a break to stuff our famished faces and silence our congested brains. We stood and stretched, our muscles cramped from slumping over our materials, then we migrated to the kitchen to sort our shares. I grabbed part of a turkey club and a fresh bottle of tea, then I returned to the living room and crashed on one end of the couch.

Shay smiled as she unwrapped her veggie selection. "Let's talk about anything *but* school."

"Amen to that," Judge agreed before tearing into his sandwich.

"Are your meatballs good?" I asked as Mia swallowed a giant bite.

She smirked and licked a dribble of red sauce from her bottom lip. "Not as good as Evan's." He choked beside her and we fuckin' lost it.

"That was a crazy night." Deck settled in with his loaded Italian option and flashed me an arrogant grin. "I barely remember the movie."

"I, um, tried to watch," I said with a slight blush, "but it was kinda boring."

"Hell, you picked it!" Shay laughed.

"Well, I wanted to see 'Anal at the Aquarium,' but Callie shot me down." Deck shamelessly threw me right under the Mia bus and shoved in a giant bite of sandwich. I rolled my eyes and waited for the wrath.

"Fuck off, Callie! You passed on an anal movie?"

I tossed my palms with an innocent shrug. "Hey, you could've picked yourself if you weren't dry humping Evan in the lobby."

"You could always see it at lunch on Wednesday," Shay offered with a giggle. "Stop by The Basement. Grab some of Joe's new ass beads. Make a day of it."

"Hmm. Maybe."

This girl.

Decker took a drink of tea and scanned the space. "What did we even talk about before we all started banging each other?"

"We talked about how much we wanted to bang each other," Evan chuckled. "Hell, Three Doors changed everything."

Fuck, that was an understatement.

"We were so worried about risking our friendship," Judge offered with a casual shrug. "Turns out we had no reason to."

"Think anything could break us up?" Evan asked with a glance around the room.

Deck waved him off. "Nah."

"Hell, I hope not!" Mia said.

Shay shook her head. "No way."

I swallowed a lump of sudden emotion, then lowered my face to hide my shameful blush.

~ • ~

After the next round of gastro cards, we collectively decided that the need for caffeine had kicked in. My eyes burned with fatigue and my hips ached from my earlier adventures. The heavy hand of guilt pressed hard on my heart. I just wanted to sleep so we could get this drama over with sooner, but tonight, my grade mattered more. I stood like a zombie in the kitchen, making fresh fuel for the crew as the others scattered around the apartment to stretch. Decker strolled in with a sultry grin and squeezed next to me at the counter.

"Need some help with that?" he asked, palming the hip of my pajama pants and peeking over my shoulder.

"Hey, now. I can't cook, but I *can* make some killer coffee," I bragged with a laugh.

"Oh, I know. You looked lonely, though."

Aww.

"I'm just running on empty," I sighed with a forced smile and blinked up at his groggy brown eyes. I filled the line of six mugs before me and shivered under my sweatshirt as he stroked my lower back.

"I'll help however I can," Deck offered quietly, "but I can't promise that my intentions are honorable. You look adorable when you're tired."

Heat rushed between my ribs and warmed my aroused chills. *Christ, he was sex on legs.* "Aren't you just a sweet talker tonight?" I flirted.

Deck scoffed with a smug smirk. "Oh, you think it's just talk?"

Oh my.

After I distributed our cups of addiction, we gathered around for another cycle of hell. As the others were settling back over the books, Evan unexpectedly parked behind me on the couch without his laptop. I yawned absentmindedly and slumped back between his thighs, staring at my handwritten notes blanketing the coffee table.

"You look exhausted," he whispered above me, his hands slipping over my shoulders into a sensual massage. His strong fingers kneaded through my tense muscles, and I rolled my neck through the pleasing pain. I whimpered under my breath as his soft tongue tickled my ear, his fingertips rubbing deep circles above my collarbones.

"If you wanna sneak to bed early, I'll escort you," he taunted. "I'll even do all the work."

Jesus.

~ • ~

Under Shay's stern eye, we curbed the sexual tension and finally finished the lesson with each friend fighting loud yawns and droopy smiles. I offered to share the index cards for more cramming in the morning, but the others waved me off, so I tucked the stack neatly into my backpack pocket. Judge hadn't approached me all evening, and I felt myself missing those luscious lips, so I motioned him over as he loaded his laptop.

He flashed those sexy dimples as he strolled across the space. "Hey, sleepyhead."

I danced my fingertips over his beefy chest and tugged him closer for a slow, soft smooch. "I needed that," I whispered against his smile.

"Oh, is that so?"

"I kinda missed you tonight," I flirted.

"Well, I didn't wanna distract you."

Aww. He was unbelievably sweet under that arrogant exterior.

"I mean, I can handle a little distraction," I teased with a suggestive shrug.

He propped a cocky brow and slid his hands lower to cup my round ass. "Like this much?"

"That's better, but I think I could take more. I'm tough."

Judge swept in with that sensual mouth and twirled his coffee-flavored tongue over mine, squeezing my cheeks and hugging me against his lightly grinding groin. My burdened brain bypassed the lingering stress as my body melted into his steamy embrace.

Shay called our selfish asses out from across the room. "Hey! Are you tonguing on a weeknight?"

Judge pulled back with a guilty giggle and tossed a palm. "I'll take the blame for the tongue. And don't worry, I'll share."

Evan piped up and palmed his hips. "Fuck, I want a good kiss, too."

These guys.

Shay tucked a shiny strand behind her ears with a flirtatious smile, suddenly willing to bend the rules. "Okay, okay. I guess we all deserve it."

"Well, come get it," Evan offered with outstretched arms.

Judge left me with a final, sultry peck and approached an impatient Mia, so Decker cruised over to fill my void. He palmed the back of my neck and swept his fingers into my blond hair, frenching me with wet lust and palpable passion before backing to his steady pace. As tingles rushed downtown, I realized that we needed to ax this fuckin' weeknight tongue rule.

"Damn, Deck," I whimpered.

"Just wanted to say thanks for making the coffee," he offered over me with a sexy smirk.

I planted my hands on my hips and laughed.

"I've been making your coffee for months, mister. You're behind on your tab."

He wetted his bottom lip, those deep brown eyes locking in. "Name the time and place," he whispered, "and I'd be happy to work it off."

Christ, was I sweating?

When Evan claimed his turn to tease me, I stood on my tiptoes and swept my soft tongue across his, my panties already warm and moist at the hands of his friends. "Thanks for the massage," I mumbled as he licked and nibbled my jaw with restrained aggression.

He rubbed circling thumbs under the hem of my shirt. "There's much more where that came from, Callie."

Fuck.

Warmth rushed to my cheeks under his blue gaze. "Can I schedule an appointment?" I flirted.

His sexy lips curled into an irresistible smile. "Sure. My bed. Fifteen minutes."

After the guys waved final goodnights and slipped downstairs to their apartment, Mia, Shay, and I offered little more than dazed, depleted smiles as we completed our bedtime moves together. Our traditional hug held a different meaning as we gathered before my bedroom door, the collective weight of both my classes and my conscience sinking my cheerful ship. When I finally snuggled deep under my comforter and burrowed into my pillow, I found myself entirely too exhausted to think, so I drifted away and relied on my dreams instead.

~ 20 ~

"*Illustrate and label the digestive system in its entirety. The illustration should display all pertinent organs in anatomically correct locations, including segments and layers, as well as all digestive bodily fluids. All labels must demonstrate correct spelling, and illegible responses will not be evaluated. Failing to correctly identify greater than five components will be considered inadequate, and no points will be awarded.*"

What the fuck?

I'd finished all the other exam questions with confidence, but this page? Is this a fuckin' joke? I stared at the paper in disbelief and subtly glanced around the room for reactions mirroring mine, finding my classmates face down with pencils grinding. The professor hadn't required this bullshit on any previous testing, and I sure as hell hadn't studied any sketching skills. I took a deep, calming breath and crafted the best digestive system I could, which ended up looking like a fuckin' alien, then reviewed my final product and shrugged to myself. The labels were correct. I could spell. My handwriting was sharp. I could only hope that the prof would appreciate my feeble attempt at anatomy art. After adding my packet to the stack on the prof's desk and flashing her a hopeful grin, I left the science center feeling mildly optimistic.

I hadn't allowed myself to think of him all day, locking the entire situation in the back corner of my crowded brain. Three Doors had strengthened my ability to compartmentalize, and today, it had become the victim of my success, screaming and pounding to escape the locked cell in my mind. I parked on a bench in front of Sunrise to collect my thoughts, check my phone, and perhaps stall the shenanigans to come. The late afternoon sunshine coated me in a warm glow, but it couldn't compete with the heat of finding his name at the top of my texts.

> Guy: thinking of you
> Guy: good luck on your exam
> Guy: we're having dinner at your place
> Guy: it's gonna be okay
> Guy: see you soon

Too fuckin' sweet.

The group thread was just below his, so I clicked to catch up with the latest crew conversation.

> Judge: dinner?
> Mia: are you cooking?
> Evan: no and neither are you
> Mia: kiss my ass
> Deck: cooking should never be an option
> Shay: we'll figure out something to order
> Shay: just come up around 7

My heart flared with shame when I considered the upcoming evening, but I'd earned that burn. I added my dinner approval and tapped back on his name.

> Callie: sorry for the late response
> Guy: all good
> Guy: how was the exam?
> Guy: morning section had a bitch of a diagram
> Callie: same, my drawing was super fucked up
> Guy: mine, too
> Callie: you ready for tonight?
> Guy: just thinking of being with you after this

Aww.

> Guy: and of pounding you more often

I laughed out loud, and a passerby looked at me like I was losing it.

> Callie: I'm headed home, catch you later
> Guy: hang in there, we got this

~ • ~

My girls were already comfy and coasting when I strolled in from class. Shay waved a goblet of red from the big blue chair and grinned. "Open bottle in the fridge waiting for ya."

"So? How'd you do on that fuckin' drawing?" Mia asked as she peeked from over the back of the sofa.

I dumped my backpack on a dining room chair. "It was rough, but okay. You guys?"

"I think I fucked up some fluids," Mia groaned. "So relieved it's over."

Shay tossed a palm. "I feel pretty good, actually. I hated the material, but I understood it."

I hooked my jacket by the front door, kicked off my shoes, and poured myself a full glass before crashing on the cushions. I sat quietly and sipped, determined to appear chill despite the remaining dread of the day. My girls weren't having it.

"You seem more stressed than usual." Mia turned to me with concern, those big brown eyes reading me like a book. "You need to talk?"

"I'm just tired," I sighed, staring at the collection of half-burned candles on the coffee table. "I need to unwind."

"Is everything okay?" Shay asked quietly. "Just school stress or something else?"

"I'm fine," I assured her, swallowing my lie with a sweet drink. "I think I'm just gonna soak in a bubble bath before dinner."

"Are you gonna diddle yourself like usual?" Shay giggled over her glass. "That'll relieve some tension, for sure."

I had to laugh. "It's been a while since you threw that one out there."

"I didn't wanna kill it with too much play."

"Good job." Mia grinned. "It's still funny."

I stood from the sofa and stretched, deciding to take my wine to the bath with me. The nightly tossing and turning had taken a toll on my ragged body. I looked between my loving friends and smiled with a guilty lump forming in my throat. "What would I ever do without you girls?"

"Eat better, for sure."

"Drink less."

"Have a boring sex life."

"Do less laundry."

"Okay, okay. I get it." I shook my head with amusement and turned for the hallway. They continued shouting the list with tipsy enthusiasm as I started my steamy bathwater.

"Still have a fuzzy pussy!"

"Never fix that ratty hair!"

"Wear old lady pajamas!"

"Adopt six cats!"

~ • ~

I soaked beneath the lavender-scented suds and stretched in the scalding water. Although I could usually work through most challenges when given quiet time to think, my mind had been occupied elsewhere and the clock was now ticking. Aside from deciding the best night to break the news of our indiscretions, my guy and I hadn't developed a convincing strategy beyond the blunt truth, leaving my part of the script resting on only my shoulders. I wanted to believe, as he assured me, that Mia and Shay loved me enough to forgive me no matter how it went down, but I still processed the potential outcomes.

Worst-case scenario? One of them stashed feelings for him, too.

Best-case scenario? They would hug me and tell me it's okay.

Likely scenario? Profanity. Interrogation. Side-eyes for claiming one of their cocks.

I shifted in the steam and sipped from my tasty alcohol, wondering just how he would describe our status when given the chance. Christ, I was rusty at this whole romantic relationship thing. What began as simply quenching my sexual thirst had morphed into something more, despite a pretty fucked up foundation. Plus, I couldn't ignore the obvious. He was a striking, sexy man in the prime of his life, well aware that my gorgeous girlfriends also lusted for his cock, but he was essentially passing on the potential to continue fucking us all. I'm guessing that many guys in his place would've chosen that multi-pussy access for as long as possible.

But *he* didn't.

He was willing to give up the game for the chance to be with me...

...and I was all in.

~ • ~

"This Alfredo is amazing!" Decker gushed over his plate, presenting high praise from our resident pasta expert.

"I think it's homemade." Shay inspected the napkin logo.

We elevated our dinner beyond the standard fast food options, sharing decadent dishes of a rustic feast from an authentic eatery across town. With a couple of borrowed chairs from our bedroom desks, we crowded the crew around our small dining room table, jawing about our classes and mocking our jacked-up drawings. My circle was all smiles as we stuffed our bellies and I almost forgot about our pending predicament.

Decker relaxed back in his chair and gestured with his wine. "By the way, Evan thinks our pathology professor wants pounded."

I raised my brows. "Oh, come on."

Evan nodded sincerely. "She wants it *bad*. You should see the looks she gives me."

Mia shot me a smirk and rolled her eyes. "Okay, I'll bite. What looks?"

"You know, like she wants me to cream her." He furrowed his brows and parted his lips into a ridiculous, seductive pout.

Judge shook his head. "Dude, stop. That's messed up."

"That's exactly how she looks at me. Tell 'em, Deck."

"I haven't seen that look, man. I was referring to her comment about your khakis."

"Wait," Shay choke-laughed, "the tight ones?!"

"They're just normal pants, but she told me that I 'filled them out nicely,'" Evan explained with flippant air quotes.

"She did not!" I chuckled skeptically.

Decker slipped in on the defense. "She really did. I heard her."

Shay patted Evan's arm with understanding. "You know why she said that, right?"

"I have a decent ass, I guess." Evan shrugged with a cocky grin, drawing sarcastic groans from the other guys.

"Oh, it has nothing to do with your ass," Mia reasoned, cutting straight to the chase and mimicking a hand job over her meatballs. "You can see the entire outline of your package in those pants."

Well, there it is.

Evan's eyes widened with shock. "What the fuck? You can see my rod?"

"It's true," I conceded with a giggle. "We've talked about it."

"You're not serious."

"The hell we're not."

"So, um..." Evan swiveled between us for help. "Should I not wear them?"

"Oh, no. You *definitely* should," Mia teased, "maybe just not to class."

"Unless you wanna pound her at some point," Shay added with a mock toast, "then wear them with pride."

~ • ~

"Anyone else want more wine?" I offered after we'd practically licked our plates clean, hoping to soften the upcoming blow for all of us.

"Sure." Mia smiled. "I think we deserve it."

Shay and Deck loaded our mess in the open dishwasher. Mia stacked leftovers in the fridge while Evan bagged the takeout trash. I popped another cork of chilled red as Judge wiped the sauce slops from the tabletop. Sentiment tugged at my heartstrings as our sixsome worked together, falling in sync like a fucked up, but functional family. I hoped with all I had inside that tonight wouldn't change that vibe.

The alcohol had exchanged my frazzled nerves for a tipsy glow and, on any other night, I would've encouraged some group groping again. I stole peeks of my partner over my cup as he cleaned, admiring his thick muscles and charming smile, and I wondered if we could pull off a quick hump after this confessional. Hell, if the girls got feisty, I may be sleeping in his bed anyway.

After we finished straightening the space, our crew scattered in the living room with our fresh drinks and crashed on the furniture in satisfied clumps. I relied on the safety of Shay's rational logic and snuggled next to her, keeping a close eye on the others as they assumed comfy positions. Evan stretched out beside us and rubbed his ripped abs under his tee. Judge made himself at home on the loveseat and gulped a giant drink. Decker relaxed back in the big blue chair, and Mia squeezed against his hip.

Okay. Just one more chug of wine and I'd be ready to spill it.

Deep breath, Callie.

Shay lightly cleared her throat beside me. "So, Judge and I fucked today," she announced casually to the room. "Twice, actually. There. I said it."

Wait, what?

My mouth dropped with sudden shock, and I stared at her pretty face in awe.

"That's part of the reason we wanted to have dinner tonight," Judge sighed with surrender. "It wasn't fair to keep it from you."

Well, this was fuckin' unexpected. I'd practiced my concession speech like fifty times in my head, but Shay had just inadvertently ripped the mic from my shaky hands. Selfish relief flooded my chest and I sucked in a shallow breath. I could roll with this. Let's see where this goes.

"You're fucking kidding!" Mia couldn't hide her shock, her eyes widening and mouth gasping. Shay cringed beside me, so I found her angsty fingers and, ironically, offered *her* a squeeze of support. This was too fuckin' much.

"Was this a one-time deal?" Deck asked.

Judge didn't blush often, but he laced his answer with adorable shyness. "I mean, I hope it wasn't."

Shay gazed at him, a delicate smile forming when their eyes met. "It wasn't for me."

He flashed a hint of those dimples, then Shay suddenly slipped from under the warmth of our shared blanket and crawled over his lap. When he cradled her in his long arms and kissed her pink cheek with those soft lips, it finally clicked. I recognized an extra layer of comfort and attraction between them I hadn't noticed before. At the beginning of Three Doors, when the guys had shown me individual attention, I'd wondered if I was the only one being seduced on the down-low. Clearly, I wasn't. I'd been so wrapped up in my own lust that I was oblivious to the genuine connections that the others were making around me.

Judge scanned the room with resignation. "Well, I guess you wanna know how this happened. I'm just gonna be straight here, guys—"

"Wait. Before you get in too deep..." Evan held up an interrupting palm. *Stop.*

"...Mia and I fucked on the side, too."

I audibly gasped and covered my stunned mouth with my free palm. Shay sat dumbfounded on Judge's lap, swerving to Mia with disbelief.

"What the hell?"

Mia scooted to the edge of her seat and petitioned for mercy with pleading hands. "I wanted to tell you, girls! I swear! I was just waiting for the right time!"

What the fuck was happening?

Decker eyed me expectantly from the comfort of the blue chair, a cocky smirk plastered across his face. "Callie?"

"Right, right," I muttered as I fidgeted with the pink fleece. "I'm sorting things here." What had I planned to say again? My speech was in there somewhere, buried in the thick wine fog just beyond reach. Luckily, my accomplice stepped up to save me.

Deck shifted forward beside Mia and rested his elbows on his knees. "Callie and I have been seeing each other, as well," he admitted with trademark confidence. Just hearing the sultry confession leave his lips practically melted my fuckin' panties. God, I loved being his dirty secret.

Mia smacked him on the shoulder. "Get the fuck out!"

Judge cocked an amused brow in my direction. "*Seeing* each other?"

Well, hell, I had to say something, right? "Seeing each other and maybe fucking a little, too," I clarified with a tipsy giggle.

Shay's mouth practically hit the floor. "Christ, Callie!"

Without prompting, Mia and I slithered from our seats and joined our undercover lovers. Deck kissed the top of my blond locks and exhaled a sigh of relief as I layered the blanket over our laps. The other newly formed couples made comfortable moves, too, caressing and smooching until we all finally faced each other.

Well, look at us.

"This is fucking crazy," Deck whispered in my ear, palming my thigh under the cover with an excited squeeze. "It's not just us."

My natural, nosy tendencies took center stage. "I know! I can't take it!"

"Well, hell, I guess I'll start," Judge began as he circled his arms around Shay's hips. "Our story is pretty simple. We had a late lab this semester, so we've been spending more time together."

"But nothing escalated until the night we went to The Back Door," Shay stressed.

"I just wanted her after that. Like really fucking wanted her. That field trip got me fired up."

Shay rolled her pretty eyes and patted his pecs. "He says it wasn't the blow job, but I'm betting it was."

"I mean, the job was great, but it was more than that." Judge scanned her face and sighed. "There's just something about her."

"*Aww.*" I palmed my chest with pure happiness for my girl, admiring the exchange of emotion between their dark eyes.

"Anyway, we started texting after the theater and basically phone fucked from that point on," Shay continued the spill. "Then, I got so fucking hot watching him kiss Callie last night, I just couldn't take it."

Jesus.

Judge licked those delicious lips in my direction. Despite being smashed against Deck's mouthwatering body, the overt flirtation warmed both my cheeks and my cooch. "So, today, we met up between classes," he snickered under his breath. "And, well, I planted my flag, so to speak."

This guy.

"So, now what?" Evan asked.

"We're just into each other," Shay explained with a casual shrug. "That's all we know right now."

"You were bailing out of Three Doors with this confession?"

"Yeah, man." Judge cringed. "I just can't do it now. Not after...I don't know. It's just different."

"Where did you fuck?" I abruptly asked, then I added a weak defense when everyone laughed. "I'm just curious, damn it." Truth be told, I kinda wanted the visual. Decker bumped my shoulder with a naughty grin.

Shay nodded to the hallway. "Oh, right here in my bed. I knew you two had different classes, so we wouldn't be interrupted." I pictured Shay's frilly comforter and posh pillows being crumpled under Judge's dark, flexing muscles. *Fuckin' hot.*

"Aww. You guys are so sweet and innocent together," Mia swooned.

Evan cleared his throat beneath her. "But Mia and I," he hesitated, searching my girl's golden smile for the perfect description.

"...we're just straight-up kinks," she finished his thought with a goofy grin.

"Details," I demanded. "All of them."

"You know it's fuckin' hot," Shay said.

"Christ, look how wild they are in front of us," Judge added with a headshake. "Can you imagine what they do when they're alone?"

Mmm. I definitely could.

Deck read my filthy mind as I squirmed with arousal against his hip, sliding his fingers higher under the blanket and stroking the moist heat gathering around my pussy. Christ, Three Doors had ignited so many new fires inside me, but this unexpected voyeurism kink burned even hotter than ever.

Evan pinched Mia's ass and offered the mic. "You wanna tell it, don't you?"

"You know I do." We all chuckled as he jokingly rolled his eyes behind her back. "Well, Evan and I started texting after the movie, too," she admitted.

This was un-fucking-real. How were we all slinking around without showing any signs? My detective skills fucking sucked. And I sure as hell didn't get any phone fucks.

"We were all into it," Mia continued, the passion in her voice spreading to her animated hands, "talking about all this stuff we wanna try and wild things to do to each other. We talk about fucking around with all of you, too. He likes it when I get down with the other guys. Like *really* likes it."

Evan squeezed her curvy waist. "I do. That's true."

"So, the last couple nights, he came up here and railed me all over this apartment after you girls went to bed." She gestured around the space for reference as if she were casually pointing out the decor.

"No fuckin' way," Deck muttered under my gasp.

Evan nodded with proud guilt. "I did."

"Where?"

Evan and Mia smirked at each other.

"Wall."

"Floor."

"Dining room chair once."

Evan shook his head with an amused grin. "Mia wanted fucked against one of your bedroom doors, but I said no."

"What the hell?" Judge laughed.

"I figured that the girls might catch us," Mia explained nonchalantly, "and who knows what could happen from there."

Well, damn.

Shay spoke on behalf of our collective awe. "You're both fuckin' nuts."

"I can't believe I didn't wake up for any of it," I challenged, furrowing my brows and considering the logistics.

Mia tossed a palm. "Credit the game, I guess. I've been working hard at staying quiet as I juice."

Oh.

"And we're cutting classes early and hitting the lunch show at The Back Door tomorrow," Evan announced as he beamed up at her. "Hope you guys will cover our notes."

Mia's big, excited eyes met his. "We'll call it our first official date."

I cocked my head, engrossed in their natural chemistry as they murmured against each other's lips. I still drooled over our beefy blond, but something wonderfully unexplainable sizzled between them. "It works, actually. I can see it."

"Okay, okay." Shay clapped her hands excitedly and shifted to me. "Your turn!"

"Yes! Tell us *everything*!" Mia squealed.

"Well, I started feeling more for Callie, but I kept it to myself." Deck paused and shot me that smokey-eyed, sexy smile that made my heart backflip between my ribs. "I didn't wanna tell her and jack all this up, but I got crazy fuckin' jealous at the theater and decided it was time to make my move."

"I felt it, too," I confessed, the trademark blush crawling up my chest. "I wanted it to be Deck during Three Doors." My new man rewarded me with a slow, thrilling drag over my plump clit, and I chewed my lip to prevent a whimper.

"So, this has been in the mix for a while," Shay called me out with a swirl of her finger. "You said you had no preference, like us."

"And I didn't at the beginning," I elaborated with the bold truth. "I mean, I'm still attracted to Evan and Judge, but it's just physical. Deck and I have something more, like this way of talking to each other. It's hard to explain."

Judge scoffed with confusion. "But why were you jealous at the movie, man? I'm pretty sure Callie was on her knees in front of your seat, not ours."

Valid question. Hell, even I wanted to hear this.

He stroked that seductive stubble with contemplation. "Honestly, it was this one fuckin' detail that I couldn't get outta my head. I was kissing her and we were really getting into it, then Evan pulled her away from me."

Evan winced. "Sorry, man. I didn't know—"

"But we *all* kiss," Shay interjected. "That makes no sense."

Decker nodded. "I know how it sounds. We fuckin' love this group thing, and hell, if it makes her hot, it makes me hot."

Fuck. Me.

"Anyway, we were all kinda teamed up that night and I didn't pass Callie off so she could have a ride with my friends. Evan literally ripped her away from my lips and my body. The chick *I* wanted. And I didn't like it one fucking bit."

My proud pussy responded with a deep throb of wet thirst as he shamelessly displayed his possessive ways. He was so effortlessly dominant and demanding, it nearly stole my breath to hear him speak of me that way.

"I had no fuckin' clue, man." Evan's brief frown of remorse morphed into a cocky smirk. "I just love kissing Callie."

Someone fuckin' pinch me.

Decker stopped him with a palm. "I get it, and I know we were all doing our thing, but I needed that shake. I crashed her the next morning while you girls were grocery shopping and told her how much I wanted her."

My fond memory of that unleashed kiss slowly faded as I moved to the last phase of our confession. "And now comes the terrible part. I've been sick all day about telling you."

Mia waved me on. "Hell, girl. Just say it."

"We cheated at Three Doors."

Record scratch.

"Seriously?"

Decker stepped up in my defense. "Don't blame Callie. I begged her to tell me what room she would be in and I was *very* convincing." Of course, he had to toss in that arrogant addition.

"No, it's on me," I admitted quietly. "I wanted to know it was him, just that one time." No one spoke as the wine churned in my nervous belly.

Mia gifted me with her soft smile. "I mean, Evan and I still rolled the dice, but I understand why you didn't." I mouthed a thank you and waited for Shay to chime in, but she stared at her lap and fumbled with Judge's fingers.

"Look, I know it's jacked up," Deck continued our plea, "but I was in too deep to take the chance of you fucking her again, and I had to draw the line. I hope you guys can forgive me." I shifted my guilt to the side for a second, admiring the honest way he spilled his soul in these circumstances. I could only wish my words flowed so easily.

Judge jumped in with acceptance. "I totally get that, man. Good for you for going after what you want."

"I feel awful," I insisted, hoping to find Shay full of forgiveness and not disappointment. "I'm so, so sorry."

"We were doing our own stuff on the side, too," Evan assured me, Mia nodding along beside him. "None of us are innocent."

"Right? Don't beat yourself up, girl." Judge flashed me a sympathetic smile. "It's not like I just tripped and fell into Shay's bed today. It's not just you two."

"They're right, Callie," Shay said when she finally met my eyes. "I can't lie, the cheating thing hurts, but fuck, we all crossed lines."

Mia shrugged. "Hell, if I'd thought of throwing the game, I probably would've done it, too. Just being straight."

"And it was only the one time," Deck promised with pressed palms. "Just this past weekend. The rest was by the book."

"It doesn't matter now, man," Judge said. "It's over."

Evan jumped in. "Plus, we agreed that if one of us met someone special, we'd end it anyway, and here we are."

"I don't think we expected that special someone to be in this room." I laughed under my breath at the irony as the others murmured agreement. We'd cultivated this wild game to remain friends, but fuck, we'd found so much more outside of those closed doors.

"So, as far as I'm concerned, we were all a little shady, but I hope we can move past it." Judge scanned the room with expectant eyes.

Mia nodded. "Same. I want all of us to be happy together."

"It's all good here," Deck said.

Evan grinned. "Here, too, man."

"Clean slate?" Shay asked with a hopeful smile.

"Fuck, I'd love that." I slumped against Deck's shoulder and sighed with relief. Hell, I'd never considered this crazy fuckin' conclusion, but the crew's collective acceptance felt like just the right fit.

Evan spoke up. "Obvious question. Are we finished messing around together?"

There was a group pause for consideration, but I decided to dump my desire first. "I hope we're not finished with each other. I like watching you guys with my girls." Deck drifted to my damp center again and massaged approval with beckoning fingers. I cleared my throat through a whimper and he laughed under his breath.

Fuckin' tease.

"I love my three goodnight kisses," Shay reminded us. "Especially the good ones."

Mia shifted on Evan's lap. "I need to watch Evan fuck around with you girls. It's too hot to give up."

"I think we can develop some new rules and make this work." Judge squeezed Shay's hips possessively. "One? This swapping stuff happens only when we're together."

Reasonable.

Evan shot us a cheesy grin. "Two? You girls stay smooth." That earned a hearty laugh around the room and, for the first time in days, I felt like I could breathe again. Shay and I enthusiastically agreed that we were never going back to a full garden. Mia for the fuckin' win there.

A soothing silence settled among us as we accepted the current status of our sixsome, paired off for the heavy moves but willing to share our partners for that group thrill we all craved. Of course, it all appeared amicable enough, and the conversation had cleared my conscience, but one lingering pitfall still threatened the peace. I decided to trigger the topic and let the crew decide how to proceed.

"So, about Three Doors," I began, the taste of apprehension thick on my tongue, "should we clear the air about the rooms?"

"As silly as it sounds," Shay said quietly, "I just don't wanna know. I think I'd be jealous now."

"Same," I said. "I wasn't jealous at the time, but things have changed." Before that fairytale kiss in my bedroom, I was willing to push my forbidden feelings aside for the sake of the game, accepting that Deck desired my friends just as much as I wanted his. But now, my heart collapsed at the thought of him rocking that thick cock inside someone else, burying thrust after thrust until he brought another pussy to its brink. *No way.*

"I don't *ever* wanna know which of you Mia fucked," Evan conceded with slight irritation. "I can handle the rest, but not that." Mia palmed his blond chin and yanked his lips to hers, offering her stance with a confirmation kiss.

"No need for me to know either," Decker added, palming my thigh possessively and rubbing slow strokes near my knee. "I got my girl. I'm good." *His girl.* The claim left my pelvis aching with raging arousal, so I draped my fingers over his under the blanket and squeezed with desperation.

"So, we keep it quiet," Shay said, then her face brightened. "But I have a general question that I've been forgetting to ask."

Judge encouraged her with a nudge. "Hit it."

"I know we're not telling *which* rooms, but how did you guys pick each week? Just random? Draw numbers or something?"

"We didn't pick."

I tilted my head at Evan in confusion. "What do you mean?"

"On preview night, we went into our own rooms," he explained. "Obviously, we could see you that night, so we knew which room you picked."

Deck scooped up the ball and ran with it. "We assumed that you'd be switching around after that, so we just stuck with the same door."

What?

My panicked eyes darted from Shay to Mia, finding their faces blanked with speechless shock, so I sat up abruptly in the big blue chair and clarified on our behalf. "Wait, so you're saying that you played in the same rooms every single time?"

Evan nodded nonchalantly. "Right. I mean, you girls were switching each time. We didn't need to."

What the fuck?

Judge went on. "After mapping it out, we figured that if we shifted, too, odds are we could land with the same girl each week. We didn't want that at the time, if ya know what I mean."

Mia palmed her mouth and mumbled through cracked fingers. "Well, that's what you got. We didn't switch either."

"Wait, what?" Deck's jaw dropped beside me. "How in the —"

"We used the same fucking method!" Shay's words hurried from her lips. "Just assumed you guys were rotating every time!"

"You're fuckin' with us," Evan snickered. "No way."

Mia shook her head emphatically. "She's not. I swear we never swerved."

I think I heard each individual breath as the crew absorbed the unbelievable truth, interrupted only by the thundering pulse screaming in my ears.

"So, all that time, we were fucking the same person?!" I practically yelled in disbelief. I'd been so sure that I'd experienced different cocks, different methods, different kisses...

This was too much. It was one thing for the crew to accept that we'd fucked each other prior to these new partnerships, but knowing that I'd come undone in the arms of only one was almost too much to comprehend. I'd loved every second of Three Doors when my heart stood alone, completely embracing the concept of landing amazing sex from this tempting trio. I assumed that keeping the details secret would level the playing field for all of us, especially now that our emotions were intertwined, but as I shifted my eyes between all of my best friends, reality blazed in my chest.

"Okay, wait. Let's sort this out. What about preview night?" Evan asked, his blue eyes swiveling between us.

"We were always in the same room," Shay mumbled our shared statement, "from preview night on. Same room."

My gears grinded for answers, then suddenly, a realization hit me like a punch in the face. "Wait! You saw us on preview night!" I practically choked and clawed at Decker's thigh. "If you didn't switch, and we didn't switch, then you guys know who you've been fucking this whole time!"

I covered my mouth as six sets of shaken eyes darted around the room. Deck's long fingers curled over mine under the cover, but I couldn't bear to look at him, aiming instead for the frantic faces of my girlfriends as fire poured over my cheeks. Christ, I wanted it to be Decker so bad, I think my heart practically stalled in my chest. What the fuck would happen now? Were the guys gonna tell us? *Should* they tell us? Would this ruin everything?

Evan suddenly tangled his fingers in Mia's wavy locks and smothered her with a dominant kiss, then pulled back and rambled against her lips. "It was you, Mia. I was with you on preview night."

"Really?" Mia gasped. "Door number three?"

"Fuck yes," he growled, tearing into her again and clawing lustfully at her back.

Mia wrestled away and met his eyes. "So, that means that first night when we..." He nodded with a smug smirk as her voice trailed off. "Jesus, Evan!

Can we go fuck right now?" They promptly devoured each other again, grinding in a filthy romp like they were already naked.

My heart, mind, and body skidded down different paths as I stared at their wet, wild tongues twisting together. I'd never seen Mia happier, so my anxious chest relaxed on her behalf and swelled with pure joy. My busy brain reminded me that Evan had been effectively eliminated from my previous pussy play, but scorching shivers rushed south when he snuck a blue-eyed peek at me during a break for breath. I clenched my knees under the blanket as that initial, raw thirst for my fellow blond emerged, but Deck didn't hesitate to assume control. His bossy fingertips snaked between my tightened thighs, then he pinched at my throbbing clit through my leggings with arrogant authority.

Fuck, he knew just how to work me.

"Mia, come on," Shay pleaded, rightfully halting the continued celebration as our ending hung in the balance.

Although only a minute had passed since Evan's revelation, each second seemed to drag like time stood still. Breath hitched in my lungs once more as we all turned to the other established couple. I stared at Shay's flawless face and silky skin, considering that Deck had shared filthy, erotic nights with only my perfect friend before he made his moves with me. My stomach twisted in knots.

"Okay. I'm ready for it." Shay shot a sympathetic glance at my partner, then she crossed trembling fingers in her lap as the last hope. I felt that.

"It was me," Judge blinked up at her with those warm, brown eyes. "My room is first."

I exhaled with recovery as Shay squealed with joy, half of me wanting to punch Deck in the balls for making me wait through one last tease. He avoided my exasperated glare with an amused smile as we listened to best friends reassure each other.

"So, that means you never—."

"And the guys never—"

"And it was always us?" Shay asked.

"Just us." Judge swept her into a suited, sensual kiss. Seconds later, she pulled back and cocked an arched brow.

"We gotta talk about that first night, though," Shay teased. "For real."

Fuck! Mr. Vanilla! Mia's eyes widened with mine as we both stifled the giggles.

Judge buried his face in her shoulder. "I was hella nervous, Shay. Don't kill my rep…"

Aww.

"Well, Callie," Deck said, finally shifting that smoldering gaze my way. "I guess it was only you."

"And only you." I caught the mischievous twinkle in his eye as my mind recounted our revealing sessions. "So, you're the one who smacked my ass," I noted with a smirk.

"Yep."

"And you mocked me when I wasn't finished."

He man-giggled and tugged me closer. "You were wiggling on my shaft and trying to get me going again. I had no idea that was you, but I fuckin' loved it."

I shook my head in amused disbelief. "Wow, Deck. Wow."

He softened his cocky grin and snuggled close, dragging his scruff against my neck and wrapping his hot tongue around my earlobe. "And you're the one who begged me to fuck her on preview night," he growled, seductively slowing each syllable against my skin.

I squirmed under the heat of his wandering mouth, his fingers circling unbearable friction between my legs. "God, I wanted it *so* bad," I moaned, sliding my hand low on his pelvis and raking nails over his steel.

"You have no fucking idea what you did to me that night," he confessed, leaving hungry scrapes under my jaw. "I know you heard me jerk my big cock for you in the corner."

Jesus Christ.

"Maybe I could start working on that coffee tab now," he taunted with a warm, wet lick, "if you'll let me, of course."

"Decker is staying over!" I announced to our deviant, dry-humping friends as I slid eagerly from his grips. "We're going to bed!" I'm sure neither couple noticed as we rushed to my bedroom door.

We decided to leave the lights on…

…this time, anyway.

~ • ~

Later, after Deck fucked me on my desk with memories of our magical morning, he threw me back on my white comforter and thrust his steel tip deep in my dripping pussy again. With no further need to silence my pleasure, I moaned like a woman possessed with each pounding pump.

A loud knock suddenly rattled my door. "Sorry! I can hear you fucking in there. I'll just be a second!"

Deck rested his forehead on mine and laughed. "Fuckin' Mia."

"Come in," I yelled.

She edged inside with a shy smirk. I raised brows at the pale green sheet looped around her bare body and the random strays frizzing around her cheeks. *Damn, my girl had been getting it hard.*

"You two look fuckin' hot in bed together," she rambled. "Callie, your hair is…"

Decker sighed over me with a smile and peeked over his shoulder. "Can we help you with something, Mia?"

"Right. Sorry. Have you used your vibrator?"

"Um, no."

"I didn't figure. Can I have it?"

Deck shook his head with amusement. "Didn't you buy one?"

Mia shrugged a shoulder. "Yeah, and I have toys of my own, but I need just one more for tonight."

This girl.

"Bottom drawer," I said.

Deck fumbled around in my bedside table, then offered the unopened purple rocket box to her greedy hands.

"You're such a freak, but I love you," I laughed.

"Mia! Let's go!" Evan demanded from her room.

"Thanks, guys! Love you, too!" She backed out the door, pulling it closed with a wild grin on her face.

"Well?" I blinked up at Deck's seductive eyes as he shifted those golden muscles over me again.

"Well, what?"

I mockingly bucked underneath his furry groin as his length waited inside me and, I swear, his boisterous laugh that followed was quickly becoming my favorite sound.

~ • ~

I woke in the morning with my face practically smashed against the wall after sharing a sleep space with my new lover for the first time. I rolled against Deck's solid frame and found him sprawled out on his back, an adorable half-grin resting on his lips as he hogged most of my mattress. His burly chest rose and fell with slow, steady breaths, so I nuzzled my bedhead under his scruffy chin while my groggy brain clocked in.

Could we really live the best of both worlds now? Could I enjoy the taste and touch of Deck's addictive friends while leaving my heart in his confident hands? What would become of our crew as we continued this erotic exploration? This entire scene seemed like a dream, but the hum of his peaceful pulse reminded me of my remarkable reality.

Deck's delicious body distracted my mess of a mind, and I considered checking his shaft status for potential. I traced slow circles over the ridges of his pecs and abs, then I decided to let him sleep instead while I slipped to the kitchen for my morning addiction. After all, he'd fuckin' earned it last night.

My snoozing stud didn't stir as I inched over his naked muscles and eased off the edge of the bed, not even when my smooth, bare pussy brushed his glorious wood. I quietly shrugged into my robe, feeling giddy to spend my morning in his arms for the first time.

I freshened up as the coffee brewed, brushing away my horrid breath and taming my tangled locks, then I dressed two perfect servings of caffeine and shuffled back to my space. I was just about to turn my knob when Mia's door opened at the end of the hall. Evan emerged wearing nothing but those low-slung navy sleepers and a sexy smile. *Fuck, he looked divine.*

"Hey," I whispered, gesturing with one of the steaming cups. "There's fresh pot ready for ya."

"Thanks." My fellow blondie grinned as he sidled up next to me, provoking that primal desire to spark downtown. He stroked his sandy stubble and scoped the low dip of my robe. "So, you and Deck? *Nice.*"

"And you and Mia." I smiled up at him and shook my head with a light laugh. "Think you can handle her?"

Evan stretched into a lazy yawn and sauntered to the bathroom. "Hell, Callie," he laughed under his breath, peeking over the red scratches scoring his shoulders, "what makes you think that Mia's the one who needs handled?"

Well, damn.

I swallowed hard as I stared, then I turned to my bedroom once more as arousal fluttered in my belly. I tried to balance the two full mugs in one hand, but Evan swept in behind me and palmed the doorknob with an assist. His warm bare chest radiated sex as he hovered over me.

"Make sure you show my boy a good morning," he exhaled over my shoulder, the heat of his raspy whisper rushing down my neck and dropping straight to my pussy. He cracked the door so I could slip through, then shot me a cocky smirk as he closed it behind me. "I'll see you later."

I paused just inside to collect my lustful thoughts, shaking off the remaining sparks that Evan always left against my skin. Deck's golden muscles still peeked from under my white comforter, and my thirst shifted seamlessly to him. I parked our breakfast on my bedside table, stripped bare again, and crawled back on the mattress, but this time I disturbed Deck's satisfying slumber. He untucked an arm from behind his head and snaked his hand under the blankets, then he swatted my naked ass with a surprising smack as I tried to sneak over his lap.

"Well, good morning," I giggled, propping myself up on his thick chest to meet his smokey bedroom eyes.

"Good morning," Deck whispered back with a glowing smile as he massaged my hips. "*Fuck*, it feels so good to say that to you."

Wow.

A bashful blush warmed my cheeks as he stared. "I made you coffee. *Again.*"

He raised amused brows and glanced at our waiting mugs, then he rocked his stiff steel between my legs. "No tab this time, Callie. I think I'll pay my bill now."

~ • ~

That weekend, our boys hosted our first official triple date. Against all known logic, they boldly attempted to cook us a romantic dinner after borrowing our cookware, ultimately serving a barely edible chicken casserole. Of course, with our hearts aflutter at the sweet gesture, my girls and I played along, praising each of them as they proudly claimed their contribution.

After cleaning up the kitchen, we paired off on the sectional and cuddled under familiar gray blankets, giggling and groping before the flickering lights of a cheesy streaming movie. I thought back to our first porn antics and shook my head to myself. Tonight, if someone peeked in on us, they would see three couples who'd stayed in to watch a romantic comedy.

Fuck, who would've guessed?

The flick ended uneventfully and we all just looked at each other, wiggling in wet panties and adjusting primed packages.

"So, now what?"

"Hour of Power?"

"We still have the shot glasses."

"And the blindfolds."

"Maybe we could see what those naughty nurses are up to," I suggested with a shameless giggle.

Our crew didn't bother retiring to any assigned rooms that night. Instead, we made each other hot with traded touches and kisses, fucked our partners in different corners of the apartment, and finally enjoyed that group sleepover on the sectional.

As I watched my beautiful best friends settle in, snuggling with blissful grins against our shared, seductive men, I knew only one thing for sure about our secret sixsome…

…our story wasn't over just yet.

~ • ~

Thank you for reading **THREE DOORS**!

So, what's next?
The crew may be coupled up,
but leftover lust is lingering...

This is the first book in a series of four,
so, if you're not ready for the game to end,
check out a sneak peek of the sequel below.

~ • ~

THREE DOORS: Beach House

I arched my back abruptly as Decker's firm, hot tongue flicked over my throbbing, wet clit. I couldn't see him through the blinding eye mask, but I felt the alluring scratch of his scruff against my smooth skin.

He preferred to watch me, especially in this enhanced version of Three Doors, but I still craved the thrill of the dark.

I'd been fucking Deck exclusively for the last few months while continuing lustful foreplay with his best friends, so I'd become quite comfortable with his moves.

I wasn't nearly as familiar with the soft, feminine fingertips massaging my hard nipples.

I was on the verge of climax as he worked his magic between my thighs, but when a different set of lips suddenly teased and tugged at my earlobe, I fell over the edge completely.

For the latest updates on the **THREE DOORS** series, as well as games, merchandise, giveaways, and general fuckery, hop on my author page @threedoorsbooks on Instagram.

I have a wild bunch of dedicated readers, and I'd love for you to join our community!

Hope to see you there!

— j

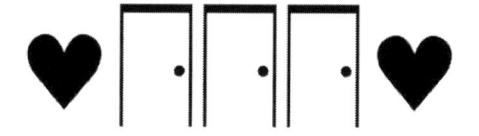

~ MY TEAM ~

Where do I begin?
I won't bore you with my writing journey.
It's not worth reading. Trust me.
Instead, I'd like to acknowledge those behind the scenes
who helped me achieve this dream.

~ • ~

~ Iffrobyn, Lauren, Luci, Paige, & Poteet ~

Thank you for giving your precious time and talent to my work,
but also for respecting me enough to pour over my words
with thoughtful, honest eyes.
Your feedback and guidance have given me the confidence
to strengthen my style without losing my voice.

~ P, P, & SS ~

Thank you for keeping me sane.
Your priceless advice, ridiculous laughs,
and unwavering support have been
a haven in the midst of this chaos.
You are my safe space, and I promise to be yours.

~ GOATS ~

Thank you for being a constant source of
entertainment, inspiration,
encouragement, and understanding.
It is my privilege to be intertwined with
such an incredible group of friends,
and I never would've taken this step
without you in my corner.

~ J, J, L, M, & N ~

Thank you for hanging out in the bubble,
listening to my rants, cheering for my stories,
and helping me sharpen my brand.
I'm honored to have you all on my team.

~ RO & RM ~

Thank you for helping me remove my blinders
and see my story in a new light.
Your praise and critique provided a valuable,
professional perspective in this process.

~ MG ~

Thank you for allowing me to spill my secrets
without fear of judgement.
You were the first person I trusted enough
to share this side of my life,
and I will never forget your early support.

~ J ~

Thank you for holding my hand
as I add another page to our crazy story.
I can't be sure of what the next chapter will bring,
but I know that you'll be with me
as we write every last line.

~ Chloe ~

Thank you for showering me with such sweet
love that my heart will never recover from losing you.
You were by my side for so much of this ride,
and I know we'll be celebrating together
when I see you again.

~ My THREE DOORS Family ~

Thank you for embracing my crazy ways.
Your enthusiasm and encouragement
have allowed me to write
joyfully and unapologetically,
with pride not present in any other part of my life.
Some of you have been with me from the first chapter,
and others are new to the crew,
but regardless of when you found me,
I am humbled and overwhelmed
by every minute of your engagement.
Your passion has fueled me to reach for more,
not only for the books,
but for myself, as well.
I appreciate our little community
more than you will ever realize.
#ilovemyreaders

~ • ~

Printed in Great Britain
by Amazon